Wendy Robertson, an ex-teacher, lecturer and journalist, was recently Arts Council Writer in Residence in a women's prison. *My Dark-Eyed Girl* is her fifteenth novel in a list which includes contemporary, historical and children's novels. She lives in the north of England.

My Dark-Eyed Girl

Wendy Robertson

HEADLINE

First published in hardback in 2000
by HEADLINE BOOK PUBLISHING

First published in paperback in 2001
by HEADLINE BOOK PUBLISHING

3

ISBN 0 7472 5979 8

Typeset by Avon Dataset Ltd, Bidford-on-Avon, Warks

Printed and bound in Great Britain by
Clays Ltd, St Ives plc

HEADLINE BOOK PUBLISHING
A division of Hodder Headline
338 Euston Road
London NW1 3BH

www.headline.co.uk
www.hodderheadline.com

For Michelle,
who gave me 'ChiChu'

Prologue

Aragon 1999

The chipped stone of the narrow path shoots away under the dusty wheels of my scooter. On my right, out beyond rocks and the thistles loom the Pyrenees, a purple smoky mass against the bright sky. The cutting wind rakes my tender scalp. The air around me is dense with the scents of peppery rosemary, undrunk wine and harvested olives. Low white houses glitter as they shoot past in late summer sunshine. The rearing stone of the sierra flows right up against the stony path then ebbs away, to surge raw and greeny-grey against the mint-blue sky.

The scooter chatters for a moment into the thin mountain air. Then it coughs and fades to nothing as I turn off the engine and dig my boots into the dust. I pull the machine back like a pony, leaving it high and dry on its rusting stand. The fabulous sun, too hot for this time of year, polishes the air and sears my arm. I scrabble in my rucksack for my factor twenty-two, and rub it viciously into my skin. For a second the blinding scent of chemicals drowns the limpid essence of the mountain air.

I untie my flapping hat from the handlebar and jam it hard on my head. Then I pick my way along the narrow path for half a mile, climb on to the escarpment at the place that we marked on the map and feel my way along the ledge to a natural refuge. Here the pathway extends to a spot not much wider than the perches used by gulls and guillemots on the cliffs at home, near Marsden Grotto.

I peer to my left then to my right. Along the escarpment there are other narrow resting-places strewn with rocks and heaped towards the edge with small boulders. On closer inspection these heaps of stones prove not to be natural. Perhaps picnickers have stacked them there to stop their children wandering off the edge and tumbling into the deep ravine below.

I feel my way to the very edge and peer down. The sheer depth is engaging, enticing. For a second I want to leap out and down into that deep shadow. I see my body tumbling: a flashback in a film. I used to rehearse my own death many times in those days when I was not well. But I am better now and I can abandon that crazy impulse to savour the way the bare hillside sweeps down to the lush valley below, where the deep green is herringboned with grapevines whose tumbling strength will, again next year, bring such biting beauty on the tongue.

I squat down, cooling the hot rock with my cooler back. I unscrew my bottle of water and glug at the contents to blot up my parched throat. I dig the heel of my boot into the dusty ground and hear the scrape as it hits some hard object. After more scrabbling and digging with my knife, I winkle out a metal object from under a round stone; underneath that there is a rag of canvas. The metal thing is like an overlarge rusty lipstick case. I slip my thumb into its hollow space and recognize a bullet casing. It's battered and very old. I close my eyes tightly. *Avia*. I say the word out loud.

MY DARK-EYED GIRL

Now in this dry, empty space the clatter and chirrup of gunfire begins to echo hollowly in my ears; some small hard object bites into the escarpment above me and spits dust on my head.

Chapter One

The Mad House

1936

Susan Cornford was used to it now. She'd become accustomed to this large echoing building sitting coiled inside its long encircling wall. She was used now to the elegant windows with their cunning bar arrangement on the bottom half; to the painted corridors, the polished mahogany and the rewashed bandages looped around the dayroom like bunting. She was used to the singing, chirruping and squawking of patients, to the occasional echoing scream and the nightly punctuation of unearthly bellowing.

These sounds, which a few years before would have sent her running, she now treats with benign indifference. Her nose no longer flares at the rank mixture of beeswax and raw antiseptic. Her ears have become attuned to the soft, lion-taming menace in Matron's voice.

She has even become used now to being identified only by her second name. 'Cornford! See to Mary Bossy in bed three, will you? She needs turning.'

'But never, never will I get used to those rats,' she said

one night to her friend and mentor, Keziah Stanton, with whom she shared a bedroom. 'They should let us carry guns so we can shoot every last one of the beggars.'

'You'd have guns on that farm of yours, I suppose? You'd sure enough have rats there as well as rabbits.' Keziah was placid about Susan's outbursts. 'Part of hospital life, honey. Rats is there always, in the underbelly of every hospital. They're the dark brothers of Matron and Dr Tordoff.'

It was eight o'clock in the morning and they were climbing into their beds, yawning after a twelve-hour nightshift. This image of the Zeus and Hera towering over the hospital universe stayed with Susan as she went to sleep. She dreamed of Matron and Dr Tordoff straddling the barn roof at home, taking pot shots at rats as big as bulls.

At twelve o'clock the following night, Susan walked down to the kitchens as usual, to collect the night tray for the staff supper for Ward Ten. Her outward journey down three staircases and two long corridors was accompanied by the usual grumbles and snores of patients, by a yelping scream followed by the soothing voice of a nurse and the distant punctuation of the dogs barking in the back yard of Dr Tordoff's elegant house on the perimeter.

In the deserted kitchen, which smelled of thrice-boiled cabbage, Susan collected the tray from the heating cabinet. She shoved a roll of towel, requested by Sister, under her arm. This, of course, made it difficult to balance the rattling tray and handle the interminable keys at each door. It was the third time this week she had done this errand, but she was used to these extra demands. Because she was different, having come to this work very late in life, she was often picked out for extra duties. They frequently used her as a kind of packhorse for the ward. It was a relief to be of use for her strength. This at least she was sure of.

She was on her way back up the first flight of shallow stairs when she spotted him on the opposite side on the top step. His bright eyes glittered down at her in the grim corridor light. His whiskers quivered. She took a breath and started to ascend close to the wall on her side, keeping her eyes straight forward. Her peripheral vision informed her that the four-legged black brother of Dr Tordoff had started to descend the stairs. Skip. Skip. Jump. Jump. Steady and slow. For a split second they were on the same step. Susan felt bile rising to her mouth. Then she stepped on and started to breathe more easily as she reached the top of the stairs, knowing that particular dark brother of Dr Tordoff must be at the bottom.

She was focusing so strongly on her relief that she bumped into a person standing stock-still at the top of the stairs. The woman put her fists on her ample hips and grinned. 'By, nurse, he was a big 'un! A granddaddy Ah should think.'

'Jane Ann!' Susan stood still while the cups and saucers on her tray regained their composure. 'Jane Ann Golon! What're you doing up out of bed? It's gone midnight.'

'Now, Nurse, dinnat gan on. Ah have to gan to the lav, haven't Ah?' Jane Ann pulled at her nightie at the back, where it had rucked up into her knickers. The voluminous garment fell to her feet. 'Ah had a wee, didn't Ah?'

'But you're outside the ward, Jane Ann. This is way past the bathrooms. If Sister Barras catches you she'll give you what for.'

'Bliddy Sister Barras!' Jane Ann's eyes rolled to the back of her head. 'Dinnet tell that *hooer*. She'll have us in the pad, sure as shot. She gets on my pips that woman. An' she canna stand me neither, so it's mutual.'

'Now now, Jane Ann. You know that's not true.' However, somewhere at the back of her mind Susan knew Jane Ann was quite right. The bristly, demanding Sister Barras definitely had her favourites among the bizarre flotsam and jetsam of Ward Ten. Among both the staff and the patients there were those who, for Sister, could do no right, and those who could do no wrong. Those who could do no right had their feelings hurt and would not take this lying down. If they were patients they might resort to throwing food or kicking trolleys. If they were staff they would flounce around and whisper in corridors, or go into sulks. In consequence patients would end up in the pad or pumped full of Largactil; staff ended up on the carpet in front of Matron.

For patients, what had started out as justified rage against unfair treatment would become actions for which punishment or containment was the only action. So Sister Barras was able to tell her colleagues she had told them so. 'There are certain patients you can never trust, believe me. Staff not much better.'

'Here, Nurse, lerrus carry that for yeh.' Jane Ann pulled the roll of towel out from under Susan's arm and fell into step beside her.

Susan moved on ahead, uneasy suddenly at the loping figure beside her. In the daytime Jane Ann was a comic, entertaining figure. Now, in the dark corridor, Susan was glad that working in this environment developed your peripheral vision.

One way or another you were always on the watch. If it wasn't the rats it was the patients. If it wasn't the patients it was the magisterial Dr Tordoff, who descended on the ward like Zeus coming down from Olympus, casting life and death around him like thunderbolts. Susan smiled to herself. Down among the mere mortals, the doctor was fawned on by people like tough old Sister Barras, who was reduced to a simpering wreck in his presence.

Susan's mind wandered to thoughts of a staff tennis tournament, not long after she'd started her training. The sight of Sister Barras and Dr Tordoff playing doubles had stunned her. Sister was surprisingly light-footed for her weight. Dr Tordoff had his sleeves rolled up and you could see the puckered war wound on his right forearm where, it was alleged, he had 'caught one' in the last battle of the Great War.

'I'll have to stop here, Nurse.' In a flurry of movement Jane Ann stuffed the roll of towel back under Susan's arm. They were standing by the internal window that lit the patients' bathroom. It was propped open with a toilet brush. 'Ah canna gan back through the clinic, can Ah? Her ladyship'll nab us, sure as shot. Clapped in the pad, or worse. Mebbe them bliddy gagging pills. Bet on it.'

Susan steadied her heavy tray against her hip. 'I should report this to Sister, you know, Jane Ann.'

Jane Ann grinned, her fine teeth glittering at her in the dusk of the corridor. 'No need for that, Nurse. Back safe and sound, aren't Ah? Yer don't wanter get us into trouble with Sister, do yer?'

'Go on then, Jane Ann. And don't you do it again.'

That grin again. 'Not till the next time, Nurse.' Jane Ann hauled herself up to the window, crawled through it and clicked it shut behind her. The corridor was echoing and empty now, dead without Jane Ann's sparky presence.

Jane Ann had been at the hospital on Susan's first day on the ward six years ago. She'd been in a side room then, under restraint. She'd tried to run away the night before and broken the spectacles of the nurse who had brought her back. The howls that emerged from the side room had sent the first dark chill through Susan.

Sister Barras had been brusque. 'Ignore that, Cornford. It's spoiled rotten, that one. Likes to get its own way. Wheedles its way round the day staff. But we see through her, mark my words.'

Jane Ann's way of displaying her spoiled nature was to smile all day at everyone. Give her an order, she smiled. Tell her to eat her dinner, she smiled through a mouthful of custard. Tell her to get into the bath, she smiled as she slipped out of her nightie to reveal her magnificent figure. Reprimand her, she smiled. All this smiling sent Sister Barras into paroxysms of fury. Jane Ann often ended up in the pad or dosed up with something extra calming which left her vacant for days. Even then she could call up a woozy smile.

For two days each month, when the moon was full, Jane Ann stopped smiling. As well as this she stopped smiling for the whole month of February. Many years ago, a week after her fourteenth birthday, she'd given birth to a baby. That scrap of humanity was the reason for Jane Ann being here in this particular circle of the underworld. Her parents, a highly respectable coal hewer and his wife, had delivered their daughter, bawling and incoherent, to the gates of the hospital. This was after they had given the baby to the hospital, once a workhouse, where he'd been delivered.

Every year during the month of February Jane Ann would cry for her child. She would cry tears for all the other women on the ward: for the nurses and the hospital, for the little town of Priorton where she was born. Then for the whole world. There were a lot of tears.

'Been to the end of the world and back again, Nurse?' Sister Barras looked up at Susan from her desk. She eased her bulk out of the chair and removed her black-rimmed glasses to reveal her watery, tired eyes. 'What were you doing out there? Sowing a row of barley?' Sister snorted the snort which in her case had to serve as a laugh.

It was quite a joke on Ward Ten that Nurse Cornford, who at thirty-two had come so late to be a mental nurse, had been a farmer in her earlier life. *Farmyacker* was whispered behind her back more than once. As she laid the table in the dayroom for the staff supper, Susan's mind went back to her first months at the hospital. She'd had to make it clear to more than one person that she had been a farmer, not a farmer's wife, up in Weardale.

'No life, that,' said one of her fellow students, the sturdy, childlike girl who was to become her friend Keziah Stanton. 'All that mud and clarts.'

'It was all right, I'm telling you,' said Susan. 'But it was hard, like you say. Cold in the winter. Had to break the ice off the water to boil a kettle.'

'If it were all right, why d'yer come here? To this mad house?' They'd been at Park View Mental Hospital for just a week then. Three of their group of ten students had run away after two days.

'Mad house?' Susan had glanced around. 'It's not bad. Better than Goshawk Shield on a freezing night with the wind howling. And my grandmother raging through it like a tornado. That was a mad house all right, in the end.'

The first time she'd come to this place, months before she registered to train there, she'd been hanging on to the arm of her grandmother, who was raving with an anger which consumed her body, and slavering with incomprehension and hatred of the world. A week later the old woman became physically as well as mentally ill. She died of pneumonia one night in the hospital, before the staff had time to send her to the General.

The nurse who dealt with Susan the night her grandmother died was a stout girl with hair as bright as a penny. She made a great impression on Susan. She'd held on to Susan's arm, listening to Susan's bitter gabble about her grandmother. How her own mother had died and her grandmother had left her with strangers, then come back to take charge in a maniac fashion. The nurse listened quietly as Susan went on and on about feeling guilty and angry at the old woman, both at the same time. Then the nurse had talked to Susan, about her own life: how her father had been killed in the Great War. How being a nurse had been her life's dream and how the work here was wonderfully fulfilling and perpetually interesting.

The woman's words stayed in Susan's mind for many months after that. In the end she came back to Park View to be a nurse, just like the girl with the hair bright as a penny. She persuaded the hospital to give her a chance, even though at thirty-two she was rather old. It was her good fortune that they were very short of recruits.

On her first day in uniform she looked around for the auburn-haired nurse.

The Sister Tutor shook her head. 'McDonald? A good nurse, that girl. She got married, you know. Pity about that.'

'A pity?'

'Never sat her finals. Not allowed to, married. A foolish girl. She'll live to regret it.'

Susan's attention swung back to the present as

members of the night staff gathered round the table for their supper. Keziah Stanton came from the clinic with the steaming teapot: a brown enamel object with a chip the shape of Africa in the handle. Sister said a rambling grace before anyone was allowed to eat.

The talk around the table was all *hospital*: the whist drive in the nurses' home; the bonfire night where they would all be ducking for apples and eating potatoes cooked in the ashes. Keziah Stanton reminded them of that time last year when a male inmate had climbed out of the men's wing and danced naked three times round the fire before being captured by burly male attendants who cuffed him about the head, scolding him for spoiling their fun.

Sister Barras relished a grimmer tale about the year a woman patient had thrown herself on the fire and had to be rushed off to the General for treatment. 'Mary Manners, that was,' Sister said, slurping her tea. 'She was up the pole for months after she got back, that one. No keeping her down.'

Susan looked at the sister's stout, confident figure: the neat collar on the black dress; the bonnet with its flying tails set on thick hair clipped back with black Kirbigrips. Sister caught her look and treated it as a challenge. 'So what about you, Cornford? Do they have things like bonfires up there in the wilds?'

Susan stared at her. She couldn't really remember whether there'd been lots of bonfires. She focused her mind. Yes, there were a few down in Stanhope on bonfire night, but that was a long way from the farm. Farm folk didn't bother with things like that. She thought hard again. Yes, on bonfire nights if the night were clear of cloud you could catch sight of the fires, small as lit matches, glittering down the length of the valley.

'No. We'd nothing like that on the farm.' She fended off the eager looks of pity. Pity was one way of looking down on people. She'd met a lot of that here in the hospital. 'But sometimes we would set the moor alight and that was a wonderful sight. It seemed like the world was burning from horizon to horizon.' She smiled at the thought.

'Now you're havin' a joke with us, Cornford.' Keziah laughed. 'Setting the moor alight! Horizon to horizon? I don't believe it.'

Susan shrugged. 'Don't believe it if you don't want to. We set it alight after the heather had bloomed. Makes the new green shoots come fresh for the next year. Cleans it all up, fire.' Her eyes caught those of Sister Barras again. This time she held her gaze till the other woman looked away.

'Now then,' said Keziah, swilling her tea round her cup and turning it upside down. 'Who wants their fortunes told?'

Park View Hospital was like a small city unto itself set in the wider landscape of pit villages and market towns that made up the South Durham coalfield. The hospital was a city contained by a city wall; a wall which did not protect the city from marauders, but rather protected the wider countryside from the marauders within.

Like any city Park View had its spires and its towers, its tall smoking chimneys, its greenhouses and gardens, its ancient oaks and its bandstand. Its population was self-sufficient. There were gardeners and carpenters, bakers and electricians, butchers and builders as well as doctors, nurses and patients. Of course, the patients didn't wander across this sylvan territory. Apart from occasional escorted walks for the meek among them they usually stayed put in their wards: the men on the cathedralesque North Wing, the women on the cosier South Wing. The Matron, Chief Attendant and his deputies lived in a neat square of houses on the perimeter. Dr Tordoff and his loftier medical colleagues held court in the grand villas by the main gates.

At the very centre of the site there was a bakery, a great kitchen block and a substantial dining hall with stained-glass windows in the Arts and Crafts style, depicting scenes in the life of St Francis. Between buildings were walkways and covered glass corridors, which provided exercise for staff and even some patients on the coldest of northern days. Every so often dances and musical concerts were held in the large central hall. It was here that the Christmas pantomime was performed. Dr Tordoff, whose secret pleasure was acting, always played the villain. He considered it one of his greatest achievements that cavorting around as Abanazer every Christmas made no difference to the iron discipline with which he ran the hospital.

On her first day at the hospital Susan had been overwhelmed by the size of it all: lost in the corridors, disoriented in the ever-extending gardens. Her head buzzed with the constant press of people, both sane and insane, after the deep peace of the farm.

The days rolled into each other: a mass of bodies and voices, screams and laughter, instructions and imprecations; people and their bulky, inconvenient bodies at every turn. As time went on she'd become more comfortable. It was as though the institution and its thick presence of people had enveloped her, had made her part of themselves.

She watched the patients as they moved on their mundane or their bizarre daily trackways, in their drab overwashed clothes. Many of them had not been beyond the ornate Victorian cast-iron gates for ten, fifteen, in one case twenty years. They must, she thought, breathe in and breathe out with the building. They must, through the years, have measured their breath, tuned their voices to the echoing heights of the room and the corridors, the constant inevitable presence of strangers. In this place, even the lowliest of outsiders, the electrician's apprentice, for instance, was more powerful than any patient.

Susan had soon absorbed the single most important lesson: the need for calm in this troubled universe; a need which was responded to with physical restraint: pills and tinctures all claiming to calm troubled souls. They used electricity too. The patients came back trembling, but they were calmer and less haunted for weeks after going down that green corridor.

Five weeks into her training, on her very first weekend leave, Susan had stood at the bus stop by the great iron gates and waited for the bus. She'd looked with shining eyes along the open, free road. She'd peered at the broad horizon with delight. She'd not known in these last weeks that her breathing had been restricted but now she'd gulped in lungfuls of fresh free air. She'd smiled through the window at the driver as the bus drew up. She'd beamed at the other passengers as she'd made her way down the bus. The clothes they'd worn, with their blues and greens, their bold reds, had seemed unbearably bright. The hats, with their felt flowers, petersham bands and feathers had seemed ridiculously frivolous. The faces, even the bloated ones, or those skinny with hunger, had seemed bright with the inner light of sanity, the spark of freedom.

By the time, several hours and three weary bus rides later, she had reached her home in the dales, she'd been drunk on sensation, buzzing with freedom.

But now, after six years, she was used to all this: the iron and sometimes quixotic routines in the hospital and the strangeness of its population – staff and patients alike. She'd survived her training where the greatest challenge was not the knowledge and skills, but staying awake in morning classes after doing a full nightshift. Despite being the oldest qualifying nurse in the history of the hospital she'd finally earned her qualification and a degree of respect from the people around her. She relished dealing with the vagaries, the challenges, even the occasional danger of hospital life: living near the edge, alongside the eccentric, the quaint and the raving mad.

'Did you never fancy getting married, like? Or a family?' Keziah asked her one night as they flopped into bed after the Hallowe'en party in the recreation room. They'd drunk too much elderflower wine (brought by the wife of the chief male attendant, who liked a party). Susan had been much in demand for the eightsome reels and the palais glides. 'You weren't no wallflower in there,' said Keziah.

'Married? Me?' Susan laughed. 'Not likely.' She pulled the starched sheet up round her neck. 'Too much like hard work for me. At some man's beck and call? No thank you.'

Keziah jumped back out of the bed and across the cold lino to click off the light. 'Don't you believe that,' she said, yawning. 'You've got that spark. The lads there saw it tonight. I'd had you marked down for one of them spinsters who'd lost her sweetheart in the Great War. There was a picture where the story was all about that. At the Tivoli in Priorton.'

'I'm not that old, thank you very much. I was at school almost until the Great War started.'

'Like I say. There's time yet. Even for you.' Keziah burrowed into her pillow like a mole and was asleep in seconds. Susan lay there in the dark and brought some words to the front of her mind from one of her textbooks. *Stigmata of degeneration.* The consequences of in-breeding. The words had jumped out at her from one of her textbooks. *Deformation, distortion, abuse, misuse, prostitution, addiction, decadence, vitiation, degradation, debasement, brutalization, dehumanization.*

Here in the hospital, there were many patients who seemed very ordinary. They could have come from anyone's sitting room, the counter of any shop. But some of the others showed these terrible *stigmata*: the twisting limbs and clenched-up faces, babbling mouths and troubled thoughts.

Susan was thirty when she discovered that she herself was the carrier of such stigmata: she was her own uncle's daughter.

She'd had the happiest of childhoods with her foster mother Rose Clare Maichin, at Goshawk Shield Farm. The only member of her own family whom she knew was her Aunt Sadie Gomersal, from Bittern Crag Farm a mile away. She'd occasionally met her grandmother there, and her uncles, when she and Rose Clare went to collect milk. Sadie had talked to her quite kindly, but the rest of the Gomersals took no more notice of her than if she were a stranger. Then her Aunt Sadie went off to Scarborough in service and even that tenuous link was broken.

Susan stayed with her foster mother, working the farm. Then one day her beloved Rose Clare had died in the yard in the act of feeding the hens. After that Susan's

Gomersal grandmother took to trekking back up to Goshawk Shield every day to haunt her granddaughter and seethe with nameless resentment. Susan mourned so much the loss of Rose Clare that she took little notice of her. Finally, unable to stand Susan's stubborn grief for a woman whom she deeply disliked, her grandmother told her this terrible thing. She raved on about how wicked Susan's own mother had been and how helpless her poor brother had been, caught in her lure. How she had been truly wicked, as was Susan now, in loving some dead Irishwoman more than her own flesh and blood.

The funeral brought Rose Clare's own daughter, Theodora, up from London. It brought her son, Rhys, from Priorton. Susan was numb to them all. She'd been too small as a baby to mourn her own mother; her grief for her foster mother was insurmountable. But she did not cry. She stayed enclosed within herself.

For weeks after the funeral, Susan was a woman of straw. She allowed the old woman to move in properly with her to Goshawk Shield. Grandma Gomersal took over the house. Susan had no heart for the chores and routines which she had taken in her stride with Rose Clare by her side. As the weeks went by the farm decayed and the house went to rot. Stock went unfed and had to forage for themselves, creating havoc in the barns. Tiles fell from the roof. Letters went unanswered.

When her fourth letter went unanswered Theodora Lytton, née Maichin, decided to take charge of things. After all, Susan was her goddaughter and Goshawk Shield did belong to her. She travelled up from London and found her own letters unopened in a heap on the kitchen table amongst a litter of jam jars and old bread. She surveyed Susan, sitting dully beside the unlit range. She cocked her ear to the raving of the old woman upstairs. Susan's grandmother was up to her favourite game, moving furniture, crashing and banging to her heart's delight.

'What is it, Susan? What's the matter?'

Susan looked at her dully.

'I know, I know! Rose Clare. She was more of a mother to you than she ever was to me. I know you must be sad. But there's more. What is it?'

Susan closed her eyes. 'How can you know? The life you live down there.' She glanced round at the mess. 'Even all this belongs to you.'

Theodora Louisa Lytton, Rose Clare's daughter, could not deny that she did have a good way of life. She lived in a comfortable house in London, wrote a popular novel every other year, went to the library, the cinema and the theatre and met her friends. She mourned her husband and son, but in general her life was good. But Goshawk Shield, where she had spent the most important part of her youth, had belonged to her since she was eighteen. And Susan was just about her only family.

'Oh Susan!' she said crossly, tears welling in her own eyes. 'I know about feeling like you do. Think of James and little Simon.' Her husband, James, and ten-year-old Simon had been swept away, like a million others, in the influenza epidemic of 1919. 'Think of my two dear ones, won't you?' Then without saying anything further she took off her elegant hat and rolled up her sleeves and raked out the range and lit it. While the fire blazed up she put a shawl round Susan's shoulders and went in search of the grandmother.

The house was a wreck. Curtains had been wrenched down; furniture had been dragged into random piles and heaped with rugs taken from the now-bare floors. The bookshelves in the dining room had been upscuttled and books were strewn everywhere. The drapes had been ripped down from all of the windows in the Pheasant Room, that wonderful hexagonal room which looked over every part of the dale; the room where as a girl Theo had written her first novel.

She found Mrs Gomersal in the main bedroom where, with the help of a kitchen knife and great deliberation, she was tearing the bed sheets to shreds. When she saw Theo she waved the knife at her, grinning.

Theo retreated, closed the door behind her and made her way back to the kitchen. The fire was now burning up cheerfully. She filled the kettle and put it to boil. Then she pulled up a little stool beside Susan and took her hand.

'What is it, Susan, what is it? For God's sake say something. I know you are sad about Rose Clare, but this . . .'

Susan raised her face to meet Theo's concerned gaze. 'She told me,' she said.

'She did what?'

'She told me about my mother.'

'But you knew. Your mother worked alongside Rose Clare here at Goshawk when it still belonged to Mrs Gervase. Your mother was a fine woman. She was Rose Clare's friend. She was strong and very good.'

'She told me about my uncle. How my mother . . . ticed him on.'

Theo's grip on her hand tightened. 'She told you what?'

'That my uncle was my father and my mother a . . . wanton.'

Theo breathed evenly for a second or two. 'It was your uncle who forced her, believe me—'

Susan exploded in a dry laugh. 'So now I have a choice? A whore for a mother or a perverted man for a father?'

'That old harridan had no right to tell you,' said Theo. 'No right.' She got to her feet and picked up a soiled tea towel to protect her from the burning handle of the kettle. She busied herself scalding the tea and pouring the cups.

Susan watched her wearily. 'You can see what she's doing, can't you? She's reclaiming me for her own. Even this minute she's spoiling this place stick by stick to show me it's not mine. That I am hers, that I belong down at Bittern Crag. Not Goshawk Shield.'

'Well, she's wrong anyway,' said Theo grimly. 'You belong to this place, just as I do. Just as Rose Clare did.' She clasped Susan's chilly fingers round the thick cup of sweet tea. Then, almost unnoticed by the exhausted Susan, she went in search of Mrs Gomersal. The sound of gushing water led her to the bathroom. The old woman was there. She watched with glee as the water overflowed the deep tub and streamed on to the soaking floor.

'Get out,' Theo shouted over the gushing water. 'Get out of my house, you old harridan, you monster.'

Mrs Gomersal picked up the bath brush and launched herself across the room. Theo ducked and grabbed the woman's arm. Mrs Gomersal wrenched herself away and launched herself again at Theo. Theo dodged to one side. The woman hurtled past her and landed in the overflowing bath of water with a splash, sending a wave into the room which drenched Theo.

The old woman sank in the water like a stone, sending a spume of bubbles in her wake. Theo waited a second before pulling her out. She snorted and spluttered like a walrus. 'Hey, missis, what yeh think yer doin'? Half drownin' us, yeh are.' She gasped and subsided to the floor in a heap. Theo grabbed her under the armpits and hauled her like a sack of potatoes across the room and bumped her down the stairs to the kitchen. In there she propped her against the wall by the fire. Then she drew a very deep breath.

Susan watched unmoving. But there was a spark now in her eyes. 'What's this then?' she said.

'It's ended,' said Theo. 'This old woman has just stopped tearing down my house, thank you very much.'

'She nearly kilt us, dragging us down the stairs like that,' Mrs Gomersal grumbled. 'She's a witch.'

'Lucky you didn't get worse,' said Susan, smiling faintly. 'Mucking up her house like that.'

'And when she's dried off she can get herself out. Away from this place for good,' said Theo firmly. 'Right out of my house.'

'I live here,' said the woman. 'I live here with my granddaughter.'

Theo looked at Susan. 'Well?'

'She's my family,' said Susan slowly.

'I'm your family, Susan. Rose Clare was your foster mother and I'm your godmother. This is your family.'

'So we're relations, are we?' Susan laughed. 'I don't think so.' She nodded at her bedraggled grandmother. 'She's my relation.'

The two women surveyed each other. Susan saw a tall, elegant woman in a smart London dress. She was pale-haired and pink-skinned and carried her fifty-two years very lightly. Theo saw a tall, rangy young woman, her broad bonny face roughened by the moorland wind, her hands strong and used to hard work.

'Rose Clare was mother to both of us, Susan. There's no greater bond.'

Susan looked down at her grandmother, snivelling now by the roaring fire. 'Maybe Rose Clare was mother to both of us, Theo. But this here's my grandmother, not yours.'

Theo glanced round the big kitchen. 'This is all too much now, isn't it, without Rose Clare? This house, the farm . . .'

Susan sighed. 'I don't know why, Theo. With me and Rose Clare it all went like a song. It was lovely here.'

Theo nodded. 'A good team. You two were a good team.' She poured herself a cup of tea and refreshed Susan's cup. 'I can't come back up here myself. Too much of me is down there now. If I came away I would feel as though I were leaving the last of James and little Simon. Perhaps I could let off part of the farmhouse and the land, and you' – she glanced across at Mrs Gomersal, who was now tossing coal from the scuttle on to the kitchen table – 'and the old harridan, if you want . . . we'll find a cottage somewhere nearer to Stanhope, where the bus goes by. You need time to get yourself better. A smaller place . . .'

Susan looked up at Theo. 'I miss Rose Clare,' she said. 'I miss my old friend like mad.'

'So do I, Susan. So do I.'

After that time life at the new cottage, even with her grandmother, was a little bit better. This place was not imbued with the spirit of Rose Clare. There was less work for Susan, fewer things for her grandmother to break. Theo sent them a postal order each week from London to keep them going. Susan began to wake up from what seemed like a long sleep. While her grandmother slipped further into the veils of madness Susan finally tossed off her low feelings like unwanted baggage. She became more her capable old self. She could think of Rose Clare with equanimity.

When her grandmother came at her with a carving knife for the third time, Susan called in the Stanhope doctor who arranged for the old woman to be admitted to Park View.

After the shock of her first visits to the hospital, Susan became more interested in what went on in there. She wrote to Theo.

> I've been thinking I might train to be a mental nurse. Proper nursing wouldn't take me because I didn't matriculate. But in this place they'll take you with a good elementary schooling. From what I see, lifting and carrying round the farm will stand me in good stead in that place. It can be heavy work. If I get in, you could rent out this cottage, as I'll hardly be there.

Theo wrote back that she was impressed with Susan's plans, but they would hang on to the cottage, as she didn't imagine Susan would be at the hospital seven days a week, fifty-two weeks a year. She would need a home base.

> You'll always have a home here in Islington with me, of course, but this is a long way to come for a weekend.

Chapter Two

At the Gun Emplacement

Maria Josep Sabater – nicknamed ChiChu after her grandmother's pet bird – could strip down and clean a rifle in two minutes flat. She could find kindling on a bare mountainside. She could light a fire with nothing more than a few roots of rosemary. She could shoot a cockerel from ten yards. She could shoot the blood-and-pus Fascist flag from fifty yards. A hundred yards. A thousand. So she said.

But ChiChu could not cook. The men on the other emplacements laughed at this. A woman along not being able to cook! Like fish without fins. The girl could sell her father's Anarchist pamphlets with her trays of roses in the narrow alleyways off the *barri* in Barcelona. But she could not cook. This was a point of laughter all along the emplacement.

In her apartment in the *barri*, ChiChu's grandmother, Juana, had cooked like an angel right up to the day of the bomb. That was a hard day for ChiChu, that day they found her grandmother's false teeth nearly sixty yards away, buried in the bark of the dusty palm tree in the corner of the square.

* * *

ChiChu's grandmother, Juana, was tall and narrow, just like ChiChu herself. The men in their family mocked them, saying they had no flesh, no covering. Wasn't that a great fault in a woman? In the *barri* they used to call Juana 'the heron'. Her husband, Josep, was called 'the hen' because although he was a great talker out in the street, he was such a craven creature in the house.

Juana stayed thin, it was said, because after producing one son, she broke the laws of God in some way and stopped her body having children. The old man must have put all his juice into one precious pot because no one could deny that their one son, also called Josep, was made of very special stuff. Wasn't he on the Aragon front at this very moment defending the Republic against Franco and his Moorish hordes? Juana was full of pride in her son and shouted insults to any man walking in the street who did not wear the red scarf of the fighter.

The old man too was proud of Josep. He told exaggerated tales of his son's courageous exploits for the people's cause in Francisco's *alberg*, a dark place where the men went to smoke tobacco and to drink the wine that sloshed from the great barrels which lined the walls.

The other old men laughed at old Josep. They would tease him, saying the totality of his own courage must have been planted in that one spurt of seed all those years ago. They all knew he was more frightened of his wife than he was of any Fascist pig cracking off shells against the comrades on the Aragon front. Some days, they observed, he was so frightened of his wife that he was driven to share a whole skin of wine at Francisco's with his friend Sol before he dare venture home.

One day ChiChu watched with her grandmother from

the window of the apartment as Sol brought her grandfather home on his back. He flipped the old man to the ground and hauled him up the stairs like an old dog. Her grandfather lay there, feigning death, and Sol called up to Juana, telling her that the old boy *had an indisposition* and for him the best medicine would be her own tender loving care, between the sheets, for preference. Then Sol whistled through his teeth in a very insulting fashion and raced off into the night.

Juana shouted after that naughty Sol, telling him he was no better than his mother and she was a thief and a whore. Then she dragged the old man into the room, her wiry hands clutching his shoulders. She hauled him to the middle of the floor, then grasped an old olive stick she kept specially to beat the washing. ChiChu watched with interest as Juana beat the old man soundly as any bed sheet. She smote him over the head and shoulders, uttering swearwords reserved only for these occasions.

Josep crawled under the heavy dresser, pulling his knees tight underneath him, so the only place his wife could reach was his heels. Then she gave her short barking laugh, gave his heel one last kick with her bare horny foot, then returned to the shelf in the corner to complete the task of decanting precious oil she had rolled in a barrel all the way from the Boquería Market. She poured the oil into returnable cans, which she sold in the *barrio*. Oil was very short these days so she considered her acquisition a great coup. She sniffed, allowing herself to gloat over the luscious harvest of oil slopping around in her old rusting can.

'Come, ChiChu,' she said, 'help me strain the oil.'

Old Josep twisted round in his strange refuge and peered at his wife before, sobered by the beating, he wriggled out to ask. 'So? A good pressing, was it, Juana?'

'The man at the Boquería told me the olives are fewer this year because of the war, but the ones he had were plump,' she said. 'Sweet as cherries.'

ChiChu shook her foot to relieve it of cramp, gritting her teeth as the spikes of pain went up her leg. She turned her head this way and that to loosen the stiffness in her neck and shoulders and peered over the barrier of stones at the soldiers opposite. They were not much more than a thousand yards away, crawling like ants behind their own barriers. The gun emplacement was one of several scattered across the escarpment, some of them spaces carved by time to accommodate the men. Men! Some were no more than children, sent up here half clad and with little training to fight for the cause for ten pesetas a day; these were the last remnants of the Anarchist militias not yet pulled in to the more disciplined People's Army.

In their section the comradeship of the early days of the revolution set the tone. No saluting. No orders given without negotiation. But the days of such democracy were numbered, even in the Republic. The talk was that such idealized respect was antithetical to discipline and would lose the war. So the old ways returned.

At ChiChu's emplacement the ground was running with mud which floated smooth as porridge over earth stamped down by three months' boot traffic. Ridges and furrows raised by months of rain alternating with hard cold or frost had been humbled and patted down by the dense spring rain. The worst of the Spanish winter was over.

Here and there, scattered along the front, buffeted by the flying roots of rosemary and thistle, were heaps of stones and sandbags which only the kindest military mind would call a gun emplacement. Each one was big enough to give shelter for five boys, or even four men, so they could take sights on the distant escarpment opposite.

This emplacement was constructed many months ago by Esteban, who was still here with the remnants of the crew. Their war had proved to be a matter of patience and holding the line, rather than heroic forays against the Fascists. They were ready to advance but orders and reorders from behind the line denied them the satisfaction of the direct action they craved. It was whispered that the Loyalist comrades did not want them to succeed here because that would be a victory for the revolution and the more timid comrades were ashamed of such radical change.

The crew was depleted, not by Fascist fire, but by cold and misery and bugs caught from rats, which had flourished in the early days of good provision and generous leavings. Scattered around the post was the detritus of the hundred-day watch: bones of dead chickens mixing with spent cartridges and butts of cigarettes. Footless boots and the ashes of rosemary fires were scattered over the crumbling remains of human excrement.

Esteban's hands were always blue with cold. He took his job seriously. His eyes peered down the barrel of his ancient Russian rifle through a gap in a long scarf, knit by his grandmother, which he had wound three times round his head.

ChiChu always took her place beside Esteban. She made sure that both his and her rifles were in a fit condition to shoot; that they wouldn't kill the man who fired them, as sometimes happened. Many of the cartridges issued to them were remoulds, which became swollen and jammed in the breech. Esteban had lost two good comrades that way.

ChiChu had just missed the bomb that killed her father and her grandparents in the *barri*, the tight web of streets in Barcelona where they lived. Despite a bad foot injury her father had returned to his home, with his comrades Jorge and young Esteban, like a conquering hero. For a week the district was full of returning *campaneros*, released after nearly a month hard fighting on the front. There was much drinking and washing of clothes and making of babies: new citizens for the Republic. The place was awash with foreigners holed up in Francisco's *alberg*, resting up hundreds of miles from home. These men saw themselves as heroes fighting for the Republic. ChiChu's father spat when he spoke of them. He said they were after their own interests.

He'd speak of Communists in the pay of Stalin, trying to divert the free spirit of anarchism into lickspittling serfdom at Russia's behest. These jokers had lessons every day on how to think in the proper way. They had to say their prayers to Stalin, he said. The revolution had got rid of the priests for this! Then he would grow angry and howl like a wolf. This madness was looked on in the *barrio* with equanimity. Everyone, even the calmest of men, got mad once in a while. It was good for the blood. People listened with respect to what young Josep had to say but after the first euphoria of leave there was an uneasiness about the place. This *barri* was firm for anarchy and the revolution. But there were spies. Josep should watch his mouth. This was said more than once.

Late on the fourth day of her father's leave, ChiChu had been sent to the apothecary just off the Ramblas to get some special ointment for her father's injured foot. The bullets were out now but it was too slow in healing.

That was when their apartment was bombed.

Even across the whole width of the Ramblas she heard the dull cracking thump and started to run. When she got there the tall building was a mass of smoking wood and stone. The remnants of the second and third floors looked out, embarrassingly naked to the world. All that was left of her grandmother were her dentures, stuck in the bark of a battered palm tree, which had struggled to life on the corner of the *plaça* which stood at the end of their narrow street.

ChiChu started to shriek. Sol, her grandfather's friend, took her in his arms and whispered in her ear. 'Those foreigners visited your father, child. They tried to get him to trim his tune, to listen to their arguments. They said he weakened their cause with the flabby chances of anarchy.' The old man pinched her arm hard. 'He was not persuaded,' he whispered in her ear. 'He was not persuaded. Your father was a hero.'

Josep's comrades Jorge and Esteban joined with ChiChu in her grief and stayed for the dark day of the funerals, which were carried out without priests. Then she went with Jorge and Esteban back to the front, a kind of surrogate for her father, a *miliciana* with her father's courageous blood in her veins. The soldiers laughed at her at first, then they taught her to shoot and move about in the mountains like any young soldier. Tall and slender, with her cord breeches and zip jacket, her cap pulled down over her tied-up hair, she could pass at a distance for one of the boy soldiers who had been pulled into the war.

But the female element in her life was not so easy to

disguise. Her comrades had to protect her from the opportunism of soldiers starved of female company and when they were told all *milicianas* were whores at heart, they stoutly defended her reputation. 'Her father was our comrade,' Esteban would say fiercely. 'And he died a hero for anarchism. This is his daughter. She is a *miliciana*.'

Esteban thrust a battered rifle into ChiChu's narrow chest. 'Call this a gun? What d'you think of this thing, ChiChu? What kind of godforsaken second-grade Russian rubbish are they sending us now?'

Esteban mentioned God a great deal in his cursing, although everyone knew he was an avowed atheist and had chased the priests and nuns from more than one convent during his extended action for the revolution. He took particular delight in opening the doors of the convents. His own sister had vanished through such a door thirty years before and gone mad before they let her out again.

ChiChu clutched the gun in her freezing hands. It smelled of olive oil and old earth, and sat awkwardly against her, without true balance. 'Mmm,' she said. 'You're right.'

Esteban nodded, then sat back against the rock, put his fingers to his mouth and blew over them. The air flowed over his knobbly fingers like the steam from a boiling kettle. Then he took a battered half-cigarette out of his pocket. He cupped his leathery hands round it, struck a flint to light it and drew the smoke into his chest with deep gratitude.

ChiChu turned the rifle over, took a sight down the barrel towards the enemy, and shook her head. 'Could you kill a half-dead sheep of a stinking Fascist with this thing? I'm telling you, Esteban, this is impossible.'

Jorge pulled his woollen cap further down over his ears and drew again on his own cigarette. Then he held his free hand out towards the fire, fuelled today by footless boots and three leather-backed books which had belonged to Marco, who had been killed just this morning by a rare bullet which ricocheted off the escarpment and smashed into the back of his head. A fact that no one mentioned was that the bullet might be one of their own, let off carelessly in the emplacement thirty yards to the left. Marco was another hero for the revolution.

ChiChu turned the gun over and over in her hands. Her store of oil, from the last of her grandmother's great cans, was running low now. It had to do for guns as well as cooking. She broke open the stock of the gun and clicked her teeth. 'See, Jorje! See this filthy rust. It wasn't young fifty years ago, this rifle, I'm telling you.'

'All there is, ChiChu.' Jorge leaned back against the stones and closed his eyes. 'All there is, little chicken.'

The news that there was a woman on the third emplacement whirred along the winter-weary line, leaping from unit to unit like an agile monkey. A woman! Many of the recruits had seen the enticing posters with tightly belted dungaree'd girls flourishing rifles and beckoning them to defend the revolution. In the early days women had fought alongside the men but that had gone out of favour. Some of them, it was said, were no better than they should be; whores who tapped the virile energies which men should be reserving for the fight. So they were pulled back and were doing fine work for the revolution now on the home front which was, after all, their place.

But this one, the whisper went, was different. She was

the daughter of a heroic comrade who had fallen for the cause. At this time, on this front, because of the girl, nightly social visits between the units were banned.

In the fourth emplacement a barber turned fighter named Enrico growled that there should be a meeting to discuss this. Wasn't it undemocratic to give an order without negotiation? He shook his shaggy head. 'We are not beasts of the field, after all.' Enrico's friend Joan leaned his head sadly on his friend's shoulder. 'A woman?' he says. 'Who knows what will happen when we see her? It has been such a very long time. They do well to keep us away.'

The order to move, when it came, was a surprise. Their section had been holding the ridge for three months through mud and the occasional sniper fire. They were used to this inactivity. Now they were to go forward at dawn, down into the gully under darkness and breach an enemy emplacement where there was a *metralleta*, a machine gun.

They did as they were told. It was a reliable order, Jorge told them, brought to them from the Anarchist channels. They wormed their way forward in small groups. But their timing was not too good, because they were badly placed as the sun came up behind them. They were sitting targets for the Fascist snipers. A shell burst in front of them. Jorge and Esteban crumpled on either side of ChiChu. She turned and Esteban put his hands, bloody stumps, towards her. Then she felt a thump, as though someone had punched her hard on the shoulder. She spun and fell. In front of her was the dead light in the eyes of Esteban. She rolled over.

Jorge was groaning, 'Get away from here, ChiChu. Get away. If they find you . . .' His throat gurgled, pulsing out blood, and his eyes closed.

MY DARK-EYED GIRL

Her nose itched with the smell of cordite. She put her hand to her shoulder and could feel the warm blood oozing through a hole in her zipper jacket. Above her the victorious shouts of the men who had killed her comrades echoed round the gully. She snaked along the ground towards a cluster of rocks which lay against the mountainside. Inching her way behind them she found a shallow hole, almost a cave. She crept in there, curled up tight, ignoring the throbbing pain in her shoulder. She knew that if she could stay here until nightfall again she would be safe. It would be a long day.

Chapter Three

Decisions

The years since making the decision to work at the hospital had flown by for Susan. The job had its ups and downs. The shifts meant that the only people she saw, from one week to the next, were people from the asylum: inmates and staff. On nightshift she only saw the people on her own ward. She slept most of the day and on her day off caught up on a week of shallow sleep.

Eddie Conlon, the chief electrician, asked her regularly to go to the pictures with him, but she turned him down. She did let him show her how to play tennis on the hospital court. Now and then she made up a four at bridge, which she and Eddie played with the pharmacist and his wife. She wrote to Theo about this intricate life behind the long wall. Theo wrote in reply: *More like a country house than a hospital! In some ways*.

Susan wrote back that she wouldn't say that if she saw Mary Thomasina trailing round the corridors carrying the log which she thought was her baby. Or if she heard the screams at night as staff bundled Sarah Lefever into a cell when she was having one of her bad dos. Or when you reminded yourself to get a struggling patient's shoes off so it didn't hurt so much when they kicked you.

'You'd 'a thought Eddie Conlon would have asked you to marry him by now.' Keziah pursued her question one afternoon when they were walking back to Ward Ten after church, escorting six patients.

'You don't know he hasn't,' said Susan calmly.

'You've turned him down, then?'

'I'm not marrying anybody,' said Susan firmly. 'I value my freedom far too much.' No good telling Keziah or anyone how afraid she was of having a child with too large a head, or a wrenched neck. Or one with an ungovernable temper like Sarah Lefever.

Eddie was four years younger than Susan. His father had been chief attendant on the male side for years. As he said too often, he'd been born in the job. He'd done his apprenticeship in a factory and had started out by saying he's rather die than work at Park View. That Mad House. But the factory had closed and like thousands of others, Eddie lost his job in the early thirties. There were no jobs to be had, so in the end he was pleased that his father could put in a word for him at Park View.

Susan went once to have tea at Eddie's house on the perimeter, just this side of the wall. It was an experiment she didn't repeat. Eddie's mother kept referring to Susan's great age and talked to Eddie as though Susan wasn't there. Eddie dismissed Susan's protests, saying this was his mother's way. She'd never been good with people.

'Well,' said Susan, 'she's quite safe. I'll not be troubling her any more.'

After that, to Keziah's disappointment, Eddie seemed to lose interest in Susan. 'You'll end up a sour old maid!' she wailed. Then her broad face brightened. 'Never mind,' she said. 'What're you doing on your weekend off?'

'Going up to Stanhope. The cottage needs an airing.'

'You can come home with me,' Keziah beamed. 'It's our George's party and there'll be a shindig.'

Susan stared at her. She'd heard tales of this family: of Jake and George and Tegger and the little sister Sweetie; of their parties and their mother's music, and the ploys they got up to to beat the means test man.

'There'll be no room,' she said.

'Don't worry about that. We'll find somewhere.'

'I suppose I could sleep in the bath,' said Susan.

Keziah exploded in laughter. 'Bath? You must be joking. The only bath there's a tin one and it's hanging on a nail in the yard.'

New Morven, Keziah's home village, was a dingy place where the vile hand of the depression had left its sorry mark. They said New Morven had the most unemployed men in an area renowned for its lack of work; an area which had spawned hunger marches and brought forth a flush of sympathy and food parcels from the guilty, more affluent parts of the country. In its worst times it had been visited by a very glamorous Prince of Wales who told its citizens that they were acting with dignity under the strain.

New Morven had once been a thriving village with two pits, a steelworks and an overlarge Co-operative Store. Now the pits and the ironworks were closed and the Co-op was boarded up. Some of those who had not tramped off to find work further south assiduously attended their allotments for basic food. Some played football and bowls in elaborate neighbourhood leagues, and made a pint of beer last a whole evening at the Fettler's Arms. Others sat on their haunches outside their gates, telling tales of times when work had been plenty, when they had bested the bosses, or how they had made their mark on the Hunger March. Some went even further back in time and told tales of their fathers: how one had fed his family by poaching the laird's game in Scotland; how another had seen a ghost in a deep mine in Wales.

As the depression ground its way through the decade three men from this village had killed themselves with despair: one by hanging from the roof beam of his pigeon loft, having first wrung the necks of his pigeons; another by walking into the deep end of the colliery pool with stones in his pockets; the third by cutting his wrists behind his shed on the allotments.

Keziah lived in the end house of a street of houses where the decade of neglect displayed itself in peeling paint and dark windows. As she and Keziah ducked washing lines and wove their way down the packed mud of the back street, the overripe stench of the privies made Susan gulp.

It wasn't just that it was a privy. She had one of those up at the cottage, but that was on its own at the end of a long garden path. These privies were in blocks of four, across a narrow lane from the back walls of the houses. Anyone needing to go there would be making their inner lives and functions very public. Susan wondered if she could manage a whole weekend without this necessity. She blushed at the thought of it.

Keziah pushed open the creaking gate and disturbed two hens that were pecking away at crumbs in a long yard. In a wide hutch two round-eyed rabbits swished through deep straw, disturbed by their presence.

They went through a tiny scullery into a kitchen where two men were sitting at a table, newspapers spread before them. By the fire, a woman with a lined face was crocheting. She stood up, smiling; her arms hung loose by her side. 'Why, our Keziah! Good to see yeh. Yeh got the bus all right?'

Susan waited in vain for them to embrace, as she would have once with Rose Clare, or as she did with Theo even now. There was no embrace. The men at the table just nodded, and sat back in their chairs. Still you could tell, they were all pleased to see this daughter of the house.

'Now, Keziah,' said the younger man. He was heavy-set with a rough beard and thick brows set over very piercing eyes.

'Now, Jake,' she said.

'Now, Keziah,' said the older man, who was short and broad like Keziah.

'Now, Dad,' she said.

Jake looked at Susan. 'Ah see yeh brought yehr marrah, Kezzie?'

'Aye, Jake,' said Keziah. 'This is Susan Cornford, me mate from work.' Her tone was deeper, her accent stronger than it normally was at the hospital.

Susan took half a step, half held her hand out, somehow impelling both of the men to stand up and shake her hand. Mrs Stanton followed suit. Her hand was soft and very dry compared with theirs. 'Will yeh sit down?' she said, removing her bundle of crochet from her own chair.

Susan took the seat, suddenly uncomfortable at them all towering above her, inspecting her as though she were a new rabbit. She smiled wanly. The men sat down again.

'I told yeh about her,' said Keziah. 'She comes off a farm in Weardale.'

'A farmer?' said Mr Stanton. 'Mebbe yeh'd like a look

at my allotment?' His tone, and the younger man's gaze, were ironic.

Susan flushed. 'Well, it was mostly sheep,' she said. 'A couple of cows. Some hens. But that was years ago.'

The tension was broken. She had admitted herself less worthy so she was all right. The men shuffled their papers and Mrs Stanton moved the kettle from the hearth to the hob.

Jake Stanton placed his hand flat on the paper before him. 'Spain, Miss Cornford! What do you think about Spain?'

'Jake,' said Keziah, 'don't start . . .'

'Spain? Well, I know there's this war now, but not much more. I haven't read a paper for weeks. Work and sleep. That's all there is at the hospital apart from the rats.'

Jake's laugh cracked into the air. 'Too busy with the bad and the mad in that mad house to know what a mad house the world is, eh, Susan Cornford?'

She was bright red. 'I'm sorry I—'

'Do you know, Susan Cornford, that in Spain the rightly elected government is being pushed out by a bunch of Fascists dressed up as soldiers supported by fancy priests with an appetite for wealth and power? And the Germans and that strutting peacock Mussolini is helpin' 'em? Gettin' together to make sure the ordinary man has no more say than them hens out there?'

'Well, I've read—'

'And Miss Cornford, do yeh know there's folks here, in this country, mebbe you're one of them, who think this is no bad thing, that the man with the biggest gun should rule.'

'Oh, Jake, get off your high horse, will yeh?' said Keziah. 'And for goodness' sake call her Susan. You make her

44

sound like a schoolmarm or sommat.'

'Complacency, that's the danger,' said Jake.

Keziah shook him by the shoulder. 'Stop it, Jake. Where's yehr manners?' He shrugged off her hand and started turning the pages of a small pamphlet which had been tucked under his newspaper.

'Now,' said Keziah, beaming, 'Ah bet Susan here'd love one of yehr cherry scones, Mam. Ah've told her all about yehr cherry scones. And Ah've promised all the staff on Ward Ten Ah'll take a bag of them back with me, so you can get baking. The food in that place isn't fit for pigs.'

'Yeh can stop making promises on my behalf, lady,' said Mrs Stanton calmly. 'Ah've plenty to do without feeding half a hospital, yeh know.'

Susan sat back, pleased that the spotlight was off her but still aware of Jake brooding at the table over his pamphlets. There was something about him which caught her attention. She could feel his energy flowing towards her. Now Keziah was off telling her stories about the wild patients, the horrible food and the rats. At that point Jake, muttering about the bad and the mad, swept up his papers and stumped upstairs.

Mr Stanton scratched his head just above his ear and looked at Susan. 'Tek no notice of the lad, pet. Out of work six years, and . . .' He glanced at Keziah.

His wife took up the explanation. 'Canna tek the fact that the only money coming in here is from our Keziah.'

Keziah looked up from where she was pouring out tea. For a second her sad face was veiled by the rising steam. 'Come on, Dad. It's not just me. There's yehr eggs. All the stuff from the allotment. People buy it off yeh, don't they?'

'Pot stuff!' He was scornful. 'No living to be made

selling folks a penn'orth of pot stuff.'

'It keeps us going, Dan,' Mrs Stanton joined in. 'And the shop gives me flour and salt and cherries for me eggs. I get me wool . . .' Her glance in her husband's direction was openly fond.

'And fish!' said Keziah. 'Me dad's a great fisherman, Susan.'

'Don't often pull a one,' said her father gloomily. 'Too many of the lads fishing the Wear for their dinner, these days.'

'More often yeh do,' said Mrs Stanton firmly. 'Now, Susan, would yeh like one of me famous cherry scones with yehr cup of tea?'

Munching the cherry scone, Susan looked around and wondered where on earth she would sleep. There was only this kitchen and a narrow little parlour visible through the middle door.

Mrs Stanton read her thoughts. 'Ah've got the beds sorted,' she announced, looking at Keziah. She poured her tea into her saucer and blew on it before she drank it. 'Yeh and Susan here can have our Jake's bed. He's gonna sleep at yehr gran's.'

'No,' said Susan. 'I'll go on to Stanhope. I couldn't—'

'It's sorted,' said Mrs Stanton firmly. 'It's nice that our Keziah brought yeh. She never brought anyone from the hospital before. Mebbe you're the one that can tell us whether these tales she brings home from there are true or not. They seem a bit far-fetched to me.'

So Susan spent the night enfolded uncomfortably with Keziah in Jake's narrow bed. Lying beside the snoring Keziah she wondered what it must be, to be part of a real family like this. At teatime, Keziah's brother George had come home dirty from the allotment; their sister Sweetie, a tiny creature who worked for pennies as under-maid in a doctor's household, flopped into the chair and put her feet on the fender. They all shared a large tasty stew, mostly vegetables, and the table buzzed with tales that they all brought in. Keziah, of course, was the centre of attention.

Susan had sat at the dinner table listening with real attention as Keziah's brother Jake argued with his father the wrongs and rights of the war in Spain. Jake, an ardent Communist, had picked up a stream of persuasive argument from his pamphlets. Some of the phrases sounded stiff and alien in his mouth, but he was very much in earnest about all men being his brothers. What he said made sense to Susan.

She recognized the feeling in him: like the feeling she had about people like Jane Ann Golon at the hospital, mad as they were. She felt a commonness with them; a desire to do right by them. Jake Stanton felt that about those poor souls in Spain.

His earnest energy seemed to ring right through her; it made her feel more alive. Suddenly she was envious. It was all right for him. He could go there and do that and satisfy his feelings. She had half a mind to go herself.

Susan had jumped when Jake seemed to read her mind. He turned to her. 'And what about you, Miss Susan Cornford? Are they not yehr brothers as well, like? Would yeh not go to fight? There's women fighting out there.'

She blushed. 'I . . . I . . .'

Keziah kicked her brother under the table. 'Leave it alone, Jake, with your rabble-rousing.' She turned to Susan. 'Tek no notice.'

'No, Keziah,' said Susan. 'He's right I suppose. We should all think about it at least.' She paused to take a breath. Then the words emerged from her mouth and she could hardly believe them herself. She turned to Jake. 'Well, I couldn't take up a gun, like. But I could help with it. I'd work in a hospital, offer in that way.' The minute she said the words, despite the fact that before this visit she had never really thought about this battle going on in Spain, she knew she wanted to do this. She wanted to do this now, more than anything she had ever wanted in her life. She had worked on the farm by the accident of her life there with Rose Clare; she had drifted to the hospital because of the accident of her grand-mother's illness. Jake Stanton's dark energy, his earnest commitment, had lit some kind of flame in her. This time she could choose.

'I'll go myself,' she announced.

Jake blinked and looked at her for the first time. 'D'you mean that?'

'She can't,' objected Keziah. 'She's no Communist like you.'

He shook his head. 'You think some poor fellow full of shrapnel cares whether it's a Communist that's doing his dressings or the blinking fancy Queen of England?' He turned to Susan. 'Are you serious, Miss Cornford? Susan? Are you serious?'

After supper Keziah and Susan washed up and Mrs Stanton took her place at the upright piano and picked out tunes from variety and operetta, singing as she went. Half a dozen neighbours came in and joined in the song.

'Your mother must be musical,' she said to Keziah through the noise. 'She plays that well.'

Keziah laughed. 'The number of times that piano was nearly sold,' she said, 'you wouldn't believe it. The last time was when I finally decided to go to the hospital. That's what made up my mind. At least being handmaiden to old Tordoff is saving the piano for me mam.'

'It makes a lovely sound.'

'She was never taught, you know. Taught herself to read music and she can sit and play anything she's heard once. We had this gramophone too, but that had to be sold. But it didn't go until she knew every tune on all ten records. They say she was up there playing seconds before I was born. Nearly brought forth on a piano stool, that's me.'

'Keziah!'

'Well, she did love to play.'

Jake listened to the music for ten minutes, then went off to his grandmother's. After he had gone, there was a change in the atmosphere. Mrs Stanton turned to her husband. 'Yeh should tell him he canna go,' she said. 'We canna let him go.'

'Tell him? He's thirty-eight, woman.'

'Well, we need him here, not fighting for some foreigners.'

'He believes in it,' said Keziah. 'Yeh canna tell him not to go.'

Her father nodded. 'It's not like he's doing any good round here. Nowt to do. Ah know that. He might just as well save the world. Save it in his head, mebbe.'

'Ah I can see why he's so mad to go,' said Keziah. 'Ah'd like to go meself. It's an adventure. And they need nurses. He told us that.'

A pin-drop silence impregnated the room. 'Keziah, Ah . . .' her mother started. 'Ah hope yeh don't . . .'

Keziah's father put a hand on Keziah's shoulder. 'Aye, love. It might be an adventure, but what . . . what'd we do without yeh? The rest of us here're on the scrap heap. Yeh knaa that.'

'It'll not always be like that, Dad,' said Keziah. 'Things'll get going here. Jake says there'll be a war here too. Hitler's beating his old drum. Sooner or later they'll have to gear up. They'll need steel, coal. There'll be work . . .'

'That's as mebbe. But till then, Kezzie . . .' Mr Stanton's quiet voice struck Susan to the core. Never having lived in a house with men, she was impressed by the authority this man carried in this house, despite being out of work since the twenty-six strike, and despite the very quietness of his demeanour.

Dr Elias Tordoff stepped out of his new motorcar and watched as Tommy Rankin, his driver, put the shining wonder into reverse gear and backed it right down the long gravel path towards the garages. Now and then Elias suffered a twinge of guilt about the fact that he did not walk from his gracious house at the perimeter of the grounds to the tall doors of the main wing of the hospital. On very bright days he did make a habit of walking to the hospital, swinging his silver-topped cane and acknowledging the greetings of the staff, right and left, as he made his way down the winding path through the trees. However, if it were even slightly windy or rainy he telephoned for Tommy Rankin. He could not turn up on the wards with ruffled hair or damp spats. That would not do. It would not do at all.

Elias Tordoff comforted himself that he ran a tight ship. He had always regretted the myopia which had scuttled a planned career in the navy, and service in the Great War. After all, he'd sailed toy boats and worn sailor suits since he came out of petticoats. His father and grandfather, two uncles and two great-uncles had seen time in the Senior Service, two of them as naval surgeons. So it was a foregone conclusion that he should follow them.

It had been his misfortune to have a mother who was a bit of a weakling, and bequeathed him this damnable short sight. Throughout school, through medical school and in all his home life, by an act of supreme self-discipline he had worked his way round this weakness. Still, the dratted navy medico spotted it and wouldn't let him in.

He had sated his frustrated desires by playing hard games of tennis and with the hobby of fencing, which fortunately led to a bad nick on the arm which allowed him the fictional virtue of a war injury. It was not an actual lie, but hints were dropped which allowed a certain heroic interpretation.

Never mind, never mind. He went back to his medical career to be the best medico who hadn't sailed the seven seas. Well, perhaps not quite the best. Not quite good enough for the big London institutions, but good enough for his present berth, the great hulking vessel which was Park View Hospital. Two thousand patients and many hundreds of staff. It was his vocation to steer this great vessel through the murky waters of New Ideas and up the treacherous creeks of Possibility.

Oh yes! Oh yes! He ran a trim ship. The key to it all was respect and trust in the man at the helm. The crew, staff and patients alike, called him 'Sir'. Some of them, old servicemen, even saluted. Elias never demanded it, but felt quietly satisfied when it happened.

The women, of course, did not salute. Ridiculous thought. But some of the older women, used to domestic service on house and farm, would bob him a curtsey and call him 'mester'. The nurses called him Dr Tordoff, and the more obsequious of them stopped just short of a curtsey and blushed when he talked to them.

It was all very satisfying. Very satisfying indeed.

Matron, broad of beam and with the face of an intelligent horse, was not obsequious. She knew her own worth, and that was very useful to him. When he was off in Scotland in August for the shooting, or when he was in Nice in December, he was perfectly confident that the hospital would tick over on well-oiled wheels. Matron knew his methods and his desires, and carried them out to the letter.

Such a level of command in one's absence must surely be proof of great leadership.

The long corridor before him gleamed. A woman in a patient's overall was on her knees, polishing the last section of floor. A second woman was reaching up to polish a stained-glass window that depicted St Francis feeding the birds. As he passed, the woman on her knees lumbered to her feet. 'Mornin', mester,' she said, going on to her back heel in the vestige of a curtsey.

'Good morning, Mary Jane Stewart,' he said, baring his teeth. She was getting old and unsteady now. When he had first come here as deputy superintendent, Mary Jane had had a bold look in her eye and a firm body. Time, of course, had taken its toll. It was not the hospital which did this. Not the hospital at all. His own wife had lost all her body tone in that same stretch of time. She slept without sleeping draughts and controlled her temper without Largactil but she too had little self-discipline. She was disconcertingly slack these days.

Elias prided himself on the trimness of his own body,

the taut fullness of his skin, all a result of his disciplined regime. This involved breathing and dumbbell exercises on rising; one game of tennis a day; a moderate diet and self-indulgence confined to a nightly Havana cigar. The problem of taping on his glasses during tennis paled into insignificance when he considered the benefits of his regime.

At the corner of the corridor he brought his feet together in the military fashion and turned sharp right. In doing so he crashed into two scurrying nurses and sent one of them flying.

That night back at the hospital Susan wrote to Theo.

As soon as Jake Stanton said was I interested I knew I was! I thought it would be very hard to do, but it seems there's a big shortage of nurses. He told me that the nurses before the revolution were mostly nuns and they're on the other side in this war because they serve the Church, which is on the side of the Fascists. So. Can you believe it? Am I mad?
    Your loving,
        Susan

PS. I was knocked over in the hospital corridor this morning by the superintendent Dr Tordoff. Now he *really is* mad.

Theodora sent her some gold coins to sew into her corset and told her that yes, she was mad and that she wished she herself had the courage to do the same.

From the arguments floating around here, [she wrote,] it seems like a very just cause. A lot of slick soldiers trying to overcome the properly elected government, however bumbling it is! But they are so unsupported. Even the Labour Party, which should know better, is standing on the sidelines. Ellen Wilkinson, that little MP for Jarrow is, however, raising funds for the republican cause. But the thought of you there! Amid those flying bullets! It doesn't bear thinking about. A bit of a change from the farm, don't you think? I suppose, though, experience in the asylum is not a bad preparation for what's going on in Spain at the moment. It must be mad out there.

The government is stopping the British volunteering just now. Still, you've got all these fellows coming back from the front and talking like heroes.

There surely is danger, though, for us from the Germans. Those in the know say war is inevitable.

Your loving,
Theo

Chapter Four

At a Small Church in Aragon

It would be unkind to say this young female patient was
an inconvenience in the clinic. It was unusual to have a
woman. Sofia, the Spanish nurse, told Susan that in the
earlier months of fighting there had been other women:
a famous Anarchist, impossibly cut with shrapnel
who died within minutes, before they could send her
back down the line to hospital. They had given first aid
to *milicianas* with smashed limbs, with flesh wounds.
Some of those women were tough young fighters, braver
than men in the face of their wounds. And, said Sofia
darkly, they'd had worse to deal with than war wounds:
in one case the tragic consequences of rape, too late to
abort.

This girl, with a clean wound in the shoulder, was
different. She was tall and slender, and looked no more
than fifteen. The story was that she'd been found lurching
about a mountain road, rambling and suffering from
exposure, by a group of Italians coming down from the
front. They were walking behind a ramshackle truck,
which held their own wounded commissar and two other
comrades who had been caught in crossfire.

The girl was wearing the dungarees of a *miliciana* and carrying an ancient but efficient Russian rifle. When she saw them she collapsed in the middle of the road. One of them picked up the rifle, examined it, then threw it into the back of the truck. Then he picked her up and laid her tenderly in the lap of his commissar, who winced and adjusted his wounded leg.

The commissar had whistled. 'Hey, Toni! One of the dratted committees must have decided to put children in the war, now.' The commissar had lots of opinions. He'd told his comrades many times that despite their idealistic views only old-fashioned military discipline would win their fight against the Fascists.

The driver forced the protesting truck into gear, then set off again. They stopped at the hospital to drop her off along with the commissar and two comrades who had, respectively, wounds in the hand and in the backside. The clinic, set up in a stripped-out, vandalized church, served to treat more straightforward wounds and send soldiers back to the front with the quickest dispatch. More serious cases were given first aid and sent on to the bigger hospitals in Barcelona. The other Italians said their heartfelt goodbyes to their commissar, re-formed in their straggling line behind the truck, and kept marching. He called to them, telling them to hurry. Leave was too precious to squander on him. He was well. He was well! he told them. They must go.

Susan had cleaned the girl's wounds, washed the crust of weeks of fighting from the rest of her body and dressed her in one of her own two nightdresses. The rough hospital issue seemed just too hard for such a young body. Susan brushed the girl's thick hair back from its centre parting. It crackled with life and shone like liquorice in the light from the narrow windows.

On the first night the girl would not let Susan leave her. She clutched at her hand and called for her grandmother, her *Avia*. She called for her father, and for people called *Jorge* and *Esteban*. Susan cursed her lack of understanding in this language. She'd tried very hard in the first weeks and could understand the very basic words of need: *water, lavatory, hurt* ... But this girl spoke in Catalan, not even Spanish. This was too hard together. The sibilant curls of the language made Susan's mind reel. She'd tried to make little cards with questions and answers in Spanish and English. But then there was the further problem of Catalan and many of the wounded could not read or write in any language. So she gave up, made do with sign language and the help of the two Spanish nurses who spoke English.

She'd travelled with three other nurses by train from Paris down to Perpignan. There they had changed trains and come through mountain tunnels into Spain. Two of the nurses were ordered on towards Madrid; she was sent to this clinic with a nurse from Harrogate who promptly caught measles and was shipped back home in a fortnight.

So this was how Susan had ended up dealing with this girl, this child who was now pouring out her heart in a language she just could not understand. She prayed for the child to go to sleep so that she too could rest. She finally slept there on the bed without knowing it.

The nurse Sofia woke her up by whispering in her ear, 'Come on, Sister. We will be without help from you if you sleep like this.' She half dragged, half carried Susan back to their shared room to finish her rest.

Another nurse came and woke her up three hours later, to tell her that the little girl fighter was climbing the walls and shouting for her. Susan discovered that the nurse had put a bed into a storeroom for the girl, and pinned her to it with tightly tied sheets. Her head was moving from side to side, her lips folded tight against each other.

Susan put a hand on her hot brow. Her eyes snapped open. '*Avia*,' she said.

'She says *Grandmother*,' said Sofia helpfully through the door as she passed by with a pile of sheets.

'Not your grandma,' said Susan, untying the sheets. 'I'll not be anyone's grandmother, pet. Not ever.' She pulled the girl's hands on top of the sheets and smoothed the rough skin. 'But I'll take care of you. You can bet on that.'

The girl started rambling again and Susan called in Sofia to translate. Sofia asked her questions and listened intently to the answers. Then she put a finger on the girl's lips to stop the flow. 'The girl, she says her father and grandparents were blown up by a bomb in her home. A *barri* in Barcelona. And her comrades from the unit are dead. She says she has no one. She says she was one of the best fighters in her unit. She says she has no one.'

'What about her mother?'

'She says her mother died many years ago. When she was born. Her grandmother took care of her. She has no one. Her comrades Jorge and Esteban were killed on the mountain, at the emplacement.'

'Ask her name. Ask her how old she is.'

'She says she is seventeen. And she says her name is Maria Josep. But her grandmother called her ChiChu. It was . . . what you call it, a pet name. A name of affection.'

'ChiChu,' said Susan.

The girl's eyes suddenly closed. Her eyes moved restlessly under the nearly transparent lids. Two or three tears squeezed below the lids before she could stop them. Then she opened her eyes, blinked and stared straight at Susan. Then she said something.

'What was that?'

Sofia shook her head. 'It is dangerous,' she said. 'It is not allowed.'

'Tell me!'

'She says you shall be her mother. That she is tired and you must be her mother.'

Susan looked at the child, whose eyes had closed again under those transparent lids. Then she shrugged. 'I've work to do,' she said. 'I can't be anybody's mother.'

As she walked along the main ward she was stopped by a growling voice which had laughter at its base. 'Hey, English nurse, do you have water for a poor soldier?' It was the Italian, Commissar Fibretti, a mountain of a man with too much hair. He lay back against his pillow like some great bear. She poured some water into a glass and took it across to him.

She put it in his undamaged hand. 'You speak English,' she said. 'That's something anyway.'

He handed her the glass and wiped his moustaches with the back of his hand. 'I was in England in 1932,' he said. 'A trade unionists' meeting. Then I stay on in London to learn the language because the Party thought it convenient.'

'You are a Communist?'

He nodded. 'All are Communists who would rid us of these tyrants. In my country I fight against the rat Mussolini and they throw me in a stinking jail. In Spain I come to help them to get rid of Franco's rats. Very simple.'

He laughed a hearty, gurgling laugh that made her want to join in. The men in the other beds stirred and began to watch and listen with interest. 'All are Communists who fight the Fascists, the dictators.'

'No. No. You're wrong, sir,' a thin man with a grey beard called in Spanish from the opposite bed. 'It is the Anarchists who started this fight. The fight belongs to them, not Moscow's lackeys.'

'What does he say?' said Susan quickly. The man spoke in the crackling tones of Catalan, like the girl. She understood that no better than the more widely used Spanish.

'He is Anarchist. They are jolly men, the Anarchists. But are children. They think wars can be won, the Fascist rebels can be routed, by some kind of explosion of brotherhood.'

'And it won't?' These confused lines of argument had been perplexing her. She'd come out here thinking she was joining a simple force of right against might. But it was not so simple.

Fibretti shook his head. 'A war needs discipline, order. This romance of Anarchy will blow away the resistance to this Fascist revolution. The Fascists will triumph.'

The man from the bed opposite was shouting now, struggling with his bedclothes: 'Fool! Fool! Italian clown.' Sofia hurried across and forced him back into bed. Then she looked over his shoulder at Susan, her eyes severe. 'No more war talk,' she said. 'Let them fight their wars, big and little, when they get out of here. They need peace in here.'

Susan tucked in the Italian's blanket more securely. 'You need to rest, Commissar. You will only get better if you rest.'

MY DARK-EYED GIRL

His face, under its veil of hair, was sulky. 'And when I get better, Sister, I will go back to the fight to stop the Fascist canker growing outwards. I will fight for the old fool across the way. I will fight for the boot-faced nurse. We will do this despite these elderly children who call themselves Anarchist. Believe me.'

'Ssh,' said Susan. 'No talk about the war. You heard Sister Sofia.'

She walked back down the ward with Sofia. 'What was that all about, Sofia?'

'You don't know? Ah. You don't know.' Sofia's tone was sour. She shrugged. 'Me, I am for the Anarchists, like the young girl in the side room, and the old man over there. They are true to the Catalan spirit. They fight for everyone to be equal, men, women. No priests. No grandees. The Communists were only little at the beginning of the war.' She glanced sideways at Susan. 'Now they ride on top; they have Russian guns and all these foreigners here, fighting their cause. The Communists want no revolution, just beat the Fascists.'

'I'm not a Communist.' Susan thought then of Jake Stanton. Jake was a Communist all right. Equal shares. Get rid of the bosses. He'd even get rid of the King and Queen of England. He told her so when they had travelled together to Paris. He was taciturn, reading his pamphlets and painfully learning words and phrases in Spanish. She was tense, worried about the extremity of his ideas, whether this was not all a big mistake. She'd last seen him in Paris, getting on a train for the Spanish border with a group of volunteers. They were to walk through the mountains to Spain. It took her papers another week to be processed by the powerful Paris committee.

'I'm not a Communist,' she said now to Sofia, 'though I know some who are.'

'So what are you?' said Sofia. 'Are you Anarchist? Are you Fascist?'

Susan shook her head. 'I don't think I'm anything, really.'

Sofia raised her thick black brows. 'That is very sad,' she said. 'Everyone must make their stand.'

'I just came here to help.' How damp that sounded. How undecided. 'Really, just to help.'

Sofia laughed heartily at this, pinched the side of Susan's arm and went on to help another sister to undo a welcome package of drugs which had on it an American postmark.

Within two days, both Commissar Fibretti and the girl, Maria Josep, were up on their feet. Each day the commissar would make his way round the ward, sitting by each bed in turn. He laughed with his own men and the others. He told them jokes, bawled revolutionary songs into their ears, talked urgently to them about the war and ways in which they would inevitably win it and how the structure and order of the Communists was the only weapon to beat the *Fascisti*.

Sofia eyed his antics sourly. 'I saw an American film in Barcelona before the war. There was a tall man in it, the villain. They said he could *charm the birds off the trees*. This one, he charms the men out of the trees. He will have them all signing party papers before he leaves. Even the old one.' She nodded at the Anarchist, who despite himself was tapping his hand against the bed rail in time with the Italian's song.

'Not you, Sofia?'

'Not me. I will not hand my soul to Moscow. Not me.'

Maria Josep, whom they all now called ChiChu, walked quietly around after Susan, watching what she was doing, listening to her words. She herself said nothing, either in Spanish or any other language. Her shoulder was mending by the day and she demonstrated her desire to do cleaning jobs and sorting jobs, to help Susan on the ward. She and the commissar became friends; each morning she would take a walk to the river with him. Sofia had told him of the terrible fates of ChiChu's father, grandparents and her dear comrades. He rumbled away to the girl in cobbled Spanish, rough Catalan and liquid Italian. She drank in every word but said nothing.

Susan started to spend time by the commissar's bed at night. It was a relief to speak English and she enjoyed hearing him talk in his exaggerated fashion about his adventures and his vigorous view on life. His chanting of the Moscow dogma was tinged with the faintest mockery. Despite his injury he had some kind of force, great energy within him that those around could tap into. Susan usually came away from his bed refreshed.

One night he said, 'The girl ChiChu must speak or she will end up with no voice.' Susan had just turned down his light and tweaked his bedclothes to a smoothness which would have pleased Sister Barras back in Park View.

'So you must teach her English,' he went on. 'The girl must be taught English.'

Wearily Susan pushed her hair back underneath her cap. 'Me?' she said. They had three nurses laid low today with some kind of fever. She and Sofia had now been working more or less round the clock for five days apart from the odd couple of hours' sleep snatched in the little storeroom. 'I can't do that. I have no time.'

He grabbed her hand in his and squeezed it in his broad, thick fingers. 'It is not enough to nurse, dear Nightingale.' He paused. 'Is that not right? Did not the English have a nurse who called herself after a bird?' He went on. 'You must give succour, Nightingale. But more. You must always leave behind more than you take.'

The next morning the nurses came back on the ward, pale but fit again, and Sofia passed on the hospital commandant's instruction that she and Susan should take the day off. Minutes later, Susan had her own message for Sofia.

'The commissar overheard you, Sofia, and says it is a fine day and we must go to the river. That man is very used to giving orders,' she said drily. 'And we are to take ChiChu with us. It seems we need to see the running water to refresh us all.'

Amused at the Italian's motherly bossiness, Sofia conceded that this was a good idea and they set off with baskets of towels and rolls, and a blanket to sit on. ChiChu walked alongside them quietly as Sofia chatted on about her family in Barcelona, her lover, who was fighting far out on the Aragon front, and the fineness of the day despite it being so early in the year.

Walking along the dusty track Susan was suddenly penetrated by the bleak isolation of ChiChu's silence. She determined that, really, it would be a good idea to try to teach her a bit of English. She'd show her how to do some proper nursing things as well. She was already a great help. ChiChu would soon be another skilled pair of hands. She was very quick.

Down by the river, Sofia lost her stolid cynicism and

became excited. She ran up and down the bank, peering into the water, letting it trickle through her fingers. She took off her shoes. 'Come on! Come on!' she said. 'We must go into the river. The commissar was right. We need refreshment.'

ChiChu smiled a little and sat down beside her, pulling off her own heavy shoes. But she went further. She pulled off her dress and her camisole, leaving only a thin shift. She untied the greasy ribbon from her hair and let the heavy liquorice-black tresses fall. Then holding up her bandaged arm, she waded in, the water rushing right against her narrow body. She waved her good arm at Susan. 'Come!' she said in English. 'Come!'

Sofia, down to her own shift now, laughed at Susan. 'The girl speaks English for you, Susan. You must come. Come!' She reached into the basket. 'I have soap for the hair.' She unpinned her own hair, then she ploughed in after ChiChu.

Much more slowly Susan removed her own layers of clothing and unpinned her own hair. Then very gently she let herself into the flowing water and let it take her substantial weight. She put back her head and let her hair flow with the stream. ChiChu waded up to her and turned back to say something to Sofia.

'Very . . .' said Sofia.

'Very . . .' said ChiChu.

'. . . pretty . . .'

'. . . pretty . . .' said ChiChu.

'. . . hair . . .'

'. . . hair . . .' said ChiChu.

Susan laughed and shook her head so that her hair moved and flowed with the rush of water. 'Thank you, ChiChu,' she said. 'You speak very good English.'

'Thank you,' said ChiChu. 'Very good English. Nice hair, Susan.'

Sofia brandished the soap. 'Now we all wash our hair. Very good. Eh?'

They helped to lather each other's hair, assiduously pulling the strands apart so each one was well rinsed in the moving water of the river. After wading ashore they rubbed their heads hard with the towel and combed their hair with Sofia's thick comb. Then they lay in the warming sun with their hair fanned out behind them and waited for it to dry. To pass the time Susan started to name objects for ChiChu to repeat after her. *Fish. Water. Sky. Bird. Grass. Stone. Wind.* Then sentences. *The sun dries my hair. The water rushes over stones. The mountain is high.*

After two hours, their hair was still slightly damp and it was hard to pin up again. They did the best they could. When they arrived back at the hospital their hair had collapsed back round their shoulders.

That night Susan put her small lamp on the side table and set about her usual round of the patients. She tucked in a loose blanket on the commissar's bed. He gave a low whistle, then reached up and brushed a tentative finger against an escaping curl. 'Pretty hair, Nightingale,' he whispered. 'Three graceful goddesses by the stream, eh?'

She pulled back from him. 'You were there,' she whispered fiercely. 'You followed us to the river. You bad man!'

'I was your protection,' he said softly, his hand now on the back of hers as it lay on the blanket.

She threw off his hand. 'You're a bad man.'

'Bad?' He took her hand and kept it in his. She let it lie

there. He stroked it with his other hand, and his touch made her want to cry. He lifted it to his mouth and kissed it and she could feel his soft lips, the soft hair of his beard. She felt a heat radiating from deep inside her and she started to tremble. He put her hand back by her side. 'Go to sleep, Nightingale. Go to your bed.'

She walked back down the ward, feeling as heavy as lead. She went to the tiny alcove at the end of the ward. In there Sofia was writing by the glow of a small lamp. Sofia looked up at her. 'The night nurse has not come. I will wait here for her. And I will come for you if you are needed. You look so very tired. You must go to bed.'

In the little room she shared with Sofia, Susan threw herself fully clothed on to the bed. She was exhausted and elated at the same time; full of foreboding yet pulsing with some odd kind of freedom. Since she had been a girl quite a few men had shown an interest in her. There were tradesmen and farmers up the dale, and those men who had shown more than a little interest at the hospital. But the warm love and companionship of Rose Clare had always been sufficient for her. Never had she felt any urgency to go further than a friendly greeting. She had never wanted to 'walk out' in the true sense, with any of these men. Then, when her grandmother made her nasty revelation, she was relieved that this had been so. She made her mind up then that there would be no marriage, no children. Things like that could miss a generation before they made their terrible mark.

But now she knew that had been a very easy decision. If she were honest with herself she'd never had the depth of feeling for anyone that would make such a decision a sacrifice.

Her head was swimming. She was aching all over. She

rubbed her sides and the tops of her thighs to relieve her ache and diffuse the heat. Then that feeling she'd had when the commissar had kissed her hand sheeted through her again.

The door creaked open. She took a deep breath and closed her eyes. Sofia must have been relieved already. Then Susan could feel heavy hands on her hair and she turned over. She could feel his hair and the heat, and weight of him beside her, but could barely see his face. His hands pulled at her pins. Then her own hands were touching his, helping him to undo her hair. He groaned and then the mouth that had kissed her hand was on her mouth. She could feel his salt tears on her lips. The heat inside her generated a dangerous certainty which she followed into a vale of pain and pleasure that before she'd never had the means to imagine.

They lay quietly afterwards, she still throbbing with a wavelike residue of feeling, he muttering in Italian, stroking her hair and crying afresh. She felt soothed beyond measure and drifted to sleep without knowing it. When she woke up he was gone. The bed was sticky beneath her and there was a cold draught from the door. She leaped up and stripped the bed, bundled it into the laundry sack. She pulled off her petticoat and stuffed it in beside the sheet. Then she put on a coat and crept outside to the laundry cupboard to get fresh sheets.

By the time Sofia was finally relieved and came yawning to bed, Susan was lying in a pristine bed pretending to be asleep. For a split second she wondered if she'd imagined it all. But the rough cold sheet told her otherwise. What had happened had happened, and although one part of her was terrified, another more tranquil part acknowledged the rightness, the logic of what she had done.

The strangest thing was that she had never called him by his given name, Bartolomeo. Even now she just thought of him as 'the commissar'.

ChiChu is sitting away from the glaring sun in the cool shadow of the overhang of the house. She is watching her grandfather's veiny old hand moving a draught on the game board that was set between them. Over his shoulder pokes the bulbous nosed face of his friend Sol, whose gap-toothed mouth is whispering words in his ear, telling him which pieces to play, urging him to make the right move.

The two old men start to quarrel and ChiChu starts to cry. Juana, her grandmother, comes up behind them. She is wearing a golden dress and brandishing the stick she uses for the washing. ChiChu feels the sting as the stick falls about her own shoulders and weeps as her grandmother berates her through a gummy mouth bereft of teeth. 'Did thou love me, nasty ungrateful child? If thou didst love me wherefore didst thou not save me from this burning, from these fires that torment me?'

ChiChu pushes her away, battling with the folds of the old woman's shawl and her beautiful dress. 'Go away, old one. You're dead; you're a dead soul. You have no place here.' Then she wakes to find herself battling with the thin blanket on the narrow cot she occupies in the storeroom by the ward.

'What is it?' Above her loomed the Englishwoman, babbling in that baffling language of hers. She looked different somehow, her face glowed, lit somehow from the inside; yet her uniform was the same, her hair oiled and clipped back in its usual severe manner. 'Why are you shouting, child?'

ChiChu pulled the blanket up around her. 'Dream,' she said in Catalan. 'I dream about my dead grandmother.'

Susan shook her head. 'English,' she said. 'English, if you can manage it, ChiChu. I am sorry, I do not understand.'

ChiChu shook her head stubbornly. 'No English,' she said. Then she pulled the sheet right over her head. But now she was wide awake and could not re-enter sleep, in or out of her dream. An hour later she was in the ward as usual, carrying the heavy jug of water, filling the glass which each man had by his side. At the other end of the ward she could see Sofia and the Englishwoman doing the dressings in their methodical way. She hoped the Englishwoman would not ask about the dreams again. In her careful way she would be sure to have checked out the words with Sofia. She was always doing that, checking out the words.

The Italian commissar, when she got to him, was sitting up on his bed, fully dressed, reading a leaflet from the pile on his table. He was immaculate. His uniform, though threadbare, was neat and pressed. His hair and moustaches had been neatly combed. He beamed at her.

'Good morning, little nymph!' he said in his quaint Catalan which was not so much fractured as curled up at the edges. 'Why would you look so sad on such a very fine day?'

She sat on the end of his bed. 'Do you have dreams, Commissar?' she asked.

He looked hard at her through his beetling brows. 'Ah. You speak, little one! I had a dream last night, little one, where I was transported to a place very near heaven and given a very fine gift.'

She pleated his sheet, bunching it into her hand. 'What gift was that, Commissar?'

'Ah, ChiChu, this thing had a beauty, an untouched beauty which I have never before seen. It was a surprise. Never in Italy, never before in Spain have I known such freshness, such beauty.'

'What thing was it, Commissar?'

'Hard to say, child. It was not quite the food you would eat, not quite the garment you would wear to keep you warm till the end of the world. Perhaps something between the two.'

She sighed.

He took her small hand in his. 'Such a great sigh for such a small chest. What is it, ChiChu?'

'I had a dream but it was no thing of beauty, Commissar.'

'So what was it, this dream?'

'I dreamed of my grandmother. I told you of her teeth, they got stuck in the palm tree in the *plaça*?'

He nodded. 'I remember this,' he said.

'Well, she was there in my dream, shouting at me, berating me with her gummy mouth. She screamed that I had let her burn in a terrible place. There was a fire after the explosion . . .' She hesitated.

In the pause which followed the murmur of the other patients and the click of Sofia's heels seemed to fill the ward. Then the commissar's hand pressed hers. 'Did you go to Mass, ChiChu, before you became a battle maiden?'

She shook her head. 'Only when I was very small. My father had no time for priests. We are Anarchists and atheists. The priests cause all the trouble. He says this.'

'Your grandmother? Did she go to Mass?'

She shook her head. 'My father's actions led the priest to banish us all from his church.'

He sat quietly for a moment. 'The old things change in these times, and for good reason. But there is calm in the Mass, and wise resolution, whether or not you believe in any god.'

'What do you tell me, Commissar?' she frowned.

'One day you will find a church with a good priest. Ask him to say a Mass for your grandmother's soul. It is a fiction but it is a fiction which tells a true story when you find yourself so very near to death.' He swung his legs off the bed and stood up straight. 'And while you are there you may ask him to say a Mass for my soul also.'

The Englishwoman was halfway down the ward. She looked up in their direction. The commissar winced a little, then drew himself to his full height, took an imaginary hat from his brow and swept a low bow. 'Good morning, Sister Susan. Are you well this fine day?'

The Englishwoman smiled faintly, her pale cheeks pink. She bent down over her next patient.

ChiChu jumped off the bed and went across to her. 'I help you,' she said.

What the commissar said had soothed her. There would surely be a church somewhere, with a priest who was not in the pay of the Fascist rebels. She would find it. She was certain she would find it. And she would learn some more English. It might be that in England there would be such a priest.

Later she helped Susan with the bathing, and had to remind her three times that you didn't need to wash a man's arm twice. She took the flannel from her. 'You already clean him,' she said.

Although Susan did not have the commissar in her eye line all the time as she worked, she could feel his presence burning towards her from his corner of the ward. When her eyes finally caught his he nodded gravely at her then smiled his beaming smile.

Suddenly the peace of the ward was rent by the arrival of the Italian adjutant Toni and two other comrades, who swept the commissar into their arms and shouted their delight at his recovery. They kissed him on the cheeks and slapped him on the back, rattling away about an action in Barcelona where they had helped the authorities to wrest the telephone exchange out of the hands of the Anarchists.

He calmed them down, talked with them, and then came across to the table where Susan and Sofia were cutting bandages into smaller rolls. 'My comrades return to the front,' he said. 'I shall go with them.'

Sofia said, 'Your leg is not properly healed, Commissar.'

'It is well enough. The air and the exercise will complete the healing. My comrades say the truck is in very good heart,' he said. 'In any case there is more crawling than running in this war.' He turned to Susan. 'Except for only one thing, Nightingale, I am delighted to return to the fight. There is no time to waste to rid us of these rats in human form.'

She tried to keep her face very steady. 'And what one thing would that be, Commissar?'

'Someone gave me a gift,' he said. 'A gift which has changed my life.'

'What gift?' said Sofia, frowning.

He placed a rough finger in the dimple on the nurse's chin. 'The best gifts, o wonderful one, are those which remain secret.' Then he picked up her hand and kissed it.

She pulled her hand away. 'In Barcelona, sir, they'd arrest you for a spy, kissing hands like a *bourgeois*.'

His large eyes bulged and he laughed across her at Susan. 'Well, Sister Susan, would you have me a bourgeois or a rough artisan?'

Susan took a step forward and kissed him on the cheek. 'Take care of that leg, Commissar. We don't want you back here.'

He looked at her quizzically. 'Is that true?' he said. 'You do not wish me back here?'

'Only in one piece,' she said.

'Commissar!' one of his soldiers called from the end of the ward. 'We move now.'

He nodded then and moved away, saying goodbye to the men in the beds, one by one. When they were gone, taking with them their smells of dust and war, an uneasy silence settled on the ward: a combination of fear and longing compounded by the tension of being left out, left behind.

Outside, ChiChu was hanging on to the edge of the truck. 'Let me come, Commissar. I will come and fight with you. I am *miliciana*.'

'It is not fitting.' He unpeeled her fingers from the metal. 'No. It is no place for you. They were wrong to let you go before. You have work to do here, ChiChu. Help Sister Susan and Sister Sofia to mend the soldiers and put them back in the fight.'

She grabbed the door again. 'No. No. I come with you. I fight.'

He took her face in his hand then and looked her in the eyes. 'No, ChiChu. I want you here, especially to look after the Englishwoman for me. Will you do that for me? Look after Sister Susan especially for me?'

She frowned at him, then let go of the door. Toni put the truck into gear. 'You do that, ChiChu?' said the commissar.

Then the door of the truck was taken away from her hand and she turned to see the Englishwoman and Sofia standing in the doorway. Sofia was waving, but the Englishwoman was just watching the truck as it clattered out of sight, her face frozen and quite old.

Chapter Five

A Dangerous Man

Susan welcomed the plunge into work after the commissar and his comrades went up the line. The ward was receiving its quota of overspill casualties from an extra flurry of action in the city: products from a mini war between the Anarchists and the Communists. One soldier had to be moved out to the tender care of his wife to make space for a young electrician who had been caught in fire from the telephone exchange. Two of the Anarchists were in a critical condition and had to be kept behind screens for two days. For some reason there was no space for them in the city hospital. The pain which throbbed in their quiet cries made the recovering men wince, their faces solid, like grey clay. For them, for a week or so, the ward had been a universe unto itself, cut off from the uncertainties of life on the front line, whether that front line was out on the sierra or on the street corners of Barcelona.

One of the men behind the screen was a welder from Birmingham; the other was a ledger clerk from Edinburgh. Sofia told Susan to sit with them. 'You sit with beds eleven and twelve. You will know what they say,' she said sourly.

Susan scowled at her. 'What is it, Sofia. What is the matter?'

Sofia glowered at her. 'Foreigners!' Susan felt that if they had been outside the ward Sofia would have spat on the ground.

'Like me, you mean?'

Sofia's anger faltered. 'Not you. Foreigners like the men.'

'Foreigners? But these men have left their own country and come to fight for the cause.'

Sofia closed her eyes then opened them. 'They come here for their adventures, like they are in a film. Douglas Fairbanks with his sword. Ha!' Her lips curled. 'At home they live the lives of clerks.'

'They could die!' protested Susan. 'Many have already died.'

Sofia shook her head, sad now. 'That might also be their final adventure,' she said. 'The real fate of Spain is nothing to them.'

That night Susan went to each of the men in turn and asked how they were. 'No problems, Nurse,' said Tom Martin.

'All right, Nurse,' said James Laurel.

'Is there anything you need? That I can get you?' she said. 'There are a few English newspapers.'

Martin shrugged. 'I'm all right,' he muttered. 'I'm all right.'

Laurel stared at her. 'Don't worry, Nurse. He's ticking a bit. Bomb blew someone's head into his lap. Then he starts running, see? And I start running after him. Round the corner and into the side of this blinking great truck. Splatter the head and wham the truck. Quite taken the wind out of his sails, you might say,' he grinned. 'Hardly the hero.'

Susan stood up uneasily. She should stay to talk to them; it should be a relief to hear her own language spoken so freely. But she wanted to get away. These men would not have interested her at home. There was no reason why they should interest her here.

The Englishmen were visited by a dapper man in uniform who was clutching a small, leather satchel. Sofia told Susan he was the English commissar, who often came when there were English patients. She punched Susan's arm. 'But not like the Italian commissar, eh?'

He talked earnestly with the men and left a small pile of leaflets on the table between them. He accosted Susan by the door. 'Laurel says that you're English, Nurse . . .' His Scottish voice chopped the air with precision.

'Nurse Cornford, Mr . . . ?'

He ignored her cue for his name. He looked round. 'Is there somewhere we can sit, Nurse Cornford?'

She led him past Sofia, who was watching them sardonically through the door, to the shaded veranda where the nurses sometimes sat in their precious minutes away from the ward. She sat down and he sat down beside her.

'Bin here long, have yer, Nurse?' His voice was deep and had the sound of the Glasgow streets. His eyes were cold and gleaming, like the tightened skin of a fist.

'Four months now,' she said.

He removed a small, thumbed book from his satchel. 'Martin there says you're the only one here. English, that is.' His pencil was poised above his book.

'Yes. There was another one. But she caught measles and had to go back home.'

He scribbled something. What on earth was there to scribble? 'And you answer to . . . ?'

'The hospital commandant. Like the other nurses.'

He scribbled again. 'Are you a member of the Party, Nurse Cornford?'

'The Communist Party? No. I'm a member of no party.'

'Labour Party? ILP?'

She looked at him steadily. The hand that wielded the pencil was small for such a big man. 'No,' she said. 'I am the member of no party, like I said.'

He pursed his lips. 'Naïve, Nurse Cornford. You make yourself putty in the hands of the Fascists. Very naïve.'

'If that's so Mr . . . er . . . what am I doing here mending the heads of lads who've been shot by the Fascists?'

He shook his head. 'Discipline, Nurse Cornford. This war will not be won without discipline. Political discipline, that is.'

She stifled the desire to tip him out of his chair and kick him very hard.

'Who's that?' he said sharply, pointing his pencil at ChiChu, who was lurking in the doorway staring at him under her sullen brows.

'That? That's ChiChu. Her real name is Maria Josep. She came here injured. She was a *miliciana*.'

'What? A *miliciana*?' He frowned. 'I thought we'd got rid of all those women fighters.'

'She was fighting with her father's comrades. Seems he was a great fighter. Then he died in an explosion and his comrades took her back to the front. Then they were all killed and she ended up here.'

'Explosion?'

Susan looked at the dusty toe of her shoe. 'Set by Communists, she says.'

'Ah.' His tone sharpened like a knife on a stone. 'They were . . . she's an Anarchist?'

'Well . . . yes . . . but they're—'

'Fascist spies and Trotskyite collaborators. We have the evidence. There are Anarchists spilling the beans in prison here and Madrid.'

Susan protested. 'She's no spy. I don't think . . .'

'So what don't you think, comrade?'

'I thought, I think . . . strange that all these explosions, these arrests . . . It must . . .' Her voice trailed off. 'It seems daft, all this fighting. I thought Franco and the Moors were the enemy.' Franco had brought his crack troops from North Africa to help his cause.

He shook his head. 'The enemy within, comrade.' He tapped her arm with his stubby pencil. She moved her arm away. 'The canker. The Anarchists at best are underground, ill-disciplined. At worst they are tools of the Fascists.' His voice droned on. She thought of the Italian commissar, singing and joking with the men, talking to them with warmth, enthusiasm. He was a commissar. How many more he would win over to his cause than this dried stick with his clerk's voice and his fish eyes.

'Well?' He was looking enquiringly at her.

'What was that, Mr . . . ?'

'What is her name? The *miliciana*?'

'I forget,' said Susan. 'Do you know, I can't bring it to mind . . . Maria Josep. We call her ChiChu.'

He clicked his teeth and stood up. 'When did you say you came over, Nurse?'

'Four months ago.'

'Did you come alone?'

'No. I came with Jake Stanton, the brother of a friend.' She watched him write down the name with his stubby pencil. 'Now, he's a member of your Party. I had to listen to songs in praise of Marx and Lenin all the way from Le Havre to Paris. On and on and on . . .'

'Were you vetted in Paris?'

She nodded. 'Mmm. This woman in long boots and a fur-collared coat just about had my sock measurement. Thought she might not let me through, at one point, mind.'

'Yes?' he said sharply. 'Why?'

'Well, truth is my nursing experience has been in an asylum. She wasn't too sure about that.' She laughed heartily.

'Is it so bleedin' funny, Nurse?'

She was pleased to have got under his skin. 'Well, experience in a mad house is not such a bad preparation for this lot. It's like a film plot gone mad. Trouble here is that the goodies are fighting among themselves and the baddies are just sitting waiting to pounce on the remains.'

He closed his book with a snap. 'That's treason, Nurse. There are men in Madrid in prison for saying less.'

'I tell you what, Mr . . . er . . . It comes to something when someone's clapped into prison for having an idea.' She looked at him steadily. This one was a bully like her grandmother and he fancied himself in the way Dr Tordoff did. Small man with too much power. But neither of these things worried her now. That's what being in this mad house of a war had taught her. She smiled slightly at the thought.

He stood up, disturbing some flies which had settled on his immaculate uniform. 'Well, Nurse, I can't see that we can be of any more use to each other, can you?'

She stood up and, tall as he, looked him in the eye. 'Would you tell me something, comrade?'

He flushed. 'What'd that be, Nurse?'

'You know I worked in a mad house before I came here. So where did you work before you came here?'

'Well, I don't think . . .'

She chuckled. 'Go on. Fair's fair, Commissar. There is no shame in these equal days. Is that what they say?'

His eyes were no longer fishlike. They had darkened to glittering coal. 'If it is so important, Nurse, I worked in a shop in London.'

'Which shop?' she said swiftly.

'Marshall and Snelgroves.'

'Ooh, Commissar, my sister gets her hats there. Did you sell hats?'

'I did not,' he said.

'What did you sell, then?'

'I sold ties.'

'Ah,' she said, slowing down. 'Gentlemen's ties . . .'

'That's enough. Enough, I'm tellin' ye! I'm not having nae more o' this.'

He turned and stomped away, raising dust in the road as he made his way to his dusty car and its dusty, cigar-smoking driver.

He lit himself a cigarette as the car pulled away, and drew on it hard before he would trust himself to say anything. 'Bloody woman!' he said. 'The weakest link. Always the weakest link. Brains in their bellies.

His driver swerved to avoid a crater in the middle of the road. 'I wouldn't tell La Passionara that, if I were you, comrade.'

The commissar calmed himself by breathing slowly; very, very slowly. You had to be careful what you said out loud these days. La Passionara, that great icon of the left, would have his guts for such an outburst. He threw his half-smoked cigarette out of the window. 'Just a manner of speaking, comrade. Just a manner of speaking. Old habits die hard.'

Seeing the commissar leaving in a huff, ChiChu came through the door. 'A dangerous man,' she said, drawing her arms across her throat.

Susan laughed. 'Just a silly, jumped-up man.'

ChiChu scowled and shook her head. 'Dangerous,' she said. 'Such men are dangerous.'

Sofia came to her later and asked her about the English commissar. Then she too shook her head. 'Policeman,' she said, 'just a policeman for those who will tear the heart out of Spain. We rid ourself of the grandees and the priests and now in its place we have commissars and foreigners.'

Susan shook her head. 'I cannot understand all this. I thought simply we must get rid of the Fascists who're poison here, just like in Italy and Germany.' It would stop the rot. That's what Jake said.

Sofia shook her head. 'Not so simple,' she said. She went on to tell Susan of a letter she had had from her sweetheart. The letter had come from a prison. 'They put him there because he objected to the arrest of his own sergeant. They said they were all spies.'

Susan shook her head. 'But they're not all like that. The Italian . . . he . . .'

Sofia put a hand on one side of her face and looked up at her like a wise, dark bird. 'Ah, Sister Susan, now that's different. He is a man with heart. And he has a bad time in Italy with the Fascists. But he is a man with good heart.'

Susan coloured but kept her voice even. 'Yes. I can see that, Sofia.'

★ ★ ★

A week later Sofia broke into Susan's rare siesta and shook her awake. 'You have a visitor. He is down on the ward.'

He was brown-faced and gaunt-looking. She hardly recognized him under his tan and his straggling beard. But the eyes were familiar.

'Jake,' she said, smiling. 'It's very nice to see you in one piece.'

He turned a hollowed face towards her. 'Yes. But I've seen things and done things . . .' he paused.

'But you're here. Still alive.'

'But I'm here.'

She took him into the small nurses' sitting space and put out the jug of wine. 'It's good to see a familiar face,' she said. 'Good of you to seek me out.'

'Ah could do naught else,' he said. 'Ah had to come.'

The dogged intensity of his tone struck her. All those months ago, he'd infected her with his desire to come here and do something for the cause. They had travelled here together. He waited with her in Paris until he got his orders. But in this time he emanated chill, impersonal zeal. It was as though she was a package he had to deliver.

She frowned. 'Why is that? Why had you to come?'

'Why, there we are, like, resting up in Barcelona. I lost three mates in the last do. Doesn't bear thinking about, what happened to them . . .' His voice faded away. 'Anyway, this feller, this commissar party wallah seeks us out the other day. Says he's talked to you. Well, he starts digging and digging. Lost me temper with him, I did, challenged him on his history back home. Said I'd match him strike for strike, action for proletarian action, and he couldn't best me.'

'He sold ties in Marshall and Snelgroves.'

Jake glanced at her. 'No shame in that, exploited by the grasping capitalists like the rest of us. Just clean hands, that's all.' He paused. 'No sin in clean hands.'

'So what did he want?'

'He started asking about you.'

She frowned. 'Me?'

'Said yeh were a Trotskyite and a weak link. Allus gannin' on about weak links, these fellers.'

'He called me a what?'

'A Trotskyite. Enemy of the Soviet State. With these lads if you're not with us you're agin us. So they look for a label. Yeh really got his goat, that one!'

'I've no idea what that means. I told him I'm not interested in any of that, not the Communist Party, not the Labour Party—'

'Ah, he said all that was a front. That you are plotting and pleading innocence.'

'He's paranoid.'

'What?'

'Self-deluded. Thinks the world's plotting against him. Ask your Keziah. We had plenty of them in Park View.'

'Anyway, he thinks this clinic is a nest of Anarchists and he's putting in his report. They'll come for yeh, Susan.'

'Me?' she laughed. 'Me? I'm not important enough for them to come for. For anyone to come for.'

'Nee laughing matter, pet. They've got women in prison. They've shot women. Ah've heard it down the line. Mebbe not an Englishwoman yet, but that look in his eye – it made me blood run cold. It could be a test of faith for him. Ah dinnat knaa what yeh said but yeh didn't half rub him up the wrong way.'

'Well, all I did was laugh at him.'

'Aye. That'd be it,' he said gloomily. 'These fellers can't stand bein' laughed at, I can tell yeh.'

They drank their wine in silence for a second.

'And he mentioned this lass, this *miliciana*. She definitely was a spy, he said. Said it was all in his report. She was the daughter of a well-known Anarchist.'

Susan frowned at him. 'So why are you here? Compassionate leave?'

'In this war? Don't make me laugh. Sign on, get trapped. That's what they're saying.' He stirred about uneasily. 'Ah can't make it out, really. Seems like he was saying for to come and tell yeh. To get out.'

'He sent you?'

Jake shrugged. 'Seems like. He fixed me three days' leave.' His brow cleared. 'I know. Yeh got under his skin and he wanted to get rid of yeh from here. Didn't like someone like you being the heroine.' He reached in his pocket. 'Ah've got safe passage documents with government stamps. And notice here about a ship which is going to Marseilles.'

'Will you come too?'

He shook his head. 'Still a job to do here, bad as this is,' he said. 'But Ah'll go with yeh to the docks.'

'What about ChiChu?'

'ChiChu?'

'The *miliciana* he talked about. The girl soldier.'

He shrugged. 'These papers say nothing about her.'

'They'll arrest her.'

He shrugged. 'Up to them. Up to her.'

'She can come with me.'

'The papers only allow one.'

'We can try, Jake. Come and meet her. She's not much older than your little sister Sweetie. Only a child. No spy.'

She went out and got ChiChu from the ward.

ChiChu was wary of Jake, stirring restlessly under his gaze.

'She dinnat look like any girl soldier to me,' he said, scratching away at his beard.

'What do girl soldiers look like?' said Susan. 'I've never seen one before ChiChu. She's very strong, despite being very slender. She says she was a good fighter.'

'What is man?' said ChiChu. 'Who is he?'

'He is my friend,' said Susan. 'Friend. From my home. You know, friend.'

'You live with him?' said ChiChu.

Susan shook her head. 'No. Yes. He is like my brother,' she said desperately.

ChiChu nodded. 'Yes,' she said. Her body relaxed and she smiled easily enough at Jake. 'Brother.'

Jake looked at her. 'She says you are a soldier,' he said, putting an imaginary rifle to his shoulder and shooting it.

She mimicked the action. 'Yes,' she said, 'soldier. Kill Franco.'

'Just a bairn,' said Jake. 'No spy.'

'I can't leave her to be locked up.'

He nodded. 'Give it a go. I wouldn't want to leave her myself.' Susan had made him think about his sisters, poor enough at home it was true. But no one had called them to arms, had put a gun to their shoulders.

Susan went for Sofia so she could explain what it was all about to ChiChu. Sofia listened with a thunderous face. 'Evil man,' she said. 'That commissar. Child killer.'

Jake shook his head. 'Some of them are like that. The end justifies the means, they say. Ideas good, people bad.'

'The Italian commissar, he was different,' said Sofia. 'Good ideas. Good person. Is that not so, Susan?'

Jake missed this but Susan thought of the commissar. The size of him, the warmth. The sheer expansion. She was returning to England, probably back to the hospital again, back to life's routines. Of course, the Italian commissar could very well be killed, as had so very many of the men they had sent back up the line. He might live; in which case he would go on fighting here or anywhere else where the Fascists stamped their boots. She would not see him again. She knew that. Perhaps she was happy about that. Perhaps it was the easy thing to do, to return almost as though nothing had happened, to reclaim her old self. Then her body sang for a second in memory of that brief time she and the Italian commissar were together. She would not forget that. She would never forget that, whatever life's routines may offer.

ChiChu looked at these two English people who didn't look in the least like brother and sister. But strange things could happen like that. Sol, her grandfather's old friend, had had a son and a daughter, one blond, fat and tall; one short, dark and stick-like. There were some jokes at Sol's expense but it was accepted in the village that they were truly brother and sister.

And now, according to Sofia, this scrawny Englishman had come to rescue his sister from the Communists. Over the sea to France, by train to Paris, then over the sea to England. ChiChu was sad that Susan was going, but argued that she should stay, patch up soldiers to send them back to the fight. Sofia told her that she was on the List. They would imprison her like they had imprisoned hundreds of others for thinking in the wrong way. She couldn't patch up soldiers in prison. She should fight by getting away; they had killed her father so she should make them work hard to kill her. 'Think, ChiChu! Think!'

ChiChu thought how much she liked the tall Englishwoman who, despite her broad frame and open face, seemed to ChiChu to need a bit of protection herself. ChiChu had lost everyone: her mother when she was born, her soldier father, her grandfather and her grandmother. She had lost her soldier friends. No. She was not going to lose her friend. Not ever. She was determined on that. She would go with Susan and with the ugly Englishman. That was the only way.

Chapter Six

Interrogation

'Susan Cornford?'

Susan watched as the tall officer wrote her name in his neat hand on the battered, heavily lined form. She noted the thick, sun-bleached hair, the slender hands, the fine handwriting. This man was her third interrogator. The others had been Spanish, easily made angry by her lack of comprehension of their language. They had shouted and harangued her but she'd not been touched. This one spoke good English with a very strange accent. She thought he might be German.

Thick blond lashes shaded his eyes as he looked at the paperwork in front of him. 'And you've been nursing near the front?'

'Yes. It had been a church before. Now it is a clinic. We only dealt with those who were less seriously wounded. Patched them up and sent them back.'

Susan Cornford. He put down the name. She tried to be patient. If she lost her temper she'd be lost. He seemed like a reasonable man, even if he were a German. She wanted to demand that ChiChu should come with her but Jake had told her not to mention ChiChu. He'd see about ChiChu. There were other ways. They'd left ChiChu at a small *alberg* in a side street off the Plaça Reial. Susan had watched the slight figure vanish in the dark doorway with misgiving, wondering if it were the last time she would see her. But ChiChu had turned and given her a cheery wave and Susan relaxed. Unlike Susan, ChiChu was in her own territory. This warren of narrow streets and high tenements was her *barri*, her village. She knew her way round here. Jake had taken Susan to a banner-draped hotel which was acting as some kind of headquarters. She'd trudged after him up the narrow marble staircase with its worn steps. He handed her over to a narrow man in a proper government uniform. The man nodded at Jake and assured him she'd be all right, that they would take care of her. His manner had been easy, reassuring. Jake, who was late for his return to his unit, had allowed himself to be reassured.

He turned to Susan. 'Yeh'll be all right,' he'd said. 'Ah've fixed things up. They've given me their reassurance.' She noted that there was still some worry in his voice.

Jake shook hands with Susan, saluted the officer and turned back down the stairs. The officer had ushered Susan into a narrow clanking lift which ground upwards for three storeys. Then he'd hustled her along corridors and finally into a room with its single desk . . .

'Miss Cornford?' The note of command in this new man's voice brought her back to the present. 'No party affiliation, it says here.' Behind him was a tall door, half open to the narrow balcony. She could hear the creak of trams and the crackle of gunfire in the tree-lined boulevard outside.

'No. I never bothered with politics. I was nursing in my

home in England and I wished to come here to help. That's all. I came with Jake Stanton, who was brother to my friend. I was here four months, then he came to the clinic and said he'd been warned that I should leave. Then he brought me to Barcelona and they said he should bring me here.'

'And where is home in England?' The strangeness of her interrogator's accent struck her again. Perhaps he wasn't German. 'Where do you come from?'

'Where d'you come from?' she said suddenly. 'Are you French?'

Angry colour rose to his narrow cheeks. 'I'm asking the questions, Miss Cornford.'

'Am I under arrest?' said Susan sharply. 'You're the third person to ask me these same questions. I imagine the things they shouted at me in Spanish were the same questions. I'd not thought it a crime to tend the wounds of republican soldiers.'

She'd had three interrogators, culminating in this tall . . . was he a Frenchman?

She repeated, 'Are you French?' She kept her voice steady.

He put down his pen. 'No, Miss Cornford, I am not French. I am South African.'

'Oh,' she said. 'I have never met a South African. I thought you were German at first.'

'Miss Cornford.' He picked up his pen again. 'This situation is serious. The Spanish officers here say that you're in the pay of the Anarchists. They say you admitted this to them. Are you aware of this?'

'How could I admit anything? They didn't understand what I was saying and I didn't understand what they were saying. Don't you see this?' She looked at him. 'The thing is Mr ... Captain ... All I want to do is go back to England, back to my home, having tried to help here for all this time.'

'But what information will you take back? Who will you talk to? You have been ... er ...' he looked at the paperwork before him, 'consorting with enemies of the state. A woman soldier. Anarchist. From a traitor family.'

She laughed out loud. 'ChiChu? She is a child, caught up in a war. She was helping me to bandage soldiers. Don't be ridiculous.' She looked at the open balcony door and window and frowned. 'You don't have her? You don't have her here? She went home. I'm to collect her. She's to come with me.'

He stared at her. 'It is not your business. But yes, we do have her. She's been detained. She has admitted being an Anarchist. She accuses the foreign comrades of exploiting and despoiling Spain, as did her father. We know who her father was. And she admits sympathies for the Fascist soldiers.'

Susan laughed at this. 'Do you not sympathize with them? They're farm boys conscripted into Franco's army. ChiChu says our soldiers call for them in the battle to desert. And they do. They call to our soldiers across the lines. They don't want to fight against their own.'

'That sounds suspiciously like sympathy to me, Miss Cornford.'

'Maria Josep – ChiChu – the young woman is my friend. My ... protégée. I'm going to help her to train as a nurse when she comes to England. I ... I have a place in a nursing college for her. That is all.' She folded her arms. 'She must come with me. I insist.'

He rifled through the file again. 'There was no mention

in your letters about a hospital. That you've arranged for her to work in a hospital.'

'In my letters? Do you mean my letters have been read?' She'd heard of this censorship. But her own letters? Her own trifling commentaries to Theo and Keziah?

He looked at her blandly. 'We're in a state of war, Miss Cornford. Censorship is necessary for national security. Even the most ordinary letter from the most ordinary person may betray the state. There are traitors everywhere.'

'In England, Commissar, I worked in a lunatic asylum. In there, we called that attitude paranoia. It's a sickness.' She looked at him bitterly. 'It is a wonder you have the energy to fight the Fascists, so busy are you fighting the enemy within.'

He continued to look at her for a moment, then started to leaf through her file. His eye stopped on an early page. 'You are from County Durham, I see.'

'Yes,' she said wearily. 'A small place called Stanhope not far from Priorton, which is not that far from Darlington and Durham. You'll never have heard of it, not in a month of Sundays.'

He closed her file and stared at it for a moment. 'This is interesting, My . . . I . . . my father came from that part of England. He went to South Africa for work at the turn of the century.'

She warmed to the more tentative tone in his voice. 'Is that so? Lots of folks have done it, I know. Canada. Australia, South Africa. Everywhere looking for work. What was his . . . ? What do they call you?'

'My name is Maichin, Aaron Maichin. Have you heard that name in those parts?'

She settled back in her chair smiling slightly. 'A very

strange thing, Mr Maichin. The family who brought me up had that name. They are my family.'

His face became blank again. 'Of course you would say that, Miss Cornford. The only name down here is Cornford, not Maichin.'

'The woman who brought me up was Rose Clare Maichin, who was an Irishwoman who had been married to a Welshman. My godmother's name is Theodora Louisa Maichin. You may have heard of her. She writes novels. She was quite well known in the twenties. Those stories still sell all over the world. You could check with your censors. They'll have a note of her address in their ledgers, or wherever they keep their blessed spying records.'

Now he was staring at her, his light eyes glittering in the light from the single lamp. 'I know this family,' he said. 'I know it. I know of this woman.'

She frowned. 'You've been in England? You've met Theodora?'

He shook his head. 'My father was connected with them, Miss Cornford.'

'South Africa? Oh, my goodness. There's something familiar . . .' She frowned at him, peering in the early evening gloom.

His chair scraped back on the wooden floor as he stood up. 'I think that's sufficient, Miss Cornford. This interview is at an end.'

'Is your father still in South Africa?' she said tentatively, trying to hold him with her. 'I could write to Theodora . . .'

He shook his head. 'No, not at this moment. He died. There was a shooting accident.' The soldier reached across the little table and took her hand in his.

He escorted her back to the small room.

Then the door clicked shut behind him and she was

left again with the light of the single lamp. She moved from the chair to sit on the simple pallet which had been doing service as her bed for two nights. Then she stood up again and shouted at the top of her voice: 'Mr Maichin. Mr Maichin. Commissar Maichin. Come here! Come here, I tell you.'

There was a rattle and some scurrying in the corridor, then he was standing before her, smiling slightly. 'What was it, Miss Cornford? You have something for me? It is always better to say . . .'

'I just wanted to tell you that I will not go from Spain without Maria Josep . . . without ChiChu Sabater. I promised I'd take her with me. I'll not go without her. I promise you. She must come with me.'

He stared at her. 'You'll be lucky to get out of here yourself, Miss Cornford. Do not concern yourself with this woman.' He turned on his heel. 'She's a traitor,' he said over his shoulder. 'A traitor to her country.'

She listened to the rattle of the keys again and threw herself on the pallet. 'She's not a woman!' she shouted. 'She's not a woman! She is a child!'

ChiChu sat down and put her head in her hands. It was hard to know how many days, weeks, they had kept her here. The time went slowly, but, looking back, it telescoped into almost nothing.

ChiChu kept her eyes closed. Her head was sore from the rough hair cut they'd given her and her stomach was shouting out for something, anything, to ease its aching hunger. If she closed her eyes she could pretend the others weren't there. On the benches against the wall sat an old woman wearing a tattered dress which had originally come from Paris, a young prostitute with a sore, running mouth, and a heavy woman in black who sat making some kind of bedraggled lace using a small wooden disc. This was the woman who had spoken kindly to her at first. But ChiChu stayed quiet. She had been warned by the prostitute to say nothing to the heavy woman, as she was a police spy. The prostitute also told her not to speak to the woman with the tattered dress, as she was bourgeoise, the wife of a notorious Fascist and therefore The Enemy.

The thought of talking further with the girl with the sore mouth, or either of the others, did not entrance ChiChu, so she sat with her eyes closed. She invoked waking dreams of her father holding forth at one of his meetings; of her grandmother scraping out the residue of olives after making the oil; of her grandfather reeling home after a late evening at Franco's; of Esteban showing her how to strip and load a rifle; of the comrades singing Anarchist songs round a scrappy fire halfway up a mountain.

When Susan had left her, the friends in the *alberg* told her that after the street-fighting, when the Communists took the telephone exchange, the assault guards had come and taken everyone. All the active comrades. The prisons were full. They were turning shops, warehouses, into prisons.

This place where they were now locked in had been a shop near the Mercat Boquería. Her grandmother had once bought shoes there: good working clogs that lasted very well. Savage men had questioned ChiChu in the back room of this shop, where once an old man had put new heels on working boots. She had tried to keep her eyes closed during the questioning but they slapped her and told her to open them, and to open her mouth and tell how she lay like a snake in the hospital spying on

Spain's heroic soldiers when they were at their weakest. They wanted to know who it was that she sent the information to. And where she was going when they picked her up in a known Anarchist café, with those other zealots who were plotting the downfall of the true government.

In the weeks of questioning, again and again she had shaken her head. All she was doing, she said, was looking for anyone from her *barri*. She had been at the front working in a hospital and now looked for her friends.

The prostitute seemed none too pleased when ChiChu returned to the cells with mere slap marks on her face. She, and others, she said darkly, had suffered worse. She must be a spy. They had sent her here to spy on them.

Her name was called again and she stood up wearily. The woman in the tattered dress looked her in the eyes and she saw sympathy there. She prayed that the woman would say nothing. Any word of sympathy from a Fascist would brand her a sympathizer and would probably make things worse for her.

She blinked in the bright light of the corridor and stumbled as the man's hand pushed her from behind across an alleyway and into a small room stacked with cabinets and heaped up with files. A man stood up behind a desk. He was tall and striking, his pale hair shining in the light from the open window. He nodded at her escort and she heard the door click behind her.

'Maria Josep Sabater? Will you pull that chair forward and sit down?' He spoke Spanish well, but he was certainly a foreigner. 'Sit down!' he said sharply.

She sat.

He frowned. 'How did your hair become . . . that?'

She put her hand up to her butchered curls. 'They cut

it because ... they said ... I had lice. When they questioned me, they said I had lice. They cut my hair with a razor. They laughed and said I had lice.'

'Did you?'

'No. My hair was clean.'

'You know a woman called Susan Cornford?'

Her face lit up. She looked round. 'Susan? Is she here? My friend?'

He shook his head. 'What does this Susan Cornford have to do with you?'

'She showed me ... about bandages. I was injured and they put me in her clinic. The old church. She showed me how to be a nurse.'

'And how were you injured?'

Her narrow face hardened. 'I am *miliciana*. I fight for Spain. I shoot Fascists.'

'And how did you fight?'

'I am part of a section where fight the friends of my father. I joined them when my father was killed.'

'Were they Anarchists, your comrades? Anarchists like your father?'

'True patriots,' she said. 'They died for Spain, my comrades. I was the only one left.' She sighed a deep sigh and there was silence in the dusty, sunlit room.

The man stood up. 'Come with me,' he said.

She felt a flicker of fear. 'Where? Where do you take me? Will you shoot me? A woman in the cell said they were shooting women.'

His tanned cheeks went ruddy. 'I will take you to Susan Cornford,' he said impatiently. 'There's no time or space in this war for children.'

He took her arm and marched her out of the room and along a corridor. She could tell that he was some important person in the way the soldiers seemed to melt away as he strode forward. The two of them walked through the narrow streets. There were crowds on the corners and at the makeshift barriers but they studiously ignored the tall foreigner who had the wriggling young woman in his grasp.

They turned out on to the broad avenue of the Ramblas and dodged a creaking tram. He stopped in front of a narrow hotel. 'Here. We go in here,' he said. She wriggled, but he held her fast.

Well, at least it wasn't another police station. Perhaps he would seduce her. The prostitute was well versed in these things. She had told her what to do. He nodded at the man lounging near the door and they took a clanking lift up three floors. He walked along a corridor, opened the door with a key and walked her in.

'ChiChu!' Susan rose from the bed. 'You brought her, Commissar.' She held out her arms and ChiChu walked into them. 'Your hair, ChiChu. What have they done to your hair?'

The door clicked behind the commissar and it was half an hour before he returned. 'I have her release papers from the prison,' he said. 'They declare her a rebel, so you'll still have a problem getting her out of the country.'

'Still,' Susan said. 'Thank you, Commissar, for your efforts.'

He surveyed her coldly. 'You have no place in this war, madam. Neither has this child.' He dipped in an inside pocket and pulled out a small sheaf of papers. 'Embarkation papers, for you both. The captain may overlook the blight in her papers. We can hope so,' he said. 'They are signed and sealed. You will travel by fishing boat to France then on to Paris. There are francs in the package for your journey to London from Paris.'

'Commissar, I have to thank—'

He shrugged. 'Do not celebrate, madam, until you arrive. Mistakes may be made.' He looked round the comfortable room. 'You'll stay here until morning when I'll come for you and take you to the harbour.' He walked to stand in front of Susan. 'This is risky, Miss Cornford. It's not without risks.'

They watched the door shut behind him and saw the key turn in the lock. Susan turned to ChiChu. 'And now, Señorita Maria Josep, tell me again about those women in the prison. And this poor hair.' She stroked the spiky hair.

ChiChu caught her hand. 'Eat, Susan. 'I am very *afamat*. Hungry.'

'Well,' said Susan, 'hungry you may be, but by the look in that man's eye, at least, I think you might just be safe.'

Chapter Seven

Theo's House

'Spain, Spain, nothing but Spain in the papers.' Theodora Maichin pushed *The Times* away from her, a faint scowl on her fair face. 'Now Franco makes for Madrid. Dratted man.'

Theo's lodger, Mr Walstein, looked at her over his glasses and smiled. His gold tooth – fifth from the back on the left – glittered in the light of the corner lamp. 'Ah, Mrs Theodora, you cannot say this. Each day you are on Upper Street, gathering newspapers like sheaves of corn, plucking each ear of news about Spain like a squirrel.'

Theodora laughed. 'Oh, Mr Walstein, it's you who should be the writer, not I.'

'Ah, dear lady, the foreign words force their way from my mouth. Never could I put those words on the page. Not in the right order, not at all.'

Theodora pulled the newspaper towards her again. 'So many commentators in these papers. How do you know that the truth is out there? Look here. The *Daily Worker* is full of pieces about Spain. It seems as though it has an ear on the front line. Then the others . . . well, at least the *Manchester Guardian* makes a lot of sense. *Daily Mail* takes Franco's line. Where is the truth, Mr Walstein?'

He shook his head. 'Never the whole truth, Mrs Theodora. They never say the whole truth. I tell you many times the truth of what happens to my cousins and niece in Germany. But we read nothing of that in the English papers.'

'But, Mr Walstein, they're full of Adolf Hitler and a kind of sublimated war fever. Look at the Olympics. What a show that was and what hands were gently wrung about the Führer's peacock ways. Some of them do hint admiration for that man and what he does. Others worry about him and the threat of another war.'

'But they don't worry about *my* people, dear lady. And, if they don't worry, they accede to these disgraceful things. I tell you, some of these people are comfortable that the Fascists call my people spies and child-killers, exploiters who plot international domination. There are English people who feel just the same as those Germans.' He was pleating the white tablecloth with his slender fingers. 'They think so themselves. I can tell this.'

'I am sorry,' said Theodora. 'So sorry.' Now she was driven to apologies suddenly for being English.

'How many of my people fight for the Republic in Spain, Mrs Theodora. They've gone through all this terror in Germany and Italy and still they help the Spanish to fight the Fascists. But in the newspaper they are called Red. Red this. Red that!'

'I know this, Mr Walstein. I do know this. You remember, my goddaughter is there is Spain? Susan? I read you her letters.'

He glared at her for a moment as though she herself were Mr Hitler, then he relaxed. 'Forgive me, Mrs

Theodora. I think of the face of my little niece Madeleine and I wish to fight the world.'

Theo had heard stories of Madeleine on many evenings, as the two of them enjoyed their late night brandy and chocolate. Wherever they had been during the evening – Theodora to her Lit Phil meetings, to the cinema, or to the theatre; Mr Walstein to visit one of his old friends in Golders Green, to play cards or listen to the wireless and share a bottle of beer. Wherever they had been, during the day, Theodora and her Mr Walstein met in her sitting room and drank hot chocolate and brandy by the dying fire.

'Poor Madeleine,' she said, knowing what was coming word for word.

'That house in Hamburg, Mrs Theodora. You would have liked it. Tall. Beautiful. Plane trees in the garden. I'm telling you. Picnics in the woods. Her father, my brother, taught at the university. Bees and bugs. Innocent things. That was what he studied. Innocent things of nature. Do you know, Mrs Theodora, the nurse who brought Madeleine into the world said the child had a halo round her head as she emerged? The woman was a Catholic, of course, but we understood the angel picture in her head. And clever! Mrs Theodora, Madeleine was the cleverest in her class. Her father taught her mathematics; her mother taught her philosophy and I taught her to play the violin. Such a tender touch she had.' His eyes filled up with tears and Theo sat very quietly while he composed himself.

Mr Walstein had been her lodger for six years. He had been sent by a man at the university to look at the large collection of violins in her house. James, her husband, had been a well-known maker of violins and had built up a very fine collection.

Mr Walstein had visited the house several times to look at the fine instruments. He delighted in them. Finally on one visit, he played them for her. His slender hands were the first to draw music from them since 1919. That was the year Theodora lost James to the vengeful influenza that mopped up survivors from the Great War. He was buried side by side with their son, Simon, who had been too young to be called up for the war. The disease was no respecter of innocents.

It was the night he first played James's violin, that Theo found herself telling Mr Walstein about James and little Simon.

'For two years after those events, Mr Walstein, I shut myself in this house. In that time, I could neither read nor write. Daylight bruised my eyes. Mrs Fawcett took care of me. I cared not what I ate or what I drank. I scratched out letters to my mother and goddaughter, Susan, up in the North and that was all.' She paused. 'In the end I realized that it was Simon I mourned most: the life unlived. With James . . . well, we'd had a wonderful life together. It seemed a sin to mourn that.'

'That was a sad state, a sad state to be in,' said Mr Walstein, as he laid the violin carefully in its velvet case. 'But you are well, now. It did not go on?'

'For two years, I was like a ghost in my own life, Mr Walstein. Then I visited Mother in the North. It was there, in the peace of the low hills, within the sound of running water, that I began to think of James and little Simon without anger. I sat again in a special room where I'd always written since I was a young girl. That was when I started to write again. That great dam of pain broke in me.'

The new novel had been a tragic love story of the

MY DARK-EYED GIRL

Great War: a time of great love and no returning. Thinking about James, Theodora worked with a strand of happiness running through her. It was a feeling of pleasure she had always had when she wrote her stories. She thought it had gone from her for ever.

Rose Clare and Susan were delighted at her personal resurrection as she set about building another life without James and the sweet sound of his violins. She had finally taught herself to still the hunger for James's music, for the touch of Simon's young hand, the clean soap-and-dust smell of him; his urgent need to take on life.

But the long evenings in the tall house in Upper Street had still been poignant, haunted by mute violins and baby toys still scattered here and there.

'Then you came, Mr Walstein, came and played the violins to me.' When she realized he lived in lodgings she offered him rooms at the top of the house. From time to time there were other lodgers. It was a big house. The money was very helpful. She'd had nearly four years with no book out at all and her novels sold at a trickle now; no longer the flood of the early days. But Mr Walstein came to stay and she was comforted again by the sound of the violins drifting down the wide staircase. She was sustained by the warmth of their cocoa and brandy just before bedtime. Even after five years, this was the extent of their intimacy. It satisfied them both.

Apart from the Madeleine stories she knew little about him. He was a private man, contained like a tightly screwed jar. She wondered if there had been a wife and children, engulfed by catastrophe like little Madeleine. But then she decided not; she could sense in him the dry warmth of a bachelor rather than the dense, contained passion of the husband.

Tonight she was sitting on the small sofa on one side of the fire, her two cats, Viv and Jen, curled in a shell-like coil beside her. It was hard to tell where one ended and the other began. Mr Walstein sat in the high-backed chair at the opposite side of the fireplace.

'Will we truly go to war, do you think, Mr Walstein? Did you read about the welcome they gave Mr Hitler in Vienna? Did you see them waving the flags? How can we stop him?'

He rolled his brandy glass in his delicate musician's hands. 'So terrible to say this, but I do wish with my whole heart that it will happen, this war. I want them to do something strong about those men of bad spirit in Germany. Spain also. But they accommodate Mr Franco and let the Spanish suffer. They vacillate, afraid of Mr Hitler and let him walk into countries with a victor's step.'

Theo frowned. Susan, never far from her thoughts, moved to the centre of her mind again. What had possessed that young woman to go to Spain? Yes, she knew that men of goodwill were still going there to join the fight, despite the ban. That the Communist Party was still recruiting here in London at this very moment. Some of her acquaintances at the Lit Phil had sons and daughters, nephews and nieces who talked of going. One young lad had been turned down by the party as 'an adventurer' with no commitment to 'the cause'. The cause? Was that Communism or the saving of Spain? Well, Susan was no Communist. And at thirty-eight, after her life on the farm and her years in the hospital, she was too sensible to be carried away in an adventure. Her letter had said: *This is not an impulse, Theo. But it seems now I am like a horse tramping round a very elaborate corn gin. This man – Jake – he talked so well of the justice of the cause. He makes me want to go. I have never felt so strongly that something is right for me. Never.*

'You worry about your goddaughter?' Mr Walstein's voice broke into her thoughts.

'So I do, Mr Walstein. She is a sturdy soul but bullets are no respecters of strength. They cut through; they cut through.'

The light of the fire glowed on his face as he nodded, the shadow on his eyes deepening. 'We worry for our own. Those tender lives.'

'Susan's more than my goddaughter, Mr Walstein, she's mine by adoption. She was born into my hands and then her mother died. In some ways she is as much to me as Simon was. She is all I have left.'

'Ah! The ties of true affection, Mrs Theodora, like those which bind you and me after our years of sadness.'

The clock ticked in the room, and Viv the cat jumped from Theo's lap and stretched herself thoroughly in the heat of the fire. Jen followed suit, joining in on the languorous display.

'Mr Walstein,' said Theo, '. . . I . . .'

Mr Walstein stood up and yawned. For a second, he was not unlike the cat. 'Now, Mrs Theodora,' he said. 'I will wish you good night. I have to rise early in the morning to miss the rush on the roads. I had to swerve the other day to miss a motorcar driver who also thinks I am a spy or an exploiter. We ended up in the gutter, my bicycle and I.' Then he was gone.

Theodora looked at the door through which he had vanished. His words of affection, mild as they were, were faintly embarrassing. It was uncomfortable to have such things made explicit between them.

She was saved from further pondering by a great knocking at the door. She checked her collar and her cuffs, peered in the hall mirror and patted her hair and went to open it.

'Mrs Theodora?' Mr Walstein was standing at the top of the stairs in a dark silk dressing gown. He was a strange, exotic creature now, standing there at the top of her stairs. She had never seen him in less than a three-piece suit and old-fashioned wing collar. 'Mrs Theodora? It is very late.' The strain in his voice held shades of other nights in another city where the midnight rattle on the door had about it the menace of chains.

His anxiety made her waver. She had never felt any sense of threat in the dark, crowded streets of this city, but it was late and this was her own home. Then she shook his fear away from her. 'It is quite all right, Mr Walstein.' She undid the bolt and opened the door to be faced by a bedraggled and forlorn figure. A woman's face beamed at her from under a very unflattering woollen hat. 'Theo?' she said.

'Susan!' she said. Theo turned and said, 'It is all right, Mr Walstein. It is my goddaughter. Come here and meet her. Meet Susan.' She reached across her threshold and pulled Susan into the house. 'But it's so late, and you're so thin. How can you be here? You are in Spain.' The gabble of her voice echoed in her own ears. Her months of worry about Susan were flowing out of her in incoherent chatter. Then she stopped. Over Susan's shoulder, she caught sight of a tall, dark-eyed girl with rough hair sticking from her head like a porcupine. Her face shone like gold white in the shadow of the porch. 'And who have we here?'

Susan put out a hand and pulled ChiChu into the

house beside her. 'This is Maria Josep, Theo. But we all call her ChiChu.' She kept ChiChu close to her side. 'She was a *miliciana*, Theo. She fought at the front against the Fascists. Then she helped me in the hospital.'

'This child fought against those dogs?' The voice came from the scarlet silk vision of Mr Walstein, now halfway down the stairs. 'She actually fought?' He was trembling.

ChiChu clung to Susan's side as this strange man reached towards her. 'This child?' He gripped ChiChu's shoulder.

Theo took his arm. 'Mr Walstein,' she said, 'do you think you could bring all those bags and packages in out of the rain? We will go into the kitchen so they can take off their wet things, then we can make a hot drink. These two will be missing the sunshine, even if they don't miss the war.'

By the time he'd brought the luggage into the hall, Mr Walstein had retrieved his equilibrium. He was just going upstairs again when Theo, on her way into the sitting room, called him back.

'Come, Mr Walstein. Come and meet my sister properly. And the little fighter.'

The two visitors were sitting side by side on the couch by the fire, ChiChu welded to Susan's side. The cats sniffed at her feet and squeezed themselves on to the sofa beside her. She stared at them in terror and sat bolt upright, rigid with fright.

Mr Walstein reached over and lifted the cats away from her, on to the carpet. 'The little one is afraid of the cats,' he said. 'Even though a brave soldier.'

Susan eyed Mr Walstein. Theo had written of her lodger but the doddering old man of her imagination did not fit him. What was this rather upright, distinguished creature in silk dressing gown and slippers? She glanced at Theo. She was a dark one, was Theo.

Theo smiled easily. 'This is Mr Walstein, Susan. Remember, my houseguest? Like your friend ChiChu here, he finds refuge in England. Mr Walstein, this is my goddaughter, my sister, Susan. Susan Cornford.'

He took her hand and half bowed over it. 'It is an honour, Miss Cornford. Your godmother speaks of you to me many times.'

Still wrongfooted a little by their intimacy Susan said, 'So she told you about me? A misbegotten waif given shelter by her mother?'

Mr Walstein was nonplussed. This happened to him occasionally in this country. He understood the words but could not at all fathom out the meaning.

Theo laughed. 'But yet she is the sister of my heart, Mr Walstein, my mother's beloved daughter. My mother loved her more than she did me.'

Susan protested. 'No, Theo. That's not so.'

'It's true. If Rose Clare were here to ask she would say I was right,' said Theo firmly. 'So don't be a misery, Susan.'

Mr Walstein walked to the door. 'I will go to bed, Mrs Theodora. You ladies will have much to say.' He turned to ChiChu and bowed. 'Now you are safe, ChiChu,' he said. 'This is a good house in which to be safe.'

ChiChu had attended carefully to this pantomime between the strange man in red silk, the beautiful fair woman and her friend Susan. The words they said had no more meaning for her than the roaring of waters or the chirruping of birds. She seemed to have lost the scraps of English which Susan had so painfully taught her on the rough sea route from Barcelona to Marseilles. On the long train route to Paris the more familiar rhythms and phrases of the French language blotted out altogether the low, heavy tones of the English words she had learned.

Any impulse to talk had been wiped from her by the damp chills of the final train journey to this big, dark city. She thought she would never open her mouth again. Then there were the cats. From their new lying place on the threadbare hearthrug the cat creatures were staring at her coldly. Their fur was tight and smooth like the fur of mice. One was pale, the colour of mushrooms. The other's coat was deeper like the stone on the escarpment with which Esteban had built the emplacement. The mushroom cat had yellow eyes, but the stone-coloured cat stared at her with unblinking eyes of bright amber. How could this woman, this sister of Susan, bear to have these animals in the house with her? In all other respects – the books, the furniture – she seemed like a civilized woman. But those cats!

After much talk and two cups of cocoa Susan hustled her to bed. 'Sleep, ChiChu. Have some sleep,' she said. 'I don't think you have slept since Barcelona.'

It had been a relief when the blond commissar had got her to Susan at last. She thought he was taking her to be raped, tortured, or even to her death. She shuddered as the lisping words of the Spanish interrogator echoed again in her ears, as he described graphically to her the execution of anarchist whores who had consorted – they had the evidence – with Trotskyite traitors.

But then the South African soldier called Maichin came for her. His Spanish was perfect. Even his Catalan was good enough. But then to Susan he spoke English. He spoke so fast to Susan that ChiChu lost track. But whatever Susan said to him worked, because he came right on to the fishing boat with them at the port, settled down and stayed with them until the ship was about to embark. He talked at length to the captain and gave him money alongside their papers. Still she did not trust him. Even when he got off the boat and it was rocking in the water on its way to France she did not feel grateful to him. It was his comrades, after all, who had killed her father. And her grandfather. And her dear *Avia*. He was not to be trusted.

In her lumpy London bed, ChiChu yawned and stretched her feet, pushing down against the starched, white London sheets. Suddenly she was very tired. She must sleep. Perhaps that would cure the growing ache in her for Spain, for her grandfather and grandmother, for her father and Esteban.

'*Avia*,' she said, turning her face up into the darkness, 'what am I doing in this cold land? What will happen?'

'Maichin?' Theo stopped poking the fire and stared at Susan. It was one o'clock in the morning. They had drunk their way down two pots of tea and the talk still flowed.

'Aaron Maichin,' said Susan. 'When he said his name, he must have seen something in my eyes and asked why.'

'And?'

'And I told him it was my foster mother's name. Then I had to explain about the adoption. That you were my adoptive mother, only really you were my sister and that Rose Clare was really my adoptive mother.'

'It's a wonder he didn't put you behind bars there and then,' said Theo. 'From what you say, everybody was putting everybody else behind bars. Especially the mad ones.'

Susan looked at her with her usual direct gaze. 'People

usually believe me,' she said. 'They believe me when I talk.'

Theo laughed. 'So they do. Straight as a die, you were, even when you were a little girl.'

'And when I said where I came from, which particular bit of the North, he believed me even more. He said his father came from there, oh, thirty years ago. More than that. Before the Boer War.'

'His father?' said Theo, leaning forward. 'Did he say what his name was?'

Susan shook her head. 'Not the name. It wasn't Stanhope he mentioned. Priorton. Gibsley. Asked me all about those places. Said his father knew them.'

Theo took in her breath. 'What did he look like? This South African?'

'Tall. Hair almost white in the sun. Very brown. She paused. 'Some people would have said he was very good-looking. He had a kind of glamour. You know – Ronald Colman, Douglas Fairbanks. The captain on the ship told me the South African said he was doing all kinds of things for the Republic. Blowing up bridges. Trains. Dare-devilish things.'

'Did you say fair?'

'Yes. Blond, you might say. A good talker. Looked at you, direct. A strange accent, though.'

'How old?' said Theo sharply.

'Younger than me. Late twenties, maybe.'

'This is extraordinary. Extraordinary.'

'What is, Theo?' Susan was feeling tired. Her back was aching; it had been a long day. A long month. A long year. She wanted to be on her own, suddenly, to continue her mourning for the Italian commissar. Even the mourning was an excuse to think about him. 'Why are you wound up like this, Theo? I suppose he might be some kind of relative.'

'You've heard me, perhaps Rose Clare also, speak of Edward, my oldest brother?'

'Yes.' Not much was said about Edward. She knew he was a 'bolter', that he ran off one time. There was something murky, something not quite right about it. Rose's husband had been a bolter too. Something of a family tradition amongst the Maichins.

'Well, Edward was very tall, very fair, and very good-looking. And a good talker. And you know he ran away?'

'Yes.'

'Well, it was to South Africa that he ran. That would be before the South African War.'

'Oh. I see. And you think—'

'Well, why was that boy so interested in Priorton and Gibsley? And his name is Maichin?'

Susan yawned, then stood up. 'He knew about you. And your books.' She stretched, her strong body silhouetted in the light of the fireside lamp, fashioned from a wonderful statue of a silver woman, arched back as though about to take flight. Theo's gaze dropped to the thickened waist, the rounded stomach. 'I'm sorry, Theo,' said Susan. 'I'm dropping asleep here. I must go to bed. Perhaps we can talk about Aaron Maichin tomorrow?' All that stuff about Edward was ancient history and nothing to do with her.

'Yes, yes,' said Theo hurriedly. 'I'm sorry, keeping you up like this. It's very late.' She frowned, thinking hard.

But when Susan had gone, Theo banked up the fire and sat back to watch the flames struggle again to take hold. Her head was buzzing in the background with thoughts of Edward. But in the foreground was the image of Susan in the lamplight. There was no doubt, no doubt at all that she was pregnant. Theo wondered if Susan knew.

ChiChu turned restlessly in her narrow bed. She was tired to the bone. She knew she should sleep. She wanted to sleep, but the gentle drone of the women's voices cut into the sleep fog each time it threw its cloak around her. Those two. Mother and daughter yet not mother and daughter. The woman Theo looked not much older than Susan. But then Susan seemed very old to ChiChu. The two of them clasped each other with warmth. They had known each other all Susan's life. ChiChu had never even known her own mother. Never felt the touch of her hand. Only the warm, dry touch of her grandmother.

Once Susan had told her that she, too, had no mother. That her mother, too, had died on the day she was born. But here was the woman Theo giving Susan a mother's embrace, as they talked of another woman, Rose Clare, who was mother to both of them. For a woman without a mother Susan was well mothered.

A floorboard creaked in the room above her. That would be the strange man in the red silk coat. The man with those deep eyes. Was he the husband of the woman Theo? But there was something different. Her grandmother and grandfather, they were husband and wife. Those two did not behave like that. Not at all.

How hard it was to know just what was going on.

Chapter Eight

New Citizens

The next morning Theo served a breakfast of eggs for them all in the dining room. Mr Walstein breakfasted early but lingered longer over coffee than usual. His habit was to be in his workshop in the music shop in the city by eight thirty but today he politely begged another cup of coffee. In this way he was still there when Susan and ChiChu came downstairs. He turned his head slightly to follow the sounds of their voices as they approached the dining room.

Theo rose when she saw them. 'Up already? I'd have thought you'd have slept into the day after your long journey.'

Susan shook her head. 'That seven hours is the longest sleep I've had in months. ChiChu here must have had ten, despite the black rings under her eyes. There'll be another night tonight to sleep in safety and many more nights after that.'

Theo turned to ChiChu. 'Did you sleep well, ChiChu?' she said slowly, looking straight at the girl.

ChiChu's face froze and she glanced at Susan, who shrugged.

'She was making great progress in Spain with her English, but now she seems to have lost it all.'

'Just too much for her, perhaps,' said Theo, nodding and smiling at ChiChu as though the nods and smiles would melt the ice. There was no response. Theo shrugged. 'Well, you should both eat breakfast at least. Perhaps that might loosen ChiChu's tongue.'

Mr Walstein stood up. He pulled out the seat beside him and gravely nodded to ChiChu, who slid silently into the chair. She sat quietly, eating her eggs with appetite as the others talked around her.

Mr Walstein announced, 'Mrs Theodora, I will take today for holiday.'

'Holiday?' she smiled at him. Surprises were very unusual with Mr Walstein. 'You, take a holiday?'

He nodded to the girl at his side. 'I will take Maria Josep for a walk.'

ChiChu looked blankly at him. He pointed to her and to himself and walked two fingers from each hand together across the white tablecloth.

She smiled slightly, glanced at Susan and nodded her head. Susan smiled back. 'You go, ChiChu. A walk will do you good.'

They all helped to take the plates and dishes to the kitchen. Theo stacked them neatly on the wooden draining board. Susan put the enamel dish in the sink and started to run water into it. Theo put a hand on hers and said, 'No. Leave that. Mrs Fawcett will be here any moment to do them. She doesn't like her routine upset. Not at all. We'll take a second cup into the sitting room, shall we, Susan?'

Susan poured tea into two clean cups. She handed one to Theo. 'What about your work, Theo? Don't you need to be writing or something?'

Theo grinned at her. 'Well, if Mr Walstein can give himself the day off, I'm damned sure I can give myself one.'

Susan blinked a bit at the language, but led the way. In the sitting room she found herself having to recount the whole of her experience from her first interviews in Paris to her return to England. If she missed details, Theo would take her back to them.

'I can't think why you're so curious,' laughed Susan. Still she felt light at the end of it, as though Theo had funnelled much of the stress and difficulty which Susan suffered into her own being, and had taken them into herself.

'So these Italians,' she said suddenly. 'Who did you say they were? I thought the Italians were helping Franco. It's in the papers.'

'They were volunteers. Communists mostly. Hated Mussolini and came to Spain to fight as part of the International Brigade. They sang as they marched. You know? A funny lot, they were.'

'But you had a soft spot for them?'

'Yes. I think I did. But every one of this group I knew was killed. So soft spots were no use.' Her tone was bleak. 'No use at all.'

'Susan. Can I ask you something . . . well . . . very personal?'

Susan went pink, then nodded slowly.

'Did you take a shine to one of these boys?'

Susan was red now. 'I don't think . . . well yes, as a matter of fact. There was one. But he died, so that was that. And he was no boy. A grown man. Anyway, he had a wife and four children in Italy. So it would never—'

Determinedly Theo drove on. 'And is it he?'

'Is it he? Is it he?' The construction was awkward on her tongue. 'What on earth do you mean, *is it he*?'

'Is he the father of this baby?'

'What?' Susan stood up. 'What on earth do you mean, Theo?' Her hand went to her waist.

Theo came to stand beside her. She put her arm through Susan's. 'Don't you know, Susie? Surely you know? You're a nurse . . .'

Susan shook off her arm. 'Don't be stupid, Theo. Writing those stories has gone right to your head. You . . . you . . .' With a kind of rapid dignity she went across the room, through the door, which she slammed behind her, and up the stairs.

A few minutes later Theo followed her and knocked on the bedroom door. She waited a second, then knocked again. A muffled voice told her to come in and she did so.

'Susan? Do you mind?'

Susan was sitting before the oval mirror. Her reflection raised its eyes to Theo. 'How can I be so stupid,' she said. 'Thirty-eight years old and—'

'Didn't you know?' asked Theo.

Susan shook her head. 'Everything has been such a tumble – finishing at the clinic, then getting myself and ChiChu safely here.'

'Didn't you *miss*? Menstruation?'

Theo had always been bold with her language. Most women called it their 'monthlies' or 'the curse'. She was very modern, was Theo.

'Yes I missed, all right. But I do go two or three months at a time sometimes. And when I was having that do with my grandmother I didn't show for six months. Same when I started working at the hospital.' She put her hand on her waist, then slid it over to her stomach. 'I can't believe it. I can't believe it.'

'Was it the Italian, Susan?'

'It can only be him. We only . . . once. We . . . you know. I wish,' she said, her face bleak, 'how I wish we had done it a hundred times.' Now her lip trembled and Theo took her in her arms and held her until the trembling was over.

She opened the dressing-table drawer and took out a lace-edged hankie. 'There, dear, here you are, have a good blow.'

Then she went and sat on the padded window seat and peered out of the window until the hiccoughing and the spluttering stopped. When she turned round Susan was red-eyed but composed.

Susan sniffed. 'I can't have it,' she said. 'Of course I can't have it, this baby. There are ways.'

'What? Why not? You mustn't mind what people say, Susan. We can—'

'It's not that,' said Susan.

'What is it, then?'

'You know how I was born, don't you?'

Theo frowned at her. 'Of course I do. I knew your mother . . .'

'And you knew all that – my uncle – what he did?'

'Well, that's unfortunate, but—'

'Stigmata of degeneration,' said Susan.

'Pardon?'

'The baby will have . . . problems . . . interbreeding. It will have extra fingers or toes. It will be an idiot.'

'That's rubbish.'

'Listen, Theo. You're the writer, I'm the nurse. I've read the books.'

There was a long, strained silence as they both

contemplated the thought. 'But that can't be true. There have been cases in history. Byron . . .' Theo's voice tailed off. The truth was, she did not know at all. Then she tried again. 'How long? How old is . . . ? How far on are you?' she demanded.

Susan frowned. 'I don't know the date. May, I think. Portugal had just recognized the Franco setup and the commissar was very angry, very angry about it.'

'May. That would be May.' Theo counted off the months on her fingers. 'Crikey! How many months is that, Susan? Have you felt it move?'

Susan pushed back the dressing-table stool and looked down at herself. 'I see it now. I thought I had some gastric trouble. I was sick. Then stomach rumbling and gurgling. Goodness. Yes, it has moved!' She pressed her hand in a downward movement, then jumped with shock. 'Yes. Yes. It's there. I thought . . . you know, gastric trouble? And the strain of those last days? Am I such a fool?'

Theo looked at her carefully. 'Well, Susan, two heads or not, you'll have to bring this baby to term. It's too late to . . . I know there are ways but it's too late. What?'

Susan was smiling at her. 'He moved again. Here. Feel.'

Theo put her hands under those of Susan and felt the magical quickening inside. 'Susan!' she said smiling. 'I feel it!'

'Him!' corrected Susan. 'You can feel him. I tell you what, Theo,' she said thoughtfully.

'What?'

'If he has two heads I'll love him twice as much.'

ChiChu Sabater was only just getting used to England. She felt safe here, but underneath she was bubbling with resistance to the greyness of it all: to the air which was like soup; to the light which seemed filtered through a grey veil. She longed for the bright, hard light of Catalonia where even the winter clouds were only a muffle for the light behind them. She longed for the rumble of Catalan voices, urgent talk, face on face, by people energized by the brisk dispatch of fate and imminent death. She wondered about the battle going on across the sea and thought about her enemies, the friends of the South African, the people who had hurt her and killed her father and grandparents. Even though they were her enemies, she had to admit they were fighting the greater enemy with his strutting foreign soldiers and deadly pilots. They might be her enemy but she wished them to grind Franco and his minions under their heel. Perhaps her own suffering would be worth it if, at least, they could manage to do that and keep Catalonia clear for itself.

She brought into her mind the early, heady days of the revolution when, elbow to elbow with her father's comrades in one of the grand cafés in the Plaça Catalunya which now belonged to the people, she had listened to dreams of finer days ahead when that dog Franco was defeated and back in his kennel, in this world or the next.

But it seemed it was not to be. On their regular evening walk, her new comrade, Mr Walstein, translated for her things out of the paper, mixing up French and Spanish so she could understand. It seemed Franco had Madrid well in his sights and there was a great battle on the Ebro which the comrades were losing, handing Valencia to Franco on a plate.

One day ChiChu and Mr Walstein walked down Upper Street, past women with baskets plodding through the dark morning; women with babies in perambulators, a baby and a toddler inside, and a larger toddler hanging on to the handle. A man stood on a corner playing a concertina; a tall man stood at his side and sang in loud operatic tones, holding out his cap for the charity of passers-by. The concertina player only had one leg and had to support himself with a crutch bound in leather, which made it awkward for the fingering.

Mr Walstein and ChiChu stood at the edge of the broad street waiting for the stream of cars and bicycles to pass by. As they waited, a tall, red bus stopped and the driver leaned over to talk to the driver of another bus. Behind the buses in both directions car drivers pipped their horns and shouted in frustration, but the two drivers completed their conversation before cranking the big vehicles into gear and lurching forward again.

Mr Walstein pulled her arm through his. 'Come on, Fräulein ChiChu, let us march with confidence.' She walked alongside him and admired his authority as he held up the traffic in two directions by waving his silver-topped cane. He reminded her of her grandfather at his most dignified when he was not in his wild drinking times. They walked through narrow lanes with dilapidated, ill-kept fronts and drunken curtains, and finally saw the glitter as water cut like a wound between high buildings.

'River,' said ChiChu, forming the word with difficulty. An image of the Ebro leaped to her mind. Blood seeping down its broad banks. She had seen that wide, shining river in Paris, while they were waiting to begin the final leg of their journey home: a very wide river, busy rattling with traffic, like the shining embroidered language of the people around them. 'River,' she said.

But Mr Walstein was shaking his head. 'No, Miss ChiChu. Canal.' He turned her to face him. 'Ca-nal. Now say it. This is a ca-nal.'

She frowned. 'River,' she said.

He shook his head again. 'No. River is diff-er-ent.'

'Different?' she frowned.

'River natural,' he waved his arms around to encompass the sky, the mountainous lumps of London architecture and the mud-packed earth beneath their feet. 'God made it,' he said.

It was her turn to shake her head. 'No God,' she said. 'No God!' Then she remembered the words of the commissar. 'Perhaps no God,' she said.

His eyes searched her face. He tried his rough Spanish. 'No God? I thought that, too,' he said. 'So many terrible things happen. How can there be a God?' Then his glance went from her to the long boat which was making its sluggish way along the dark waters of the canal. It trailed another boat equally piled with rusting ironware. Other rivers in a brighter landscape came into his mind.

She put a hand on the sleeve of his Crombie coat. 'Sir?' she said timidly, trying to bring him back from the strange place in his mind.

His face cleared. 'No, child. A canal is not a river. Men dig it.' He made digging actions.

Still she was puzzled. He smiled and put his arm through hers again. 'Oh, child, I remember what it was to be like you. In this dark city with only the music of my mother tongue in my head, the lines and the rhythms of the old German poets singing there and me not understanding a word which was said around me. But it will pass, my dear, it will pass.'

ChiChu, understanding almost nothing of this, walked quite happily alongside the old man. For years now it seemed her life, like that of her father, had had only one purpose. To kill the Fascists alongside her comrades. Then to survive, when those she thought comrades turned on her and her family. Then to stay by Susan on that impossible journey from Barcelona to London. But today there was something soothing just wandering along aimlessly with the old man, beside this straight-sided river he called a *ca-nal*.

'Your Mr Walstein seems to have attached himself to young ChiChu,' said Susan two days later, when Mr Walstein for the second time had declared his desire to see the zoo.

Theo nodded. Those two had wandered the streets of Islington, arm in arm, every waking hour. Mr Walstein, having not had a holiday for six years, seemed to declare himself on holiday every other day. And the two of them walked. They walked as far as Smithfield, even as far as Blackfriars, so he could show her the bridges and the broad reaches of the Thames, so that she now knew the difference between a canal and a river.

He asked Theo to lend ChiChu her bicycle and they cycled through the city so that she could see the palace where the King and Queen lived with their little daughters. On that trip she told him that perhaps she thought that kings and queens, like priests, were no good for the revolution.

He laughed at this and told her not to say this too loudly or she would offend the English, who were giving her succour. Every day she would come back from the walks with twenty or thirty new words, even half a dozen useful phrases.

'Yes, they seem quite attached,' said Theo. 'I've never seen him so lively. So dedicated. Look how much English she speaks now.'

'Bit of a heavy German accent, though,' said Susan. 'A

128

Catalan girl speaking English with a German accent. What a thought.'

'Oh, that'll soon wear away. With you talking to her. Sometimes she sounds like you.'

Susan grinned. 'So that will mean she has a northern accent instead. She should listen to you. Now you're the one who can talk for England.'

Theo shrugged. 'In London you can make up your mind what you want to be. That's the beauty of it.' She thought briefly about the time when she was a child when she had begged an old woman to teach her to talk properly, so she wouldn't wear her Welsh accent 'like a billboard round her neck.'

'It's better that she should talk like you,' said Theo. 'She could do a lot worse than talk like you. Such soft tones. I forget how nice the northern voice is.'

Susan hesitated. 'That Mr Walstein, Theo, he's a bit of a strange man. Very quiet and ... well, somehow ... driven. The way he looks at ChiChu sometimes makes me uneasy.'

'Don't worry about him, Susan. He thinks of Madeleine, who was his niece. Her parents, that whole family, were taken off by the police in his country. He thinks they are all dead.'

Susan shuddered. 'Awful. But ChiChu ... he shouldn't—'

'He'll be all right with her. I promise you.'

The nights in Theo's house were not always restful. One night ChiChu wakes and thinks she is back on the escarpment, but this time the emplacement so carefully built by Esteban is, stone by stone, falling down the hill; and that she and Jorge and Esteban are clinging wildly to each other as they, too, tumble and lurch into the green valley below. Another night, she has the same dream but this time, instead of clinging to her two old friends, she is now a tiny child clutching her grandmother round the waist, and her grandmother's swollen, wrinkled hands are trying to brush her away.

Some days she would go shopping with Mrs Fawcett, or ride on the trolley bus with Theo and Susan to the West End of the city. She was used to the press of people in the streets of Barcelona. She had seen the fine shops on the wide boulevards outside the old city. But here in London she felt buffeted by the weight of people, by the panorama of faces so fair and undefined. Her grasp on the language, being so carefully nurtured by Mr Walstein, entirely deserted her on these trips and she would be unable to speak for a day after this. The very worst thing was the problem of clothes.

A shopping trip on Upper Street with Susan and Theo produced a layering of clothes, which was like a gag in her mouth: dress, cardigan, petticoat, knickers; and a pink horror with hooks which they called a corset. ChiChu shook her head. 'I not wear this,' she said. 'Stupid thing.'

The women exchanged glances. 'She hardly needs a corset,' said Theo. 'She's as narrow as a wand.'

'What about stockings?' said Susan. 'She can't go barelegged. It's too cold, for a start.'

Theo frowned then led the way to the children's department and bought three pairs of knee socks in white, blue and black. 'These should do the trick.'

Dressed up in her new clothes, ChiChu looked such a strange cross between child and woman that they all smiled.

Susan said, almost sorrowfully, 'A far cry from the

dungarees and a zip jacket of the *miliciana*. She looks years younger than she is.'

'Wouldn't we all like to do that?' said Theo, smiling.

One wet Saturday, Mr Walstein stayed at home to teach ChiChu to play Twenty-Ones. Theo and Susan had a special appointment to see Theo's doctor in his shabby surgery just off Oxford Street. He confirmed Susan's pregnancy and made arrangements for her confinement in March in a nearby clinic. Now, for Susan, her fate to be a mother seemed settled and solid. On the surface she was tranquil but deep inside a new battle raged between fear of the stigmata and sharply renewed memories of her short time with the Italian Commissar. She pondered at the thought that, even though he probably died for a free Spain, the commissar had bequeathed her and the world a spark of his life. And this, even when around them all another, greater war was beginning.

Even so, she had no regrets for her actions. How lucky that she was here with Theo in this condition. She was anonymous. A stranger in a strange town. She thought of the girls stuck in the Park View asylum for life as a consequence of just the same careless act. Girls whose families had sent the unwanted child for adoption and hidden their deviant daughter in the asylum. Anything was better than that.

They bought a ring in a small jeweller's to make her look married and so when she arrived at the clinic, birth imminent, she was put down as 'Mrs Cornford'. The nurse asked if her husband would be in attendance but she told them he had been killed in the war in Spain. The nurse tutted sympathetically and, for a second, Susan missed Bartolomeo as though she had known him all her life. Later the rage of the pain drove any thoughts, guilty or otherwise, out of her mind.

Theo, banished from the hospital the night before, came early the next morning; she brought roses and a vase to put them in. She also brought ChiChu, who surveyed the pristine surroundings with interest.

Susan looked tiny and shrunken in the bed. Hearing them rustle at her bedside, she opened her eyes and smiled weakly.

Theo put a hand on her arm. 'Bad time?' she said. 'They wouldn't let me stay.'

'Bad time. That's right. I think you'd call it a bad time.'

'Oh, Susan!' said ChiChu, tears welling in her eyes. 'Oh, Susan. Bad time for you.'

Susan gave a ghostly grin. 'I am very well, ChiChu. Honestly.'

The nurse was hovering. 'I'm afraid Mummy left it a little late for the first one, didn't you, Mummy?'

Susan exchanged a look with Theo.

'Now, Mummy, shall we get baby so he can see his grandma?' And the nurse vanished in a swirl of starch and TCP.

'That puts me in my place,' said Theo. 'I thought I looked quite smart today.' Her hold on Susan tightened. 'The baby?' she said quietly.

Susan struggled to sit up properly. 'He's fine,' she said. 'Wait till you see him.'

The nurse bustled in with a tiny bundle and arranged it in the crook of Susan's arm. 'There now!' she said. 'You show him off, Mummy. Five minutes, mind you! That's all!'

Theo and ChiChu leaned across from different sides of the bed. Susan pulled away the flannelette hospital sheet to reveal a small, pink face topped by a mass of greasy dark curls.

'Look at that hair,' said Theo. 'My Simon was bald when he was born. Not a hair on his head.'

ChiChu started to laugh. 'Susan,' she said, spluttering. 'Susan, the commissar!' She ran her fingers over her chin and started to growl somewhere in her throat. His beard and his voice. 'The commissar. He likes you so much.'

Theo looked at her sharply. 'What? What does she say?'

Susan laughed. 'I think she is saying that he only needs a beard to look exactly like his father.' She ran a finger down the baby's round cheek, and suddenly she was crying. 'That he looks like the commissar.'

'What is it, Susie?' said Theo. 'Don't cry. There is no need to cry. The baby is fine. Look at him! He's round and fat and quite beautiful. Not a stigmata in sight.'

Susan shook her head. 'I was thinking about the girls, the women in the hospital. Not me.'

Theo frowned. 'In Spain?'

'No. Here at home. The asylum. Women stuck there like prisoners because thirty years before they had a baby . . . a baby out of wedlock like me. They went all through the torture I went through last night. I never realized till now. Thought . . . well . . . all women have babies so it couldn't be too bad. But it was bad. I'm telling you. And then they give the baby away. I always thought it was a terrible thing, but I never realized just how terrible until this very minute.' She held the baby up. 'Could you give him away?' she said. 'Could you?'

'Nobody's going to give him away.' Theo patted her arm. 'Believe me.'

After their visit Theo and ChiChu walked up Oxford

Street and had afternoon tea in a tearoom. They tucked into cress sandwiches and cream cakes. They talked in a halting fashion of Susan and the baby. ChiChu nodded wisely at Theo. 'The commissar was very nice man. Very merry. Very wise. He tell me to find a priest.'

Theo frowned. 'A priest? But I thought you . . . that your people did not believe . . . the revolution. I read somewhere . . .'

ChiChu nodded. 'Is so, they burned churches. Chased priests,' she said. 'My father say priests and princes are the lackeys of the Fascists. My father, he burn a convent, one time.'

Theo shook her head.

'He kill no nuns,' said ChiChu. 'Just invite them to join the revolution. I think that.'

'Well, men. Why do you want a priest? Now?'

'My grandmother hang in the air.'

'What?'

'She hang in the air between heaven and hell. She need a Mass.'

'But,' said Theo helplessly, 'I thought you didn't believe—'

'No, no,' said ChiChu impatiently. 'I not need it, but she needs. So she hangs around. She comes in dreams and she beats me.'

'So she needs a Mass?'

'So says the commissar. He say get a priest.'

'I think your commissar was very wise.'

'Perhaps he hang around with her? In the air too?'

Theo shuddered. 'No worry for you, Theo. I will find a priest and he'll say Mass for two.'

Theo did find a priest, a friend of her editor's wife. His name was Father Anthony and he was very old and a little

134

unsteady on his feet. He came to the house in a taxi and had to be helped up the steps to the front door. He sat in the upstairs sitting room and listened to their tale. Mr Walstein tried his best to translate for ChiChu.

Susan, at home now with the baby, found herself suddenly concerned for the commissar's soul. Perhaps he really was tangled up there in the ether with ChiChu's toothless grandma.

They finished their story. There was a rather stressful silence, then the old man shook his head. 'I don't know. I truly don't know.'

'The child is very troubled,' said Theo.

Then the old man nodded. 'Well, I suppose there is a need for it.' His eyes dropped on ChiChu. 'The Church fared ill in Spain at the hands of your people. That is not right. I cannot condone it.' His thin voice wavered in the air like steel thread.

There was an awkward pause.

'I nursed there in Spain.' Susan spoke up from the sofa. 'There was a shortage of nurses where I was because . . . because the nuns only took care of the Fascist wounded. That couldn't be right either.'

'Are you baptized?' he said suddenly to ChiChu.

She shrugged, then said rapidly to Mr Walstein, 'My father said he could not stop them. My mother came from a place in the forests called Vic. There were many believers there. My mother died with a priest's blessing the moment after my birth. The moment after that he christened me. Maria Josep. My father could not stop him. He was very angry.'

Mr Walstein translated.

'Good,' said Father Anthony, with some satisfaction. 'And the commissar, was he christened also?'

'Yes,' ChiChu nodded vigorously. 'The commissar told me to get a priest. He knew about it.'

'Well then, I can do this.' He turned to Theo. 'There will be . . .' he hesitated.

Theo burrowed in her bag and a white five-pound note crackled as it was passed between them. 'I'm sure your charities could use this.'

He turned to ChiChu. 'You may attend the Mass, but you may not take part. You are not in a state of grace,' he said stiffly.

His wandering gaze lit on Susan, sitting there with the baby on her lap. 'And this child, will he be christened?'

'I have not thought of that yet. His father, for whom you'll also pray, was a Catholic. But about the child, I don't know.'

He shook his head. 'Beware, my child. A baby in limbo is a thing of pathos and no dignity.'

They all went to the service, which took place a week later. They sat at the back of the large church in the shadows. Susan left the baby with Mrs Fawcett, who had had three children of her own and knew how to handle a bottle as well as the next woman.

The deep shadows in the church were pierced by shafts of dusty light, which lay like rulers from the window to the stone floor of the nave. Here and there, random as fireflies, tall flickering candles reached up to lick the velvet dark. Father Anthony was assisted by a young priest and two very young boys. There were only eleven members in the congregation and the service was a liquid flow of Latin, unintelligible to the group at the back of the church. ChiChu's brain caught some of the phrases like fish snagged in a net – quicksilver things that glittered and swam away from her consciousness in a second. In that stream of words, Susan caught the name Bartolomeo Fibretti and ChiChu caught the names of her grandmother. She remembered her grandmother's mutter over her beads, many years ago, when her son and husband were out of the room. And now in this gloomy, foreign church it was as though her grandmother was muttering in her heart and she was content. They sat to the end of the service, and watched the worshippers leave. They sat on for ten more minutes before Father Anthony came hobbling down the aisle. 'That is all,' he said rather fiercely. 'That is all. You may go.'

He followed them to the arched doorway. Theo insisted on shaking his hand. Following her example, ChiChu caught his dry small hand and Susan did too. Then Theo took out two crisp, white notes from her bag and pressed them on him.

'Five more Masses,' she said quietly. 'Five more Masses for their souls, Father.'

'Yes, yes.' He pushed the money deep in his cassock and shuffled off. 'I will add their names.'

'We come five more times?' said ChiChu miserably as they walked away. 'We must come five more times? I do not want this. Dark church. My father not like it.'

'No,' said Theo. 'That will not be necessary.'

'And my grandmother will move on?' ChiChu asked anxiously. 'She will not stay and press her arms round my waist?'

'We shall see,' said Susan. 'We shall see.' The whole business had made her feel very uncomfortable. Perhaps the commissar, wherever he was, would laugh at her going to such lengths following the old ways. Perhaps not.

They stood in a subdued group at the bus stop when

ChiChu suddenly grabbed Susan's arm. 'See, Susan! See! Franco! All lost now.' Beside the bus stop was a newsstand whose poster behind its iron grille declared 'MORE FRANCO VICTORIES'.

'It is all over,' said ChiChu. 'All finished.' As she started to scream the other people on the bus stop edged uneasily away. One woman glared at Theo angrily.

'I'm sorry,' said Theo. 'But she's very sad. She comes from Spain, you see. Her country has just been stolen and nobody has done a thing about it.'

Chapter Nine

War

Susan and Theo registered the baby as Bartolomeo Fibretti Cornford and named his father with the word 'deceased' underneath. They called the baby Barty and this child thrived in this household of three women and one elderly man. ChiChu was afraid of him at first, as she had been of the cats. But he pulled at her finger and in a few weeks was smiling at her, and she could not resist. Sometimes she even allowed him to accompany her and Mr Walstein on their London walks. The two of them shared the handles of the perambulator as they walked the city streets.

ChiChu's hair was growing now and Susan brushed the thick curls behind a bandeau, which she fashioned from a silk scarf of Theo's. But they could not get her to wear corsets. She wore the long socks and although she was tall, she continued to look much younger than her eighteen years.

As soon as she herself was fit, Susan became restless. 'I should do some work,' she said to Theo. 'You can't keep all of us here. I'll get a job. In a shop or something. I want to work.'

Theo shook her head. 'How long is it since you had Barty? Three months? Anyway, the house is to keep whether you are here or not. Another two and a very small half make little difference.'

'To be honest, Theo, I feel a bit like a leaking tap. If Barty were on the bottle properly, then Mrs Fawcett could feed him. Or ChiChu. I want to do it,' said Susan. 'I want to work.'

Theo threw up her hands. 'Suit yourself,' she said. 'You know that between the rest of us, Barty will be well taken care of.'

'I must earn some money. There were all those clothes for ChiChu and you keep us going, week by week.'

'Work then! Work if you want to. It really will make no difference to me. But that has to be your choice. The books don't make a fortune any more but the money drips in. We can manage.' In fact all the recent dramas had rather taken Theo away from writing. In truth the publishers were in no hurry for her next novel. There was talk of a paper shortage. The paper stock was being conserved for more important documents than fiction. War has a hungry mouth.

ChiChu would no longer speak of Spain, and walked from the room when Susan and Theo exclaimed at the bad news from Spain. She was happiest now with Mr Walstein, who was teaching her the violin. He never talked about Spain. The rest of the household, unwillingly tolerant of the unearthly scrapes and wails which came down the stairs, knew that Mr Walstein was going to lose the battle with ChiChu the violinist. The cats cowered under the chair in the hall. In the matter of the violin at least, ChiChu was no Madeleine.

So preoccupied was this household with its newcomers

and its settling-in dramas that Theo had less time than usual to peruse the papers, so she did not attend too closely to the gradual gathering of opinion against the Prime Minister for his last-ditch peace-waging. She spent less time with her old literary friends in town so she missed some of the political gossip, the distilled worry, the sublimated thrill focused around the inevitable forthcoming war. Where formerly she would have been outraged at the British Government's lack of action when the Germans walked into Czechoslovakia, it was merely another irritant on a day when Susan was out working in her shoe shop and Barty was teething. About the time the Government released Czechoslovakian gold to the Germans, Mrs Fawcett went down with measles and Theo had everything to do herself. She had quite forgotten what one did about a screaming baby with flag-red cheeks.

But even into this household the world finally dipped its dark fingers. In 1939 Franco's troops finally took Barcelona. There were their military parades in its streets and its services of thanksgiving in its churches. Theo handed the newspaper to Mr Walstein and he went to find ChiChu. ChiChu was stricken. She locked herself in the room she shared with Susan and shouted terrible vengeance on this monster who had despoiled her city. Then she became silent and for days did not seem to hear even Mr Walstein's voice.

The news of Franco's final defeat of the Spanish Republic was all but drowned as England contemplated its own war: a war against a people who were still called in common talk by the massively singular name of the Hun.

The announcement of war, half expected for many months, was greeted in many households in grim despairing silence. Parents listened to the measured tones of the newsreader on the wireless and looked at their young ones in hidden, anticipated mourning. Old men dreamed of yellow smoke slipping silently over muddy terrain and woke up shuddering. Dark memories of sons and brothers killed on the Somme were revived at the sight of young men, not yet shaving, strutting the streets of village and town, in raw khaki uniforms.

Susan first heard of the Germans driving their tanks into Poland from one of her customers, a stout woman who wore a good deal of jewellery and had dainty feet and high insteps.

'Are you new here, my dear?' said the woman, easing her bulk into the leather and chrome chair.

Susan kneeled at the woman's feet and carefully removed her shoes. 'Yes. Well. No. I've worked here some time now.'

'I thought so.' The woman flexed her foot, pointing it like a ballerina, turning it this way and that. 'I do have terrible feet, I have,' she said complacently. 'Terrible.'

Susan fell into the trap. 'Oh no. These are wonderful feet, madam. Soft. Nice shape. Unspoiled.'

The woman smiled, her second chin lapping into her fur collar. 'But too long, dear. Even the narrowest fitting sometimes won't do.' She looked around the crowded shop. 'But here, I can usually find something.'

Susan glanced at the stack of ten shoeboxes which she had gathered on the woman's orders. 'Yes, madam, I hope we can.'

She was shoe-horning the elegant feet into the fourth pair of shoes when the woman, bored now with the process, said, 'I see he's in Poland.'

Susan was fastening a resistive buckle. 'Who?' she said. 'Poland?'

'Hitler. I see he has those black boots of his in Poland. Tanks against cavalry, says in the papers. Nasty piece of work, that Mr Hitler.'

Susan looked at the foot, and allowed it to slip to the floor.

'War's inevitable, my husband says. Sure as night follows day. Any day now. He'll be at England's gates in no time, with his tanks.'

Susan stood up. Barty. She should be with Barty. And ChiChu. What am I doing, fussing over the feet of vain women? Barty. ChiChu. I should be with them. War. I know what war could do, don't I? What it can do with people. What it can do with cities. I shouldn't let them out of my sight. How can I let Barty and ChiChu out of my sight? What have I been thinking of?

Her customer stared at her. 'What is it, miss?' she said. 'Are you ill?'

Susan kneeled down again, completed the sale with her usual painstaking care and took the money. Then she put on her hat and her coat and, ignoring the protests of the manageress, strode out of the shop and made her way home. When she got there she made straight for Barty, who was lying peacefully in his cot, and swept him up and held him close. He opened his mouth and yelled.

Then the routines of war invaded them all. The early threat of screaming sirens. The rush for black curtaining for blackout. The gas masks in their ugly cases because the Germans would be sure to use gas. The issue of shelters against the inevitable bombing. Drawings in the newspapers about the safest place in your house if you got caught. Talk of rationing and doing your bit. Heroic stories from the Great War of British courage in the face of the Hun. The elaborate definitions of those who are with us and those who are against us.

ChiChu and Mr Walstein had walked into new territory that day. South and east along the river. ChiChu was used, now, to the houses, with their different shapes and sizes, and the press of people. Barcelona was a great city with its old buildings and its vast dockland. But you could walk it in a day. This city, she thought, would take a week to walk. She and Mr Walstein had walked many streets. Now she was more attracted to the distant tangle of cranes and the looming ships and gaggle of boats in the river. It reminded her of the port in Barcelona. Even the smells were similar. She asked Mr Walstein if she could go nearer, see the ships and boats up close.

They wandered about among the rearing warehouses, watching the tanks and lorries that streamed in and out of the docks. They drew curious looks from the beefy workmen there. What an odd couple they were, this old man in his well-cut suit and silver-topped cane, and this tall gypsy-looking girl in her long white socks and red bandanna round the mass of her hair.

After walking for more than an hour, Mr Walstein became short of breath and had to lean against a wall. ChiChu took his stick from him and stroked and patted his back, unsure of what to do. Across the road was a narrow shop frontage with 'Handley's Restaurant' scratched in peeling paint on the fascia above a smeared glass window.

She took his arm. 'A restaurant. We go there, Mr

Walstein. They give you water to drink,' she said. 'Then you feel better.'

A narrow counter dominated one side of the restaurant, which was really a very mean café. Half a dozen tables and their attendant chairs were scattered across the bare floor. Men in work clothes were sitting at three of the tables with half-drunk pints of beer and the remains of a meal scattered before them. They turned and watched as ChiChu shepherded Mr Walstein to a seat, then asked the man behind the bar for water.

'Water?' he grinned at her, showing cracked teeth. 'Now that's a funny request. Ain't never been asked for water before.'

'Ill,' she said, gesturing towards Mr Walstein. 'Man ill.'

The attention of the men turned up a notch at the sound of her voice. What about those new warnings now regarding strangers on the docks. Beware the enemy within. That was the whisper.

'I have a dizzy fit.' Mr Walstein's voice came from behind ChiChu. 'Stars before the eyes. A glass of water, if you please. That will help.' He slumped back in his chair. '*Gott in Himmel*,' he said, putting a shaking hand on his brow.

A man at the back of the café whispered across the table to his mates. 'Listen to that. German, that's what they are. Bloody Huns! Knew it when I heard the girl. Hun lingo that is. Bloody Huns we've got here, mates.'

The words buzzed from table to table. A small, red-faced man with sparse ginger hair left his table and came to lean on the counter. 'And where might you be from?' he said directly to Mr Walstein. 'Where d'yer hail from?'

'From Islington,' wheezed Mr Walstein. 'Truly.'

'Hey! An' I come from bleedin' Berlin!' The ginger

man sniffed. A murmur went round the room again.

ChiChu came to stand behind Mr Walstein, her hand on his shoulder. 'Islington,' she said. 'Islington, we live.'

The man turned his attention to her. 'And you! Proper little Mata Hari we got here, ain't we, mates?'

She frowned. 'Mata Hari?'

He sniggered. 'We shot her in the last do. Yer might not look like a bloody Hun, love, but yer sound like one, sure enough.' He turned back to Mr Walstein. 'So you live in Islington? And where were you born, old man?'

'Well, in truth it was Frankfurt, but I should explain . . . My name is Walstein. Hermann Walstein.'

'Walstein!' A man at the nearest table repeated.

The others had left their tables and were forming a loose circle around the old man and the girl. The word 'spy' came from the back of the crowd.

'I am no spy!' protested Mr Walstein. 'I promise you . . .'

The man behind the counter gave the glass a final polish, then bent down and whispered something to the boy who was sweeping the floor. The boy put down his brush, wiped his hand down his green apron and made for the door.

The ginger man leaned down and put his hand on Mr Walstein's shoulder, his face close to the old man's. 'Well, sir, I think we needs go down the cop shop with you. I think the cops'd like to talk to the likes of you.'

Strength flowed back into Mr Walstein. His breath started to come more easily. He flung back the ginger man's hand and pushed him away so that he fell awkwardly to the ground. Then unsteadily, Mr Walstein got to his feet.

The ginger man leaped up like a cat and started to

dance around Mr Walstein, poking jabs at him like a man shadow-boxing. 'Well, boys, we got a live Hun here. What say we sort him?'

Two other men pushed their chairs back and leaped at Mr Walstein, pushing him to the floor. ChiChu, no longer scared rigid by the angry faces, jumped on the back of the man nearest to her, shouting. '*Ruffia!* Get off him, you bad man, you ruffian.' She took his hair and pulled back his head with one hand and battered his face with the other. '*Pinxo!*'

Brawny hands pulled her off and held her tight round the waist while her arms and legs flailed the air. She stuck a foot out and kicked over another table and chair. She could hear the sounds of whistles and running feet. Then the remaining space in the place was filled with two fleshy policemen, helmets in hand.

The men stopped kicking Mr Walstein and looked up at the ginger man who had been surveying their work with approval. 'Afternoon, Sergeant Coghill. We've got two live ones here,' he said.

The sergeant scowled. 'Live what? Mackerels?' He turned his attention to the man sitting on Mr Walstein's chest. 'Git up, you.'

Mr Walstein scrabbled for his glasses. 'Sergeant,' he said, 'these men have attacked me and this lady here.' His guttural tones rested on the air.

The ginger man smiled his satisfaction. 'See, Sergeant? Condemned out of his own mouth. These two was loitering on the docks lookin' at the army loading up. I seen them earlier. Peering here. Peering there.'

'Did you attack them?' said the sergeant. 'Bloke looks bruised and battered to me.'

'Restraining him, sir. Restraining him only. And this

little hellcat here. See the scratches on Ronnie's face? Helping her accomplice, she was.'

The sergeant looked from one to the other, then turned to Mr Walstein.

'Name?' he said, taking out his notebook.

'Hermann Walstein,' said Mr Walstein. He rubbed a trembling hand down his once immaculate coat.

'And are you German?'

'No. Yes. Well . . .'

The policeman licked his pencil. 'Nationality German. Address?'

The old man looked round nervously, then stammered out Theo's address.

'And how long have you lived at this address?'

'Nearly six years now.'

The policeman wrote this down, then his gaze turned to ChiChu and she gave him look for look. 'And the lady, sir, is she German?'

'No, sir, she is Spanish . . .'

'Bleedin' International Conspiracy,' muttered the ginger man. 'Spies. The lot of 'em.'

'And we are not spies,' put in Mr Walstein. 'It is ridiculous.'

The policeman stared at him. The men who had recently attacked the old man were back at their tables, slurping their tea, picking up their neglected newspapers.

'It isn't ridiculous to protect your country against its foe, sir,' said the sergeant, shutting his book with a snap and tucking it into an inner pocket. 'P'raps, sir, we'll be more comfortable at the police station. We should leave these people to their well-deserved dinners.'

Mr Walstein shook his head. 'No. No. You cannot do this . . .'

The policeman took him by the upper arm. 'Oh yes we can. Now, sir, don't cause trouble. Be quiet now.'

Mr Walstein turned his haunted eyes on ChiChu. 'Mrs Theodora,' he said. 'We need Mrs Theodora, ChiChu.'

She ducked under the arm of the policeman and ran out of the shop, up a back alley, as fast as her legs could carry her. The men jumped from the tables and gave chase, whooping as though it were all now some game.

ChiChu ran lightly, swiftly, as she had in the mountains running messages for Esteban. She soon outstripped them. When they had given up on her, she stopped and looked around. The narrow houses and the scattering of workshops were only vaguely familiar. She frowned. Fifty yards down the road was a bus stop, and drawing up at the bus stop was a big red bus, with a familiar name and a familiar number. She jumped on, offered pennies for her fare, and glued herself to the window so that she would get off at the right stop.

'I'm coming, I'm coming, I ain't a bleedin' greyhound, you know.' Mrs Fawcett shoved her duster in her pinny pocket and padded to the door, which was shuddering on its hinges like a ship in a gale.

She opened the door and ChiChu pushed past her and ran from room to room until she found Theo in her upstairs study.

'Theo! Theo! It's Mr Walstein. The *milicia*. They take him. Then beat him. *Milicia* take him.' She gulped in air and started again. 'Mr Walstein—'

Theo was on her feet. 'Where? Where is he, ChiChu?'

ChiChu frowned. 'We were walking near the docks. No bicycles. No inner tube. I need a new inner tube.'

'The docks? How did you get back? How long ago? Wait! I'll get my coat.'

In minutes, they were back on the pavement. 'Now where? ChiChu, where?'

ChiChu's brow cleared. 'I come here on the 74 bus. Big red bus.'

'Right. We'll get on the 74 in the other direction. We will go back. You tell me where you got on and we will get off there.'

It took them two full hours to find their way back to the café. The man behind the counter was still wiping glasses. He glanced at ChiChu and looked blandly at Theo. 'Can I help you, love?'

Theo smiled brilliantly at him. 'I'm sure you can. Were you one of those fellows who beat my friend Mr Hermann Walstein?'

He scowled at her. 'That foreigner?'

'Mr Walstein is my guest. He's my friend.'

'You want to watch who you make friends with, missis.' He blew on the glass and gave it another rub. 'The police got him.'

'Someone hurt him.' She looked round the deserted café. 'Who was that? Who hurt him?'

The man shot a heavy-lidded glance at ChiChu. 'All they did was . . . er . . . restrain him till the sergeant got here.'

'Which police station?' she said. 'Where is the police station?'

'Just round the corner, it is. Lucky that, for your friend. If the coppers'd been much longer, I don't know that I'd've been able to restrain my customers. Patriots, they are, to a man.'

She pulled on her gloves, her face now grim.

'You should be ashamed of yourself, sir.'

He called after them, his voice sliding off the greasy glass of the door. 'I'd watch what company you keep, lady. Beware the enemy within.'

At least they hadn't put Mr Walstein in a cell. He was sitting looking very woebegone in a corner of the main office at the police station. The sergeant, though extremely mannerly, was of the same basic opinion as the café proprietor. 'It's risky, ma'am. Big feeling against foreigners these days. And Germans! This man is a self-confessed German.'

'That's ridiculous, sergeant. This man came here in 1933 to get away from the Germans. They killed his family. He works here in London in a music shop and has for several years.'

'Well, ma'am. That's what the word is. They worm their way in till you think they're harmless as a new babe. I read about it in the paper.'

'Sergeant, I know this man. Now, will you let me take him home, or are you going to arrest him for a spy? One or the other. The one and I'll take no action. The other and I will most definitely take action, to your detriment.'

The sergeant was rather enjoying the show: this quite distinguished woman losing her rag, the big-eyed dark girl beside her. 'This could all be a spy deception,' he said. 'You. This foreign girl here. The old man there. You could all be in on it. What did you say your name was?'

'I didn't. But it's Theodora Louisa Lytton . . .' She paused. 'I do have another name.'

He licked his bottom lip. 'An alias? Yes, I know about aliases, ma'am. I read about them.' There might be something in this spy thing after all. 'Another name?'

'Theodora Louisa Maichin. That's my name.'

He frowned. That did ring a bell. He took in her fair good looks, her rather fancy appearance. He peered into her eyes. 'Actress, is it? The name sounds familiar.'

She shook her head. 'No. But you might have seen one of my stories at the pictures. *Rich Cargo* – Greer Garson played the lead. That was from my novel. My novel was called *Rich Cargo* too.'

He beamed. 'Well, I never. You're that one, are you? You wrote that story?'

'And would you think I could harbour a spy?'

'Well, Mrs . . . Miss Maichin. No harm intended.'

She smiled at him. 'So . . . Mr Walstein can come home? He can come home with me?'

He frowned for a second. 'Well, I will have to enter his name and address. All foreigners now are being asked to register.' He paused. 'There's talk of internment, you know.'

'But that would just be . . . well, suspicious people, Sergeant. People who'd shown they were a threat.'

He shook his head. 'Well, miss . . . ma'am. Who do we know is a threat? Who should we be suspicious of? Spies is, by definition, devious creatures. The best of 'em you'd never be suspicious of, would you? Damn good at it, the best of 'em, you must admit. I've read about it.'

'Well,' said Theo firmly, holding out Mr Walstein's coat so he could put it on, 'my friend here is not one of those. He is a quiet man, a musician. And he was persecuted and his family has been killed by that horrible setup in Germany. Do you honestly think he could be a spy?'

The policeman handed Mr Walstein his hat. 'Well, ma'am, if you vouch for him . . .' He stood back and folded his arms. 'We do have your address. And your names.'

ChiChu watched this performance: the 'grand lady'

had come in her grand clothes and showed the ordinary people how to do things right. Something was clutching at ChiChu's heart and she didn't quite know what. An echo came in her head. Her father's voice: '*Bourgeois*.' He would spit the word out like a swearword. She remembered an argument between her father and grand-mother over the harassing of a cotton buyer in the early days of the revolution. The merchant had been benevolent, and had saved the poor people from many a difficulty with his generosity. Her grandmother had condemned the comrades for harassing him.

'*Don't be grateful, Mother. Exploitation is the source of his wealth and his generosity. That exploitation means he can be generous with you. So he makes you smile on him, bless him, curtsey to him. You have no dignity*.' His voice hammered the walls of their small house; his exultation that at last the people's time had come was palpable.

Then in the early, heady days of the new government, when Barcelona belonged to the people, ChiChu saw this same man, the cotton buyer. He was wearing the cap and smock of a workman, slipping down the narrow road in the old city. By that time the bourgeoisie had fled the city or gone underground, taking on the dress of workers to pretend they were of the people. They were heady days. The shops, the cafés, the manufactories were all in the hands of the workers. There was no false respect, no grateful squirming for favour.

Now ChiChu was witnessing this sweating policeman, the militiaman, who had been very much the boss in the workers' café. Here he was squirming at the behest of Theo Maichin because of her bourgeoise style, her forceful charm.

In a moment, ChiChu's ears were longing for the balm

of her own language, even the lisping Castilian of the other Spanish people. Her blood was crying out for the heat and clear light of the Spanish sun in this grey city, which smelled of old leaves and made you blind with its swirling, yellow fog. Inside her, her very organs seemed hardened to lead, and the words being passed between these people were alien, foreign things which made no sense to her. At this moment she could only see Theo, who had been her benevolent patroness, as one of the exploiters her father had despised.

She sat unnoticed in the taxi, as Theo fussed over Mr Walstein and bewailed his sad experience. Theo bundled them both into the kitchen, but ChiChu escaped and went to the bedroom she shared with Susan. She touched the objects in the room. Brushes, ornaments, water jugs, mirrors. They were barren, alien things. She peered at herself in the mirror: the face with its dark eyes; its halo of black hair, the pearl-buttoned cardigan signified a stranger. She flung herself on the bed and stayed there in the darkening room until Susan, sore-footed, came home from work.

'What is it, ChiChu?' said Susan. 'Theo says you won't come down, that you'll not eat. What's up now?'

ChiChu looked at her with dead eyes. This was a familiar face but the words coming out were scrambled sound which made no sense. But Susan's troubled face brought some energy into her leaden head. '*Spain. I wish to go home, to my own country. This is not my country.*' She said this in her own language: the language of her father, of her grandmother and grandfather.

Susan struggled to understand. 'Spain is not your country now, ChiChu. It is Franco's country. They've won. The Internationals are home now. There was that meeting here in London. A Reunion. It is all over. Your country has to be here.'

'*Spain is my country*,' said ChiChu. '*I was a soldier for my country*.'

'If you go back,' Susan searched in her brain for the word, 'you will be imprisoned. Or worse.'

ChiChu put her head in her hands. '*The men in the café knew. I am a foreigner. I do not belong here.*'

Susan sat on the bed beside her. 'You belong here with me, ChiChu. England is your home now.' She tried to say in Spanish: '*England is your home now*.' But ChiChu refused to be consoled and Susan, exhausted by her day, went back downstairs to report to Theo and Mr Walstein over dinner.

Mr Walstein unbuttoned his napkin from his waistcoat.

'She would not speak in English,' warned Susan. 'I could not get her to speak English.'

'We will see,' said Mr Walstein.

The next thing they heard were the haunting sounds of what could only be Spanish music on the violin. In half an hour the strands of tension which seemed to web the house loosened and everyone began to breathe easier. Hours later Mr Walstein came down, flexing his fingers and welcoming the cup of cocoa which Theo thrust into his hands.

He shook his head. 'She was frozen with sorrow,' he said, 'missing her family and her country. This I feel with her. Now she sleeps, but I do not think the sadness will go. Not for a long time.'

That night, ChiChu's sleep was punctuated by dreams of Spain. She is small again and her father carries her on his shoulders. His friends laugh at him for being both a mother and a father to his small daughter: 'Leave it to the old woman, friend. That is woman's work.'

'Ho!' he says. 'Do our ideas live only in your mouth, comrade? Ancient attitudes about women reflect the bourgeois patriarchs. New times these. Unless we take the ideas to our hearts, not just live with them in the mouth, there'll be no revolution.'

Now, she is in her father's workshop and he is teaching her how to cobble shoes. She learns the tricks of his trade so that, after the revolution, she will make her living shoulder to shoulder with her comrades. She drives the small hammer on to her thumb and cries out. He waits for her to stop crying and then he shows her his hands, scarred and split from many misfired blows. 'That's a comrade's life, little one. A cobbler's life. If you want soft hands you must be a laundress or a cook. A cobbler's hands are as leather. Like to like.'

Now she is supporting her grandmother at her father's funeral, holding her arm tight so she won't fall down. People are crowding round like dark birds, offering respect, mumbling outrage at the assassination of a fine man, a comrade who was a shining example. Now she throws off her grandmother, who falls into a hole in the ground and she screams at them to stop talking, stop laughing. They start to laugh at her, and she pummels their chests with her hard, leathery hands. She looks up and the man she is beating is her father. She turns to the next one and he is her father too. And the next. And the next. She races across to the coffin and prises open the lid with her hard hand.

She wrenches it back and her grandmother beams toothlessly up at her from her silken resting place. In her wrinkled hands, crossed over her breast, she clutches her rosary which, instead of its usual silver cross, has her false teeth hanging from it.

ChiChu pulls her out of the coffin and, holding her frail figure in her arms, runs right through the *barri* to their house. But the house is not there. Almost not there. There are huge shell holes in every wall and the roof has been burned off. The only thing still standing is the tall dresser, under which her grandfather is sheltering, his feet sticking out of the end, his toes trembling.

Her grandmother leaps out of ChiChu's arms and grabs her washing stick and starts to berate her husband as a drunkard and a coward. Then another shell explodes and everything is gone. The house. Her grandmother. Her grandfather. Everything.

Then her grandmother is dancing before her, swishing her shawl and stamping her feet like some gypsy. ChiChu lets out a whimpering laugh. '*Ho, Avia!* Stop it, stop it, will you?'.

'What is it, ChiChu?' Susan's voice came from the other bed. 'Are you all right?'

'Mmm. Mmm.' ChiChu turned her face into the pillow, pulled the eiderdown higher round her shoulders, and feigned sleep.

This dream – or variations of it – had visited her several times since she had been in England. Only here in England did her father and her grandparents come here to haunt her so. In a strange way, she enjoyed the dreams, hugged them to her. Tonight, after the frightening time in the café and the police station, it was a special comfort.

She had lost her ability to say English words and she was among strangers. But inside her, in her head and in her dreams, she still had her father and her grandmother and her grandfather. Her grandmother had stopped admonishing her now; she just kept playing the games with the coffin and the crucifix and the teeth, practising some strange joke. She must be satisfied with the Masses they had said for her in the English church. Now she just came back to cheer ChiChu up with her ghostly conversations.

ChiChu had started to talk back to her. And the talking was a comfort.

Chapter Ten

Avia

As time went on ChiChu, stunned and silent now, found nightly comfort in telling the events of the day to her grandmother. Sometimes the old woman seemed to be sitting in the windowsill swinging her rosary beads. Sometimes it was as though she were lying on the bed beside ChiChu, her breath smelling of olives. Her listening presence made up a little for the more terrible dreams which ChiChu had in her sleeping hours.

At first, Avia, this war seems like no war. You and me, we know what war really is, don't we? The click of shells and the drone of planes. It's the smell of cordite, the click of a rifle on a street corner and men in torn clothes with red scarves, standing up in trucks. But here in this cold country the war is sandbags blocking the doorways of great buildings, more and more men in uniforms, very neat, on the streets. It's the little boxes which people carry around against the gas and the black curtains at every window. It's little Barty in his own little leather boat against the gas. It's me and Mr Walstein painting our bicycles white and making funny hoods for the lamps. Susan read of a cyclist mown down by a bus in the blackout, so she made us do

159

this. This war is men with great cans of white paint who steadily, steadily, paint the edges of pavements.

I see pictures in the newspaper, Avia, of little children gathering at stations to be taken into the country away from the bombs. This is called in English evacuation. But there are no bombs. Then Mr Walstein reads the paper and tells me of children made wild with homesickness on first evacuation returning home to mothers wild with relief. He explains to me homesickness and I know very well what it is. There is no night, no day, when I do not feel homesick for your kitchen with its great cupboard, for the slop of fresh olive oil in your big jar. And the taste of your pickled fish.

Mrs Fawcett, Theo's servant – did I not say Theo was bourgeois? – well, this Mrs Fawcett evacuated herself and her four grandchildren to her sister's house in place called Wales and came back a month later saying evacuation wasn't all it was cracked up to be and could she have her job back? So she's back taking care of the house again, which is a relief. Perhaps I am turning into a bourgeois myself. That is the danger.

Susan and I had to go to an office to get little books for food and we must be careful with our supplies. Well, that is familiar, anyway. We knew how to do that, did we not?

But there are no bombs. I have no sense of danger. There is no smell of cordite, no flying shells to puncture the walls of the houses.

A bitter winter has set in and keeps us all inside. It was cold on the hillside, with Esteban and the others, sharing a blanket in the mountain night. But not so cold, so damp, as this place. In the morning there is ice inside the glass window. My teeth chatter and my lips are blue. They notice this, so in this house there are fires, great fires which you must feed with black coal to keep warm.

Theo, the lady who is Susan's friend, or sister, or mother, I can't quite make out which, is truly a bourgeoise. My father would not approve of her. She sits with a blanket round her in her little room scratching and scratching away at sheets of paper, writing furiously as though the very action will keep her warm. She has cats. Did I tell you she has cats? Well, they sit at her table beside the pile of paper poking their nose through the black curtains at the window. Then a man bangs on the door. Did you hear him, Avia? He bangs on the door and tells us to put the light out. And all the time it was the naughty cats poking their noses through the curtain.

The rest of us sit beside the hot fire. We play games with cards which Mr Walstein has taught us. Sometimes he brings down one of Theo's violins and plays it to us. I had one try to entertain them. I tried to play the tune for the sardana so they could all dance, like we do in a circle. But they all moaned: even Mr Walstein who is my friend moaned, so I stopped. Each night we listen to the wireless to hear what is happening with the war. But I cannot understand the words and Mr Walstein tells me all about it. It seems to me that it is a time of teasing, like the very beginning of a bullfight.

Sometimes a great siren sounds, as though in one second great planes will come and rain down bombs and death in that way we know. But that has not yet happened. I say to Mr Walstein how strange this thing is, this war which is no war, but he tells me that in distant places there is going on a terrible scramble to make weapons, to build aeroplanes. They all get ready. And with these, he tells me, the Fascists will be vanquished. He is sure of this. He is a very clever man, Avia.

Susan was disturbed by the nightly muttering which emanated from ChiChu's corner of the bedroom, but she did not mention it. She thought perhaps ChiChu was praying. Perhaps the stream of Catalan was some kind of comfort to her in a foreign land. She wasn't talking in English these days but at least she was listening to English in the daytime, which was something.

Susan talked to Mr Walstein about this muttering in the night, this stream of Catalan. They were sitting round the fire with Theo, drinking their late night cocoa and brandy.

The old man shook his head. 'She has lost many words. It is hard for her, to be the foreigner. I try hard with her English but now she stops learning.' He frowned, then he turned to Theo. 'Perhaps it is best, Mrs Theodora, if the child learns her English from you. It is a terrible thing these days for the child to learn to speak English with a German accent,' he said solemnly.

Theo looked at these two, who were now her family and her dear companions. 'She doesn't like me,' she said abruptly. 'She looks at me under those dark brows with big questions in those dark eyes. She would not take lessons with me. She thinks I am something . . . I don't know what. But she doesn't like me.'

Mr Walstein ignored her protest. He sipped his cocoa. 'And, with your kind permission, Mrs Theodora, lessons for me also. This way ChiChu will come to you. ChiChu and I will be your pupils. All the time I am in England I think I speak English. Now I find that I have been speaking German these seven years without even knowing it.'

Theo was right. ChiChu did take some persuading. It took both Susan and Mr Walstein to get her to agree. But in the end they did have their lesson each evening in the hour after supper and before the nine o'clock news. Theo had them lifting their heads, stiffening their upper lips and loosening their bottom jaw as they read the poetry of

Yeats and Lord Byron. Despite herself, ChiChu proved the apter pupil. One morning she made them all laugh when she corrected Mr Walstein's pronunciation of 'marmalade'. 'Theo says the "e" is silent, Mr Walstein. Remember?'

He shook his head sadly. 'The old dog and the new tricks, they go not together.'

Each night ChiChu still dreamed of her father and her grandmother and explosions on the escarpment. Sometimes she was in the centre of the scene, running with terror. Sometimes she was watching it all again and again from the outside as though through the wrong end of a telescope. But as her English improved, her nightly waking conversations with her grandmother became less regular. Still, though, she took comfort in the nightly watching presence, the lingering smell of olives and pickled fish.

Susan, persuaded to return to the shoe shop by Theo, became exhausted and bored with her work there. In the early weeks there had been a flutter of panic among her well-to-do customers which led them to buy shoes in multiples. There was an elderly nun who bought six pairs of black lace-ups, size fives. A young woman bought her pouting six-year-old six pairs of black bar patents, sizes eight, nine, ten, eleven, twelve and one.

Susan looked up from fastening the buckle on the size eight shoe. 'Well, madam, these should see the war out. If there is a war. Seems like it's all gone quiet, just now, like. Not like a real war.'

The mother, sitting with knees closed together, crocodile handbag clasped in gloved hands, frowned down at her. It was as though a chair had spoken. 'Oh, there will be a real war, believe me. My husband says so.'

'My daddy is a very big soldier.' The child turned this way and that, wriggling on her bottom. 'He says the Germans will bomb us to bits. I'm going to America to stay with my cousin Joanna. I must go to America because London will be bombed and all the children will be killed. Now I will have lots of English shoes to take with me. Not those nasty American ones.'

Susan glanced at the mother, whose face stayed frozen.

'And Mummy can't come, can you, Mummy?'

'Do be quiet, Eva. Do be quiet!' The annoyance and despair in the woman's voice, strapped down under her polished assurance, struck a chord with Susan. The woman was thinking of life without her child. She wondered why she herself was kneeling at the feet of one child while her own child was miles away, on the point of being bombed to bits? She completed the sale, then went to the manager, Mrs Tregoning, to tell her she would leave today.

She was treated to a rare spark of annoyance. Good workers were hard to find. 'This is the second time you have done this, Mrs Cornford. This is inconvenient. Very inconvenient, Mrs Cornford.'

'I have to be with my son, Mrs Tregoning.'

'Are you evacuating, then, Mrs Cornford?'

'Yes . . . yes. That's it, Mrs Tregoning. We have to go north. My family comes from there.'

'I gathered so, Mrs Cornford, from your talk,' she said stiffly.

At Theo's house that night, Susan didn't tell them what she had done. In the usual early evening bustle the opportunity did not seem to arise. But Theo did bring up the subject of the war. 'Well,' she said cheerfully, 'it looks as though Mr Hitler has decided a war is not worth the biscuit.'

Mr Walstein shook his head. 'Do not trust him,' he said. 'The man is a sneaking fox. He is lying in his lair, planning our doom.'

Theo laughed. 'Don't be so gloomy, Mr Walstein. What a sobersides you are. He's had time to ponder his challenge. Think of the last time. He cannot unleash such a thing again.'

'Last time was different.' Mr Walstein placed his knife and fork carefully together. 'Last time, I myself fought for my country. For Germany. Last time, being German still held honour. That war was a scramble, a terrible mess, the result of posturing. But this time, evil is unleashed. Like the story of Aladdin. The genie is out of the bottle.' His voice cracked with rage and despair.

The three women looked at him in astonishment, not sure whether their surprise was at the revelation of Mr Walstein as a soldier, or that he knew the story of Aladdin.

'You fought in France, Mr Walstein?'

'I was called to arms in the service of my country, Mrs Theodora, and I responded. In the Imperial Army, however, I was merely a clerk in a central store, and never fired a shot at another human being. For my country I was sorry then, but now I am happy.'

'Well,' said Theodora easily, 'perhaps again there'll be no shots fired in anger. Perhaps Mr Hitler'll be satisfied with the countries he's grabbed already.'

'What rubbish, Theo! What wishful thinking,' said Susan. 'Of course there'll be a war. Read the papers. Conscription! All this talk of war production. All this stuff about rationing. We are digging in, getting to know the feeling that we are at war.'

'Sabre-rattling!' said Theo briefly. 'Just sabre-rattling.'

'What do you know about it, Theo? Scribbling away here in your room, sometimes without knowing the time of day, or buried in the British Museum checking just how they told the time in Saxon times.'

Theo's face hardened. 'I'm sorry, Susan, that you think my activities so childish, so reclusive, but it is those activities which put bread on our table, you know.'

Mr Walstein unbuttoned his napkin, stood up and quietly fled.

ChiChu, wide-eyed, was staring from one woman to the other. Her glance moved between two women who, living at one remove from each other, had never exchanged a cross word in their lives. Beside their benevolent calm, the strife-ridden hearth in her own home in Spain seemed infested with long wars. Now these two women looked like Theo's own elegant cats, squaring up for a fight. For some reason, this cheered her. Here was real feeling. Susan would win against the bourgeoise. ChiChu's eyes sparkled.

'I am sorry we are a burden to you,' snapped Susan.

'No! No!' Theo clapped a hand on her forehead. 'I don't mean that, Susan. But if you see what I do as childish rubbish—'

'I didn't say that. I said you don't give attention to what is happening in the world outside.'

'And you do? Working in your superior shoe shop?'

'Well. Now you ask. Today I served a woman six pairs of shoes in rising sizes for her daughter. She's the wife of a soldier. She's packing off the daughter to America for the duration. That's what she said, for the duration. And guess what that means? For the duration of the war. The war, Theo!'

'Some hysterical woman. Mad. Buying six pairs of shoes. She'd be doing that anyway. She needs a good floor to scrub.'

Susan did not know where the anger came from. 'Smug. Smug, always so smug. Here you are, sitting here in London writing your books, meting out judgement about what's going on, pontificating about all the hard things in life. Writing about the twenty-one strike. The twenty-six strike. Showing all the best feelings. Outrage. Good liberal feelings. You even join the Labour Party to nail your colours to the mast. You write me letters. You tell me what to think about the world. I had to look up to you between getting the cows in the byre, feeding the hens, and telling the sheep-shearers what for.

'Then you come like an avenging angel to release me from my lunatic granny. Very good of you. I am very grateful. Somehow from time to time you convince me I am your blood, not hers. But that's not true. I am her blood. Her lunatic blood. Double distilled. And what chance have I? Trying to tend mad folks because I can see their side of the coin? Wrapping the wounds of poor Spanish souls who have their madness distilled in turn with the fire of freedom. Then I come back home here into the madness of a war which is not a war. The madness of old men who go on mending violins despite the fact their mothers and fathers, their sisters and brothers, their friends and comrades, are all dead, killed by the insane desire for some strange thing. Old times. Simple times. No strangers . . .' Her head was going from side to side now, her eyes closed, the thoughts welling into her brain with unceasing force. 'But I'm always inferior, Theo. Always down there somewhere with my crazy grandmother and my miscegenated conception. I might have been a daughter to your mother all those years, but no sister to you. We're all in awe – in awe of your achievements these years. Blushing with pride at the sight of your name in a bookshop. But not, never your sister . . .'

ChiChu, not following the rambling tirade, was frightened now by the tears in her friend's voice. 'Susan! Susan!' ChiChu shook Susan's arm, forced her to turn and look at her. 'Come, come. Baby cries. He wants you.' She pulled Susan to the door and up the stairs.

Theo stared at the door and tried to breathe more slowly and by sheer willpower stop the tears coming to her own eyes.

ChiChu followed Susan as she marched to the bedroom and picked up the roaring Barty. The solid weight of the baby calmed Susan. As she comforted him she was soothed herself.

ChiChu picked up a hairbrush from the mantelpiece and quietly sat on the bed. She pulled off her bandeau and started to brush her hair, watching Susan silently as she pulled at the tangles. She put the hiccoughing Barty up against her shoulder and rocked backwards and forwards whispering the mantra, '*Golden slumbers kiss your eyes. Golden slumbers kiss your eyes . . .*'

In five minutes he became even heavier as he dropped off into a deep slumber. She placed him gently on his pillow and pulled his blanket up to his chin. Then she stood up and flexed her back against the strain of holding him. He was getting very solid, was young master Barty.

ChiChu held out the hairbrush to Susan, who took it and started to pull it through ChiChu's strong hair. She brushed it until all the tangles were smoothed out and it fell, shining in the lamplight, on to ChiChu's shoulders.

Then she put the brush back in its accustomed place on the mantelpiece. ChiChu pulled on her bandeau and shook her hair back. Susan smoothed the curls on ChiChu's forehead.

'There now,' she said. 'That's more like it.'

ChiChu caught her hand and held it tight. 'Theo is good, Susan. A good woman. Mr Walstein, he likes Mrs Theodora.'

'I know, I know.' Just at this moment Susan did not really want to hear this good thing about Theo. She cast around in her mind for something to say. 'But she is not my sister. She says she is, but she is not my sister,' she said lamely.

ChiChu grasped her other hand. 'ChiChu is your sister, Susan. Like Theo. We choose, me and Theo. You. We both choose you.'

Susan freed herself and went across to the window to rearrange the heavy blackout curtain. Then she turned round.

'What a wise girl you are, ChiChu. Now perhaps you can tell me what I should say to Theo to make up for bawling at her like some mad woman, no better than my loony grandmother.'

The next day Susan's problem of what to say and what not to say to Theo about the previous evening was swept away by some men in dark suits who came knocking at the door asking for Mr Walstein. The men were polite enough. They showed Mr Walstein and Theo their government documents and waited while Mr Walstein put together a change of clothes and a case with his most precious possessions. He took some books, a small box of letters from his brother and his niece, and his least favourite violin. 'They will not take this from me, Mrs

Theodora, I am sure. And music will take care of the hours.'

Susan and Theo had to explain twice to a weeping ChiChu what was happening to her old friend.

'He will be fine, ChiChu,' said Susan. 'The Government is gathering all the foreigners in one place. There, they will sort out the sheep from the goats. They say there are spies in our midst.'

'But Mr Walstein?' said ChiChu. 'Is no spy. They shoot him?'

'No. No. No. The people there will not be spies,' said Theo patiently. 'The Government needs to be sure. He will soon be back.' Privately, she was furious at the crude 'scoop-'em-all-up, collar-the-lot' mentality. But she could not show this in the face of ChiChu's despair at losing her old friend. 'I promise you I'll go to the police station and make the strongest objection. I'll write letters of objection and faith in Mr Walstein's loyalty to some important people I know.' She took ChiChu by the shoulders and looked her in the eyes. 'He'll not be there long, I promise you.'

The day after that whirled by, with Theo writing letters and bustling up to town to see people she knew. Susan and ChiChu went up to put Mr Walstein's rooms in some order. ChiChu insisted on clearing and setting the fire so that it would be all ready to light the second he came back.

An exhausted Theo came back at seven o'clock without any news. She placed her hat wearily on the table. 'I've spoken to everyone, anyone I know, and they say there is nothing we can do. Nothing will happen till it's all shaken down. We have to wait awhile and then start to enquire. We can only wait.' She sat down heavily in a chair.

'Nobody can help. They have a war to fight and till then these "aliens" are nothing but a nuisance!'

ChiChu did not understand all this but she did understand the pain and despair in Theo's voice. 'Mr Walstein dead,' she said.

Later, after Susan had settled Barty and held ChiChu's hand until she seemed to fall asleep, she went back downstairs, with heavy steps. Theo came into the sitting room with a tray in her hand on which were two steaming mugs of cocoa and two crystal glasses of brandy. 'Mr Walstein would hate it if we did not keep our old custom,' she said. 'I'll write and tell him we drank to his health and to his freedom.' She put a glass in Susan's hand. 'I suppose this makes me very involved in all this, in spite of my scribbling, don't you think?'

Susan flushed, and stared down at the glass which she rolled around in her hands, focusing on the glint of fire on the crystal. 'I was tired, Theo. Out of order. None of it was fair.' She proffered the glass slightly towards Theo. 'Well, here's to Mr Walstein, Theo. A nice man, if ever I saw one.'

Theo held up her brandy and drank. 'He has been a dear friend. He *is* my dear friend. Tomorrow,' she said, 'I'll write more letters.'

Susan reached for her cocoa and drank it slowly. 'Tomorrow,' she said, 'tomorrow, ChiChu and Barty and I, we go up to Durham.'

Theo looked at her thoughtfully. 'You're right, Susan. From what I heard up in town today, there's no question about this war, no question at all. You're right and I was wrong.'

Susan looked at her, fond again of this strange woman she had known all of her life. 'You should come too, Theo.

For safety. You need to be safe.'

Theo shook her head. 'I've lived here thirty years now, Susie. James and little Simon died in this house. I'll not leave them. Or Mr Walstein. Blast Mr blasted Hitler. I'll stay here and work.'

'Those things I said, Theo . . .'

Theo shrugged. 'What's that, Susie, between sisters?'

Susan wriggled a bit, uncomfortable at Theo's magnanimity. As usual Theo had said the right thing. She wished she had taken the opportunity to be magnanimous, but the moment had gone. Somehow, Theo always had the upper hand, even if she didn't need to take it. In her calmer moments Susan knew that Theo meant all of this for the best: all the advice and help and sisterly comfort. She knew that Theo could be bewildered, sometimes even hurt when Susan turned cross and rejecting. But she didn't realize just how hard it had been to be on the receiving end of such kindness for all of a person's life. That had been one reason why working in the hospital and helping out there in Spain had been so very good. In the hospital and out in Spain it was Susan herself who had been doing the helping; she had been solving problems for others.

At last she relaxed. She touched Theo's arm, smiled slightly. 'I suppose nothing matters, really. Barty and ChiChu – they're what count now in these dark days.'

Theo put a hand on hers. 'I can't quite tell you, Susie, what it means to me that you're here. Up in Durham or here, it's no matter. It was strange when you were in Spain, so far away.'

It was funny, Avia, seeing those two women quarrel. I've never seen Susan with so much fire in her. But, can you believe that

172

MY DARK-EYED GIRL

I was sorry for the bourgeoise? She had such a sad look on her face. Perhaps she is not so bad after all.

Chapter Eleven

The Volunteer

To Theo's relief Susan's decision to go was delayed in the next few days by the problems of packing for a long stay and the trouble of getting hold of train tickets.

She was walking down the stairs with her arms full of washing when there was a very loud knock on the door.

'Can you get that, Susan?' Theo's head came round the door of the sitting room where she had been working all morning. 'I'm just tussling with something here and I can't think where Mrs Fawcett's got to.'

The man standing on the step was tall and fair. He was only faintly recognizable in battered civvies. His ragged blond hair was stuffed into a broad cap.

'Yes?' she said, frowning. Then her brow cleared. 'Oh. Grief! It's you, Captain Maichin. What would you be doing here?' The difference in him was astonishing. Gone was the natural authority of a man who might hold another person's fate in his hands: the steady focus of a soldier who might blow up a bridge or a person with surgical precision. Here was an ordinary man. Aaron Maichin looked tired and unkempt. She would have passed him in the street without noticing him.

'Miss Cornford?'

Susan opened the door a little wider. 'What can I do for you? How did you know where to find me?'

'Your letters. To Theodora Maichin.'

'Yes,' she said. 'In the censor's file. So you're here, not in Spain?'

'That all finished, didn't it? I did go back to Jo'burg. Then the show started here so I came back.'

'I see.'

'Then I was in France for awhile. Then I came back to London to meet some people and felt . . . I knew where you were. So . . .' He peered past her.

She looked uncertainly at the long, empty hall behind her. 'You should come in, I suppose,' she said. She led the way, country fashion, to the kitchen, then thought she should have taken him to Theo in the sitting room. Too late.

'Will you sit down?' she said. The chair scraped on the tile floor as she pulled it out. She turned to fill the kettle with water. The gas popped as she lit it with a spill taken from the fire. 'So what brings you here, Captain? This is a long way from Barcelona. Or from Johannesburg, for that matter.'

His presence made her uneasy but she was moved by the sight of him. She did not know whether this was for his own fair self, because he saved her and ChiChu; or for the sense of Spain that he brought with him into the dark London house: the scent of dust and oranges; the sour bite of cordite. Those days were so far away now.

Aaron Maichin lounged easily in the kitchen chair. 'I know we met under strange circumstances, Miss Cornford, but I was in London to see these people . . .'

'So you said. I read of the Brigade meeting – last year,

176

was it? The reunion meeting? Large crowds, so I read. Some kind of celebration?'

'Celebration?' he grunted. 'For losing everything? I wouldn't come to that. Vainglorious. No. I've been in France. Now, I'm back here. There are bigger fish than Franco to fry these days. Fascism incarnate, is old Hitler. Stamping away on the borders of France, just now.'

'Will you volunteer?' She was pleased to have the busy job of making tea. His energy filled the kitchen, made the air prickle. She didn't know whether she liked this man or disliked him. As soon as he got into the house, his tramp-like exterior had fallen from him like a husk and she sensed the power and menace she'd felt in that small room in Barcelona.

'Any decent man would sign on for this fight, Miss Cornford. I fought Fascism there in Spain. I'll fight it here. You know that, after what you saw in Spain.'

'I saw a lot of wounds, Mr Maichin. And some men die. A lot of pain, brother fighting against brother.'

Then, from the top of the house came a baby's wail. She handed him his tea and excused herself. 'I'll be back in a moment. Little Barty wants his bottle.' She coloured. This man knew nothing about Barty, of course.

His minder gone, Aaron looked round the room. Blazing fire. Clutter with a sense of order somewhere behind it. Bills by the clock on the mantelpiece. Plates on a rack on the wall. No sign or symbol of the woman who really interested him.

A head popped round the door. Fair, lined face, fair hair looped loosely back with a velvet band.

'Susie, I—' Her glance fixed on him and her hand went for a second to her throat. 'Edward?' she said. All of her senses vaulted through her body to her mouth and back again. 'Is it Edward?'

He leaped to his feet, coming forward, one hand stretched out. 'Theodora Maichin? I am Aaron Maichin, my father's . . .' He took her hand and held it tight. 'I'm the son of—'

'Edward,' she said. 'You're the picture of him. The spitting image.'

'I can see that doesn't please you, that I look like him.' His gaze was direct, challenging.

She ignored this. 'At least you don't sound like him. Not at all. Of course you must be—'

'South African. Born and bred.' At last he took her hand and held it closely in his. 'And I'm not Edward, I'm Aaron, son of Elisabet. My mother was German and I'm at least half her if not more.'

There was a note of pleading in his voice. She wondered what he knew about Edward. He must know about Edward, his father. He must know all about him, being born in this house.

'And Edward?' she said. 'He . . .'

'Is dead,' he said, watching her carefully. 'He left me and my mother when I was ten. The last I heard, he was shot in Jo'burg for killing a woman.'

She stared at him, unblinking. Her face showed no shock.

He frowned at her. 'You knew about him? You knew what he was like?'

She pursed her lips. 'He left here under a cloud. Oh, 1902 it would be. He could be very cruel, your father.' She would not tell him the truth. She could never tell him the truth.

'So my mother said.' He watched her carefully. 'I know

enough about him. I've come to find out something about you. About my other family here. Since my mother died, I've no one left in South Africa.'

'You'll live in England?'

He shrugged. 'I was in the Brigade in Spain. We failed there and now I'm here to join up properly, so who knows where I'll be living in a year's time?'

She stared at him. Tall, narrow and blond, he was a reincarnation of his father. Like his father, too, he seemed to fill the room with his presence. In his days as a preacher, her brother Edward could have a whole hall full of people in tears, men and women alike. She sensed the same power in this man. Edward also had great charm which he could use to ruthless ends.

The door clashed and Susan came in with Barty on her arm and ChiChu lurking behind her. The room was now filled with women. Susan laughed at Edward's glance towards the child. 'The Spanish war left you with an unfulfilled desire to kill more Fascists. It left me with my own little anti-Fascist. This is Bartolomeo Fibretti Cornford, my son.'

'I wouldn't . . . I didn't . . . You're too . . .'

'Old?'

His perplexed look made them all laugh. He turned to ChiChu, who had grown inches since he met her and, though paler, was round as a plum. Her hair, which had been almost shaved when he first saw her, was tumbling over her shoulders, only barely contained by a bandanna. 'Now, you've grown, Miss . . .' He frowned, but they did not supply him with ChiChu's name. He searched his memory. Sabater. That was it. Maria Josep Sabater. 'Miss Sabater.'

He looked at Susan. 'I had this Spanish friend who

fled to London. Seems that he was picked up. Interned. All aliens. "Collar the lot." They say Mr Churchill said that. Miss Sabater must not have been registered.'

Susan looked at him defiantly. 'Well, the police have her name, but I suppose we filled in no forms. I say to people she's my daughter.' She put an arm round ChiChu's shoulders.

'You should be careful, or you'll be behind the wire alongside her,' Aaron said absently. He was staring at ChiChu as though he was trying to commit her face to memory.

ChiChu looked at him sullenly, then turned to Susan. 'Soldier comes for me? Like Mr Walstein?'

'Walstein?' he said too quickly. 'Who's this?'

'We have an old friend, a Jewish musician, who lived here, Aaron,' said Theo easily. 'They came for him yesterday. He'll be behind barbed wire somewhere by now. We need to find where he is.'

He shook his head. 'This is what happened to my friend from the Brigade. Here for refuge, having fought for the Republic. Back behind the wire. Our friend becomes our enemy.'

'Why not you?' said Susan. 'You're a foreigner, after all.'

He smiled easily. 'Oh, British citizen, me! I've got papers to prove it. Now I'm here to volunteer to fight. I think they will have me. I speak German from my mother. I have information for them from France. My Spanish experience makes me useful. Not much use behind the wire.'

'Where are you staying?' asked Theo abruptly.

He looked at her. 'Well, I'm not quite set up anywhere yet. There are some small hotels. This is only for a week or so till I get my papers.'

'Stay here,' she said. 'Of course, you must stay here.'

He beamed. 'This is kind . . .' he said.

'You're my flesh and blood,' she said abruptly. 'How can I do less? There's a war on.' She looked around the room. 'D'you have no luggage?'

He laughed out loud at this. 'Well, I must be honest Mrs . . . What can I call you? . . . I have a bag but I tucked it behind the bush to the left of your front gate.'

She stared at him. 'Aunt Theo. I suppose I must call you Aaron. As I said, you're my flesh and blood.'

So Aaron came into Theo's house and Susan and ChiChu's flight was postponed. He was not welcomed with open arms. It was no return of the prodigal. ChiChu was openly fearful and suspicious. Susan was civil but very wary. Theo was uneasy, not really able to separate this tall fair-haired creature from her brother, Edward, who had wreaked his own havoc in her early life.

Aaron stayed in Mr Walstein's room. ChiChu did not speak to him, but made excuses to go into the room when he was elsewhere to check that he had not disturbed things. He would come back to find an ornament returned to its original place on the shelves, a violin returned to its original angle on its hook.

He came back one day to find her leaning across his battered case to return a book to a shelf. He put a hand on her shoulder and she turned and started to beat him in the chest. He held her off. Then he dropped his hands and spoke to her in Catalan. 'You must keep away from my room, ChiChu. It makes me uneasy when you come in and out like a shadow. This is my private space.' Very deliberately he leaned down and clicked his case shut.

She stared at him. 'It is not your room. It is the room of Mr Walstein.'

'I know this. But for these days I stay here and this is my kingdom. I will not be here always.'

She made for the door. 'It is Mr Walstein's room,' she said over her shoulder. 'You are an invader.'

Then she was gone.

Each day he went out at eight o'clock and came back very late, and one day he came back early with an address for Mr Walstein. He handed the paper to Theo.

'Perhaps you could write to him, Aunt Theo. I understand people send things. Food. Socks. You would know.'

She smoothed out the crumpled sheet. 'This is good of you, Aaron. You didn't have to . . .' she frowned. 'Your contacts must be very good.'

'The least I could do, Aunt Theo.' He glanced at the watchful ChiChu. 'After all I have stolen this man's room. Perhaps I owe him some home comforts?'

She stared at him. There was something very cautious, very watchful about him. He was polite and helpful. He went away each day to God knew where and she wasn't on the terms with him that would allow her to ask where he'd been, what he had been doing.

He talked with her about the progress of the war. Sometimes he talked with Susan about the Spanish War and its regrettable outcome. Occasionally he spoke with ChiChu in Catalan, but ChiChu would run from him rather than stay. She mistrusted him now as much as she had on the first day, when he came through her door with his battered bag. She knew he had got her and Susan out of Spain but she still thought of him with the other commissars, those who would say that a patriot like her father should be killed.

There was no doubt, however, that the presence of this stranger in their midst somehow lent a festive air to the house. They had their evening meals now in the dining room, the dense blacked out room lit by candles. Each day Aaron continued to go up to town and come back at dusk. He did not tell them where he had been or what he had been doing. He had his hair cut, bought new clothes: soft tweeds that sat easily on his tall figure.

'Don't you think he looks like a different man?' said Susan to ChiChu one night as they prepared for bed. 'He doesn't really look like the man we met in Spain.'

ChiChu shrugged. 'He is spy,' she said.

'A spy?' Susan looked at her.

'He creeps into house and out like a spy,' explained ChiChu.

'He was a friend of Spain,' protested Susan. 'You know that.'

'He killed my father. And my grandmother and grandfather.'

'He didn't,' said Susan. 'He fought for you, for Spain.'

'His friends,' said ChiChu indifferently, 'friends of Stalin – they killed them. Just the same. He is a spy for Stalin!'

'No, no. You have it wrong!' said Susan.

But ChiChu would not be convinced and she stayed away from Aaron Maichin. If he was in one room, she was in another. Susan watched him notice this: saw his eyes flicker round the room before he settled down.

On the eleventh night of his stay, this tension was brought to an end by German bombers who, in their first real sortie of the war, bombed the London docks, and dropped two very effective bombs on the die-cast factory and a row of houses by the canal where Mr Walstein and ChiChu had so often walked.

Theo told ChiChu this and her eyes sparkled. Perhaps

the tormentors of Mr Walstein had not survived the raid. 'Perhaps they die. Who knows?' She smiled slightly.

'Never mind about them,' said Susan sternly. 'What about us? It's time we were getting out of here. It'll be us next.'

Chapter Twelve

Intruders

'Here you are, Mester Strophair. Post. Ah'm not called on to come up here too often.' It had taken Harry Tills nearly five minutes to thread his way up the narrow track, through the hens and dogs, the waste wood and dropped cowmuck of the Goshawk farmyard.

Barry Strophair threw down the wisp of hay he had been using to rub the fell mud off Cobber. The sturdy pony had carried him on his morning survey of the lambs dropped under hedges and out-jutting stone on the lower reaches of fell which butted on to Goshawk Shield Farm. The number was up on last year. Not a bad season, considering.

Barry rubbed his hand down his old tweed trousers and took the large white envelope from Harry Tills. It was not the envelope he was looking for. He'd watched Harry Tills' progress up the bank through the side of his eyes and had thought it might be a letter from Jack. Not that Jack was a great letter writer, like. But this one was not from Jack. An army letter would be brown and small, not large and cream. It would not be addressed in this flowing, familiar hand. He pushed the letter inside the baling string

185

which, tied tightly round his waist, stopped the wind getting through his tweed jacket.

'London postmark,' said Harry Tills, stamping his feet to keep the blood flowing down there. 'Unmistakable.'

'Aye.' Strophair picked up another handful of straw and attacked the pony's muddy rump.

Harry blew on his clenched hands. 'Parky day, like.'

'Meself,' said Strophair, 'Ah find that keeping moving stops the cold setting in. Keeps the blood flowin'.'

Harry abandoned any thoughts of a warming brew. He turned and started to pick his way back across the cluttered yard towards his old bike, which was leaning against the ornate stone pillar, on which swung the broken farm gate. He steadied the bike and jumped on it, hoping that Mrs Robson, down at Bittern Crag Farm, would be grateful enough for her post to brew him a cup of tea. He needed that to warm his blood on this freezing spring afternoon. That would set him up for the helter-skelter bike ride back down to Stanhope.

Back at Goshawk Shield the letter stayed tucked into Barry's rope belt all day. He worked slowly, stumping about the yard and the fields. Clinging like a crab to his back was the sure certainty that he would not get through all the work that was waiting for him. It was too big a farm to work alone. His son had never bothered about that, of course. Off with those play-soldiers the minute Hitler rattled his sabre. In the year before that the Territorials had been Jack's excuse to get off the farm on weekends. He'd complained for years of never getting off the farm, whining about how he'd done a man's work on there since he was ten or so for no pay. When he was younger he was too frightened to voice his complaint.

But from the day he was sixteen he'd spoken up and they'd fought over it; with fists and sticks from time to time.

Barry gave up on his son after that, watching Jack's antics as a 'play-soldier' with contempt. He knew well enough that Jack had worked for his father for not a penny piece for himself from when he was ten till he was thirty. The money for himself, for the pints at the Black Bull in Stanhope, Jack earned from breeding rare black sheep and selling them at agricultural shows. The Territorials was his first stab at freedom: for the first time he saw a pay packet of his own.

Chamberlain came back from Munich saying there'd be no war, and Jack, not believing him, had slipped off before dawn one morning to walk down to Stanhope to sign on for the Army proper before the real war whistle had been blown. And Alfie and Jim Gomersal, who had worked alongside him on the farm, sloped off too, despite the fact that Barry had reluctantly told them both that he would plead for them at any tribunal. 'You're needed here on the land, no question about it!' he had growled. But still they went.

Strophair struggled to take off his damp coat in the cluttered porch, and the white letter fell to the ground. He stepped on it before he saw it. He picked it up and threw it on the table. He pushed his weekly pan of stew to warm up on the fire. Then he held his hands under the cold tap to warm them up a bit before he rubbed them on a well-used cloth and sat down to open the letter. It was from Her, of course. Time to time, She deigned to let him know that she was alive; that this whole shebang really belonged to Her; that he only rented rooms in the house and leased the land.

That he was here at all under sufferance.

He had to put on his steel-rimmed glasses to read the flowing, looping hand. You'd think, Her supposed to be a writer, that She'd have learned to write clearly.

Dear Mr Strophair,

I hope this finds you and Goshawk Shield both in good heart. The news of the war is very grim here; you will have read about it in the paper. They say our troops are in France so I imagine your Jack will be with them. Wasn't it brave of him to volunteer straight away?

Strophair threw down the letter in disgust, then picked it up to peer at it again.

We've finally had bombs here, as you will have read in the papers, so London is not so safe at all. The thing is, my half-sister, Susan Cornford, is here with a young protégée, a Spanish girl. I feel they should be in a place of safety. Of course, I thought of Goshawk Shield. It must be the safest place in England, up there in the Durham Dales. Susan has a small child who is called Barty. Susan married while she was nursing in Spain and very sadly her husband was killed in the fighting.

So will you make arrangements for them to stay at the house? I am sure they will be no trouble and perhaps may be a help, now that you are working single-handed.

I thought those upstairs rooms overlooking the fells would suit. Can you get them aired? They will arrive this Friday or Saturday, depending on the trains.

    Relying on you,
    Yours sincerely,
      Theodora Maichin

He stared glumly at the letter. *My half-sister!* Susan Cornford Gomersal, more like. Another of the Gomersal bastards. Her mother'd been no better than she should be, just a skivvy to the Maichins. She pops the bastard, that Susan, then she dies. And those Maichins took the girl, took her away from the Gomersals, so they did. Drove poor old Mrs Gomersal loony. Died in an asylum, that one.

And who was this baby She talked about? The baby belonging to Susan Cornford? Had her own bastard now, did she? Dead in action? That was an old one. And a *protégée?* What on earth was one of those? A refugee maybe. England was flooding with them these days. Foreigners all over the place, running things. There'd be no England left in the end. Should put them all in a boat and push them out into the channel and pull out the plug. No problem about who they were and where to put them then. *Collar the lot.* Mr Churchill had it right. You couldn't trust one of them.

Barry screwed up the letter and threw it in a corner with the other rubbish. Then he lifted a pudding basin from the draining board and splashed it clean with water. Then he ladled broth into it from the pan on the fire, crouched over it on the table and spooned it into his mouth. Get those upper rooms ready? Who did she think he was? One of those skivvying Gomersals?

              ★   ★   ★

The soldier left us, Avia, and Susan tells that we must come from London with all its explosions, we come away and stay on a farm. This makes me happy. I think of you, Avia, with your basket of olives when you were a girl and my grandfather came to your village. You're exchanging a word squeezing your eyes against the savage light of the sun. Your skin glows like copper in the yellow light.

So all the way on that interminable journey I am thinking of you, at your door, the cockerel scratching the dust at your feet as though he is some great bull. A very nice horse lives in the stable here. I think of the horses on that old farm when I visit with my father. I am very small and from between his legs I watch the yearling move in circles on the long rope. All the time the sun beats down.

We travel to this place on a train with lots of soldiers and people in sour clothes; women with frozen faces and bewildered children. Their gas masks in cardboard boxes would look festive if only the faces would smile.

Then we heave our cases and bags on a bus that grinds its way into the hills and we get off and walk a long way up a mountain to this place. Susan has Barty tied to her back with a shawl, like some hill woman. Then we get here. All mud and snarling dogs, hens screeching and clucking behind doors. And I am frozen to the bone. The joy at going to a farm, away from that town, has leaked from me.

Susan led the way through the corridor into a big bedroom at Goshawk Shield. 'You and I and the baby can sleep in here, ChiChu. We can pull another bed in. And we can make the next one into a little sitting room.' She opened the door and peered in. 'This is the fire that warms the bathwater so we'll need it on. Look at this view. You can see for miles.' She tried to keep her voice bright, to cover her despair at walking into this house, the cosy haven of her childhood, now a dark, rural slum.

The house had been open and deserted when they arrived. Susan had disturbed a bull bedded down on muddy straw in the back dairy. And what about the Pheasant Room, window-lit on four sides out of six, where young Theodora had done her writing? The Pheasant Room now had chickens roosting on the desk and the chairs. ChiChu had laughed at this and 'clucked' at the chickens, pleased when they fluttered and clucked in response. But ChiChu had never known the house before, when Theo's mother, Rose Clare, was in charge: immaculate and shining it was then, with flowers in jars standing in windows.

'I cold.' ChiChu shivered now. 'This house very cold, Susan.'

Susan thrust Barty into ChiChu's arms 'We'll light the fires, ChiChu. Bring the baby down beside the kitchen fire and we'll light fires in both these rooms. I can't think what has happened. Theo said the rooms would be ready. She sent old Strophair a letter.'

She was very annoyed but still, within an hour, she had both fires blazing and had riddled the kitchen fire to make it shine brightly. She found two vast clotheshorses in one of the pantries and set them before the fires in the rooms upstairs. These she draped with mattresses and blankets from one of the deep cupboards on the landing. 'We need them aired before they go on the beds,' she said. The air became tinged with must as the damp of years came out of the linen.

Rejecting the sour stew on the fire hob, Susan went out and milked the single cow in the back barn and brought a bucket of foaming milk, which she heated on the stove for the baby and themselves. ChiChu grabbed the warm cup with gratitude.

The light had almost faded when they heard clanks and movements outside. The door creaked. They waited till the farmer came through the door from the scullery. He looked at them and sniffed. 'Oh. So you got here, then?' he said. 'Ah saw there was some upscuttlin' in the yard.'

'Did you get Theo's letter, Mr Strophair? Theo said she sent a letter.'

'Aye.' He nodded towards the rubbish in the corner. 'In theer somewhere.'

Susan looked at the mess. 'Well, you must have been mistaken about the date, Mr Strophair,' she said slowly. 'But no need for you to worry. I've lit the fires upstairs and am airing the bedding. We've warmed ourselves here, and had some milk, so you don't need to worry.'

'Ah wasn't worryin'.' His face stayed rigid, and his eyes moved to ChiChu. 'An' who might this be?'

'Oh. And this is Maria Josep Sabater. We call her ChiChu. She's from Spain.'

'A Spanish type? I thought they'd locked 'em all up. Foreigners and spies. Get rid o' the lot. That's what I say.'

'ChiChu's with me. And they will not take her.' In truth, this was one reason why it was a relief to get away from London. The police had a note about ChiChu somewhere, from the day she and Mr Walstein were accosted by the dockers. That chicken would come home to roost in its own time.

Strophair's glance dropped to the bundle sleeping peacefully now on the settle. 'Aye. Theodora Maichin said you had a bas— baby.'

'Yes. This is Barty. Perhaps you'd like to lock him up

too, Mr Strophair, him being half-Italian.'

He shrugged. 'The letter said you'd be no bother. Wouldn't get in the way. I've got nee choice. Nee choice at all. It's Her place. She's allus gannin' on about that.'

Susan looked at him steadily. 'I see you've hens in the Pheasant Room. And a bull kept inside too.'

He shrugged again. 'Cold winter. Roof flew off the barn in a big storm in last back end. Empty space going to waste.'

'Mrs Lytton wouldn't be pleased.'

He looked at her and sniffed. 'Mrs Lytton teks no interest. An't been here in five years. Stays in London scratchin' out those books of hers. And now and then lets me know the place is hers.' He paused. 'Got no help here at all now. Our Jack's fighting Hitler. Your Gomersal cousins left us in the lurch too. Went to save their bliddy country. No hands to plough and plant. Teks me all my time to see to the stock.'

She frowned. 'Cousins?'

'Gomersals. Alfie and Jim. You know, Gomersals. Yeh might call yerself Cornford, hinney, but everyone round here knows ye're a Gomersal. No mistakin' it. Tall and gangly.'

She raised her brows. 'You know as well as me, Mr Strophair, I've always been Cornford, just as I was christened, but I've never denied I was a Gomersal, Mr Strophair. Indeed I took care of my Grandma Gomersal . . .'

'Aye, put her in a loony bin, so I heard.'

Susan gathered Barty into her arms. 'Well, Mr Strophair, that was because she *was* a loony. It was the best place for her.'

'Aye,' he said. 'Yeh'd say that, like.'

She stared at him. 'Suit yourself, Mr Strophair. Anyway, I'm down to Stanhope in the morning to order some coal and to get paraffin for lamps. Supplies too, for you've nothing in your pantries. Can I get you anything?'

'Well, not coming from London, like, with fancy ideas, I've all I need here.'

'We'll get those rooms sorted upstairs, but we'll need to use this kitchen.' She glanced around the cluttered, dirty space.

'Like I say, suit yehself.' He moved to the fire and pushed the stew on to it. 'Now, I need me tea.'

ChiChu watched these two, listened to their stilted conversation. She could not understand a single thing the man said, but it was easy to see that he did not welcome them; that he despised her and loathed Susan. That was quite a start to their stay in these cold, northern parts. Quite a start.

Later, when the chill was off the upstairs rooms and the sheets aired, ChiChu and Susan made up the beds and fell into them to sleep off the long, cramped train journey and the savagely cold welcome at Goshawk Shield.

In the next few days they played a very elaborate game of cat and mouse with Barry Strophair. He was out on the farm or in the barns most of the days, and at night he vanished into some lair at the far side of the house. If they heard him clattering in the kitchen, they stayed away from there. In the intervening times they got the kitchen and pantry cleared. They caught the bus down to Stanhope to fill the pantry with basic stores. They got the oven in the range working properly and Susan re-baptized it by making a batch of bread. The first batch burned but the second was perfect. She knew the temper of the iron monster from all those years she had worked here alongside Rose Clare. The kitchen had sung bright contentment in Rose Clare's care and she determined, with Barty and ChiChu to care for, it should be no less bright.

The only traces they had of Barry Strophair were the sound of his shambling movements and the modest raids that were made on their stores. They would find half a loaf where there had been one, or a lump cut out of a piece of cheese.

ChiChu often caught sight of his back as she wandered the farmhouse and the outhouses, but he ignored her and she did not greet him. One afternoon she made her way down the corridor to the Pheasant Room and opened the door. Hens leaped from their perches and settled again. From the top of what had been a bookcase, a magnificent cockerel shot her a beady glance. Despite the mess, the poultry seemed well cared for. There was water for them in a bin lid on the floor, and one of the six windows was propped open for them to come and go freely. She moved among them, clucking into their faces as she had seen her grandmother do in the country. There were rough plank-wood nesting-boxes at the back of the room. She padded across and disturbed two very well settled hens in the far corner. 'There now, pretty ones, what do you offer?'

She returned to the kitchen with five warm eggs folded into the front of her top jumper. She placed them carefully on the table, which Susan had just scrubbed. 'There is food everywhere here,' she said. 'We will not starve.'

After that she went along the back corridor to the large back dairy to see the bull. The window was so dark with grime that barely any light came through. But he was there, black and gleaming and radiating strength.

'*He, toro!*' she whispered, grinning. 'The old man has you in prison, does he not? Me, I was in prison once with an old bourgeoise and a street whore. Now here you are with old Susan and me. Good company, eh?'

The bull skittered on the stone floor and pulled in vain against the rope which was fed with painful efficiency through the ring in his nose. His eyes rolled towards her, glittering in anger. But underneath the anger there was something else which made her freeze. There was the sense of the familiar, the known.

I am standing on a box, my father's arm tight round my waist, my back to his front. I am perfectly safe. But before me there is all danger. There is the smell of blood, the sticky ooze from the pricks on the great beast's back. There are the lunges and the clattering charges as the slight, upright figure teases and taunts him with a fluttering cloth and turns his vengeful charge into a thing of clattering ridicule. The crowd calls and whistles, breathes out and breathes in with the proud discipline of the toreador. The bull canters near to where we stand. I can see him close. His eyes roll towards me and I press back against my father. Those eyes are clouded with pain but somewhere, somewhere there is still a spark. He shakes his head and the swords attached to him clatter. The blood oozes down the matted coat.

'Yeh want nowt in here!' The voice behind her made ChiChu jump back and she was against the chest, not of her father, but of Barry Strophair.

'I . . . I was looking at him.' She turned to face him. The English words came to her from nowhere.

'Were yeh?'

'He's very small but he is still fine. But poor horns. Very small horns.'

'Dexters. Small breed. Good line, this one. That's what he's here for.'

'I'm sorry?

'Farmers round here'll pay a lot to have him serve their cows.'

'Oh yes. I see this,' she said uncertainly.

He put a hand on her shoulder. 'Let's have yeh out of here, lass.'

She twisted back to look at the beast. 'He looks very sad,' she said. 'This bull is in the dark. No like dark.'

'Dinnet yeh worry about him,' he said. 'He enjoys himself, time to time with the cows. Other time he's in here. For safety, like.'

And she was thrust out of the door, which was slammed behind her. She stood very still, bringing back into her mind the heat and the roars and the smell of the bullring. She must put these thoughts from her. She would never return there, to that heat and dust. Not to that place. Never again.

After that, every day she waited for Strophair to leave the farmhouse and went to see the bull. She watched him quietly until those rolling eyes came to rest on her. Then there would be the struggle, the fight with the rope, the flash of anger in the eye. Then he would settle again, his eye dulling to blunt fear. Sometimes, she stayed to rub the window with a rag so that a little of the daylight would seep on to him. Or she would shovel away the rank straw and rake some new hay down from the bale that Strophair had wedged in the second makeshift stall. All this gave her comfort, she did not quite know why.

'*He, toro!*' she said softly. '*He, toro!*'

Chapter Thirteen

Toro

ChiChu noted a change in Susan in the weeks following their arrival at Goshawk Shield. She had been a giantess of calm in the Spanish hospital: brisk, efficient and very much in charge. When they'd been waiting in fear in Barcelona, wondering whether or not they would get out of Spain, Susan had been bracing and dogged. She had made sure the soldier came to find her. She seemed then to be in charge of the world.

Then down in London, she had seemed younger, less certain, subdued and somehow shrunken in the elegant shadow of Theodora. Here at Goshawk, as the days went by, she seemed to grow again. She was very much at home, striding round the house and the farm with Barty on her hip, or tied on her back with a shawl. Gradually she cleared the place. She scoured the cluttered pantries and leaded the black range; she baked bread and scones twice a week and exchanged eggs for goods on Stanhope market day. She combed the hedgerows for fruit and made jam in the dozens of jars rescued from the dust. She and ChiChu mucked out the bull properly and carted the muck to a heap, downwind of the farm, before scrubbing out the dairy and his stall and putting out fresh hay. They rooted out hammer and nails from a shed, and Susan held the rickety ladder while ChiChu mended the roofs of the hen crees. That done, they moved the hens and protesting cockerels into the crees, freeing the Pheasant Room of their feathery clutter and sweet, rank smell.

After they had moved the poultry to the hen crees, ChiChu discovered where Strophair stored the meal and fed them herself each morning, adding the meal to the kitchen scraps. She smiled at Susan about this. 'I feed them. They give us eggs.'

It took them three further days to take the cobwebs off the walls and ceilings in the Pheasant Room, then three more days to scrub it out and polish the windows to let in the streaming moorland light. One day Susan walked down to Stanhope with a basket of eggs on one arm and Barty on her back. Three hours later she came back in a rackety taxi laden with new paint. They used this to paint the walls and ceiling of the Pheasant Room a yellowy cream; the window frames a dark, slatey green.

The day they finished was bright and clear. All four windows presented a different framed picture of the long pasture leading to the fells. The two of them stood together in the centre of the room, turning almost a full circle. The light reflected now from the walls and seemed to create its own pale sunshine.

'Is beautiful, Susan. So beautiful.' The words forced themselves from ChiChu's mouth.

'Aye,' said Susan. 'I wanted to do this so you'd see there is more to lovely places than the bright sun and the blue sky of Spain. My mother, Rose Clare, loved this room. Theodora was always in here when she lived at Goshawk, writing and that.'

ChiChu moved to her friend's side and took her arm, hugging it closely to her. 'Is very beautiful, Susan, this room.'

Susan kept her voice steady. 'I thought we'd make a playroom for Barty here, and mebbe the two of us could sit here and remind ourselves that it's not all that ugliness, not all killing. That madness out there.'

'You think of the commissar, Susan?'

'So I do.' Susan nodded. 'Now then. I've been up in the lofts and there's some real thick mats there and some chairs and things. I found a cradle that was mine. A man who lived in this house made it for me.'

While the women made their commotion in the house and the yard, Barry Strophair moved in and out, backwards and forwards, like a dark shadow. He still ate his stew at the end of the day, but Susan scoured his pot and remade the stew at the end of every second day. Strophair continued only to wash his hands and face at the kitchen sink; he carried a foetid smell around with him. They knew when he'd been in a room even when he was not there. That was how they knew he had been in the Pheasant Room and their bedroom. But they said nothing.

Susan continued to take their egg surplus down to Stanhope and did quiet deals for flour, for paraffin, even for the rackety taxi she needed to get back home. The advent of rationing made discretion very necessary.

Down in Stanhope the signs and symbols of the Home Front were manifest. Some windows were crisscrossed with tape, although the danger of bombing was small in such a remote town. The blackout was strictly observed, policed by those who had seen more direct action in the

Great War. There were notices chalked on the board by the newsagent's, sketching out the brave and optimistic enterprise of the early stages of the war. The cinema played to packed audiences, many there to see the newsreels with images of men in uniform embarking for unknown destinations, of women in trousers welding tanks or submarines. In the church and chapel they rehearsed well-turned prayers for the sons and daughters already out there saving their country.

Out at Goshawk Shield, apart from the scratchy tones of the nine o'clock news and the occasional letter from Theo in war-weary London, the war had little impact on their everyday lives. Theo's news made Susan fear for her safety, and ChiChu was still fighting her own Spanish war in her head. Strophair suppressed images of his son helping him with the lambing. But none of this was mentioned, day by day, as they got on with the routines of the farm.

ChiChu visited the bull each day to make sure he had clean straw and food in his manger. He still rolled his eyes at her and she had to tie him very close while she took a brush to him to clean his muddy flanks, and found clean sacking to bring something of a shine to his black coat. His great muscles and massively contained presence afforded her some comfort.

Susan came one day to watch her at her work. 'Funny, that you like him so much. What they do to them in your country . . .'

'Funny?' ChiChu frowned.

'Strange. Strange that you like him so.'

ChiChu ran the soft brush down his flank again. 'Is a fine beast. Proud. He is locked in a jail. Just like me in those days. I was locked away. The man locks him away.'

'But . . .' Susan watched her closely, 'in Spain they kill the bulls. It's a great performance, like the Church. But they die bleeding. Vanquished by a man in a suit of lights.'

ChiChu shrugged. 'They test the high courage of man against the stubborn pride of the bull. Like play with swords.'

'Duel?' Susan laughed. 'But there are three, four, five of them, one of him. How can that be—'

'The bull has great strength. In Spain he is twice as big as this little *toro*. Only great matadors can combat a great bull.'

'But it's cruel.'

ChiChu hunched her shoulders again and scowled. 'You not understand, Susan. Even the foreigners who love the bullfight and make great romances, they do not understand. They do not understand.' She stood back and threw her rag on to the edge of the manger. 'There. Is he not a fine *toro*?'

One morning, Harry Tills brought two letters in brown envelopes for Barry Strophair. Susan was by the gate in her great galoshes, swilling the last of the muck on the yard with her bucket before tackling the sludge with her great broom.

'By, missis,' Harry Tills said, 'yeh've made a reet difference here.' He handed the envelopes to Strophair, who had just come out of the barn, dogs at his heels, stick in his hand. 'Two for yeh today, Mr Strophair. Yeh can only hope it's good news, can't yeh? Dunkirk! Bad business, that. Callin' it "the great retreat". That's what they're calling it on the wireless. Heh! Retreat all right. They got thousands of those lads back, papers say. But how many dead on the beaches? That's what I say. How many marched off to Germany, wounded an' all?'

'Mr Tills!' said Susan. 'Mebbe better if you'd have some tact.'

He shook his head. 'Tact doesn't bring them back, missis. Dozens from this dale in that expeditionary force. Ministry envelopes by the dozen I've bin deliverin'. Tact doesn't mend that. Not easy bein' the bearer of bad tidings in these days.' He looked expectantly at Strophair.

The farmer scowled at him and tucked both letters in his rope belt, picked up his stick and whistled for his dogs. 'Standin' here gabbin' won't get the work done,' he said. Then he marched past them through the gate towards the fell. The dogs slunk after him, tails down.

They both watched him. 'Hard man, that Strophair,' volunteered Harry Tills. 'Hard as nails. Ah've delivered fifteen of those letters in this valley, and the families are tearing them open to get at them. White at the gills they are. Ah've seen some tears, and some wild laughter this week, Ah'm tellin' yer.' He rubbed his hands. 'Parky this morning, like. Freezes the nails off, I'm tellin' yeh. What Ah wouldn't give for a nice cup of tea. No sayin'.'

'Tea?' Susan leaned her brush against the fence. 'I'm sure we can find you some tea, Mr Tills.'

She led the way. Later, sitting at the table cradling a warm mug between his blue fingers, gratitude made Tills offer her one of his own special titbits. 'That other letter, that's from the Government, not the Army.'

'Government?'

'Delivered a few of them an' all, them from the ministry coming to talk about the women.'

'Women?' She was feeling very stupid.

'Women to help on the farms,' he said impatiently. This one obviously never read the papers or listened to the wireless. 'They're calling up the women to make up

204

for the men. Factories. Shipyards. Farms too.' He gurgled a hearty drink and sighed with satisfaction. 'Canna see it working, meself. Women doing farming.'

She raised her eyebrows.

'Different with you, missis. Anyone'd see it were different. You.'

'Hard job for us all if it doesn't, isn't it, Mr Tills? All pull together, isn't that what Mr Churchill says?' She paused. 'So, this other envelope?' She regretted the weakness of forcing the confidence, but if it was to do with the farm she wanted to know.

'Mrs Rasket read hers out ter me. Says a man from the ministry'll come, then farmers can get some of these land women to help'm. Mind yeh, looking at that yard, and yeh with your brush, old Strophair's stole a march on them, seems to me.'

Later, in his cluttered room at the end of the house Strophair fingered the two letters and held them to the lamp. He opened the ministry letter first. He stared at it blankly. Eh well. Let'm come. All of 'em. Ministry man. Farm women. No good looking a gift horse in the mouth. He was ridden with women these days. Couldn't turn round without falling over some woman or other. Couldn't get a night's sleep without a caterwauling brat waking you.

He smoothed the other envelope on the bedside table, then peeled it open. Jack. Not dead, then! *Last seen alive, but a prisoner.* Strophair screwed the envelope into a tiny ball and threw it in a corner. No matter. It was Jack's own fault. He could have been here, helping with the lambing. Ploughing the back field. Mending the roof on the barn. Mebbe he could have kept this woman in check too. Stop her rampaging over his farm with that brown-skinned foreigner in tow. He could have stopped that brat of hers caterwauling.

He reached into the cupboard beside the fire for the long bottle. Bugger them all, that's what he said. Bugger the lot of them.

Chapter Fourteen

Encounter in the Lane

I've called him Toro, this little bull. I know I should not do this, dearest Avia. A foreign name will take away his English power, his strength. But here in this cold place it is good to hear such a name on my lips. Toro! He is only a poor thing, dear Avia, compared with our brave bulls, but it is a hard life he has here in his dark stall, which is really an old storeroom in the house.

For days now he has been suffering. I change his straw and feed him well and call him by his name. Toro! His ears prick usually when I say it. Do you know?

But for days his ears have been forward. His head down. He rolls his eyes no more. He has even stopped pulling at his ring. I call his name and he pulls up breath from deep inside and does not snort so much as sigh.

I say to the farmer that the bull is sick and needs a bull-man to attend him. But a stream of words comes out from his mouth, mean as a snake's, that I cannot understand. I go to Susan to ask her, but she is worried now about the baby, whose temper tantrums make his cheeks as red as our flag (trampled now in the dust by the beast Franco. I know this now.) Did I scream, dearest Avia? Were my cheeks red as flags? I have no one to ask this in these days; not a single person who knew me when I was a baby. No one who knew me when I kicked my legs and started to walk. No one who heard me say my first words. The stream of words about me here is a wall of fear. Only when Susan or Theo speak in that special way do I begin to understand, like grasping flowers in the mist.

The only one other who was easy to listen to, who seemed to read the words from my mind, was Mr Walstein. Remember I told you of him? He was taken off with the policeman and Theo writes to him where he is, behind the wire. I cannot write to him in this language so he is lost to me. Susan tells me that he says in his letters 'How is ChiChu?' So he does not forget.

Where was I? Yes. Toro. Toro is sick. Perhaps he is just tired of his prison. But I have an idea. Something to cheer him. Something to make his eyes roll, Avia.

Barry Strophair, free these days of the animal care close to the house, could go up and check his sheep and the far dry-stone walls more often. Sometimes he went up on the fell and crouched under a holding wall, smoking a cigarette or taking a nip from the flask he always carried. He would stare with increasingly bleary eyes down towards Goshawk, occasionally seeing the stir of movement as Susan Gomersal and that girl went in and out of the house about their business.

He would place his shotgun across the lichen-covered dry-stone wall and take a sight of them. *Click!* That's you, Madame hypocrite Gomersal. *Click!* That's you, little Spanish spy. He could clear the house in two shots. Get his own life back again. He lifted the gun down from the wall. They were out of shot, anyway. He'd have to make do with a couple of rabbits, or maybe that sparrowhawk which had been buzzing the lambs. *Crack!* That would do for him, no more wheeling in the sky and diving down on harmless sheep.

He stood up and peered down the fell towards the farm once more. Well. What was that Spanish bit doing? Out on the yard there with his bull. Leading him round and round. Outside! She had a long stick with a rope on it tied to the ring through the beast's nose and was walking him around as though he were a pet lamb.

Strophair set out running down the hill, yelling and shouting, 'An' what yer think yeh're doin', ye bliddy idiot? Get that feller back inside. Only one use fer 'im.' He ran out of breath and had to come to a stop. That's when he started shooting his rifle in the air. *Crack! Crack! Crack!*

That was when the bull pulled against ChiChu and wrenched the stick from her hands. He turned his head towards her, his eyes rolling. Then he lowered his head and cantered towards her, the stick trailing painfully from his nose. Running half backwards, half sideways, ChiChu raced for the heavy kitchen door, then slipped inside and locked it behind her.

Frustrated, the bull nudged the door with his horn, knowing his quarry had gone. After a couple of half-hearted charges he left the door alone and trotted around the yard, dragging the stick with him. His hoofs clicked on the stone of the yard.

Strophair scrambled down as fast as he could, frustrated by the tussocks of grass, the hidden boulders. He splashed through the narrow beck that coiled round the base of the fell like a snake. He stopped once and shot again into the air. 'Stay there,' he shouted. 'Stay there, you bliddy stupid beast.'

The bull sniffed the air, moaned at the pain in his nose from the hanging stick, then cantered across the yard, out of the open gate and down the rough track towards the road. He had only gone twenty yards when his way was barred by a small car, a black, bull-nosed Morris inhabited by a bald man in a crumpled three-piece grey suit and yellow pigskin gloves.

The bull pawed the ground, investigated the car radiator with the tip of one horn and exchanged stare for stare with the petrified motorist.

'Oh, my God!' muttered Strophair. 'My good God, what has she done?'

Inside the house, Susan and ChiChu leaned across the wide, cluttered windowsill and watched the encounter.

'ChiChu, what have you done?' said Susan, trying not to laugh.

'Poor Toro,' said ChiChu. 'He so sad. Strophair shuts him in. Ties him down. In prison. He has no pride. I take him for a walk.'

'Not short of dignity now, is he? Setting his cheek up to a car and scaring the wits out of that poor man inside.'

'You think Strophair will shoot him?'

'The man in the car?'

'No. Toro. Will he shoot Toro?'

'Well, the bull is very valuable,' said Susan. Strophair was behind a wall, cursing at the bull. 'But I think he's mad enough to . . .' She turned round, but she was alone. Now she could see ChiChu slipping quietly across the yard and down the road. She watched as the slight figure edged nearer the pawing bull. Even Strophair stopped shouting. For a second the wind stopped pushing its sharp way over the rocks and through the low trees. The whole fell was unnaturally still. The birds had stopped singing, the hawk was absent from his regular patrol. The eyes of the man in the car were wide; one yellow pigskin glove was held to his mouth, a bead of sweat dropping into his eyes.

ChiChu started in a low voice, almost saying, 'Now, Toro, shshsh, shshsh.' She heard her father's voice, her grandfather's voice, singing through hers. The bull's head moved at the sound of her voice. His eyes were no longer dull, his ears were straight up. He pawed the ground, one rolling eye still interested in the chugging car.

'*He, toro,*' she moaned, keeping the edge of the bonnet between herself and the bull. 'Come on, dear Toro, come with ChiChu.' He tried to shake his head, pull away, but that was too painful with the stick pulling down. He pawed the ground.

Above them a flight of six aeroplanes in battle livery hummed on their way further North. The bull snorted.

ChiChu's voice broke the silence below. 'Come with ChiChu.' Her voice was firm. She lifted the stick so it did not hurt his nose too much and tugged him gently. 'Come on, old friend.' The bull started to move away from the car, then suddenly submitted to her, allowing himself to be led quite tamely towards the big door that divided the house from the dairy.

Strophair followed her from a distance, his heavy step echoing on the stone yard. The man jumped out of the car, locked it carefully and followed Strophair. Susan came out of the kitchen and went along the back hall to the dairy. They all got to the dairy in time to see ChiChu locking the gate that held the bull in his makeshift stall.

Susan clapped her hands. 'Well done, ChiChu. Well done!'

'Well done?' Strophair spluttered behind her. 'Wouldn't have happened if the lass hadn't had him—'

'Thank you, miss. You got the beast inside.' The polite,

clipped tones of the stranger came from behind Strophair. 'I think the shots, sir, if anything, enraged the bull further.'

Strophair's hands rolled into fists. 'Oh, you do, do you?'

Susan put a hand on his arm. 'Mr Strophair, mebbe we'd best take the visitor into the kitchen. It's cold and damp out here. No wonder the poor old bull was miserable.'

She led the way. Strophair and the stranger followed. ChiChu stayed behind to watch Toro settle down, not particularly interested in Strophair or the stranger.

'Now, Toro,' she murmured. 'Is better? See the wide sky. No sun but the sky is very wide and blue today.'

In the kitchen, the stranger introduced himself. 'Becket-Stroud, Mr Strophair. I wrote you a letter?'

Strophair scowled. 'Letter?' he said.

'About the possibility of you having help on the farm. War food production. You will have heard of it?'

'Women?' Strophair spat on the floor. 'Farms are no place for women.'

Becket-Stroud raised his eyebrows at Susan, who was looking on with interest. 'It seemed we just saw an example of a young woman being very good about the farm. Is that so, Mrs . . . ?' His glance strayed from one to the other.

Susan laughed. 'I'm not Mrs Strophair.'

'What?' said Strophair.

'Sorry . . . er . . . ma'am.'

'I am Susan Cornford,' said Susan. 'My family own this farm. Mr Strophair is our tenant. He is the farmer. We're just staying here. Won't you sit down, Mr Becket-Stroud? You'll take a cup of tea?'

MY DARK-EYED GIRL

The thing now was out of Strophair's hands. He would have been happy to turn this snoopy sneak off his land with the shotgun. But that bull and the Spanish brat and Susan Gomersal had put paid to that idea. He flung himself into a hard chair by the table and sat impatiently while Susan Gomersal fed this man with tea and ginger biscuits.

Mr Becket-Stroud relaxed, his fear of the bull firmly put behind him. He turned to Strophair and began his rehearsed speech about farming and the war, handing out leaflets from time to time from his battered briefcase. Strophair pushed the papers away and they fluttered to the ground.

'With help, Mr Strophair, you could produce even more for the war effort. One or two more cows close to the farm. I saw two fields unploughed. Potatoes, perhaps? Onions?'

'Ah canna get round it all as it is,' said Strophair. 'All right you comin' here in yer black car, like—'

'But that's why I came here, Mr Strophair. A great source of labour for the land. Women! Keen to help the war effort, to do their bit. You can show them how to do it, and they will work with you. Help you and your farm to do their bit.' He put on his glasses and peered at a small notebook. 'I think I'd be correct in saying that two women could be assigned to Goshawk Shield. So Goshawk Shield can make its contribution to the war effort.'

Strophair scowled. 'Goshawk Shield has done that,' he grunted. 'Me own lad is my contribution to the war effort. Taken at Dunkirk.'

Mr Becket-Stroud coughed and, for a second, he had nothing to say. Then, 'I am sorry about that. But don't you see, Mr Strophair, bringing to strength the productivity of Goshawk Shield, that's your contribution to bringing your son back from behind the wire. To ending the war, so he can come home safely. Wouldn't you want that Mr Strophair? Wouldn't you?'

Chapter Fifteen

Recruitment

'Are you sure?' The mild-faced woman looked up at Judith Sowerby over her glasses. 'It's very hard, dirty work you know.' She glanced down at Judith's perfectly manicured hands, her immaculately cut suit, her handmade shoes. 'What about the WRAF or the ATS? Good opportunities there for bright girls.'

Judith laughed. 'I have a problem there, Mrs Cator. I don't usually tell people this, but I suppose here . . .' she glanced around the improvised office, '. . . the truth is I never did learn how to read or write. The parents wept, the teachers wrung their hands, but those jumpin' shapes would never make a single word of sense to me.'

'We-ell.' Mrs Cator was in difficulty. One of the wonderful things about this war was that it got one out of the house. One met all sorts of people, people one would never come across in the normal run of things: shopgirls and housewives. Maids and matrons. Many of these were illiterate; working on the land would, for them, be a valuable contribution. But to have someone drive up in a low-slung red Citroën, in her handmade shoes and her couture suit and have her flaunt her illiteracy – well, you

215

learned something new every day.

Judith Sowerby leaned forward and looked the woman in the eye. 'Honestly, Mrs Cator, you bet I can do it. Happiest time of my life on my Uncle Hugh's farm in Bellingham. Bit of milking, bit of ploughing in the spring holidays; bit of reaping and potato picking in the autumn. Rum old cove, old Hugh. Same as myself. Couldn't read or write. Even so, the Army took him in the Great War. Never more than a private, though. His brother, my Uncle Joseph was commissioned, became a brigadier—'

Mrs Cator held up a hand to stop the torrent of talk. 'I am convinced, Miss Sowerby. I am convinced!' she said, putting a tick on the sheet before her. 'There'll be a medical; if you're reasonably fit you will get in. They need every pair of hands they can get their . . . er . . . hands on.'

Judith smiled her open, untroubled smile. 'Oh, I am fit,' she said. 'Fit as a sparky yearling.'

The next woman to see Mrs Cator was a much easier task: miner's daughter who was trained as a mental nurse. The sturdy figure lounged in the chair in front of her. Mrs Cator frowned. Some of these girls were so slack. Never been taught to sit with their knees together. Did not know about the straight spine.

'Why would you choose to come out of nursing, Miss Stanton? Surely you are needed there in the hospital?' she said.

'Well, ma'am, I've worked at the hospital ten years. Feel like I've done that now. Me brother volunteered early and I wanted to do my bit too.'

'You didn't fancy the other services? The ATS perhaps?'

Keziah Stanton shook her head. 'I see it like this, ma'am. I've already spent ten years under military discipline in the hospital. You should see our matron, fiercer than any general. And Sister Barras! Worse than any RSM. I've had a basinful of that.'

'There is discipline in the Land Army, you know,' put in Mrs Cator. 'It's very hard work. Don't think it's not.'

'Aye. I realize that. But I reckoned you'd be mostly outside, feeding hens and ploughing and stuff. Not so much standing to attention. You know?'

Mrs Cator surveyed her for a second. The woman looked fit and strong, at least. Being used to hospital discipline would be an advantage. 'Can you read and write?' she said abruptly.

Keziah shot her a hard glance. 'Course I can,' she said. 'I've got my school-leaving certificate here, and passed all my nursing exams. Better at the practicals, of course. But reading and writing, that's a detail. Everybody can read, can't they?'

'I wouldn't take that for granted,' said Mrs Cator, putting a tick on the sheet in front of her. 'I'm sure you'll make your way in the Land Army, Miss Stanton.'

Keziah stood up. 'Is that all right, then?'

'That's all right. You'll be notified about when to report and there will be a month's training on Plumfield Farm in North Durham. Then you'll be assigned a place where you'll work.'

Susan woke with a start. What was that noise? It wasn't Barty. He was lying beside her, quiet as a lamb, breathing slowly and regularly with little puffs. She slipped out of her bed, went to the window to peer into that deep, Goshawk Shield darkness. Gingerly, she lifted the sneck and pushed the window open. The dense silence of a country night enveloped her, fought to slip past her into the room where Barty and ChiChu slept. Her mind battled with it, then she shut the window again with a click.

'Is something?' ChiChu's voice came to her in the darkness.

'No. No. I just wanted some air,' said Susan. 'It seemed so warm in here.'

'Is a very cold night,' said ChiChu, burrowing further under her bedclothes. 'The window makes colder.'

'Sorry. Sorry.' Susan climbed back into bed beside Barty and, shivering suddenly herself, pulled the plump eiderdown up to her nose.

Then for no reason at all the hospital popped into her head. Not the Spanish hospital, that whitewashed, stripped-down church which mourned its bright symbols and icons. No, it was the long, prison-like corridors of Park View that flashed on her inner eye, with Jane Ann sneaking out at night to prowl forbidden territory. The hospital with Dr Tordoff making his way with the delicacy of a ballet dancer from his palatial house on the perimeter to the columnated doors of the main building with its mutters and moans in the night; its loud laughter and its occasional despairing scream.

She shivered, despite the heat of the heavy bedclothes.

Then the merry face of Keziah Stanton was before her. Was she still at the hospital? Was she still going to her house in New Morven on her weekends off? And how was Jake? Susan thought of the gaunt, bearded face of Jake Stanton as he was the last time she'd seen him in Spain. Had he survived those last months in Spain? There were so many deaths just near the end. So many after. The fighting had stayed desperate even when the cause was lost. Then afterwards all those executions. She shuddered.

Aaron Maichin for one – he had definitely survived. Quite perky settling in there at Theo's. So sure of himself. She could just see him in some beleaguered French town at this minute, pretending to be German and discovering something important. Susan was still not certain about him. She'd observed him being charming and respectful with Theo; but he was peculiarly watchful with ChiChu. There was something unnervingly hawklike and secretive about him.

Barty chuntered a little in his sleep and she stroked his cheek until they both fell again into deep sleep.

The next morning after breakfast, Susan's nighttime thoughts impelled her to write a long letter to Keziah Stanton. Then she went in search of Mr Strophair to ask if she could borrow his cob to go down to Stanhope to post it. He told her he needed the horse to get out to the Barrow Field where he was doing some fencing. Anyway, there were the potatoes to hoe up. She and the girl were to do that. Wasn't that what they were doing for the war effort? Helping on the farm?

She scowled at him, turned and stumped away and was treated to the sound of him coughing, coughing and spitting behind her. She was just walking back through the yard, not so cluttered now, when she caught sight of Harry Tills pushing his bike up the hill towards her. She waited for him. 'Just the man!' she said. 'What a sight for sore eyes you are, Mr Tills.'

His face twitched in a gesture, which was half wink, half nod. 'Now there's a welcome, Miss Cornford. Ah was just thinkin' what a parky morning this was an' how a nice cuppa tea wouldn't come amiss, and here you are.'

Two minutes later he was ensconced at the kitchen table, a cup of steaming tea in front of him. Only then did he produce the mail from the depths of his bag. There were two letters. One from Theo, and one she noted, her heart jolting, from Keziah Stanton! It had been sent to Theo's house and readdressed twice but still arrived within a week of its dispatch.

She pushed a plate of ginger biscuits in front of Harry Tills and asked him to excuse her. Then she went to the Pheasant Room and opened her post. Theo's letter was full of the bombing and the disturbances in her life caused by it. She had finished her book, although the publishers said there might not be enough paper to print. She'd written to Mr Walstein and had letters back. She said she'd seen Aaron again. It seemed he'd signed up with the Army and was doing special duties. *One dare hardly speculate but I imagine with his blond looks and being able to speak German he is quite useful. He brought me a dusty bottle of French wine last week, which I like to imagine came straight from France. Of course, I ask no questions.*

On another matter: *I've sent on a letter from Durham for you which came to me here.*

Susan opened the letter addressed in Keziah's familiar round hand: the usual chirpy tone, with the usual fragmented bits of news. The rationing. The increase of horses and carts in Gibsley, there being so many fewer cars and vans; what few cars there were up on bricks. There had been this appeal for men to stay in the pits instead of dashing off to war. *Our George and Tegger are back at the pit and earning good money.* There was talk of conscripting men for the pits. Oh, and Jake had been home from Spain long enough to have a shave and eat two or three of his mother's meat-and-tatie pies. Then he'd gone off to fight again. This time for England. *But he's, like, subdued now. Doesn't let his mouth run away with him like he did. He's changed all right. Not the lad he was. He said he saw you in Spain. Talked about you quite a bit.*

And last but not least:

Guess what? I'm leaving the hospital to do war work. Not that I have to. Nursing's protected, as you know. I put my notice in and old Dr Tordoff came personally and asked me to stay. Can you believe it? When I said I was firm he was all right. In fact he told me he was volunteering as well. I told him I didn't realize the army was full of lunatics and he gave me such a look.

Our Sweetie is doing all right as she's been signed up for the Royal Ordnance Factory where they make bombs to drop on the Germans. She's gone a bit wild, though. Earns a good bit of money and goes dancing three times every week. Well, it's a short life.

Your friend,
     Keziah Stanton

Susan smiled as she tucked the letter back in its envelope. She turned over the one she'd already written to Keziah. On the envelope she wrote: *Received yours of the 14th inst. Will reply.* Then she went down, poured Mr Tills a second cup of tea and asked him if he would kindly take her post down the post office for her.

'Aye. That'll be OK.' He reached into his bag. 'Ah've got one here for Mr Strophair.' It was small and brown and had OHMS on the corner. 'Ah was thinkin' mebbe he was getting called up but then thought on that'd not be possible. Bit long in the tooth Ah'd 'a thought.' He seemed taken with his little joke.

Susan took the letter and put it on the mantelpiece in a prominent place in front of the clock. 'Thanks, Mr Tills. I'll see he gets it. I don't know about getting called up. He'd fight for the Germans, that one.'

The Stanhope bus picked up a second passenger wearing land girl togs and with a lurch of gears set off again. The girl stopped beside Judith. 'You'll be goin' to the same place as me. They told us you'd be on the bus,' the girl said. She nodded at Judith, also dressed in the corduroy of the land girl, and plonked herself in the seat beside her.

Judith Sowerby looked her companion up and down. Small. But strong, perhaps. Not smart, though. Judith knew the uniform on her own trim figure looked smart and businesslike. But on her companion it looked as though she were wearing her big brother's cut-down khaki jumper and wellingtons.

'Well,' said her companion, 'looks like we're stuck together in this place, wherever it is. My name's Keziah Stanton. What's yours?' She stuck out her broad hand and shook Judith's with a very strong grip. 'I never saw you at Plumfield. Where d'you train?'

'Judith Sowerby. I come from Gosforth, just outside Newcastle. Trained in Northumberland.'

'Did yer volunteer for this?' said Keziah, suddenly suspicious. 'Yeh sound like yeh'd be better in the Army, or the Navy. Yer dinnet talk like a land girl.'

Judith smiled. 'Now why would you think that?'

Keziah paused. You could hardly talk about the problems of having a cut-glass accent. 'Well, yeh just seem . . .'

'Well, it was either this or an arms factory. I couldn't

bear to be shut in some dirty place and come out smelling of gunpowder. What a fate! And the other things? Well. No. I do think fighting Hitler is a good thing. But I haven't a fighting bone in my body. So they gave me no choice. The Land Army or nothing.' No need to broadcast the state of her literacy. She was used to concealing it. It had been useful with Mrs Cator, who had really needed persuading, so she could go on the land. But normally there were lots of ways round it.

'What d'you do before, like?'

'Me?' Judith's laughter was like a bird chirruping in grass. 'Nothing. Not a thing, my dear. Help my mother run the house. Go to the Theatre Royal for plays. Concerts. Tennis. Dress fittings. It felt quite busy, to be honest. Spring and summers I'd work on my uncle's farm, which was fun. Bit of ploughing. Lots of riding. But when you boil it down it was nothing.' She paused to light a cigarette. 'What about you? I'll wager you've been doing something real.'

Keziah scowled at her. 'Is that a crack, like?'

Judith puffed on her cigarette. 'Honestly. It wasn't a crack. What did you do?'

'I was a mental nurse,' said Keziah. 'Worked in an asylum.'

Judith raised her finely plucked brows. 'A nurse? One would have thought that would be useful, say, for the Army. They'd grab you. All those shell-shocked boys.'

'I nursed mad people, man,' said Keziah crossly. 'The only wounds I dealt with were self-inflicted.'

Judith shrugged. 'Madness is war, my dear. Madness is war. No less than two uncles of mine returned from the Great War mad as hatters. Perfectly sane before. When Uncle Toby got back he slept in a cupboard for three years. He went in the cupboard at night and roamed the streets of Gosforth by day clad only by a copy of the previous day's *Times*. Then one day he returned to the cupboard altogether and stayed there. There was talk of an asylum for him. My mother told me that in the end they only got him out at the point of a gun. And a German one at that. They acquired one specially.'

'Did he go to hospital?' said Keziah, thinking of the man who pranced round the flames at Park View that bonfire night.

'Hospital? My dear, Sowerbys never go to hospital. No. In the end they set him up in a kind of horse breeding place in the wilds of Northumberland. I used to go there for my school holidays. Loved it, my dear. Him too. Horses and all that. Uncle Toby used to climb in bed with you . . .'

Keziah clutched her arm. Heads on the bus were turning round. 'Shsh,' she said.

Judith lowered her voice to a stage whisper. 'Didn't matter, of course. You kicked him out and he was a whimpering cur, slavering at your feet.' She dropped her cigarette on the cluttered floor of the bus and ground it under the heel of her handmade leather riding boot. 'So were you a good nurse, then?' She lit another cigarette.

'I was all right.'

'So why d'you leave it for all this?'

Keziah was sick of the focus on herself. 'I'd this friend. She nursed alongside me. She went to Spain to work. Was there in thirty-seven. She was a good nurse. I envied her going off like that. Freedom and that.'

'Is she still there? In Spain? That show's all over now, of course. I saw those pictures of Franco's army marching into Barcelona.'

'No. She's home now. She came back.'

'Is she an army nurse here?'

'No. She has family now. She's living with her sister in London.'

'London! Can be fun but I wouldn't go down there now for a diamond tiara. They're having a bad time there with the bombs. The pictures on the newsreels . . .'

They talked and half slept as the bus trundled along. Then, at last the old bus creaked at their stop. The conductor shouted down the bus. 'Here y'are, ladies. Get off here.'

They picked up their bags and made their way down the bus, ignoring the dark looks from passengers scandalized at the tone of their conversation. The bus wheezed into action and left them in the dense driving rain at the bottom of the fell.

Keziah stood with her back to the wind and looked at a printed fragment of map which she took from her pocket. 'That's it.' She nodded at a narrow, barely marked path on the other side of the dry-stone wall. 'Up there and turn left behind that big hill and we should be there. Goshawk Shield Farm.'

'That's miles,' moaned Judith.

'D'yer wanter shout the bus back, then?'

They threw their packs over the wall then clambered after them and started to trudge along a faintly marked path with sodden, whiskery grass growing up in the middle. They were halfway up the track and had skirted round an upjutting rock when they came upon a slender, dark figure, muffled to the eyebrows, leading a small compact bull with a ring through his nose.

Judith took shelter behind Keziah. 'We're looking for Mr Strophair,' said Keziah. 'Goshawk Shield Farm?'

The dark figure continued steadily past them with the

bull. 'House up there,' she said, flinging her arm vaguely in the direction of the fell. 'Is there.' It was the voice of a girl, not a boy. White teeth gleamed at them in the mist.

They waited until she and the bull were well on their way before they went on, and rounded a heavy rock ridge which gave on to a whole new vista of fell and sky. Sheltering under the ridge was a tumble of buildings clustered around a fine doorway which had brambles curling up to the elaborate knocker. The building reared up almost black in the filtered light of the moorland afternoon. Half of it was hung with the unkempt generations of Virginia creeper. Its windows stared eyeless towards the fell.

'Oh my God!' Judith clutched Keziah's arm. 'This isn't a farm. It looks like Dracula's castle. I saw the film at the Odeon. Boris Karloff, I think. Ugh!'

'There,' said Keziah. 'That gate at the side. More like a farm round there.'

The gate creaked as they opened it. They stepped into a farmyard scattered with stone troughs and the detritus of ruined farm machinery, edged by buildings with doors whose peeling green paint had bleached to silver. In one corner some hens were harassing two cats, which vanished into the dark interiors of a barn. A man appeared suddenly at the shadowy doorway of a barn, bolstered in a bulky jacket tied with string, his eyes deeply shaded by his deep cap.

'Aye,' he said. 'What is it? D'yeh know yer trespassing?'

Judith's chin went up. 'We've been sent here,' she said.

'Who sent yeh, like?'

'We've been assigned here by the Land Army. They would inform you. We're here to help you with your war effort.' Judith spoke very slowly as though to a deaf person.

He spat on the floor. 'Too much help round here as it is.'

'We saw a . . . girl, I think, with a bull.'

'Spaniard,' he growled. 'Filthy Spaniard. Should drown the lot.'

'Yeh should 'a got a letter from the Ministry,' Keziah tried. 'Mebbe they forgot to send it. These farms are agreed. We were told that.'

He sniffed. 'Wait here,' he said. The dog at his heel growled. 'Dinnet try anything, mind.' He strode to the open kitchen door. The dog growled again. Judith walked across and squatted so she was face to face with it. 'Now, boy,' she said, 'I think we should be friends, you and me.'

Susan had been enjoying a peaceful afternoon on the back landing, disembowelling the linen of decades from the deep landing cupboard on the top floor. She had tied Barty by a long scarf to a bedroom doorknob. He could toddle two yards in every direction but could not reach the top of the stairs and tumble down.

She had just finished sorting mendable sheets from sheets only fit for dusters when clashes and bangs from downstairs raked the air and Barty started to whimper. She untied him, put him on her back, and jogged along the landing and down the stairs to cheer him up. 'Gee up, horsy! Gee up!'

In the kitchen, Barry Strophair had flung all the ornaments off the mantelpiece and had stripped down the dresser. Pans were bouncing off the stone-flagged floor. 'What is it?' she shouted over the din. 'Why are you doing this? Stop it, Mr Strophair!'

He paused and looked blankly at her. Then his look cleared when he realized who she was. 'Letter,' he said. 'A Ministry letter. I've got women here, who say . . .'

Susan put Barty on to the floor and picked up the brown envelope which was there, with the scattering of papers from the mantelpiece. 'This must be it. Came a fortnight ago. I left it there for you. You never opened it.'

He tore it open, and held it towards the fire to read it. 'Feller who came,' he said, pushing the letter towards her. 'I'd 'a thought the bull would 'a done for him. He says we are on the list for the Land Army. Look at those rates of pay. Can you see here! Rates of pay for help you didn't ask for!'

She glanced at the letter. 'These Land Army girls are coming?'

'They're here,' he said, turning his face towards the door. 'In the yard.'

'Good,' she said firmly. 'That'll be a hand for you. You say there's too much to do. The potatoes to clear, the field to plough.'

'Too many women here already.'

'Don't you start that again, I keep telling you. There's a war on. Now. These land girls?' She moved towards the door.

He blocked her way. 'You mind your business,' he said. 'Get on with what you've got to get on with. Farm's my business. I'll see to'm.'

He shut the door behind him and she stared at it blankly. Then she said, 'Well, Barty, let's go up and finish the sheets. We're not wanted here, what d'you think?'

Barty looked up at her under his mop of black curls and his face split into a very wide, toothless grin. For a second she could feel the bright sun of Spain and the warm heat of Barty's father's presence. She blinked. 'Come on, my boy,' she said. 'We've got work to do.'

Outside, Barry Strophair strode across the yard to where Judith Sowerby was on her knees, cuddling his dog as though it were some lady's poodle. He took two steps and kicked the beast in the midriff so that it went six feet, into the peeling door of the old stable. The dog squealed and barked, baring its teeth at Strophair. He walked across to kick it again. It crouched back, then slunk away into a corner, whimpering.

'Stop that, you filthy beast.' Judith started forward, then hesitated.

'Mr Strophair!' protested Keziah. 'There's no need for that. Dog did nowt. Nowt at all.'

He eyed her and she went closer to Judith, slightly in front of her.

'Yer friend here's probably ruined dog with her pettin'. He'll be to train all over again.' He sniffed. 'I found yon letter. It got mislaid. Well, seein' as yer here, there's plenty work to do. Might as well stay. Ministry feller'll be on me back if you don't.'

Keziah looked at their packs, then turned to look at the farm buildings. 'Where will we stay, Mr Strophair? We'll need to put our things somewhere.'

He pointed to the door against which he had just flung the dog. 'Stable over there. Rooms on top of the stable, the Gomersal lads stayed when they worked here. Kitted up for sleeping in there.'

A sharp wind cut down the dale, whipped through the chimneys of the house and speared its way down into the yard. Judith shivered. 'And perhaps we could have a hot drink, Mr Strophair? It's been a long journey.'

He shrugged. 'Stow yer stuff, an' help yourselves. Kitchen's over there.' He looked around. 'Then there's plenty ter make yerself useful for a start. Hoss to muck out. Cow to milk. An' we got a field of taties to pick. Yer'll find us in the top field.'

'Today?' said Keziah. 'We just got here!'

'Ah thowt yer came here ter work,' he said, then turned on his heel and left, whistling for the dog, which slunk after him, its ears down.

The stable loft did have two truckle beds in and a battered cupboard, but apart from that it was just a stable loft with rubbish and old tack shoved into the corners. There was one small window so thick with cobwebs that it was impossible to see out. Keziah poked her finger into these and brought them away like a hank of old wool. 'Ugh!' she said.

'You've said it,' said Judith. 'Ugh! Ugh! Ugh! So this is how we'll save our country from Hitler.' She sat down on the truckle bed which creaked under her weight. 'Bloody bloody *bloody*! What have we got into?'

Keziah lifted a tattered blanket from the other bed and it fell to pieces in her hands, showering mouse droppings on the wooden floor. 'Come on!' she said. 'We'll go and make ourselves a nice cup of tea and decide what to do next. Ah don't know what yeh think, Judith, but Ah'm not working for that old monster and Ah'm certainly not sleeping in this hole. Not for one night. Get your kit.'

They made their way across the yard, through a ramshackle porch and into the kitchen. A bright fire crackled up the chimney but the room was in a mess. Keziah filled a tin kettle and lit the gas. Then she rooted in a cupboard and found a tin of tea. She retrieved an enamel teapot off the floor and sorted out two whole cups from the broken ones beside the dresser.

Judith stretched out her boots before the fire. 'Rum sort of place, this,' she said. 'Talk about country idyll.'

The tea was just brewing when they heard a baby's howl from somewhere in the house. They exchanged glances. 'There must be a Mrs Strophair,' said Keziah. 'Must be quite a slut if this is anything to go by.'

The door creaked open and a tall woman stood there: the curly-haired child holding her hand was bawling his head off. The woman smiled. 'He got out of his tether and fell down five steps.' She frowned and looked harder at Keziah. 'If I didn't know better . . .' she said.

Keziah steadied the teapot, which she had nearly dropped. 'Why, yeh bloke!' she yelled. 'Susan Cornford! Don't tell me you're Mrs Miserable Bleedin' Strophair.'

Susan's laugh rang out. 'Me? That one? Never!' Barty suddenly stopped crying and put a thumb in his mouth, looking closely at these strange people. Susan went to shake Keziah warmly by the hand. 'So you're the land girl! Old Strophair only found out about you today. He stormed the kitchen, as you'll have seen. He's messy at the best of times but he's excelled himself today.' She turned to Judith. 'And you're land girl two, I imagine.'

Judith held out her hand. 'Judith Sowerby, for my sins. As you say, the second land girl.'

'This is the one I was telling you about,' said Keziah. 'My friend the nurse. She was in Spain, bandaging the soldiers.'

'The nurse?' Judith looked at this tall, wispy, rather plain woman. Didn't look like a textbook heroine. Not at all.

'The friend who went nursing in Spain. I told you on the bus.' Keziah bent down and tickled Barty's cheek.

'And what have we here?' she said, looking up at Susan. 'Handsome little brute. Spanish, is he?'

Susan laughed. 'Long story,' she said. 'He's mine. Not Spanish. Italian.'

'We saw a dark-eyed girl out in the lane,' said Judith. 'Leading a bull by the nose. Old Strophair was after drowning her. Called her a dirty Spaniard.'

'That's my young friend ChiChu with Toro,' said Susan. 'All part of a long story. My letter must be chasing you around or you'd have known at least some of it. But that'll keep. First, you look nithered, the pair of you. I'll make you a hot drink and summat to eat. And I'll clear this clutter while you eat it. Old Strophair did all this looking for that letter about you. He's a monster. No doubt about it.'

'Couldn't agree more.' Judith was looking at Susan with open curiosity. She'd thought Keziah's friend would be younger. Like Nurse Cavell, whom the German's shot in the Great War. She'd seen a film about her at the Odeon. And what was this baby about? The woman was old enough to be its grandmother.

They told Susan about their barn-loft billet and the mouse droppings. She laughed. 'No need for that. Plenty of rooms in the house, give or take lighting a few fires. They'll need opening up and warming through, but he can't put you in there like a couple of chickens in a coop. Not while I'm here.'

By the time Strophair came looking for the newcomers, Judith and Keziah were ensconced in a long room in the eaves above Susan and ChiChu's bedroom. They'd eaten two fried eggs between slices of Susan's own bread, and were quite different women from the frozen waifs who had presented themselves in his farmyard three hours before.

'Ah telt yeh to come and find us,' he grunted, reaching for his regular meat stew. 'Work to do.'

'We'd just arrived,' said Keziah. 'Needed to find where we were. Get dried out. We can start tomorrow.'

'I've put them in the apple loft here in the house,' put in Susan. 'No need to put them in the stable, out in that rat hole.'

'Stable's good enough for yer own Gomersal cousins,' grunted Strophair, dipping a hunk of bread in his stew and sucking at it. 'Good enough for your bloody cousins. Why not these?'

Susan's face hardened. 'It was never good enough, even for them,' she said. 'You don't want reporting to the Ministry, do you? And you must be pleased to have this help for the potatoes?'

He sniffed. 'I've gotta pay them. They're not a present, you knaa. Dinnet care where they stay,' he grunted. He glowered at Keziah. 'Just get yersel' in the yard tomorrow six o'clock sharp. An' dinna touch the dogs or I'll shoot 'em. No use to me softened up with women's touch.'

The women exchanged glances. Susan went to the door. 'Well, Mr Strophair, we'll just leave you to yourself. Let you have your tea in peace.' She nodded to Keziah and Judith, who followed her to the Pheasant Room. There on the threadbare carpet before the fire crouched ChiChu, acting as a climbing frame for a giggling Barty, whispering in his ear in Catalan.

'Sit down, won't you?' smiled Susan. 'With the old terror out of our way we can let our hair down, can't we?'

Keziah looked at ChiChu, glowing in the light of the fire, her abundant hair tossing this way and that as she played with Barty. 'Now then, Susan. What was this long story you were talking about?'

* * *

Toro is feeling much better from his walks, Avia, though I hear in my ear the voice of my father that he will be no good for the corrida. Too much talking, too many soft touches. Like Mr Strophair says when you touch his dogs. Then I say to him I know this, that Toro with his strange looks would never make sport. But he is my companion and my memory of home. The very smell of him is good.

The farmer is angry that I take Toro into the field and into the lane, that I walk and talk with him. But I pretend not to understand. I wait and take him out when the farmer is on the hill. But still he watches us from up there. I see a shiver of movement from the hill opposite. My eye is sharpened with looking for Fascist snipers. Remember? I sit on the gate watching Toro, but my eye also is on the hill and I see the farmer moving about with his rifle.

Today I saw him with his gun at his shoulder. Pointing at me. One day he will shoot me. What do you think, Avia? Susan was in the yard with Barty and I was in the field with Toro. And there he was on the hill with his gun at his shoulder, peering down the barrel..

We all ignored him but he came down just the same, tramping through the yard like an old dog, past me as though I was not on this earth.

And there are two women here, did I say? One is tall and thin with golden hair, like that American woman we saw at the cinema in Barcelona. Do you remember? She was petting the old sheepdog and the man kicks the old dog. Just to frighten this woman. The other one is smaller and is Susan's friend. She too took care of mad people. There is much more talk now. A wall of harsh, clattering English around me. I understand very much of it but a whole day of it makes my head ache. Sometimes my bones ache so much with longing for home that

MY DARK-EYED GIRL

I can hardly walk. I can hardly rise from my bed in the mornings, my eyes will hardly open on this grey world.

But still I rise to help Susan and to take Toro out of his prison and into the light. And what do I care if the farmer doesn't like it?

Chapter Sixteen

Sorting It Out

'We need to get this sorted out properly,' announced Susan, looking round the crowded kitchen table.

'What?' said Keziah, with her mouth full.

'This business with Strophair. You're supposed to be working for him, remember. Land Army girls? I read about you in the paper.'

'We do have lots to do,' said Judith, spreading out her fingers with their broken tips. 'Potato picking must be the filthiest, coldest job in the world.' It had taken them days to harvest the field of potatoes, hand digging and sorting them. The potatoes were now in muddy pyramids at the end of each row, in danger of rotting.

'Yes. But it's me telling you to do this thing. I'm not the farmer.'

'You're a farmer yourself,' said Keziah. 'Always said so. Why don't you make a job of it? Yourself?'

'Yes. Yes,' said Susan impatiently. 'But Strophair's the tenant. It's his farm, isn't it? I'm doing his work for him. You're working for him but never see him. It needs sorting.' Her tidy mind was offended. She'd known the farm when it was in good heart.

'What are you going to do? He's always off up at some far end of the farm, counting sheep, killing foxes or fixing fences or whatever he does.'

'Killing rabbits,' said Keziah gloomily. She'd had the job one day, of skinning and gutting a pair of bloody rabbits which he dumped in the kitchen doorway. They made a good stew but Keziah could not bring herself to eat it. 'Can't eat a thing whose blood you've had on your hands,' she said that night, reaching for a lump of bread to eat with her turnips.

On the evening after the morning discussion the women waited until Strophair was sitting in the kitchen with his head down over the stew, and gathered in the kitchen. Keziah leaned against the sink, Judith sat in the chair by the fire and ChiChu sat on the floor with her back to the press, carving a stick with her sharp knife. Susan sat at the other end of the table from Strophair, Barty on her knee.

The farmer's spoon scraped as he finished his stew. He looked up, wiped his mouth with the back of his hand and growled, 'What's this, then?'

'Well, first, Mr Strophair,' said Susan slowly, 'do you want me to take on Goshawk Shield or would you rather run it yourself? I've run it before an' I could do it again. Don't worry about that.'

'What yeh on about? This is my place, here. My farm.'

'Aye. I know that. But there's a war on, if you haven't noticed. Listen to the wireless. We have to feed the nation. And here we have three fields unplanted and your taties only just picked and not dispatched—'

'None of your business,' he interrupted. 'It's my land.'

She paused, not wanting to bring Theo's name into the conversation. She would attend to this by herself. 'Look,

Mr Strophair, mebbe we have got off on to the wrong foot, barging in here. But the land's there. And you've got two hefty girls . . .'

'Thank you very much . . .' said Judith.

'. . . sent here to help you. There's me, and there's—'

'I need no help from foreigners,' he snapped, glancing sidelong at the silent ChiChu. 'Else what's this all about? Need to keep foreigners out.'

Susan glanced at ChiChu, but did not comment. 'So, what do you want to do? Do you want to organize all this yourself, get us all working? Or do you want me to sort it all out and you do the sheep and the far fields, like you've been doing?'

For a few seconds all they could hear was the scrape of ChiChu's knife as she whittled her stick.

'That way, the farm'll be productive and the government man won't come and requisition it – the land. If you don't work the land the Government will requisition it and put someone else on to work it. It says so in the papers. On the wireless.'

He stood up. 'No choice, that what yer sayin'?'

'I'm saying you have a choice. I run it or you run it properly. For the war effort. Manage these girls and get the farm into some decent heart.'

'Suit yehself,' he growled. 'My hands are full with the stock and the fences. Suit yerself.' He made for the door.

'The tractor,' said Susan, frowning. 'There was a tractor. Theo lent you the money for it. Did you sell it?'

'Our Jack packed it away in the cow shelter by the Old Stream field. Nae use fer it meself. Horse is cheaper an' does it just as well.' He barged out of the door, which swung back so hard against ChiChu she howled with pain.

The others crowded round her, commiserating and shouting curses at the vanishing back of the farmer. ChiChu stopped howling, rubbed her thigh and scowled up at them. 'Bad man,' she said. 'Very bad man.'

Half an hour later, they were attacking the rusted wooden padlock on the old cow shed with a small axe. At last the door creaked open and there was the tractor. It sat on its haunches, hardly visible in the light from the crowded doorway. The bonnet was scummed up with dust and festooned with cobwebs. The air reeked of dust and old slurry. The shed was so cold they could see their breaths in the air. But they could make out two large wheels and two small wheels, a steering wheel and a cranking handle. 'All the bits are here,' said Susan. 'Look! Jack's wrapped the tyres in oilcloth.' She poked behind the tyres. 'And here's the sledge we used to pull things over the field.'

They opened the door wider and set to levering the tyres on to the wheel hubs. When this was done Susan climbed up on to the seat. Keziah grasped the crank-handle. She tried, and failed to turn it.

Judith leaned against the door, arms folded. 'No bloody good,' she said. 'No bloody good at all. I can drive a tractor, but I can't bloody drive this one. Engine is kaput.'

ChiChu moved past Keziah, pulled up the bonnet and peered inside. Flakes of rust dappled her black hair as she withdrew her head from the tractor's dark interior. 'Is bloody good engine,' she said. 'I fix.'

Susan climbed down and peered into the engine. 'Are you sure?' she said. 'It looks complicated to me.'

'Is bloody good.' ChiChu's voice was an eerie echo of Judith's. 'I fix.'

'How can she?' Judith looked at Susan. 'She's just a

kid. Can't know anything about engines.'

'Oh yes she does.' Susan put an arm round ChiChu's shoulders. 'She's a *miliciana*, is that not so, ChiChu? And she is no kid. She's nineteen.'

For a second, ChiChu's face lit up. '*Si*,' she said. '*Miliciana*. And nineteen years.'

'*Miliciana*? What's that?' said Keziah.

'She was a fighter in the Spanish war and, so I was told, could strip down a gun or an engine as good as any man.'

Keziah whistled.

'Smashing!' said Judith. 'A soldier in our midst. I'd never reckoned on that.' She'd not taken a great deal of notice of ChiChu up to now. The dark-eyed girl was just a slender waif who lurked at the edges of Goshawk Shield, whittling her wood, or tending her beloved bull and her hens. Judith found her vaguely irritating, contained so much within her own bubble, uninterested in anyone except Susan and Barty and the dratted bull. Judith was used to people falling for her charms.

'Well, ChiChu, now you're a soldier on the home front,' said Susan. 'Fighting Hitler, not Franco.'

'One day,' said ChiChu, 'I fix tractor in one day. Then you can drag potatoes to market.'

The tyres were worn but not perished and, on moving the tractor, they discovered a working trailer upended behind it. And behind that, three rusty cans of petrol, only half evaporated. 'This'll do to start. Susan will need to apply for coupons after this,' said Judith.

In the event it took ChiChu two days to do the job. Still, the others heaped praise on her for the workmanlike way in which she excavated every removable bit of the engine, scraped off the rust, cleaned it, oiled it and slotted it back into its correct place. At the end of the second day Judith climbed up into the driving seat. Keziah performed her cranking task and they all jumped as they heard the engine sputter, then roar into life.

'Now then, comrades,' said Susan. 'At the very least we can move the potatoes and get them down to the market. We can plough the bottom fields. Plant some oats, mebbe. Stir the land again. Make it feel wanted.'

'And what about old Strophair?' said Judith.

Susan shrugged. 'That old devil can skulk up in the top fields as much as he likes. We can get on with things down here. We don't need him.'

'He won't like that, from what I see of him,' said Keziah.

'Well, hard cheese, that's what I say to him,' said Susan. 'Hard cheese.'

Chapter Seventeen

Keeping a Secret

Toro these days only emitted the occasional roar in anger. He pawed the cobbles on the yard only for effect. He had a good life. His improvised stall in the dairy was now clean and sweet. ChiChu saw to it that he had fresh straw every day and food as a matter of routine. His coat was clean and his hoofs shone with ChiChu's attention. He appeared to relish his daily wanderings with her in the lane and the field. He did not even object too much when she attached her stick and rope to his nose ring to lead him along. She even washed the mud off his hoofs when they returned to the dairy.

Every so often a farmer from another part of the dale would come with a trailer to take him off to play the sire with another field of cows. The better farm-keeping at Goshawk Shield was noted. The benefit of the land girls was mooted in the district. It seemed that these women had certainly brought Goshawk Shield into better fettle; they and that Gomersal woman who was there with some foreign children. Old Strophair complained at the Thursday market that his place was crawling with foreigners.

Still it was acknowledged that Susan Cornford Gomersal had been no mean slouch in the years she held Goshawk Shield. Be she a woman. But Strophair might not be wrong about the Spanish girl who had charge of the bull. She was probably all right, but she didn't seem able to speak a word of English. It worried you, that. There were all those warnings on the wireless. Things in the paper about rescuing foreigners. Strophair might just be right.

Toro's performance at stud proved very effective and more farmers showed interest in his services. Strophair benefited. It was he who talked to the farmer; he who pocketed the money. He complained to the farmers about the Spanish girl but still allowed her to lead out the big bull and walk him up the ramps of the customers' carts. That way the bull was no trouble: never any trouble when he was handled by the Spanish girl.

Judith and Keziah worked shoulder to shoulder every day. They ploughed the potato field and got two fields, which had been let fallow for two years, ready for planting with oats. They helped with the chickens and reopened the old pigsties to house four young pigs whose only interests in life were rolling in mud and the source of their next meal.

Judith took the Welsh cob into her special care. When she observed that Strophair had left him behind, she groomed him. She took every chance to ride him in her crowded daylight hours. She used him for some of the farm tasks. But this was only possible when Strophair was away from the farm.

One afternoon she asked Susan to ride pillion and they rode the boundaries of the farm. Susan pointed out and named the fields and farms which pockmarked the green lowlands and the grey highlands of the fell. She pointed out Bittern Crag Farm where her mother had been born and where she had first opened her eyes.

Back at the farmyard, Susan hauled her aching bones off the horse and watched as Judith jumped lightly down. 'You like all this, the land and that,' she said. 'I wouldn't 'a thought you the type.'

'Love it. I'd forgotten how good it was. Used to do it for fun up in Northumberland.' She surveyed her muck-set hands and broken fingernails. 'Though, to be honest, I was never so filthy, never worked so hard.'

They watched ChiChu march across the yard, a towel over her shoulder for her evening tryst with Toro. 'What a strange child that is.'

'I've told you. She is not a child. She is a young woman.'

'She seems one. Locked away there in her own little world. Never speaking.'

'She does speak,' objected Susan. 'In Spain she was a real chatterbox.'

'That would be in her own tongue, of course.'

'No. English as well. She learned quite a lot. And then some more in London. Now she seems to have lost much of it. Though she knows what goes on.'

'So she's kind of dumb?'

'No. Not at all.' Susan thought of the stream of Catalan which ChiChu muttered at night in those strange prayers of hers, when she thought she was unheard. 'I think she's not so happy. Has kind of gone into a shell. It's not about the English. Like I told you, she understands everything we say.' She paused. 'When I was at the hospital – the mental hospital, Park View? You'll have heard of it? – there was a woman there, dumb as a cluck. Couldn't say a word. But up to twenty years old she could talk as well as anyone. Well, she had a baby and . . . it died. They said she did it. Killed it, like. Though it was never proved. Something clicked in her and she never spoke again. Twenty years she was in there, she never spoke.'

'You're not saying ChiChu killed a baby!'

'No. No. Though who knows what happened when she was fighting? But her family has all been killed. Blown up by a bomb from her own side. Such a waste. Now she's stuck here in this country. Maybe it is just too much. There's times, though,' she paused, 'it seems to me she's not too unhappy. Not all the time.'

Judith nodded. 'She loves that bull.'

Susan smiled. 'He reminds her of Spain, though he's a midget compared with those Spanish bulls. He is some kind of comfort.'

'Did you ever see a bullfight?'

Susan shuddered and shook her head. 'Never got to that. But some of the people I met had a great love for the bullfight. It's special to them. Not much of it in the war. Bullfighters mostly fought for the other side.'

'It's strange, though. Such a strange thing to do. How can she pet that bull, knowing what they do to them in Spain? Primitive, when you think of it.'

'No stranger than fox-hunting, when you think about it,' Susan echoed her words. 'I bet you've been blooded along with those other hunters and shooters.'

Judith laughed. 'Now there you have me,' she said. 'Clever Susan. More to you than meets the eye.'

That night after supper Judith took a lamp and walked round the buildings on the nightly check which Susan had inaugurated. She ventured into the dairy and even before she saw him, she could feel Toro's breathing, rustling presence. She drew nearer and held the Tilley lamp up high. She moved across to the bull's stall. She could see little more than the bull's sturdy hindquarters and swishing tail. She stood on her tiptoes till the gleam of the lamp caught his rolling eye as he twisted his head towards her. For one second his eye surveyed her, then he bellowed. The hair on the back of her neck stood up, her grasp loosened and she fell back against a rough tweed coat.

'Now then,' a voice growled behind her. 'Disturbing me bull, are yeh? Fancy yersel', nae doubt.' A hand grasped her upper arm. She could smell him. She pulled it away.

'I was just—'

His hold tightened on her. 'Yer knaa, it's dangerous in here. This'n's no lady's pet like yon dog. Yer want nothing just doing anything in here.' Then he pulled her round and had her pressed against the stall. He put his face against hers. She could smell smoke, whisky and half-digested food. She turned away, pulling her face as far away from his as she could. She opened her mouth to scream and his seamy, leathery hand pressed over her face. His lower body was pressing on her and she could feel his knuckles as he scrabbled and pulled at the string round his waist to loosen it.

Beside them in the stall, Toro pawed the ground and snorted softly to himself. Judith closed her eyes tight and pulled away as far as she could from the pressing hand, the enveloping body. The smell of old sweat and alcohol was making her heave. She heard the door scrape open and the light voice of the Spanish girl. '*He, Toro!*'

Strophair let Judith go and turned to face the Spanish girl, who stood before him, her eyes glittering in the light of Judith's lamp, a long hayfork in her hand. She jabbed this towards the farmer. '*He, Toro!*' she said, poking his shoulder. He tried to grab the fork and she flicked it away from him. Then she jabbed again, this time near his face. He flinched, ducked under it and edged back to the far wall, towards the door. She jabbed at his legs and he jumped a little in the air.

'Bloody foreigners,' he spat at her. 'Get back to your own place, will you? Spies, every last one of you. Germans, Eyeties, Spanish. Put the lot of you all behind bars.' He'd felt his way now to the door. He slipped backwards into the darkness and they could hear his voice rasping towards them. 'Bloody foreigners. They should shoot the lot of you.'

Judith breathed out. She rubbed her right arm down her face with the sleeve of her jumper, trying to scour away the marks of those leathery fingers. 'I say, thank you,' she said to the watching ChiChu. 'You saved me from . . . well.'

'Is all right?' said ChiChu.

'I'm all right. No harm done,' said Judith.

'Harm done?' said ChiChu.

'I am all right,' said Judith. 'Thank you.'

ChiChu went across to the stall and peered at the restless bull. 'Toro all right,' she said. 'I hear him shout.' She started to murmur at him in Catalan and Judith felt on the edge, left out. She picked up her lamp and made her way back towards the house.

Seconds later ChiChu caught up with her. Judith stopped and faced her. 'Don't say anything,' she said. 'Don't say anything to Susan or Keziah. About Strophair.' She took the other girl's arm. 'Do you understand? Don't say anything. I wouldn't fancy the fuss. You see? Too boring. Keep it a secret. It's better all round.' She had learned that with her uncle: you just kept quiet. People could be very boring.

ChiChu nodded. 'Is secret,' she said. 'Better all round.'

Chapter Eighteen

Dancing Lesson

With the advent of the other two women in the household Susan began to look more closely again at ChiChu, seeing them a little through their eyes. She'd become accustomed to the girl's quiet ways about the house and the farm, to the nightly flood of prayers in Catalan, to her dour presence in the kitchen whittling her wood. She missed the bright chirpy girl who had helped her so willingly, with such laughter, at the dressing station in the white-washed church on the edge of the sierra.

One night she waited until ChiChu had finished her nightly prayers, then she spoke herself. 'Do you pray to God, ChiChu?' she said very slowly. 'You seem to be praying so much now. What is it that you pray for?'

ChiChu's face was blank. 'God. No God. There is no God, Susan.'

'But every night. You pray long prayers . . .' She put her hands together and bowed her head. 'Pray to God,' she said.

A rare laugh escaped from ChiChu. She shook her head. 'I not pray,' she said. 'I talk to my grandmother. My *Avia*.'

251

Theatrically, Susan looked round their room. 'But there is no grandmother here, ChiChu.'

ChiChu tapped her head. 'She is here. I talk to her and I know who I am.'

'Does she talk to you?'

Again that strong, pealing laugh. 'No. No, Susan. She is dead. I have told you this.'

Susan shook her head. Then she pointed to herself. 'Me, ChiChu. I will listen. You can talk to me. We talked in Spain.'

'Is different then. Is my home. I talk to you. In those days I talk to Sofia in my tongue. Is mixed up but is all right. But is different here. Is your home. The words crackle in my ears like bullets. To my grandmother I talk in my heart's language.'

Susan went to the bed and touched the narrow shoulder, rigid under the blanket. 'I'm your family now, ChiChu. You're my dark-eyed girl. Just like Barty there is my little boy. This is my country and so it is your country, and his. This is my language and somehow it has to be yours. Speak with your *Avia*, ChiChu. Speak with her. But you will have to speak with me and with all the people here. You must try. Or you'll be lost.' She thought of the poor lost creature at Park View who never spoke. 'I don't want to lose you. You're my girl. I am alone and you are alone so we must be together.'

ChiChu turned sideways and kissed the hand that was touching her shoulder. 'Is all right, Susan. You see.' Then she closed her dark eyes and seemed to sleep in an instant with Susan still sitting beside her.

Susan sat there as the room sank into deeper darkness, wondering if ChiChu had understood what she tried to say. Living here in Theo's shadow, and in the darker shadow of her grandmother, she had often felt that she belonged nowhere, to no one. Even at the hospital with its almost vexatious comradeship she'd always felt somewhere out there on the edge of things. Then in Spain, in the end the only Englishwoman in the clinic, she was still the outsider. But then ChiChu came along with Bartolomeo in her wake, and things changed. In her mind the two of them were linked together with her. For a time they were a temporary family of war, a fleeting, fragile thing, like a half-unfurled butterfly. Now time had moved on and the three of them were solid, like a stone chapel. This was the way she wished to keep it. She could not have said all this to ChiChu, even if she could have spoken it in Catalan. The fells were a quiet, still place and those who grew up there knew that keeping a still tongue was one way of retaining the calm. The keeping of secrets was a way of living together.

The next day, it seemed that Susan's words had had some effect. ChiChu went out of her way to ask Judith about the tractor. She oiled the bolt which held the trailer secure so that Judith could uncouple it more easily. She pointed to Judith's hands. 'You hurt hands,' she said.

Judith surveyed her split fingernails and laughed. 'Do you know, ChiChu, I used to paint them every night. My fingernails?'

'Paint them?'

'Yes. Red of the Orient, the colour was called.'

ChiChu grinned. 'Yeah,' she said. 'Like Carole Lombard. Red nails. Great film star. I see her at the cinema in Barcelona.'

Judith laughed. 'Carole Lombard? You're full of surprises, ChiChu.'

Keziah came into the shed. 'I am going to Stanhope,' she announced. 'Susan knows a butcher who'll exchange our spare eggs for sausages.'

'Ooh! Bangers,' said Judith. 'I love bangers. Sizzling in a pan on a cold night. On bonfire night. Ooh!'

'If you give me a lift down to the road,' Keziah nodded at the old tractor, 'I'll catch the bus from there.' Later that day, she walked back up the hill with her shoulder sack full of sausages, a bag of nails to mend the cowshed roof and some off-coupon lining material.

ChiChu held the fabric and turned it in the lamplight, exclaiming how it changed colours in the light. 'Very pretty,' she said.

'Guess what?' said Keziah. 'Dance down in Stanhope on Friday. Girl in the butcher's told us. They're supplying pies and there will be beer. The soldier boys from the camp go there to dance. I thought I'd fake up a blouse or scarf or something with this.'

Judith picked up the fabric. 'I can make you a blouse with this.'

'You! Sew?' said Keziah.

'Don't snort,' said Judith. 'I used to make my own blouses with two silk handkerchiefs, with a kind of halter neck. So!'

'If you think you can,' said Keziah doubtfully.

'It will make a lovely blouse,' said Judith. 'And I can make you a bandeau too, to match. The soldier boys will not resist you.'

'Will you come?' asked Keziah. 'You come too.'

Judith frowned. 'Me. I don't know that—'

'Too snobby to come?' said Keziah. 'Officers only, is it, for your lot?'

The other girl shrugged. 'I'd go for the fun of it.' She

turned to ChiChu. 'You go too, ChiChu. Let's make a party.'

'Yeah,' said Keziah. 'You can dance the flamenco. I saw it at the pictures.' She stood up, stuck her chin in the air, gathered handfuls of trouser in her hands and stamped hard on the floor. 'Oh lay!'

ChiChu laughed loud and hard, finally sitting down and holding her sides. 'Oh, Keziah! So funny.'

'Well then,' said Keziah. 'Worth that to see you laugh, young'un.'

On the following nights, after their supper, and after Mr Strophair had stumped off to his back room, the three young women plotted what they would wear for the dance. Judith, as she hinted, was a fair hand with a needle and made a very good job of Keziah's handkerchief blouse. She even embroidered the matching bandeau. For ChiChu, she shortened a green skirt belonging to Susan and took in the seams of one of her own cream blouses. ChiChu stood bemused but compliant as these garments were pinned and tucked around her. She was swept along into attending the dance but warned the other two very primly that there would be 'No flamenco, only *gitanas*; gypsies do flamenco.'

On the Friday there was serious discussion about ChiChu's legs. 'You cannot wear socks,' said Keziah. 'They would think some school kid had tagged along.'

'School kid?' ChiChu frowned.

'Little child who goes to school,' said Susan from the table, where she had some ministry forms spread out before her.

'I no school kid,' said ChiChu.

'Then you must wear stockings,' said Keziah.

'No need,' said Judith. 'Pull up your skirt, ChiChu.'

She yanked the girl's skirt up around her thighs. 'Brown legs, see? Better than any stockings. Doesn't even need gravy browning.'

'Bare legs!' said Keziah contemptuously. 'Not respectable, bare legs. Me mother would have a fit.'

'We'll paint her a seam and no one will notice the difference, you'll see.'

So they did. At six o'clock on Friday evening, they were all dressed and ready to go. Judith had larded her special Pond's cream on all their weathered faces and lent Keziah her lipstick. They had tried lipstick on ChiChu but she had rubbed it off, saying only very bad girls wore paint on their faces.

When they arrived, a small man in an unmatched suit was scattering white powder on the floor and the band (which consisted of a pubescent girl with a trombone, a grey-haired woman on drums and an old man on the piano) was just wheezing into life. There were cups of tea for sale from a table at one end of the hall, but no signs of the promised beer. There was a scattering of men, but no sign of anyone in uniform.

Keziah groaned. 'Why did we say we would come? What a disaster. All this effort.' She looked good. The halter neck showed off her pretty shoulders, and a night of agony with rag curlers in her hair had paid off. Susan had assured her she was the very spit of Margaret Lockwood.

'It was your idea,' said Judith, lighting a cigarette. 'Now you'll just have to grin and bear it.'

The old man at the piano asked the smiling, scattered crowd if they would take their partners for the foxtrot. Judith tapped her cigarette in the ashtray until it was cold and then put it carefully back in her silver cigarette case.

'Might as well teach old ChiChu here to dance. If she can't even do the flamenco, she'll have to do something.' She dragged the protesting ChiChu on to the floor and, taking the part of the man herself, she began to demonstrate the steps. At first ChiChu stumbled, half laughing, half falling on the floor. Then the music clicked inside her and it was easier to follow Judith's strong lead. After that the rhythm changed and Keziah showed her the waltz. Then they changed over and Judith waltzed with her. Then Keziah did the foxtrot. After four dances, they collapsed behind the long wooden table and Judith went to get them some more tea.

She came back and announced that the town boys had arrived, and so had the soldier boys. She nodded towards the doors with their battered scout notices. Bringing in the night cold air and the smell of tobacco ground into cloth, came soldiers of every size and shape. They trickled in ones and twos: tall ones and short ones, fat ones and thin ones, those who wore their uniform like a tailor's dummy and those who looked as though they had tied on their khaki sackcloth with string.

'Now,' said Keziah. 'This is more like it.' She sat there and eyed the throng, while Judith and ChiChu sat with their backs to the dance floor which was now filling with people.

Keziah agreed to dance with a corporal with a very fetching moustache and was whirled away in a Viennese waltz. ChiChu turned wary eyes to Judith. 'I will not dance with man,' she said. 'They talk.'

'Don't worry.' Judith stood up. 'We'll go to the ladies' and powder our noses.' They set off down the dance floor, Judith's arm firmly through ChiChu's. Halfway down, they were stopped by a short soldier with fair, bristling hair. He put a hand on ChiChu's arm. 'You dancin'?' he said.

Judith pulled her away. 'No, she's not dancing,' she said.

The man clung on to ChiChu's arm. 'Whassa matter, sweetheart, got no tongue in yer head, is that it?'

ChiChu pulled her arm away. 'I not dance,' she said stiffly.

'I not dance. *I not dance*,' he said. 'What have we here? A foreigner. Eyetie if I'm not mistaken. Mussolini Mata Hari? I thought we'd shipped those fancies out.'

'She's not Italian,' said Judith firmly. 'She's Spanish.'

The man made another grab at ChiChu. 'Same difference,' he said. 'A Franco special.'

ChiChu's eyes flashed. 'Franco?' she said. 'Franco?' Her hand came back and she punched him so hard she caught him off balance and he fell to the floor. A girl shouted 'Shame! That lass has felled him, see that? That gypsy's cracked that lad.' Heads turned; there was a general swell of movement in their direction. Judith grabbed ChiChu and hauled her through the gathering crowd to the safety of the ladies' toilets. They stayed there for five minutes while Judith peeped through the door. Three feet away from the door stood the blond soldier with a mate who seemed twice as big. She shut the door with a click. 'Why d'you do that, ChiChu?' she said crossly. 'Those chaps are out to get the pair of us now. Why d'you do it?'

'Franco special?' said ChiChu steadily. 'If I have a gun, I kill him.' Her lips pressed together in a tight smile. 'I cannot let him say that about Franco.' In fact it had given her great satisfaction to land that blow. All the difficulties in this strange cold land, had, for a second, been resolved in that single action. She nodded at Judith. 'I cannot let him say it.'

The music swelled and faded outside. Girls came in and out of the toilets, eyeing them curiously as they leaned towards the mirror to outline their mouths in precious lipstick. The story of the foreign girl felling the soldier had spread quickly through the hall and some of the women came here answering not the call of nature, but their own scandalized curiosity. Some of them muttered things about foreigners and traitors into the mirror but no one challenged the two women in the corner.

The word of the fight finally reached Keziah and she came bursting into the little room, saying, 'What have you done, ChiChu? What have you done?'

'All she did was sock this fellow who was getting above himself,' said Judith. 'I'd have done the same myself.'

'Well there's nine of them waiting outside now,' said Keziah. 'You'll never get out that way.'

'The window.' ChiChu nodded at the window above the sink. 'I climb through the window.'

'Yeah,' said Judith. 'We could do that. But then we've gotta get through the town. And then there's the bus. They'll catch us at the bus stop.'

Keziah frowned. 'I know. I've got it. Lad I'm dancing with is keen as mustard, an' he's purloined a Jeep. I'll get him round the back and he can get us home in the Jeep.'

Judith frowned. 'Will he do that, do you think?'

Keziah grinned. 'He will if I dangle a carrot in front of him, won't he?'

Keziah took her time. She washed her hands carefully and put on fresh lipstick. Then she went out of the door and walked calmly through the gathering crowd of soldiers.

Inside, Judith opened the window wide, scrambled through and jumped into the alleyway beyond. She waited until ChiChu appeared and held out her arms to break the slighter girl's fall.

ChiChu started to laugh.

'Sshh!' said Judith. 'They'll be howling round here like dogs.'

A horn pipped from the end of the alley and Keziah's voice came hoarsely to them. 'Come on, you two. Come on, will you?' They jumped into the back of the Jeep and fell on to coiled ropes and a heap of waterproof capes. The engine revved up and they were away, out of the town and along the country tracks, retracing the route of the bus that had brought them here.

The Jeep raced along the lanes, despite the pitch-darkness of the blackout and the headlights being reduced to a mere slit of light. They thought the soldier would drop them at the bottom of the hill at the bus stop, but he turned the wheel and careered up the hill in the tracks of the old tractor.

Shaken and sore, they jumped out of the back and came round to the front to see Keziah's grinning face. 'Good ride, eh?'

Judith leaned inward to catch sight of the soldier who was driving. 'Thank you. Saved our lives, I should think.'

He coughed nervously. 'Don't tell no one,' he said. 'Don't tell a bleedin' soul.'

'You just go in,' said Keziah. 'Tell Susan I'll be in in a minute.'

Susan listened carefully to their tale, then peered through the kitchen curtains. 'I hope she's all right.'

'A carrot,' announced ChiChu. 'She is giving him a carrot.' She looked very young indeed in the light of the lamp. 'Keziah say she give him a carrot.'

Susan adjusted the blackout curtain and glanced at Judith.

Judith said, 'ChiChu, I—'

ChiChu shut Judith up with a flutter of her short fingers. 'Is all right, Susan. There was much carroting in my war. Is useful, sometimes.'

Judith and Susan were still smiling when Keziah came in twenty minutes later. 'Well?' demanded Susan.

Keziah groaned. 'Don't come the old mother on me, Susie. He was a nice man and he did us a great favour and he is posted, he knows not where, tomorrow.'

Judith said, 'ChiChu called it "carroting". She said they did much carroting in her war.'

Upstairs ChiChu heard their laughter. She twisted and turned in the bed. She had started to tell her *Avia* about it all but for the first time her words fell into the empty darkness.

'*Avia . . . Avia*,' she said. But her grandmother was not there. She'd floated away into the cold winter night, up above this pale, dark country, back to the brightness of the southern sun. ChiChu pulled the blanket right up to her chin. Well, there was Judith to talk to now, as well as Susan and her friend Keziah. They'd have to do. It would mean she would have to cobble together words in this scratchy language of theirs. But that would have to do. Her grandmother was no longer tied to her. Now she could go free.

Chapter Nineteen

No Longer on the Sidelines

Theo Maichin surveyed the thin, resigned face before her. 'So how are they treating you, old friend?'

Mr Walstein looked back keenly through his glasses. 'It is uncomfortable here, Mrs Theodora, but no more uncomfortable than the conditions of our soldiers in North Africa.'

She glanced round. 'This looks so very grim.'

'There are unhappy people in this place, Mrs Theodora. People who love this country and are troubled by the suspicion which falls on them.' He paused. 'But they say that this must happen. They accept it, as I do.'

'How do you pass the time?'

'There is a library. I mend violins and violas. There are some good musicians in here. The greatest of these is a German fellow who played once with the great orchestra of the Vienna State Opera. He played in a café in London before they came for him.'

'Does he play in here?'

'We have a little orchestra and we listen to some very fine music.'

'So it is not so bad?' Her heart was heavy and she was

looking for his permission to feel less guilty about this impertinent incarceration.

'The body is well, Mrs Theodora. Sustained by the warmth of comrades who suffer also. But the spirit . . .'

'The spirit?' she prompted, her heart sinking.

He grasped her hand so hard that her rings cut into the flesh. 'It is very low, Mrs Theodora. Perhaps God has let me see a measure of what my brother and his wife and little Madeleine suffered before—'

'No, Mr Walstein,' she protested. 'We're not like that! They were animals, those people.'

'Perhaps it started like this.' He sighed. 'Perhaps we are all made animals if we feel under threat. They are not so . . . terrible here, I suppose. Doing their job. But they are suspicious of each one of us. As though we would hurt them. Sometimes my spirit wishes to cry.' He caught sight of the tears in her eyes. 'No, dear lady, no! You cheer me. The very sight of your dear face cheers me. I will not have you here and make you sad.' He handed her his handkerchief, neatly folded although slightly washed out.

She dabbed her eyes and handed it back, smiling with some effort. 'It's I should be comforting you, Mr Walstein.'

'And you do, dear lady. And you do!' He looked at her over his glasses. 'Is there news of young ChiChu and your sister with their baby? Are they safe?'

She smiled more easily now. 'Well, Susan's not the best of correspondents, but it seems they are all well there up in the country. Susan has just about taken over the farm and ChiChu has found herself a bull to take care of. And the farm has land girls.'

Mr Walstein frowned. 'These are . . . ?'

'The Government sends strong young women to help on the farm.'

'The Government sends . . . So they will know about ChiChu, the Government?'

'I don't know.'

'They will put ChiChu in a place like this,' he said sadly. 'They find out and intern her.'

'No. No. She's a child.'

'She is a young woman, made into a child by being a stranger in a strange land. It makes children of us all. There are real children here,' he said. 'Some very nice children.'

Theo glanced at her small gold watch. 'I must go,' she said. 'I'll miss my train.'

He stood up, clicked his heels together and bent his head over her hand. 'Do not worry about me here, Mrs Theodora. I am safe here.'

'I promise you . . . I promise you I will do something.'

He shook his head. 'Do something about young ChiChu. She should not come here, or any place like this.' His voice was desolate and Theo knew he was thinking not about ChiChu but about Madeleine, his lost niece.

Later that day, as Theo made her way through the dim London afternoon, her mind was on the problem of Mr Walstein. Coming out of the underground she was so preoccupied that she bumped into a man and was held at arm's distance for a few seconds before she recognized him. In officer's uniform and smart cap he was very different from when she'd last seen him. 'Aunt Theodora. In a brown study? Is that not what they call it?'

'Aaron Maichin,' she said. 'How did you jump from nowhere?'

'I saw you from the other end of the platform and ran

to meet you this way. Turned a corner and we clashed.'

'Well!' She pulled her sleeves down and smoothed her jacket. 'What are you doing in Islington? I thought you were abroad, in some mysterious place.'

'Coming to see you, and the others. I've a day's leave before going off to . . . going off. Thought I'd check how you were. The bombing has been bad.'

'We don't need checking,' she said sourly.

'Sorry about that. I just wished . . . to see you all again.'

She smiled suddenly. 'I'm sorry, Aaron. I'm a bit preoccupied. I've just been to see my old friend Mr Walstein, locked up like a criminal for the crime of being one of Hitler's victims,' she said glumly. 'Anyway, come home with me. It'll be dark soon, and these roads get pitch-black without the streetlights.'

He offered her his arm. 'Where've you been? An internment camp, wasn't it?'

'Such a very sad place.'

'They had to do it, you know.'

'They didn't intern you and you're not English.' She picked her way delicately round a wire fence placed to stop pedestrians falling into a substantial bomb hole.

'So you said, that other time. But there must be thousands there who can prove their absolute loyalty. It's not their fault but it's a wise precaution. I say that and I've had some friends taken.'

'It's so undiscriminating.'

'Yes. Well. I heard that Mr Churchill insisted on an absolute clean sweep. To get rid of the uncertainty, you know? Fifth column and all that. Foreign types in our midst.'

Theo pulled her arm away and hurried on ahead of him. 'Mr Walstein is not a foreign type. He's an individual.

He's loyal. He loves this country.'

Aaron caught up with her and took her arm again. 'It's sad, I know, but in this war to think of the individual is dangerous. It's like the army. An individual has to be sacrificed for the good of his brigade, his side. That's what he signed on for.'

'But civilians don't sign on, Aaron. They get swept up in things. Mr Walstein did sign on by coming here to England, I suppose, and not going to America. But they take no notice of that.'

'Sometimes such things are necessary.' His tone had stopped being conciliatory. Now it was hard as ice. She shivered, glad that the house loomed before them and she could distract herself with the issue of keys and doors. There was something, something about him that made her think again of his father, her brother Edward. She set him to stoke the kitchen fire and put the kettle on while she went upstairs to change.

When she came back down he looked much less intimidating. He had his cap and jacket off and was standing in his army braces, pouring out tea. He smiled at her. 'I heard you coming so I started to pour. I hope this is all right?'

She sat down at the table and pulled her cup and saucer towards her, suddenly at ease with him and, to her surprise, trusting him. 'My manners tell me I must say how nice it is of you to call again.'

'My instinct tells me you are not really pleased at me calling.' He frowned slightly. 'To be honest, I would have thought it not a bad thing, to find a long-lost relative. That you might welcome it.'

'Well . . .' she hesitated.

'It's my father, isn't it?' he said abruptly.

She found herself blushing. 'He was young when he left,' she hesitated. 'He was quite a cold person.'

'Cold as ice,' he agreed.

She looked at him very carefully. 'He had been very cruel to . . . people. He had—'

Aaron interrupted her. 'He met my mother just after the war with the Boers. She said he dazzled her. Like a golden god, she said, with a silver tongue.'

Theo nodded. 'He broke hearts in Wales, where we started out.'

'My mother's father was like your friend from Germany, but he came away after the Great War. He had a large shop in Jo'burg and had funded somebody who went off for gold and reaped some rewards. My mother and father had this grand wedding in too short an order to be respectable because a child was on the way. My grandfather gave them a good house. And I was born.'

'They were happy?'

'Yes. For a time they all thought he was wonderful. Sincere Christian and all that.'

'Then . . . ?'

'Then my mother had a son who was stillborn and he was horrible to her after that. He continued to be horrible to her but they hid it from my grandfather.' His jaw tightened. 'I remember I was only six but still I tried to get between them, but I got a good beating for my pains.'

'He could be very cruel,' she said with feeling. 'Then . . . ?'

'There was a scandal with a . . . well, a low woman who came to the house and begged for some help from him. The woman vanished then, and the police came for my father.'

'The police?'

'He took all the valuables in the house, all the gold from my grandfather's safe, and ran.'

'That was it?'

'Well, no. My mother was pregnant again and the baby and she were both lost this time. The beatings . . .' His voice faded away for a second. He coughed. 'Well, there was only my grandfather and me and we managed. He died in 1935 and that was when I decided to go to Spain. I was useful there, with my German. Hitler's spies were everywhere.'

'And Edward?' she said. 'Your father? Did you see him again?'

'Well, yes. In a manner of speaking. Just before my grandfather died, it was all over the papers. He had . . . well, there were another two women missing, who were found dead. He was arrested, but he escaped. The brother of one of the women tracked him right out in the country and shot him. It was all over the Jo'burg newspapers. Then my grandfather had his heart attack. After, I left for Spain.' His voice was hard and dry.

'So you knew him as a terrible man,' said Theo slowly. 'And he was a terrible boy before he left the country. So why would you want to come here, to search for me, to talk to me? I would think you would want to forget him and anything connected with him.'

Aaron leaned over and poured her another cup of tea. 'Well, I knew about you. Your books were sold in Jo'burg and he boasted about you. Then I met Susan Cornford in Barcelona. She mentioned the name. I knew my father and I loathed him in me. I wondered if there is another side to being a Maichin. In meeting you . . . well, to be honest . . . it's a relief.'

Theo relaxed. 'I am pleased. Pleased for you. There are

other Maichins up in Durham. It could be that some day you'll meet them. Get to know that other side. We are very ordinary. Mundane, even.'

'I don't believe it.' He smiled, and looked again, disturbingly, like his father, Edward. 'One day, though, I'll see them all. The war first, all this second.' He reached into the buttoned pocket of his shirt and took out a fountain pen and a small book. 'Now, I want you to tell me the name of your Jewish friend and the place where he's interned. Perhaps you can write a detailed letter to vouch for him and I will see where we can send it so it has the most effect. Maybe this kind of thing is a useless sacrifice of an individual. What cause is served by imprisoning an old man?'

Theo's heart lifted at his tone but one part of her still remained wary. He had his father's charm and liquid voice and he had been using them for an hour on her. She wondered even more so now that she knew he was half-German. Why had the authorities not picked him up in their clean sweep? Did his spying in Spain for the republicans excuse him? Did his fluency in German and his cross-cultural demeanour make him useful to intelligence here so they could forgive his indelicacy in having a German grandfather? She closed her eyes.

He leaped to his feet. 'Oh, you're tired, Theo. That long journey and all this talk has worn you out.'

His warm tone made her cross, but she was too tired to put him in his place. 'What about you, Aaron? Will you stay the night?'

He was already buckling on his tunic. 'No, no. I have to go. I have to meet someone in Central London in half an hour.'

'Aaron! It's half-past nine at night.'

He grinned at her, and looked suddenly very young. 'There's a war on, Auntie Theo. Had you not guessed?' He picked up his case and made for the door, pecking her on the cheek as he left. 'T.T.F.N. Is that what they say now? Ta-ta for now?'

She listened as the front door clicked shut behind him, muffled by the heavy blackout curtain slung behind it. She touched her cheek where he had kissed it. For a second, she felt young again herself. How nice it must be to be kissed on the cheek with intent. She had a number of men in her circle of friends and acquaintances, all of whom had been warm and attentive since her husband died. But she had never been tempted. Life was good and she had had one great love and would not tarnish that by scrambling around with ersatz imitation.

But that kiss on the cheek from the son of her errant brother had sent a ripple of life though her, had swept some surface clean which had been cluttered up within the past. The words came unbidden to her lips. 'I'm part of the human race again. I'm no longer on the sidelines.' She smiled wryly to herself. 'A fine time to discover that!'

Chapter Twenty

Cornered

Barry Strophair had stopped coming into the kitchen for his stew. He rode out every morning on his cob, his dog snapping at the clopping heels. Susan had seen him return one evening with the late dusk, the dog across his saddle. The next night the dog did not follow him out. She left it two nights and, having transferred the stew to one tin carrying cup, filled another with milk. Then she went down the corridor and knocked on the door of his room at the far end of the house. She could hear the breathing signs of life from inside, but there was no answer.

'Mr Strophair! Mr Strophair!' she shouted. 'I'm coming in with your dinner.'

'What is it?' The voice came to her from the dark recesses of a wooden porter's chair which had been pulled up to the sooty, glowing fire. 'What is it yer want?'

She put the two mugs on the mantelpiece. 'You didn't come for your dinner,' she said. 'I kept it for you.'

'I want nothing of your dinners.'

'You need something, out there on the fells.'

'Who says I was out on the fells? Who says I need dinner?'

Her eyes, used now to the gloom, caught the glitter of his from under his cap. 'Everybody needs dinner, Mr Strophair.'

He stood up and very deliberately tipped the contents of both the mugs on the fire, which spat, sizzled and smoked and settled down to fade away altogether.

He sat back into the chair and a waft of pure alcohol cut through the fug towards her.

'You've been in the Black Bull!' she said.

'They make you welcome there.'

'Did they feed you?'

'The missus gave us some of her hotpot.' There was no argument about that. He had paid her over the odds, from his bull money. She had been happy enough.

'Food went to waste here. Bad to waste when there's so much need around.'

She jumped as a cackle emerged from the dark shade of the chair. 'Pot of stew gunna win the war, eh?'

She folded her arms. 'What is it, Mr Strophair? Why won't you come for your dinner?'

'Lot of blasted witches. Set to poison any man.'

'That's not so.'

'Dinnet tell me it's not so. Yeh bring a foreigner in here, and your own bastard, and overrun the place with . . .' he paused then, chose his words carefully, '. . . bitches on heat.'

'Mr Strophair!'

'Yeh tek away me farm and me livelihood—'

'But you weren't farming it anyway. You'd not paid any rent to Mrs Lytton for two years. You were feeling low because of your Jack going away. It got too much for you.'

'Thieves and whores, the lot of you. I'll not eat food that you've touched, nor a drop that you've poured. I don't have to stay here, you know. There's other places.'

She grasped the edge of the table to stop herself lashing out at him. 'That's quite enough, Mr Strophair. I would not make you so much as a meat paste sandwich now. I take it that you'll fettle for yourself?'

He grunted and leaned forward to poke the fire and expose the last pale glowing cinder in the heap of silver-grey ash. 'Shut the door, behind yer, will yer?'

'He's gone potty,' she announced to the others, back in her own sitting room. 'Doolally.' She glanced at Keziah. 'Paranoid delusions to me and Keziah, who know about these things. I've seen saner people in Park View.'

Judith shuddered. 'He'll murder us in our beds,' she said.

'No,' said Susan comfortably. 'He's like a sad old fox in his lair. Toothless snarls are all he is up to. Talking about snarls, have you seen that dog of his around anywhere?'

'Delusions?' said ChiChu. 'Mr Strophair?'

Judith put her fingers to her head and made winding movements, then crossed her eyes. 'Mad! Mad! ChiChu.'

'Ah, *boig*! When he try kill you. He mad!'

'What!' said Susan.

'He had a go at me in the bull's place one night,' said Judith. 'But ChiChu here saved me with the hay fork.' She paused. 'It was something else he wanted. He didn't want to kill me.'

'You didn't say this,' said Susan. 'How d'you not say?'

'A secret,' said ChiChu.

'I'd 'a done him with more than the hay fork,' said Keziah, 'if I'd known.'

'Not worth the fuss,' said Judith. 'At the time. But now, if he's getting worse . . .'

'He didn't seem threatening to me.' But Susan was not

so sure any more. 'Like I say. He's just an old lame fox in his lair.'

'What about the dog?' said Judith. 'Was the dog there?'

Susan shook her head. 'No sign of the dog.'

'He'll have kicked it to death,' said Judith gloomily. 'You can bet on that.'

'So how was Jake? I see you had a letter.' Susan turned to Keziah.

The thin letter with its prison camp headings had arrived earlier that day. Keziah had taken it off to the bedroom to read it and then gone out to the beet field where she and Judith were working.

'Oh, he sounds quite chirpy, considering. They have classes and concerts and that. Not enough food but, like he says, there is a war on. He's probably covering things up but at least the letter got through. He mentioned you. He says that he remembers Spain and hopes you are all right. He says mebbe you could write to him.'

'Me?' Susan thought for a second of Jake in his mother's house arguing the rights and wrongs of Marxism. And in Spain, gaunt as a ghost, embittered and disillusioned. 'Why me?'

'He always liked yer. Right from the first.'

'News to me, that!'

'You couldn't see the signs. I've lived with him. Know the signs.'

Susan thought of the Italian commissar. 'I'm not too good at signs,' she said. 'Caused me many a slip.'

'Anyway, the more letters for him the better. Reminds him of the world out here. They don't all get through, so the more that go, the better chance he has of getting one.'

'All right. Though what I'll find to write about I don't know.'

MY DARK-EYED GIRL

As time went on she found a great deal to write about in her fortnightly letter to Jake Stanton. She wrote about Keziah and Judith and the battle to keep the farm productive; she wrote about Barty and how he was talking, how she wished she could teach him some Italian; she wrote about the coming of Captain Maichin like some kind of well-pressed angel to help her with the rescue of ChiChu and how she was closer to her than those of her own blood with the exception of Barty; how it reminded her of herself with her beloved foster mother, Rose Clare. She wrote about Theo, there in the London bombings, worrying about Mr Walstein who was in an internment camp which would not be as bad, she hoped, as the camp Jake was in. She told him how she worried about Theo, independent as she was. London was no place to be in this war.

In time she was to get a trickle of letters back. Jake wrote how he had enjoyed their conversations in the old house. How he had enjoyed their meetings in a foreign place – he never mentioned Spain – and felt she had done good work there. How he hoped to meet her in the future when he knew they would be the best of friends. He told her of the remarkable characters of the men he met in the camp, chaps he would never have met on the outside in a month of Sundays.

Keziah teased her when she got letters, pretending jealousy that Susan was the preferred correspondent. 'He's taken a shine to you, no doubt about it,' she said. 'Didn't I tell you?'

In the end Strophair stopped coming into the house altogether. He left the cob and went off to the fields with a pack on his back. Judith followed him on the horse and came back to tell them that he had holed up in one of the field barns by the Bottom Stream Field. He emerged and wandered the perimeters now and then. When Susan and Judith checked, the sheep seemed well enough out on the fell.

One day ChiChu took Toro for his customary walk round the yard, into the field and along the pathway. As always, the rope and the stick sustained a respectful distance between the two of them. Still, she felt easy with him, murmuring and reassuring him in Catalan as they made their way between the hedges. It was a crisp day, very clear. The crag before her was etched in grey against a silver-white sky.

Suddenly Toro stopped in his tracks and turned towards her, lurching too fast, too close.

'No, Toro! No!' she said.

Then there was a crack like the breaking of a sharp winter twig. The bull lurched right on to her and she was covered in blood, pinned by his hindquarters to the muddy earth. He moved and wriggled, exhaling bellows like the end of the world, and then he was still.

That was when she realised that the blood on her was his, not hers. It was pulsing from a gaping hole in his ear and spreading across her chest like a scummy red tide. Not for the first time, she could smell the blood of a new kill. She began to scream and her scream reached across the field to the farmhouse.

Keziah, who was milking, looked up, left the pail half full and started to run. Judith, who was feeding the pigs, started to run. Susan told Barty to stay exactly where he was and started to run. 'ChiChu!' she shouted. 'It's ChiChu.'

* * *

The snipers opposite have got to her in the end. One by one they have picked off the others. Then Esteban is blasted twice where he stands. His blood is pouring over her, it sticks to her hands as she tries to scrub it off her arms and her thighs. The smell of his blood is in her nostrils, inside the fibres of her head, it is rich, searing, too strong for a man. They are all there scrambling to get her, shouting in her ear. Jorge. Esteban. They are all leaning on her now. Their dead weight is unbearable. She cannot breathe. They are squashing the very breath from her body. But how can they do this? They are her friends, her comrades, her bosom mates. How can they do this?

She draws in the best breath she can and shouts, 'Esteban! Get off! Get away from me!'

Still in her dream, she was shouting in Catalan.

Keziah stopped heaving at the bloody inert body of the bull. 'What's she shouting?' she said.

'What do you think?' said Susan grimly. 'She's telling us to get this thing off her.'

Judith stood up. 'The tractor. I'll get the tractor and the rope.'

They tied the rope round the hindquarters of the bull and tethered it round the seat of the tractor.

'Gently now!' said Susan. She pushed at the head and neck of the bull, and Keziah pushed at the body so the weight of the bull as it was hauled did not drag on the unconscious ChiChu. 'Now!' called Susan. Swearing with desperation, Judith cranked the engine into life, then leaped on the tractor and put it into gear. 'Slowly,' Susan called again. 'Slowly.'

At first the tractor had no effect at all, it seemed to stand up on its back wheels in a paroxysm of effort. But then Judith put her foot hard on the throttle, the front end of the tractor started to move and the weight in the hands holding the bull off ChiChu's body became lighter. Inch by inch, the massive body was hauled on the dusty road and ChiChu was free.

Judith jumped off the tractor and ran to where Susan and Keziah were kneeling beside the bloody, inert body of ChiChu. 'The bastard!' said Judith.

'What?' said Susan. 'Poor old bull. It's hardly fair—'

'Not the bull. That bastard Strophair. He shot the bull. There. See? You can see to the bone. Behind his ear. The bull saved ChiChu. He would have got her. The bastard.'

Susan was feeling ChiChu through the sticky blood. 'She's not cut. The skin's not broken. This is all blood from the bull.'

'Bastard. I tell you he was aiming for her.' Judith pulled her khaki handkerchief from the pocket of her dungarees and started to wipe ChiChu's face. 'Bastard.'

'Judith!' protested Susan at last. 'No need for that.'

'There are worse words I wish I dare use,' said Judith rubbing away at ChiChu's neck now.

'Leave that,' said Susan. 'We need to get her into the house.'

She was surprisingly heavy for such a slender person and it took three of them to get her into the kitchen. Susan swept all the dishes and cutlery off the long table and they laid her on there, her limp arms arranged by her side. She stood looking at her.

In the corner, Barty howled. They ignored him and, working in grim silence, they stripped ChiChu down to her underbodice and pants and, with warm water, washed the blood from her body. 'Bad bruises to her shoulder and her chest,' said Susan. 'Can't tell whether there is a break. Inside, perhaps. She could have a broken rib.'

'She needs the hospital,' said Keziah.

'We need to get a policeman,' said Susan. 'There's that madman roving the hills with his gun.'

'We need to get the slaughterer,' said Judith, 'to move that poor beast from the pathway. Did you see his eyes were still open? Red-eyed anger wasn't in it.'

In the end they all went down to the town, Judith driving, the others in the trailer. Susan clutched Barty with one hand and held ChiChu still with the other. Keziah cradled ChiChu's head in her lap. She exclaimed as the trailer swung and bumped, Judith called back that there was nothing, nothing that she could do about it.

When they reached the road at last, the quiet air cracked with another snap of a rifle, and a bullet smashed the corner of the trailer.

'Hurry up!' screamed Keziah. 'Put your foot down, will you?'

They roared down the narrow track, then into the wide road. Here, the hourly bus passed them and the passengers peered out but it did not stop. They ignored as well the curious looks at the strange entourage as they drove through the town streets, their eyes on the groaning ChiChu.

The doctor came out in his waistcoat to look at ChiChu. He shook his head and told them to follow him into the hospital. There, two hefty female porters came and lifted her on to a stretcher, and she vanished through the doors. The doctor turned to them. 'They'll examine her closely, make sure nothing is cracked or broken. Come back later. They'll be able to tell you what's what then.'

'We should stay,' said Susan uncertainly, intimidated afresh by doctorly authority. She cursed those years at Park View for drilling that into her.

'I'll stay here,' said Judith, looking the doctor in the

eye. 'I'll stay near her. We're her family, Doctor. We need to watch over her.'

Barty was bawling again. The doctor looked at him, and at these scruffy farmer women, with some irritation. Bulls, bullets, and wild hill men! Isolation had its effects. Some of the new psychology in the journals referred to it, although battle trauma was more popular these days, it had to be admitted.

Outside, Susan said, 'We have to go to the police station to tell them about Strophair.' She was pleased to be out of the doctor's disdainful presence.

The police were as polite as had been the doctor but, given the wild appearance of the women, just a bit disbelieving.

'Just come and see the bull!' said Susan. 'What farmer would kill his own bull? Worth a lot of money, bulls. He was income, was this one. At stud. Much in demand. No, Strophair was aiming for ChiChu. At the girl who was injured.'

The sergeant licked his pencil and raised his brows. 'ChiChu,' he said. 'Now how would you spell that?'

'Her real name is Maria Josep. MARIA JOSEP,' she spelled it out.

'Looks foreign to me. And this is your daughter?' His brows climbed higher into his sandy hair.

'She is my foster daughter,' said Susan firmly. 'She is from Spain.'

'A gun, you say?'

'Yes,' put in Keziah with theatrical patience. She started to speak very slowly. 'He shot at ChiChu – at Maria Josep who is at the hospital – but missed her and hit the bull. The bull fell on her and, we think, cracked her shoulders and her ribs. She is at the hospital now, this minute.

Strophair is up there with his gun. He took another potshot at us as we came away with the trailer. He hit our trailer. You can come and see that if you want. It's outside. You can see the hole.'

He licked his pencil again. 'Trailer?'

'We brought her down on the tractor trailer because we did not wish to waste time.'

'Mmm.' He shut his ledger and called for a constable. 'Constable Meadows will return with you and . . . er . . . check the premises,' he said. 'You can take the bike,' he said to the constable. 'These . . . er . . . ladies'll give you a lift up an' you can ride back down, Meadows.'

Keziah told him to sling the bike into the trailer and hang on to it. 'Mind the little lad, mind! And my friend there.'

'We should go to the hospital,' said Susan. 'ChiChu—'

'Judith's there. She'll come and tell us. You'll see,' said Keziah. 'We need to see to this madman up at Goshawk Shield before we do anything else. Before he does any more damage. And Barty wants his dinner. He's been very patient, when you think of it.'

Chapter Twenty-One

A Bag of Money

Now the Spanish lass'd lost him his bull. Worth summat, that little feller. Jack had bred him up from a young 'un. Great breed, those Dexters. Tough'ns they were, even being so little. Cheap to feed. Sired half the dale had that'n. Farmers liked his offspring, all right, and would pay for it. Come to think of it, it was that bull caused Jack finally to go off to the Army. Stubborn was Jack. Thought the takings from the bull should be his own. No one'd have that. No sane father'd see that money go into someone else's long pocket, even his own son's. Kicked up a fuss, did Jack, but he'd stuck to his guns. He'd had Jack up against the doorway and told him clear into his face. 'My bull, son, d'yer hear? My bull, so any money for hiring him out's mine, see?' Jack was bigger than his father and stronger, but only rarely had he raised his hand to him. He'd had plenty to say for himself but had rarely struck out.

This time was no exception. He had handed over the sovereigns as meek as a lamb, even while he was mouthing obscenities at his father.

And when Jack was not there the next morning, not in

his bed, nor anywhere else on the farm, Strophair had said good riddance to bad rubbish. The money'd go in his own long pocket now. And it had done, ever since. Till yesterday.

Strophair went across to the crude window in the bricks in the side of the field barn which gave him a perfect view of what was going on around the farm. The beast was still there, legs stiff. What a waste. The butcher wouldn't take it. It'd go to Charlie Simmonson the slaughterer for dog meat. What a waste. No profit in that.

Strophair wiped the spittle from his face with his broad palm.

It should have been all right, really, with Jack gone. So much less of his particular lip made for an easier life. But them Gomersal lads got lippy in their turn and ran off to the Army. He only hoped they were lying now in some foreign field, their gizzards slit by some German bayonet, or their heads blown to pieces by some German gun. Even that would be too easy for them, the lazy kites.

It was *her* fault the beast died, of course. That foreign bit. *She* should be lying in some foreign field, slit by some German bayonet, or her head ripped off by some German gun. Instead, there she was with that flurry of old witches, and his poor old bull was dead on the path. She must 'a known. She moved deliberately into the shadow of the bull. He'd her heart lined up. Lined up proper, and she pulled back the bull's head in that last minute to protect herself. Now there he was, eyes rolled back, dead as mutton in the roadway. Not worth a penny.

He should never have let her, that foreign brat, take on the bull like that. She'd beguiled the both of them with that feeding and petting, that cleaning and brushing. It pleased the farmers to see the little bull, hoofs shining and head up. They'd not demurred when he put up the fee. So, then, he'd tolerated all that stuff.

But it was a mistake letting her make the bull her boon companion like that. That wily old thing had scented what was in the air, had read his thoughts. He had put his head up and scented the danger in the air, then took the bullet intended for her heart.

Strophair pulled back from the slit window and scratched around in the corner for the last of his food, the knuckle of bread in the white sack with the last of the whisky beside it. He swilled the drink round in the bottle for a moment, held it up in the dim light of the sheep pen. Then he put it to his lips and swigged it down.

He put his hand in the pocket of his corduroys and fingered the coins which were the last of his money. No matter, there was the roll in the house with the money from the last lamb sale. Good cash crop, lambs. And the ewes, no good to him now, got a fair price for them. Good money for a hard year's work. Tucked away safely. He frowned. The problem was, he was not quite sure where he'd put it. Of course he had celebrated the day of the sale, and crept home through the night. And he could remember rolling the money tight and tucking it . . . where? Somewhere. Somewhere in that house. He would have to find it. It was his. The bitches would not get it.

'He's not there.' The young constable filled the farmhouse doorway, a black shadow against the white light of the late afternoon. 'The old boy's gone. Place stank like a public house and there was an empty whisky bottle there.'

He was not a young man but his face had that peeled look of a young boy.

'Was the gun there?' said Keziah.

He shook his head.

'Didn't see him at all? He's up there on the fell somewhere with that gun,' said Susan.

'Are you sure there is a gun?'

'Did you see the bull in the drive?'

'Aye. Charlie Simmonson is over there with his block and tackle hauling him into his cart. I just passed him.'

'Well, that big hole just behind Toro's ear wasn't made by a cricket bat, I'm telling you. And, truth to tell, the bullet that killed the bull was not aimed at his precious bull, it was aimed at ChiChu,' said Susan.

'The girl in the hospital?'

'Yes, Constable.'

He looked at the women, who were eyeing him tensely. 'I really . . . well, mebbe I should get back, like. To report to the sergeant. There'll be no light at all soon and you canna even mek out the town with the blackout.'

'So you'll leave us up here then? Alone on the fell with a madman with a gun?' said Keziah.

He passed his helmet from hand to hand. 'Well, missis, I've no orders to stay. An' anyway, it could all have been an accident, like, an' the ole boy has panicked.'

'That ole boy, as you call him, has just killed a bull in mistake for a young girl. He has no money. He has no food. And he's out there on the fell. What do you really think your sergeant would say?'

Constable Meadows relaxed a bit then. The decision was made for him. In any case, a wobbly ride on his bike back to the station in the pitch dark would be no picnic.

'You're right, missis. I'll stop on. I'll just go down and ask old Simmonson if he'll drop a message in at the police station, like. Then the sergeant knows what I'm up to.'

'Right,' said Susan. 'You'd better get up and tell him and get yourself back here.'

He must have sprinted. He was back in a minute.

'Get yourself a seat,' said Keziah from the stove. 'I'm just brewing up.'

'Don't mind if I do.' He placed his helmet on the table under the window, and sat up to the table. He smiled up at her, a peculiar sweet smile. Keziah blinked at him, then poured his tea and put sugar in without asking him. He took a sip and smacked his lips. 'By, yer wouldn't think there was a war on. Two sugars.'

Keziah was pink. 'I . . . I . . .' she said.

'Don't you worry, Constable,' said Susan. 'It's off Keziah's coupons. I'll make sure of that.'

The constable slurped more of the dark, warm tea. 'Why, it's very nice of you . . . Keziah, is it?' He thrust a podgy hand out and grasped hers. 'Colin Meadows. Constable, that is.'

Keziah shook his hand hard, then dropped it. 'Constable Meadows,' she said.

'Colin. Colin. If that's all right,' he said comfortably. 'Seein' like we're gunna spend— well . . . I'll be here watching out for yeh.' He looked round. 'Do you have a wireless at all? I always like to follow the news. The war, you know.'

'You were blushing!' said Susan to Keziah later when they were making the most of the last of the sitting-room fire. 'That young policeman made you blush.'

'Get away,' said Keziah. 'Nothing of the sort, I'm telling you. He's very short for a policeman.'

'He has a nice little face, though,' said Susan thoughtfully. 'Kind of shining.'

Keziah stared at her. 'You noticed?' she said.

'I noticed you,' Susan said. 'I noticed your face.'

Keziah turned off the lamp. 'Bedtime,' she said, pleased that the dark was hiding her blushes.

'I wonder how ChiChu is,' said Susan as they made their way along the corridor.

'She's in the hospital,' said Keziah comfortably. 'And old Judith is there. She's in good hands.'

But Susan lay wide awake, listening to Barty's snuffling in the deep country darkness. ChiChu was on her mind. ChiChu with the viscous blood of the bull spilling on her jacket and splashing like deep red petals on her sallow skin. It seemed that on this fell pathway in the cool North, the sierra wind blew and the braided vines pushed forth their velvet grapes in spite of the spit of snipers' bullets.

Downstairs, Constable Colin Meadows wriggled to a more comfortable position on the long settee. He didn't quite know whether he was happy with this assignment. There was this mad farmer lurking round with a gun. And there were two women and the caterwauling child. But that younger woman, the one with the brown hair, she looked strong, nice. A man might do worse than that. In fact a man might do worse than a nice warm billet away from blackout breakers and petty thieves making the most of the dark streets.

His complacency lasted half an hour. After that the hard bench started to stick like knives into the small of his back. He sat up and cursed the settle he was lying on, the house that contained it and the women who inhabited it. Even if one of them had this turning-up nose and hair the colour of an old penny.

'What? What?' Susan shook herself awake. 'What is it?'

Keziah was beside her bed. Her face was close to Susan's. 'Can you hear it?' she whispered fiercely.

'What?' she whispered back.

Barty stirred and she stroked his cheek to settle him. As his bubbling moan faded she heard it. Furtive shuffling and things being dropped down below.

'The policeman,' she whispered. 'He's going outside to the lavatory.'

'Nah. It's the other end. Beyond the pantries,' whispered Keziah. 'Beyond the pantries. It's Strophair.'

Susan picked up the sleeping Barty in a bundle of bedclothes, took him on to the landing and deposited him in the big linen cupboard. He turned over in his new nest and returned to his profound sleep. She locked the door behind him. 'Now!' she whispered to Keziah. 'Let's see just what it is.'

They crept down the stairs. The noise of some wild activity became bold, unsecret. It emerged from Strophair's room at the far end of the corridor.

Susan clutched Keziah's arm. 'You go and get that policeman. Now!'

'You come.'

'No!' Susan turned away. 'Go and get him,' she whispered over her shoulder. 'He'd sleep through the blitz, that stupid copper.'

She edged along the dark corridor towards the room which now emanated crashes and bangs. The intruder had given up all thoughts of caution or subterfuge. She opened the door a crack and watched Strophair as he opened doors and cupboards and ripped the last blanket off the bed, pushed stools and chairs over.

She opened the door wider. 'Mr Strophair,' she said quietly. 'It's you.'

He whirled round and peered at her in the early morning gloom. 'What is it?'

'We were wondering where you were,' she said. 'What are you doing? This is a right mess in here.'

His mouth pulled back against his cheeks and his eyes gleamed. 'Where is it? Where've you put it, you old witch?'

She took a step forward. 'Where's what, Mr Strophair?'

'My lamb money. It's gone. The money for the lambs.'

'Where d'you put it? I didn't know you had it in here.'

He was silent for a second. 'It was in here. You bin rakin' around in 'ere. My money's gone.'

'Nobody's been in here,' she said steadily. 'Nobody ever comes in here.' She could see the rifle now, leaning against the fireplace. She did not look at it but she could see it. 'You know that. No one ever comes in here into your space. We'd not want to.'

Keeping his eye on her, he pulled open another cupboard.

'Was it a tin?' asked Susan, taking one step nearer. 'Was it a tin, Mr Strophair?'

He stared at her through bleary eyes, then shook his head. 'No. An oiled sack. Linen.'

'Well,' she smiled, keeping her tone casual, 'do you know, I did see one such jammed in the space between the big clock and the wall. In the kitchen, like. Getting up there to rake the biggest spider's web you ever saw. It's still there.'

'You stole it. Thieving witch,' he grunted.

'No, Mr Strophair.' She paused. 'I swear to you I did not move it, on my child's head; that it's still there.'

He sniffed. 'Bastard head. Not worth a light.'

She winced, fought down the well of anger inside her. 'Just go and see, Mr Strophair. You'll see if I'm lying. It was tied with baler twine. The stuff that keeps up your britches. Perhaps you put it there when you were . . . er . . . tired and forgot about it.' Another step forward. Now she was directly in front of him. 'Just come and see, won't you?' Her hand, palm up, went out towards him.

For a long second he met her gaze, his breath coming in heavy snorts.

Behind her, there was a clatter and Constable Colin Meadows' voice bellowed out, 'Hold it there, Strophair. Not a step! Stay just where you are!'

In a whirling movement Strophair grabbed Susan with one hand and the rifle with the other. She could feel the rifle rammed against her back like a second spine, the muzzle nestled against the base of her skull.

'You get back,' growled Strophair. 'Get yersel' back off here. Canna think why yeh're after me. These women, they're who you should be getting, witches all. And thieves. Stole one hundred and six pounds off me, they did. All I did was come back here to get it. Get me own money.' His voice rasped in her ear. She could smell tobacco and rotten teeth.

The constable had his hands up, palms out. 'Now, now, Mr Strophair! There's no need for any of this.'

Behind his worried baby face Susan could see Keziah's

face, wide-eyed and grey-white in the early light. 'Don't worry, Keziah,' she gasped. 'Mr Strophair, he's just made a mistake.' She gulped a breath. 'You, Constable, you just go back by the door there. That's right. Just by the door. You're crowding Mr Strophair, can't you see? He doesn't like to be crowded.'

She could feel Strophair relaxing behind her. The muzzle was not so tight to her skull. 'Now then, Keziah,' she went on. 'Are you there? Is that you in the passage?'

'Are you all right, Susan?' Keziah's terrified voice came from behind the constable's shoulder.

'Yes. Yes. But Mr Strophair is worried.' She waited for him to clutch her tighter and stop her speaking, but he didn't. 'He's lost something and he's very worried about it. Some money. But I think I know where it is.'

'Careful, Mrs Cornford,' said the constable. 'This man is dangerous.'

Strophair pulled her closer.

'Oh, Constable, will you shut up!' she said sharply. 'Keziah! Listen to me. The clock in the kitchen. Tucked up behind it, where you cannot see, there is an oiled bag. Linen. Like those bags we keep for scissors. You know. There's a bag with some papers in it. Some five-pound notes. Bring it here. That's what Mr Strophair wants. Go on, Keziah! Stop gawping. Use your initiative.'

Keziah scuttled away and the room was quiet again. She seemed to be away a long time. She must have run off. Who would blame her? It was certain death in here. Susan could smell Strophair's sour breath over her shoulder. She thought of the blood of the bull oozing over ChiChu's narrow chest. She was certain that Strophair would kill them all without compunction. Shoot her behind the ear just as he had shot the bull.

She thought of Barty in his blanket-nest in the cupboard upstairs; his curls and his smooth skin. She thought of Barty's father. If I am to die now, thank you, God, at least for that. For that time with him. But let Barty stay asleep. Don't let him find him. They'll come. They'll miss the constable at the police station and they'll come up quick. And they'll find Barty. So one good thing'll come out of this. No, two good things. At least ChiChu was all in one piece down there in the hospital. Her dark-eyed girl would survive.

Keziah's heavy tread echoed in the passage. Susan breathed out again. Keziah, flushed now, came into the room. She had a folded canvas sack in her hand. 'Is this what you meant, Susan?'

'Bring it over here for Mr Strophair.'

Slowly Keziah edged forward, her hand straight before her, proffering the package.

'Right here, Kezzie. Give it to Mr Strophair.'

Strophair's hand came out for his package and Susan flung herself at Keziah and they both fell to the floor. The rifle went off crack into the ceiling and the constable leaped forward and grabbed it out of Strophair's hands. Strophair was left in the middle of them all clutching his linen bag.

Susan and Keziah got to their feet and stood before him.

He scrabbled in the bag. 'This an't it,' he growled. 'This an't me money.' He lurched towards Susan. 'What've yeh done with it, yeh—' Now the constable had him pinioned, but he babbled on and on, shouting and raging, lost in some black world of his own.

Constable Meadows, holding on tight, looked at Susan. 'Is there anywhere we can lock him in, Mrs Cornford?

Till I get a police car up here to tek him down?'

Susan thought for a second. 'The bull room,' she said. 'Nice stout lock there. Strophair insisted on it.'

Two hours later they were standing down at the bottom field watching the constable load the yelling, swearing Strophair into the black car driven by the sergeant, when the bus drew up and Judith, less than her immaculate self, alighted.

'He was always absolutely insane, that man,' said Judith when they told their tale. 'Plain as the nose on your face. Should have been committed years ago.'

'Well, he was left up here on his own, struggling with the farm. His son left him to cope alone,' said Susan. 'He's a poor man, really.'

'Don't you go defending him,' said Keziah. 'That feller was one second short of shooting you, like he shot the bull. You count yourself lucky!'

'I thought you'd have run away, Keziah. High-tailed it out of here,' said Susan. 'Pleased you didn't.'

Keziah grunted. 'I was as quick as I could be. Took me a long time to find a linen bag and cut up sheets of the *Northern Echo* to fit.'

'Anyway, it did the trick. Distracted him for that minute. You did all right, Keziah.'

Keziah turned to Judith. 'She was brave, all right. You should've seen her, Judith. Cool as old milk.' She slapped Susan softly on the arm. 'So where is this bag of money? The one he hid?'

'Don't know anything about that.' Susan started back up the hill. 'Now then, Judith, how's ChiChu? They kept her in?'

'Well,' said Judith slowly, 'it's funny you should say all

this about Strophair . . . about him being mad, you know?'

Susan stopped. 'What is it? What are you saying, Judith?' She took the other woman's arm.

Chapter Twenty-Two

The Small Room

Avia? Avia? You're here. Did you come back? I can't move. I can't. My face is hot. I need to scratch it but I can't get my hand to move up to my face. I'll try blinking my eyes, get them wide open. Then screw them tight, like I did when you prayed when I was very little, Avia, can you remember? Then open them wide again. This room's tall and narrow. A light as small as a candle near the ceiling. The walls rear up like cliffs, the colour of those dirty sail canvases you see in the port at home. I'm pinned down somehow. Canvas strips. Not even in a bed. On the floor. This is a very bad dream. Worse than the dreams of Esteban and the snipers.

There was that other dream. Red, sticky blood seeping all over me. Into my eyes, into my mouth. My hair. I can still smell it, that blood. It's still in my hair, Avia. The bull had tossed me like he tossed the careless picadors and my blood gushed out into his eyes.

No. The bull. This bull. This little English bull would not do this. I call him Toro, Avia, but he should be called George or Peter, so English is he. No. The dream is worse than this. It is me. I gored him. Poor little Toro. Somehow I have horns and I put my head down and gored this poor little English bull in his neck. And his blood spurts out like a fountain over my face, into my hair. He falls on me and my bones creak under the weight of him. But it is me. I have killed him. He is dead.

I am screaming, screaming, Avia, but the soft, thick walls of the small windowless room eat up my cries and they are nothing. My cries are held in this room just as the straps on my arms, across my body, muffle this same body and hold me down. Yellow, yellow, smelling of dust and old death. Why have they tethered me here like some dumb animal? Is this punishment for killing Toro? But that was a dream. No, this is a dream. Is it?

Get me out, Avia! Make me free. Where are you? Will you not answer now? Are you gone? The padded door opens and brings in a gale of sadness, a rush of air. They speak in their quacking language. This is a dream, is it not, Avia? Why can't they speak in my language? My dreams. My language. My dream. My language.

'What is she saying?' said Dr Tordoff. 'What is the girl saying?'

'Who can tell?' said the stout sister. 'Jabbering away. It might seem unchristian, Doctor, but you'd think we'd have enough on our plates tending our own. There is a war on.'

'Yes, Sister. That is very unchristian. She's under sedation?'

'Yes. It took some getting into her, I'm telling you, biting, kicking, scratching. She took a lump out of Sister Mellor.'

'And the chest injury?'

'They bound it in the usual way at the General Hospital. That was when it all started. Ripped off her clothes trying to get the bandage off. They say she ran in the street half-naked. Doctors and police all ran after her. Keystone cops, it sounded like. So they got her back to the station and our Dr Smith had to go to get her from the police cell. Then this stream of language! What a babble! They had to restrain her in the van all the way here.'

Can you hear them, Avia? What do they say? They talk over me like I am some stone on the hillside. What do they say? That one in army uniform – is he in charge here? Must be a military prison. Oh God. He's feeling my face, my neck. There! Nearly got him there.

'Don't touch her, Doctor. I told you she was a biter, Doctor. You should be careful.'

Dr Tordoff's nose twitched. 'What's that, Sister? What's that dreadful smell?'

'It's blood, Doctor.'

'You didn't wash her?'

'Did our best, what with her flailing about. But the smell's blood. See that! Clogging up her hair. Soaked right through. I was saying to Sister Mellor, there'll be no washing it.'

'Is it her blood? Whose blood is it?'

'Well, the notes from the hospital say it's bull's blood. How it got there . . .' She paused and said thoughtfully, 'I did say to Sister Mellor the only way would be to cut it. Too thick and curly. No getting at it.'

'Do what you must, Sister. I'll have no patient of mine stuck up with blood. Bull's or otherwise. It smells foul and it's damned unhygienic.'

They're looking at me as though they're going to throw me into some pot and eat me, Avia. I'll close my eyes. Close my eyes. A dream. It is a dream. When I wake up I'll be back with Susan in the pale white land. Toro will be moaning, wanting his walk. The hens will be squawking. The pigs will be snorting and shuffling.

They're back again. Their scissors glitter in the light of their lamp. They will dig my eyes out. I am screaming, screaming, but no one will hear. Not you, Avia, not even you.

'I must go to see her,' said Susan. 'Think of that place, Keziah! Those wards. Sister Barras! ChiChu'll be terrified.'

Keziah looked sullenly at Judith. 'Why d'you let her go? Why d'you let them take her?'

'Couldn't do a thing, old dear. Went crackers as I watched. Screaming and kicking. Got away from us. We all chased her as far as the cenotaph before a couple of brawny nurses and a policeman got her. You should have seen her, in her petticoats, bandages streaming.'

'You should have stopped them,' said Susan gravely. 'You should not have let them take her, Judith.'

Judith threw up her hands. 'How could I? They got her back to the hospital and had committed her before I knew what was happening.'

Susan looked at her and wondered just how hard she had really tried. ChiChu was nothing to her but a kind of entertaining doll, an exotic distraction. 'She is very brave and very sane,' she said. 'This should not happen to her.'

'Park View,' said Keziah. 'What a place to end up.'

'She's not ending up there!' said Susan sharply.

'Funny, though, isn't it? That being where we started out, so to speak.'

'Funny?' said Judith.

'And ChiChu and old Strophair ending up in the same loo— er . . . mental hospital.'

Susan looked round. 'There's things to do here,' she

said. 'The hens. The milking. Listen to those poor old cows. And the pigs are eating the door of the pigsty.'

'Not too much to do really,' said Judith. 'A few sheep on the fell. The rest are gone. The hay's all in. The oats are sown. Only two cows to milk. I'll keep my eye on that.'

'The chickens, pigs.'

'I'll feed them,' said Keziah. 'And I'll watch Barty. You go and see our old friend Dr Tordoff, Susan.'

'Dr Tordoff?' said Judith.

'He is the emperor of Park View. Queer old stick,' said Keziah. 'Better you than me, Susie.'

'I'll take a bag and stay at Uncle Rhys's in Priorton. That's in striding distance of the bus for Park View. I can stay while I find out what's what. Then I'll come back here and we can make a plan. You watch, we'll get her out.'

'Easier said than done,' said Keziah. 'You know that place when it closes its doors on someone. Doesn't open then for a generation. We've met those women. Locking up does something to them. We'll have our work cut out, Susan. I'm telling you.'

Chapter Twenty-Three

The Spy

When her street was demolished in a bombing raid, Mrs Fawcett, who took care of Theo's house, had finally retired to Wales with her daughter and grandchildren. In the Islington house, Theo restricted herself to the kitchen, her writing room and her bedroom. She wrote to Susan:

> Just think! When we moved to Priorton from Wales when I was little we lived there in three rooms. Then for much of my adult life I've lived in ten rooms and now I am back to three. It's perfectly adequate, when you think of it.'

Aaron Maichin had called at the house several times now. He was courteous, cool and watchful as ever. Sometimes he would stay one night, sometimes two. Sometimes he would go up to London during the day and arrive back in the evenings in the blank dark of the blackout. He usually arrived in his immaculate captain's uniform but one night Theo hardly recognized him at the door. He had a two-day growth of beard and was bundled in a dark grey greatcoat which had mud on it and smelled of dogs.

'Good grief, Aaron,' Theo said. 'You look like some Buchan villain.' He smiled faintly at that and headed straight up to the bathroom and she heard him clattering around, and whistling while he shaved. Later, as they ate together, she tried to penetrate his easy cloak. 'Am I not supposed to ask where you've been?'

He nodded at her over his laden fork. 'No. You're not. It wouldn't make sense to you if I told you.'

'It looks as though you've been somewhere very dirty,' she said. 'It smells as though it were a very dirty cart with dogs in it.'

He smiled at her. 'You might be right. But as you said, you're not supposed to ask.'

'Can I ask you something different?'

'Ask.'

'Why do you come here? Not some glamorous officers' mess? Or one of those swish dancing places that appear to be one way, according to the papers, of showing Hitler that business is as usual in spite of the bombing?'

He pushed his plate away. 'I can play around any time anywhere. I'm curious about you and my family. This might be my only chance to find out.'

'Is it risky, what you do?'

'I said. You're not supposed to ask.' He was frowning. 'Now then, can we talk about something else? The price of blackout curtaining or whether you think Gracie Fields should have taken up opera rather than screeching out her homely ditties on the wireless?'

Theo stood up. 'I'm wasting your time,' she said. 'And I've got work to do. I'm climbing my way out of a novel and I have an article to write for *Good Housekeeping*, about the old household skills that are coming back in wartime. Now that's easy. I just close my eyes and think of Rose Clare. Your grandmother, that is.'

She stomped out and he waited for the door of her writing room to crash before he leaned over and turned on the radio. She left him alone that evening, and the following morning there was no sign of her at breakfast and no sound of her when he departed.

The next time he turned up, his uniform immaculate, his arm was in a sling.

'What . . . ?' Theo said, nodding at the arm.

'Nothing to worry about,' he said. 'A bit of a knock, that's all.'

Over dinner that night he was very attentive. He asked about the progress of her novel. 'Is this one about the war? I read the one you wrote about the Great War. *Picardy* – wasn't that the one?'

She raised her eyebrows. 'You have been doing your homework. This one, though, is about England during the Napoleonic Wars. About a family in London who gave shelter to someone who appeared to be a spy.'

He looked keenly at her. 'A spy?' he said.

'Perhaps I should tap into your experience?' she said.

'Now, how would that be useful?'

'Well, you were in France recently, weren't you? Colour. Culture. Travelling with dogs and breaking your arm. You know. I imagine you know all about this spying thing.'

He laughed and to her relief it was a much more open and explosive sound than ever emerged from his father, Edward. Edward had conserved his charm and his joy for when there would be an advantage, a benefit to himself. He never wasted laughter on Theo.

'Well, perhaps I could do that.' He looked at her under level brows, then he shrugged. 'Perhaps I was indeed in

France yesterday. Or all of last week. Perhaps I did escape in a van which was transporting German dogs. Perhaps I did take a shot from a German rifle.'

Her attempt to sustain deep disinterest crumbled. 'What!' She looked round at the cluttered kitchen. 'Have you not heard, Aaron? Walls have ears. Loose lips lose lives.'

'I've told you this to show you I trust you, even if you don't trust me. I know in my bones that you don't.'

She ignored the challenge and pressed on. 'Well then, are you a spy for Stalin, as young ChiChu says? Susan told me a story of a portrait of Stalin as big as a theatre draped across a building in Barcelona.'

'Theo! So you pumped her too? I will tell you I'm a Communist. I worked for a while for this Jewish fellow in Jo'burg who had studied it all out, saw how the world should be. He was one of my teachers. I became a Communist in South Africa when I was in college. When I went to fight for the Republic in Spain. Because I was a Communist I was in the thick of it in double-quick time. The Russians were supplying guns, know-how. They were keen to defeat the Fascists. That doesn't make me a spy for Stalin. But even if I were, isn't he our ally now?'

She laughed. 'He was Hitler's ally when it suited him. We don't have to be happy about that. I have heard some stories—'

'I won't argue with you on it,' he said, suddenly stiff again. Their truce was over. 'I'm not happy with certain things that go on in Russia. But I'm less happy about the march of Fascism; wherever it stamps its ugly foot. The end has to justify the means, Theo. Even if the means makes us uncomfortable.' His tone brooked no reply.

She smiled slightly. 'In that, you are like Edward,' she said.

'In what?'

'He too, when he was arguing, managed to sound twenty years older.'

They ate in silence for a few moments. 'Isn't it dangerous?' she said.

'What?'

'Whatever you're doing in France?'

He laughed, then shrugged. 'No more dangerous than the tanks our soldiers in North Africa are facing. Or the Russians as they wait for the Germans in the East. Front-on conflict is not my cup of tea. For me, the darkness is my cloak. German's my mother tongue and I speak French well enough to pass. This is my weapon of refinement. I can be all things to all men. Much better than facing tanks.'

Theo looked at him thoughtfully. 'Just like—'

'Just like what? Who?'

'Just like your father,' she said. 'He was very good at deception. Being all things to all men.'

'Again?' He put his knife and fork neatly together. 'What is it about my father, Theo? What was it that he did here? I know what he did in South Africa. What exactly drove him from England; from his family?'

She stared at him. 'You want to know the truth?'

He shrugged. 'It can't be worse than what I know already.'

'Well, where can I start? He nearly killed me when I was twelve. After that he killed an old derelict man by fire. Then it seemed to me, though it wasn't proved, that he killed a woman who was carrying his unborn baby. Will that do? And all the time he played the good man, and looked like an angel. He spoke like a wise man.'

Aaron blushed, his jaw hardened. 'My mother thought he really was one of the angels when they married. But he hurt her and hurt me when I tried to defend her. Then he ran away with the money her father had given them. Years later the brother of one of his victims actually caught him out at something and shot him.' He was avoiding her glance, looking into the fire. 'I told you, didn't I? Not a pretty story. But does all that make me suspect, Theo? Am I tarred with the same brush? If I am a victim, can I be the same as he is?'

She caught his gaze and held it steadily. 'Are you?' she said. 'Are you like him?'

He stood up abruptly then and went to his room. She heard him bashing around.

She was still in bed the next morning when she heard the front door bang. Two nights later she was just securing the blackout and locking the door when she heard the knock she had come to recognize as Aaron's. She was pleased about this.

'Aaron, I—' Then she stopped. He was standing there, in his immaculate uniform but beside him, small and shrunken, was another familiar figure.

'Mr Walstein,' she said. She leaned forward and pulled the old man inside. 'Come in. Come in. The blackout . . .' She hustled them in and secured the blackout behind them.

The three of them filled the narrow hall. She put her arms round the old man and hugged him. He struggled a little in her embrace but smiled all the same. 'Mrs Theodora,' he beamed. 'I am home again. Here I am.'

She led him through to the sitting room. 'Come in, come in. How did this happen?'

Mr Walstein pulled away from her. 'Captain Maichin. He was my saviour. He came to the camp with a handful of papers and everything was well.' He looked around. 'He brought me home.'

Theo turned to Aaron. 'What is this? How did you do it?'

'It's a token, Aunt Theo. A token of my good faith.' He looked her fully in the eyes. 'To show you I'm not like him, like my father.'

Mr Walstein tugged her sleeve. 'How are Susan and little ChiChu?'

Theo explained about Susan and ChiChu, and Mr Walstein listened with grave attention. 'I will write the child a letter,' he said. 'A letter in Spanish about my rescue.'

'Miss Sabater is in hospital?' said Aaron quickly.

'It seems she was injured in some shooting accident and then had some kind of brainstorm, poor thing. She's in a hospital—'

'A hospital?'

'Well, worse really. It's an asylum. A mental hospital.'

Mr Walstein lifted his head. 'An asylum? This is a place for mad people.'

'She'll be all right. Susan is worried, of course, but I'm sure she will be all right. They can't keep sane people in mental hospitals these days. Come on now, take off your coat.'

They placed Mr Walstein's meagre belongings in his room, celebrated then with a glass of Christmas port followed by beef hash (rather short on beef) for supper.

Mr Walstein told tales of the internment camp, which

were not all bad. 'I could remind myself that I was not alone in my situation. There were others with their own hard tales. So I had comrades. I wrote to you about the other violinists. A viola player there was also. We played music. But many times I am very sad, Mrs Theodora. I missed you and this house.'

Later, Theo sat with his hand in hers in the shadowy room, listening to his repeated avowals of present happiness. She looked at Aaron, who was sitting on the opposite side of the room, smoking his pipe in the same darkness. To her own consternation she found herself wondering if this new gesture, this new demonstration of his power, was a reason *not* to trust him. Edward, in his time, could also be wily and appealing. He also knew how to get useful people on his side.

Aaron read her look and his face closed up.

He was away the next morning before she was out of bed. Mr Walstein was also up and about, smart in a fresh shirt and jacket from his wardrobe. He ate his breakfast with relish. 'I read in the newspaper that the theatres are opening again. The musicians thumb their noses at Hitler. Today, I will go to the music shop,' he said.

Theo blinked. 'Your job? Oh, Mr Walstein. Perhaps they found someone else.'

He shook his head. 'I am sure they will find me something, Mrs Theodora. Repairing violins. Not everyone can do it. I will pay for my place here, Mrs Theodora. I have to pay you for my room. It is important.'

She laughed. 'There is no need. Surely we are friends, Mr Walstein.'

His lined face lit up. 'If we are friends, Mrs Theodora, then it is all more important for me to work, to get money. Friends do not take advantage of each other.' He stood up and unbuttoned his napkin. 'Now! I will have to blow up the tyres of my bicycle. I am sure they will be quite flat after these months.'

Chapter Twenty-Four

Patients

Rhys Maichen, Theo's older brother, lived in a big house on The Avenue in the busy market town of Priorton. While the pit villages and towns right across the region still bore the blight of more than a decade of unemployment, Priorton – the farming as well as the commercial and manufacturing centre – still managed to thrive. In these days the businesses generated by war and the close proximity of army camps added a buzz to its High Street; a further lustre to its self-importance.

Rhys Maichin was one of those who flourished in the flush of wartime wealth. He was a large, bluff man in his late fifties, his sparse yellowing grey hair the only reminder of former russet curls. He owned a substantial hardware emporium in Priorton as well as an iron foundry, which had been going great guns since the phony war of 1939.

Rhys's wife, Ruth, was older than he, but it was widely acknowledged in Priorton she carried her years well. Unusually slender for a woman of her age, she had retained the old-fashioned style of long skirts and wore her long hair piled up, which flattered her, making her look like a figure from a sepia photo album.

315

When she realized who was knocking at her door, Ruth opened it wide. 'Well, Susan Cornford! This is a turn-up for the books. We hear all about you in Theo's letters. How long must it be . . . ?'

Susan shook her hand heartily. 'Ten years. I was still nursing then. Your Peter was getting married to that teacher.' They stood surveying each other in the hall, which smelled of spice and old lavender, and shone like good butter.

A shadow fell across Ruth's face. 'Of course we lost him. Our Peter.'

Susan blushed. She knew about this, but had forgotten. Theo had told her. Peter had been killed in the retreat from Dunkirk. Machine-gunned on the sand, his mate had told Rhys. 'I knew about that, from Theo. I'm sorry, really sorry, Auntie Ruth.'

'No. It's not fair, is it? He was a good boy. Lots of good boys are being lost. You can hardly read the papers. There's . . .' She turned abruptly and led Susan into the sitting room, where Rhys was sitting behind his papers. 'Look who's here, Rhys! Susan Cornford, of all people.'

Rhys stood up in a rustle of paper and a shower of cigarette ash. 'Ah, Susan.' His plump hand enclosed hers. 'Sure it's good to see you, lass. Our Theo talks of you in her letters. Adventures in Spain, no less.'

'The war out there's well lost,' she said briefly. 'I'm back here now. Back up at Goshawk Shield with my farming boots on.'

'So Theo said. You must have been up there some months now. We hoped you'd call.'

'Anyway, here she is,' said Ruth brightly. 'Why don't we sit down, and I'll get you some tea?' She hesitated.

Susan sat and looked up at their watching faces. 'Say if

it's impossible, but I hoped I might stay here a couple of nights. I've something to do down here. Something to see to.'

'Stay and welcome!' Rhys's plump hand flashed in the air. 'Is that not so, Ruthie?'

Ruth stood at the door. 'Stay and welcome,' she said.

Rhys looked fondly after her and then turned back to Susan. 'So, Susan Cornford, what's this mission of yours?'

'Well, I've to go to Park View.'

'The mental hospital? Didn't you work there once? Is that not so? Will you work there again? Is that what this is?'

'No. It's not that. I've a young friend, a Spanish girl. She's been committed to the hospital. Certified. It's a mistake, of course. Definitely a mistake. I want to get her out, though I do know that's not so easy, once a person's in there.' Her eye strayed then stayed with a silver-framed photograph on the mantelpiece. Staring out at her was a young man with a handsome, fair face and steady eyes, in some kind of military or naval uniform. The face was chillingly familiar. 'Who's that?' she said sharply. 'The photograph?'

'That? Why, that's our Ellis, the oldest. He was in the Fleet Air Arm. See the uniform? We did think him out of harm's way in America. He was training Navy pilots. Well regarded, so his commanding officer wrote. Marked out for promotion. Then he has to go and dive into the sea.'

She shook her head. 'No! I didn't realize. Auntie Ruth didn't say. She said about Peter . . .'

He shrugged. 'Hardly to terms with it even now, is Ruthie. Wouldn't let me put it in the *Echo*. Says they'll find him in that water off Florida. Some island, p'raps . . .' His voice faded away. Practical man that he was, he too hoped for that voice from the deep.

Susan coughed, embarrassed at the pain in his voice. 'Uncle Rhys, I . . . I can't say I knew him. He was always away at school when I called with Rose Clare, or Theo. Then . . .'

'Then we all get on with our lives,' he said quietly. 'Don't we? We were never a close family.'

Susan stared at the photograph. She most certainly did recognize the man portrayed there. He was the double of that other Maichin whom she'd first met in Spain in the uniform of the International Brigade. Aaron Maichin was so like his cousin he might just have been his twin. She shivered a little. Then Ruth came in and she put the thought to the back of her mind and concentrated on the silver tray of tea and bought cakes which Ruth placed on a small round table.

The next morning Rhys Maichin apologized for not taking Susan to the hospital in his car. 'Petrol coupons very scarce, I'm afraid. No more jaunts for us till after the war, eh, Ruth?' He glanced at his wife, presiding over the breakfast table with her dark morning face.

Rhys walked to the Market Place to remind Susan which bus to get for the hospital. 'Poor old Ruthie. Not been the same since . . . well, since the boys . . .' He cleared his throat. 'Bloody war this, if you'll excuse the language, Susan. Ah, here. The Favourite! That's the bus you need. The good old Favourite. It'll take you straight to the hospital gates. But you'll know that, no doubt.'

The last two or three miles in the bus sent Susan's heart swooping. She was invaded by the feelings that had settled on her like a fog in the days when she travelled on this same bus to visit her grandmother in hospital: a grudging attention in her grandmother's raging last days. Her spirits lifted as her thoughts moved to happier times, when she would return to the hospital with Keziah after a day out in Priorton or a weekend at Keziah's house in Gibsley.

For a second Keziah's brother Jake rose in Susan's mind as she had last seen him, gaunt and embittered in Spain. Perhaps he'd been happier, fighting with the British in this bigger war.

She remembered a tale Keziah had told her about Jake in Spain. Apparently Jake's accent had been recognized by the MP Ellen Wilkinson, visiting the Brigade with Clement Attlee. He said the little MP had taken him to one side and reminisced about the Jarrow March, and 'her' miners and 'her' shipworkers. *You'd think they were her dolls*, he'd written to Keziah. I couldn't make out whether Jake was pleased about that, or sorry, Keziah had told Susan.

Susan had been standing for ten minutes in the spacious, highly polished main entrance of the hospital when a woman in sister's uniform passed.

'Do you want something?' the sister said very directly. This attitude was familiar to Susan. Obsequiousness was really antipathetic to the nursing soul except in the face of senior doctors.

'Yes. Yes, Sister. I'd like to see Dr Tordoff.' She hesitated. 'I worked here before, you know. Then I went abroad to work. He asked me to come to see him when I got back.' She crossed her fingers behind her back.

The sister nodded, satisfied. She pointed towards the stairs which winged in two directions in the grand mansion style. 'Up there. Third door on the right. His name's on the door.' She frowned slightly. 'But then, you would know that, wouldn't you?'

'Yes. Of course,' said Susan lightly. She didn't know it. She'd never been in the doctor's office. She moved towards the staircase, keeping her back to the sister. She was relieved when she heard the retreating click of the sister's stout shoes behind her.

She began to mount the stairs. Ahead of her she could see the hospital shoes and the sturdy rear end of a patient kneeling down to polish the stair edges. Susan mounted steadily, passing close by the figure.

A voice rapped out from behind her. 'Why, if it an't Nurse Cornford!'

Susan turned round and grinned in recognition of the beaming upturned face. 'Why, if it an't Jane Ann Golon!'

'So what're yeh doing back at this cold old jail-place? Me, Ah thought you'd escaped. Years gone. Left us long-termers to sweat it out.'

'Off the ward now, are you, Jane Ann?' She looked around her. There was no supervising nurse. 'They must trust you.'

Jane Ann grinned. 'Aye. That's it. Ah must've been a very good girl, mustn't Ah? Good as gold. Ah used to clean the ward. Did a good job there. Now promoted to the front end. Spit and polish. Spit and polish.'

'Well, well. D'you like it, Jane Ann? Working here?'

The smile on Jane Ann's face stilled for a moment. 'Well, Nurse Cornford, it's all there is, an't it?'

They looked at each other, silent for a moment.

'Where'd you like to be, Jane Ann, if some fairy waved her wand? If you could be anywhere?' Now why had she said that?

Jane Ann stood up, put her hand in the small of her back and looked around the gleaming hallway with contempt. 'Why, Nurse, Ah came here when Ah was thuteen. It's all Ah know. What good 'd green fields and running streams be for me? Nowt. Nor would any big shop with sweets piled high on one side and these bright scarves to the ceiling on the other. Ah dreamed of that, once. D'yeh know that, that shop, Nurse?' She sniffed and rubbed her cheek with the back of her hand. 'Aye, why . . . Ah'd better get on then. Sister'll be after us.'

Susan knocked on Doctor Tordoff's door and obeyed the rapped out order to 'come in'.

The room was as busy as a box of gems. There were wonderful nineteenth-century engravings of the structure of the brain; a white head sculpture on the desk; leather-bound books in matching sets lined the wall; glass-fronted cupboards hid bottles and boxes in their dusty depths. Light streamed down from the stone-mullioned windows on to Dr Tordoff, who was sitting, head cocked like a bird, behind his desk.

'Yes?' he said.

Susan blinked. He was in military uniform, the light glittering on the brass buttons of his tunic and his small round spectacles. He looked up at her. Something about her demeanour made him stand up. 'Yes?' he said. This woman was somewhat familiar. He frowned. Her plain dress and her wispy hair told him that it must be something to do with the hospital rather than his wider county acquaintance. 'Is there something?'

Susan blinked and took a breath. 'Doctor, I was a nurse here at the hospital a few years ago. Then I went to Spain.'

His puzzled look cleared. 'Ah. You are the nurse who went to the Civil War,' he said. 'Nurse . . . Nurse . . .'

'Cornford,' she said.

'Yes. And how was it?' he said blandly. 'How was it?'

She looked at him blankly. 'How was what?'

'The war?'

'We lost. You would read it in the paper.'

His little round cheeks flared like two red apples. 'Brave fight in Spain. Brave fight indeed. The Fascists continue to plague us yet. Although I fear Hitler outdoes Franco in terms of wickedness.'

Her glance dropped to his tunic. 'You joined up yourself, Doctor? You're in the Army yourself?'

He coughed. 'Needed here at the hospital, of course, but I have insisted on serving at home. In the Home Guard.'

She looked more closely at his uniform. 'You are a captain,' she said.

'That is so,' he said. Elias Tordoff did enjoy his nights and weekends of training. Here was a tailor-made role: the opportunity to serve his country at last. Local leadership. He knew that he made a trim figure in his uniform; wore it with pride. Wearing his uniform in the environs of his hospital was an important way of showing support for the fight. Like a chaplain wearing his dog collar to witness his faith.

He fought down the desire to protest all this to the pale, intense woman before him, but he didn't. He coughed and pushed his spectacles further up his nose. 'Now then, Miss Cornford. Do you wish to return here? Is this why you have come?' How had she got past the gorgons in the entrance? Why had he had no note about her presence? Something would have to be done.

She shook her head. 'No. I have my hands full running my farm now. In Weardale. I've come on personal business: to enquire about a friend of mine.'

He stared at her. Then at last he waved at a chair and she took it. He sat down behind his desk. 'Is this a nurse, Miss Cornford? The woman here? We do have one or two nurses here.' He smiled at his little joke.

She shook her head. 'She was admitted the day before yesterday. Maria Josep Sabater. She's Spanish. Well, Catalan, actually.'

'Ah, yes,' he said. 'The young, dark woman. She is very traumatized.'

'She came back with me from Spain. She's in my care.'

He stared at her. 'Not unknown, such trauma. Strange country. Strange language.'

'Dr Tordoff, it was not the war. This one, or the one in Spain.' She took a breath. 'She was rolled on by a bull who had just been shot with a bullet intended for her, shot by a farmer who had just gone berserk. That would traumatize me, or even you.'

'Bulls? Bullets? Berserk farmers?' He smirked. 'Doesn't sound like Weardale to me.'

She surveyed his glittering buttons for a second. 'Well, perhaps you should remember there's a war on, Dr Tordoff. Strange things happen in wartime. In Spain, ChiChu saw her family and her dearest friends blown to bits. The man who shot the bull was Mr Strophair, the farmer. He has a son taken prisoner at Dunkirk. I myself have just learned that my two cousins have been killed in the last year. It's enough to send anyone berserk, don't you think? War!'

He flushed again in that ugly fashion. 'There is no need to take that offensive tone with me, Miss Cornford.'

'Well, perhaps that's the effect of the war, Dr Tordoff. I am not immune.'

He pushed some files into an even neater pile. 'The farmer concerned – he is here too.'

'Yes. I know this.'

'You cannot see the girl. She is in restraint.'

Susan stood up. An image of the tiny, close-padded room flashed before her eyes. 'What? This girl is troubled. Damaged. You should not have—'

'She was spitting and biting. There is no holding her when she is conscious.'

'Conscious! You mean—'

'She needs her sleep. She is in deep rest.'

'I want to see her.'

'You can't. You can see Mr Strophair. He is in Ward Seven.' His tone was flat, without emotion: a tone perfected in many years of dealing with the hysterical relatives of insane patients.

Susan thought quickly. Bullying and blustering would not work with this man. He would love a battle, just to prove he could win. All this drama was on his territory, after all.

She smiled broadly at him. 'I can see your position, Dr Tordoff. I'll be very pleased to see Mr Strophair. I was wondering how he was. But I would really like to see my young friend.'

He started to shake his head.

'Dr Tordoff! I nursed here at the hospital for six years. I am familiar with . . . I know how difficult it is here. I am not an *hysteric*. I just want to see my friend. To reassure myself and her other friends that she's in reasonably good fettle in the circumstances.'

He breathed hard down his nose. 'I don't know about reassurance.' He pulled out his watch and glanced at it. 'I have a meeting here in two minutes. I will find someone to take you to see Mr Strophair. If you return to my office I will take you to see the Spanish woman myself.'

Down on Ward Seven Susan hardly recognized Barry Strophair. He was sitting up straight in his chair in a thick, checked dressing gown. His hair had been washed and was parted and combed to one side. His skin was scrubbed and shining and the gaze he turned on her, wide and questioning. He looked twenty years younger than when she'd last seen him.

'Susan Cornford,' he said. 'It's you.'

'Mr Strophair. You look very well.'

There was a crackle of starch as the nurse beside Susan folded her arms. 'We're very pleased with Mr Strophair. Back on his feet. Nicely sorted out.'

Susan glanced at her.

'Three square meals, a bit of a warm. Does wonders for these hill folk.'

'Hill folk?'

'Shut off in the country. Stop taking care of themselves. Stop eating. Talk to the cows. Myself, I think it's a matter of what they eat. Two weeks of good dinners and talking to human beings. Good as any electric shocks, if you ask me.' She said all this in Strophair's hearing, nodding at him like a fond mother. 'Use that chair, miss,' she said, nodding at a chair on the other side of the bed. 'Don't sit on the bed. Sister'd not like it. She doesn't like it at all when people sit on her beds.'

Susan sat down.

'Prattles on, that woman,' said Barry Strophair.

'How're you feeling, Mr Strophair?'

'All right, seeing as you ask.' He stirred in his seat. 'They say the girl was hurt. Was she hurt?'

Susan didn't know whether he wanted her to say yes or

no. 'Yes. She's hurt quite bad,' she said. 'The bull fell on her. Crushed her.'

He frowned. 'The bull? The bull fell on her?'

'Can't you remember?'

He shook his head. 'What happened to the bull?'

'You'll remember,' said Susan. She didn't want to tell him about it. It was his fault, all this, and she didn't want to tell him. Outside, up at the farm, she'd have told him. But here in the hospital her training was too strong. In hospital you don't harm your patients. 'Just leave it, Mr Strophair. You'll remember in time.'

'Mr Treesting at Green Hill, he wanted the bull to come to stud. That was next week. Or is it this week? You'll need to get the bull to him.'

'Don't worry about it. It'll come back, Mr Strophair.'

'She shouldn't be here, the Spanish lass. It's wrong.'

'No. I know she shouldn't be here. She should be in a proper hospital. She's not mad.'

He frowned. 'In the hospital?'

She stared at him. 'What do you mean, she shouldn't be here?'

'Foreigners,' he said. 'Spies every last one of 'em. Spanish. Eyeties. Wogs.'

She stood up so abruptly that the chair clattered over behind her. The man in the next bed started to cry. The nurse's shoes started to click along the tiled ward. Susan put the chair to rights. 'You take care of yourself, Mr Strophair. You're a nasty man, but I'd not wish you ill.'

He sat back in his chair and smiled at her. 'Nice of you to say, Susan Gomersal. Nice of you to say.'

The nurse met her in the middle of the long ward. 'Anything wrong, Miss Cornford?'

'No. No,' she said. 'It's quite all right.' As her feet

pounded the long corridor she thought that it *wasn't* all right. Perhaps the isolation and poor food had tipped Strophair's scales into temporary madness, but the man underneath, the man before the madness, was a mean soul anyway. He'd killed his dog, his bull. He'd driven his son off his own farm, and he'd driven off her own Gomersal cousins. He had probably been a very mean child in school. It wasn't difficult to think that that meanness of spirit could slip very easily into the shooting of the rifle. She thought of those people in Germany who'd seized Mr Walstein's niece Madeleine and her parents, who shot them, or did whatever they did: ordinary people like Barry Strophair, perhaps.

Dr Tordoff was waiting in front of his office door. When he saw her he took out his watch and nodded. 'On the nail, Miss Cornford! On the nail!' And he set off on his very quick hospital walk which ensured that everyone, whatever their size, had to scurry after him. Susan lengthened her considerable stride but still had to break into a half-trot.

ChiChu was not in a padded room. She was in a small side room with a high window. Her eyes were closed. She was wearing a rough flannel nightie and her head looked like a porcupine. Susan cried out, 'What have you done to her? You cut her hair.'

Tordoff's nose twitched. 'It was necessary to cut it. It was full of . . . er . . . animal blood. Very unhygienic. And she would not get into a bath, or allow the nurses to wash it out.'

Susan glared at him. 'Do you know, Dr Tordoff, the last people to cut ChiChu's hair were some really evil people in Spain. I'd not thought she would meet such people here.'

He looked at his watch and then fixed his gaze on the high window. 'It was for her own good, Miss Cornford.' The ribbons on the high starched cap of the sister at Dr Tordoff's shoulder trembled in the air as she nodded her agreement.

Some attempt had been made to wash ChiChu's face. Susan put a finger on her cheek. It was very cool. 'She's unconscious. She's not asleep,' she said flatly. 'You have her unconscious.'

'She had to be sedated,' said the doctor.

The bed looked very freshly made. 'Has she just been moved here? Out of the pads?' Susan looked directly at the sister.

The sister glanced at Dr Tordoff. 'She is much calmer now. We thought it wise—'

Susan gritted her teeth. 'Of course she's calmer, she's out cold.'

'She was very disturbed. Shouting and disturbing everybody.'

'What was she saying?' said Susan. 'What did she say?'

The sister's hard jaw set harder. 'I couldn't tell. She was gabbling so.'

'She wasn't gabbling,' said Susan fiercely. 'She was talking in her own language. Just because it's not English doesn't mean it's a gabble.'

'Well,' said the sister primly, 'perhaps she could seek care in her own country.'

'If she goes back to her own country she'll be shot. Is that what you want?'

The sister shrugged.

Susan looked hard at Dr Tordoff. 'Can I sit with her on my own for a bit?'

'Doctor—' said the sister.

Tordoff nodded. 'A few minutes. I have patients to see on this ward. I will return for you.'

They left the door open and Susan could hear the controlled anger in the sister's voice as she scuttled along the ward beside Dr Tordoff.

Susan pulled a chair closer to the bed. '*Hola, ChiChu. Com es das?*' She put her lips closer to ChiChu's ear, very visible now the hair had been hacked off. '*Hola, ChiChu. Com es das?*' She cursed her lack of Spanish, almost entirely extinguished since she returned to England. '*Hola, ChiChu. Com es das?*' ChiChu moved restlessly and threw out an arm above the bedclothes. Susan took her hand and stroked it. She looked closer. There were restraint bruises on her wrists and her upper arm. Rage boiled through Susan. She stood up. Then she sat down again. She could do nothing. Tordoff was as powerful in here as any dictator in his kingdom. She would have to think of a less direct way.

She placed the hand neatly under the blanket and tucked the blanket up under ChiChu's chin. She walked along the ward to where Tordoff and the sister were standing by a patient. They talked and pointed, and the sister made marks on a chart.

'Dr Tordoff?'

He looked up. 'If you will wait, Miss Cornford—'

'No,' she said steadily. 'I'm going, but I will be back with . . . with some authority. And if I discover that young woman has been put back into restraint, or harmed in any way, I will bring the police here. I promise you.' She stalked off, her steps echoing and resounding off the fifteen-foot-high walls of the ward.

'How rude,' said Sister. 'How very rude.'

'Hysterical relatives, Sister. We have met them many

times, have we not?' Tordoff said lightly. But when he'd finished his round he entered on the Spanish girl's notes that she was to stay in the side ward, sedated as appropriate.

Back in his office he looked out down the long drive towards the gateway of his domain. He stood up straight, his shoulders back. He was looking forward to the Home Guard meeting that night. It was 'Recognizing and Disarming an Alien Intruder', followed by 'General Drill'.

How very nice to be doing one's bit. Very nice indeed.

Chapter Twenty-Five

Pot Models

With a family visitor in the house, Ruth Maichin was livelier than she'd been in months. The morning Susan went to hospital Ruth visited Rhys in his office at the foundry and allowed him to show her the new assembly lines where they were making side panels for tanks which would be sent on to a factory in the Midlands to be finished and assembled.

'All part of our war effort,' he said proudly. 'We've all to do our bit. Every last one of us.'

Ruth smiled with something of her old liveliness. 'I don't think we're losing out, Rhys, are we? Every bit counts.'

Rhys was pleased to see her taking an interest. She always used to. The foundry had originally been her father's; he'd been working there as a storehouse boy when he met her. How long ago those days seemed now. In the old days she used to know the business inside out. Know as much about the setup as anybody in those days.

Rhys had been angry, then sad when his sons had not followed on at the foundry. But Peter had been keen to go off and be a schoolteacher and Ellis, well, he was down to

Portsmouth to join the Royal Navy as soon as he left school. So when, years later, war broke out, he was well on his way. Well, it was all one now. No school. No Navy. No factory. No nothing. No sons.

He walked Ruth back through to the gates. 'I see the Rainbow works has a new manager. Woman it is, they say, a young relative of old Mrs Rainbow.' Rainbow's had become a rival manufacturer through the years but it was an empty rivalry now. There was more than enough work to go around for them all. Old Mrs Rainbow could sleep safe in her bed.

Ruth took his arm and pressed it to her side. 'You watch that young woman doesn't show you how to do it, Rhys.' He watched her walk down the lane and thought how, in forty years of marriage, she'd never failed to charm him. Perhaps they were allowed that, in recompense for losing the boys. Boys! Ellis would be nearly forty now, and Peter, thirty-five. He sighed, and turned with some relief to walk towards the massive door into the works. This place had been a great comfort to him in these last hard years. At least he had this place. And he had Ruth as well, even though she was half the woman she had been. All she had was him, and sometimes that was very hard to bear. Very hard indeed.

The early afternoon dusk intensified the gloom as the Favourite Bus wended its way through the high-hedged lanes and pit villages blanked out by the blackout. The route, so familiar to Susan from her pre-war journeys, was made strange by the dark. Doors and alleyways were dense black holes and the figures passing by were slippery shadows, their skins shining like fish in a tank. Occasionally, there was a flash of light as the door of a house or a public house opened to suck in a hurrying figure from the darkness.

Susan's mind was racing. Bumping along in the damp shadowy bus, she thought of the still, small figure of ChiChu on the iron hospital bed, all the life and fire bleached out of her, her wonderful hair cropped like a small Samson. Then she thought of ChiChu bouncing around the clinic in the stripped Spanish church: how she would swing around, talking and chattering, pausing only momentarily to wince at the pain in her arm. Susan thought of her passionate stories of the bravery of Esteban, of her father and his passion for Spain. Even after the painful questioning in the hotel in Barcelona, the rebel spark was still there. They'd cut her hair there, but couldn't cut her spirit. The ebb and flow of that crushing war in her own country could not defeat her; punishing interrogation had not defeated her. But the pressure of being a foreigner in a foreign land; the hatred of a half-mad farmer; drugs pumped in in a grim, foreign clinic: these had now defeated her. She was as good as dead. Susan took out her handkerchief, blew her nose and dabbed her eyes.

Susan wondered just how long it would take her to get ChiChu out of that place. Every time she surfaced from the drug she would kick and bite. Then they'd give her more of the stuff to quieten her down. Soon she'd be numb and leaden, like some of those other women Susan had known in her days in the hospital. How thoughtless and accepting she'd been then. In those days she'd accepted that numbness as part of the inevitable reality of asylums. She'd not thought too much about the real person under the fog of chemicals. Biters and kickers were always a problem. The simple women like Jane Ann

Golon had been easier to understand, to sympathize with than the biters and the kickers.

So ChiChu had to come out of there soon, before she was entirely lost in the highly polished, snake-walled world of Park View. Another doctor, an outside doctor might help. But which outside doctor? No one had treated ChiChu here in England. If only she could find someone who could speak Spanish! This would comfort ChiChu and bring her back as her own self into this world. That should convince even old Tordoff. He was a simple man in some ways, not deliberately wicked or ill intentioned. But there he was overseeing ChiChu, just rescued from her padded room, being punished by injections for the crime of having a dead bull fall on her.

A sharp laugh escaped from Susan at this thought. A woman in the front seat turned round. She regularly used this route to travel to and from the house of her aged brother. It was not unusual to come across loonies on this bus: talking to themselves, laughing to themselves. Foaming at the mouth. She'd seen it all, on this bus.

I heard some voices, Avia, quacking, quacking. I've stopped opening my eyes now. But I see through my eyelashes. Red faces. Red eyes. Hard hands. The smell of wasting and sweat. And fruit! Fruit that's all bruised and gone off. There is the one with grey curls in a bush. She smells like Grandfather did when you beat him so he ended under the sideboard. Wine! He loved his wine. But they would not have wine in this, this prison, would they, Avia?

I can still smell him, old Toro. I can hear him pawing in his place in the dairy. My head hurts but I can't scratch it with my hands. They've cut off my hands, Avia. What I have done in this strange prison that they would cut off my hands? Esteban! You remember him, Avia? His smile with the broken teeth. His hands were so bloody after the explosion. Just bloody stumps. Blood. I smell it. I taste it. It was Toro. He roared and fell. See blood. Blood and death.

Now there are more voices, but this one doesn't quack. It's smooth and soft. Ah. It is Susan. I told you about Susan, didn't I, Avia? She's my friend, my good friend. I can see her through my lashes, talking to that old soldier by my bed. The soldier with spectacles. Susan! Susan! I shout in my mind but my mouth just won't move, Avia; my eyes won't open beyond the curtain of my lashes. My head! I can't move it. I can't. Her soft hand tucks me in, her voice murmurs but I can say nothing, do nothing.

And now she's gone. I must be dead. This must be a place of the dead, Avia. You know? Where they lay out the dead? Susan has made her last visit and they will send me on to you. They will all be there, won't they? Esteban and the others. Perhaps Mr Walstein. I told you about Mr Walstein, didn't I? He was my friend, my true friend, and they took him away. Perhaps this is what they do. They bring them to places like this and preside over their death. Hands. Feet. Faces. Bit by bit they are taken away.

But no. Look! I can move my arm. I can sit up. I can open my eyes wide. I can see the red-faced one with the white apron. She has a white dish in her hand, like Susan had in her clinic. No. No. The sharp needle. Stop them, Avia. Susan! Stop them!

'Missis! Missis! You have to get off.' Someone was shaking Susan's arm. 'This is the terminus.'

Susan opened her eyes and peered out at the winter dark of Priorton marketplace. 'Yes. I have to be off here.' She pulled down her coat, tied her scarf more tightly under her chin and followed the conductress down the bus.

The conductress, a fat, yellow-haired woman who, like Dr Tordoff, wore her uniform with pride, stepped back so Susan could squeeze past. Then she pinged the bell. The bus eased off its brakes and left Susan alone in the deserted marketplace. Susan watched it vanish into the shadows, a lumbering shape with no interior lights and the merest pencil slits of headlight to betray its existence to any cruising Nazi bomber above.

She set off at a stamping pace, suddenly angry at this dark war world where all these measures – the absence of lights, the heaps of sandbags, boxed gas masks swinging from hips – brought threat to your very doorstep: this twilight world where the hoarding and doling of coupons, the salvaging of waste paper and iron pans ensured that every single person felt responsible for the country and the war. For a second she mourned the disorder and the chaos of the Spanish war with its banners and its barricades, its summer dust and winter sunshine. For the first time in many months she thought of Bartolomeo: his face was fading from her now but inside her head she could hear his deep resonating laugh.

A knife of wind whipped round the corner and raked her face. She shivered. How she wished to be before a roaring fire at Goshawk Shield, with little Barty chuckling and practising his new words on her knee and ChiChu crouched by the fire whittling her stick. She shook her head and turned to climb the hill towards The Avenue. Before anything else, before even Barty, she had to sort out this thing with ChiChu.

'Excuse me, ma'am. I'm looking for The Avenue. Can

you direct me?' A hand on her arm, a voice came to her out of the darkness.

She stopped and turned her head towards the questioner, a tall, fair man in military uniform. Then she laughed. 'I was just wishing for a bit of Spain and then I hear that queer accent of yours. Hey presto! My wish was answered!'

'Susan Cornford?' Aaron Maichin put his face closer to hers in the blackout gloom. 'Well, of all the—'

'Coincidences?' she laughed, and took his arm. 'Well, sir, I can show you The Avenue, all right, as I'm on my way there myself. What number?'

'I'm going to see a Maichin uncle and aunt. Theo directed me. I have some leave and I thought I'd make myself known to this uncle and aunt. So why are you here? I thought you were in the depths of the country? And what's this about Miss Sabater?'

They climbed the hill and she told him about the farmer and the bull and ChiChu's present dilemma. 'I was just thinking I needed someone to talk to her in Spanish, to kind of bring her back to herself. I don't know. She's like the living dead. And she's been committed. Hard to get them out when they're committed.'

Aaron hugged her arm to his side. 'We'll see what we can do. We can't let young Sabater languish there when even the Spanish prisons couldn't hold her, can we?'

She frowned. His jollity was strange, unexpected.

It was Rhys who came to the door when they rang. He moved backwards as they stepped into the light of the hall from the dark avenue. 'Susan, we thought we had lost you. And who . . . ?'

The hall light gleamed on Aaron's blond hair as he

took off his peaked cap and put a hand out. 'I'm pleased to meet you, sir.'

Rhys staggered, then recovered himself. 'You're . . .'

'My name is Aaron Maichin. My Aunt Theo suggested that I should come. My father was—'

'Edward.' Rhys grasped Aaron's hand in both of his and pumped it up and down. 'Well, I never. Well, I never. And you're in the British Army. Captain, is it?'

Aaron shrugged. 'Looks like it.'

Rhys held on to his hand. 'And your father? He—'

Aaron shook his head. 'No. He died some years ago now.'

A range of emotions chased each other across Rhys's plump countenance but none of them was sorrow. 'Well . . . well,' he said helplessly. 'In the Army now, I see. Have you seen action?'

'Hard to say,' said Aaron. He was used to keeping secrets but for a second he wanted desperately to tell the truth to this kindly man who was his uncle. 'I do this and that.'

'He was in the International Brigade in Spain, Rhys,' put in Susan. 'Blowing up bridges and things.'

They were still in the hall. Susan was puzzled that Rhys seemed to be blocking the way, preventing them from going further into the house. Ruth, hearing the talk, came to the sitting-room door. 'Rhys, what is it?' Her glance rose to Aaron. Her eyes widened and then she slid down the doorpost in a faint.

It was Aaron rather than the unfit Rhys who lifted Ruth on to the chaise longue. Susan sat beside her, patted her hands and told Rhys to go for a glass of water. He came back with the glass in one hand and a picture in a silver frame in the other. He handed the picture to Aaron.

'That's why,' he said. 'That is why Ruth fainted. I knew there'd be trouble the minute I saw you.'

Aaron stared down at a laughing, fair-haired man in some kind of navy uniform. He could have been looking in a mirror.

'This is our son Ellis. He ended up in the Fleet Air Arm. His plane did something funny when he was low flying in America and it went in the sea.' He laughed bitterly. 'Hard to lose your son in the war but not in battle. Really hard.'

'Ellis?' Ruth struggled to sit up. 'I dreamed that Ellis was alive, Rhys.'

'No, no,' said Rhys hastily. 'You were mistaken. But we do have a visitor. This is Aaron, Ruth. Edward's son.'

Ruth closed her eyes tight.

Aaron moved into the light. 'I'm sorry if I frightened you, Mrs . . . Aunt Ruth.'

'You're so like him; so like our Ellis.'

'Aye. You're the pot model of your da, Aaron. Our son, Ellis, he took after my side of the family, didn't he Ruth?'

Ruth nodded. 'Sit down, won't you? You too, Susan. Rhys!' she commanded. 'Why not dig out some of that port from the back pantry? Let's celebrate this family occasion.' She turned resolutely to Aaron. 'So Edward must have stayed on in South Africa,' she said steadily.

'He's not alive now,' said Rhys. 'He died.'

Aaron tried to fathom the dark look bestowed on them by this woman. He would have sworn it was relief.

'And was he as big a scoundrel in South Africa as he was here?' she said, her voice hard.

'Ruth!' warned Rhys, coming in with a tray of glasses and a dusty bottle.

'Don't worry, Uncle,' said Aaron easily. 'Yes, Aunt Ruth.

My father was a bad type. My mother and I escaped from him when I was a boy. I saw him only a time or two after that. And I was not sorry.' His voice was as hard as hers.

She nodded. 'You were well rid.' Then she smiled and it was like a crack of sunlight in a dark room. 'But you, you're very welcome here, Aaron.' She took a full glass from Rhys, waited for the others to take theirs, then held up her own in a toast. 'So, Aaron, welcome to the family. You have come to us out of the dark.'

As Susan lifted her glass and tasted the sweet liquor she noted an uncharacteristic flush on Aaron's cheek. She listened to Ruth's happy laughter and felt a niggle of curiosity. What was happening that would make Ruth flush, her hands move around too busily, moving her glass, the cloth on the table, the belt on her dress?

That evening the drama of Aaron's arrival in a household, which so entranced the older couple hungry for the sight of their deceased son's double, prevented Susan talking to him about ChiChu at any length. She did mention the hospital but at that point Rhys came in with a plump album packed with images of Ellis and his younger brother, Peter, at each stage of their lives: right from childhood through school and college and then, finally, in their military uniforms.

Ruth, Rhys and Aaron were still poring over the photos when Susan went to bed. She pulled the blanket over her head and reflected on her own orphaned state. There must be Gomersals around but she did not go seeking them. Her own family, the family of her heart, of her babyhood, her childhood and her upbringing, were the Maichins: Rose Clare above all. It was Theo who had officially adopted her although she seemed like her sister. At one remove, there were Rhys and Ruth, who were always kind to Rose Clare's placid foster daughter. Perhaps it was her close, loving relationship with Rose Clare which had led to her taking up with ChiChu so easily. The close love and the assiduous affection of her own foster relationship made it easy for her to take ChiChu to her heart.

But once again it was brought home to her that there were connections between people over and above those of choice. She was, and always would be, an outsider. Inside the family there was the connection of the mirror: how drawn we are to those who look like ourselves. (Keziah had once joked how people resembled their dogs. She counted four people on her fingers who, she claimed, were the 'pot model' of their pets.)

Now look at the excitement of those two old people at the sight of Aaron! He was a total stranger, a foreigner to boot, who spoke strange English and whose life experience had been entirely alien to theirs. Yet the sight of him with his sharp bones and blond good looks had put them in a tizzy. There was no doubt that he was one of them in a way which, despite a lifetime's acquaintance, she could never be. She pulled the sheet down, turned on her side and burrowed her head in her pillow.

For her, though, there had been this gift of the Italian commissar. She knew that he liked her, felt kindly towards her even if she knew also that he had not loved her in any fairy-tale fashion. But between them they had made Barty and across his growing features she saw the big Italian. So now and then, very occasionally, she saw a little mirror of herself. Now she was part of it all.

The next morning, when she went downstairs, the only

sign of Aaron and Rhys was the detritus of the hearty breakfast they had enjoyed half an hour earlier. Ruth, still drinking tea at one end of the dining table, was reading the *Northern Echo*. She put down the paper as Susan slid into her chair.

'I see our boys are making a go of it in North Africa,' she said. 'As far as you can tell, reading the papers. There are boiled eggs in the bowl, Susan. So good of you to bring them down from the farm. Such a shortage in Priorton now.' She pushed a letter across to Susan. 'We had a note from Theo. No doubt you'll have one when you get home. A good correspondent is Theo. But she should be good, shouldn't she? Her stock in trade, writing. Go on. Read it.'

Susan picked it up and glanced down the page.

. . . so happy that my friend Mr Hermann Walstein is back with me, released from internment by the machinations of – guess who! Aaron, son of our bad brother, Edward! Aaron, you will be pleased to know, is not bad at all, but I guess doing a bit of good in the Army in the secret service line. He does not say, but I think this may be so. It seems he has some leave on his way up to Scotland and I have given him your address so that he can look you up. He seems to have no problem with rail warrants, etc. He must have some pull somewhere . . . I am sure you will like him. There is something, something about him. He has a look of your boys.

Ruth smiled at her. 'Aaron beat the post!' she said. 'Isn't that wonderful?'

Susan looked at the stacked plates. 'Has he gone? I

342

thought . . .' Bang went her idea for him helping her with ChiChu.

'Gone?' Ruth laughed. 'No, he has leave and he's staying here. He said so. Anyway, he and Rhys have gone down to the foundry. He seemed very interested in what Rhys is up to. I haven't seen Rhys with such a spring in his step for months. Years, perhaps.' She stood up. 'You just finish your breakfast and I'll clear.'

Ruth was a very efficient housekeeper. Before the war Maisie Craggs, a girl from New Morven, came every day to help. Now Maisie had a good job in the Rainbow factory, as did all her pals. Domestic work was not wanted by anyone. But Ruth had found the scrubbing and cleaning, the polishing and ironing an escape from gloomy thoughts in recent times. She did it for the first time in her pampered life, and found it soothing. It passed the difficult days.

Susan helped her with the drying up, the putting of the chenille cloth on the table with the crystal vase at its centre.

'There!' said Ruth. 'All shipshape and Bristol fashion.' She turned to face Susan. Her eyes were very bright. 'Susan!' she said. 'Can I trust you with a secret?'

'A secret?' said Susan.

'Will you cross your heart and tell no one?'

Susan sat on a chair by the fireplace and looked up at this woman who was nearly but not quite her aunt. 'I cross my heart,' she said lightly.

'I am serious!'

'I do cross my heart,' Susan smiled. 'Honestly.'

Ruth sat on the seat opposite her. 'I have to tell somebody or I'll burst.'

'Tell!'

'Well. It's an old story. Ancient history. Forty years old.'

'Ruth!'

Ruth took a breath. 'Aaron. You know, you see how much like Ellis he is? He is his double.'

Susan nodded. 'Yes. There is a very good likeness. You can see from the photograph. Very striking.'

'Well.' Ruth paused. 'Aaron is my Peter's half-brother. Younger, of course.'

Susan frowned. 'Half-brother?'

Ruth took a breath. 'Forty years ago I had been married just a while. Edward, Rhys's brother, was around. He was very ... well, charming. We didn't know then what we knew later. What a terrible man he really was. I had some inkling, although Theo always knew. But that made him risky, more charming. D'you see? But by then, the deed was done.'

'The deed?' Susan frowned again, then the penny dropped. 'You're telling me that Ellis was Edward's son? That he and Aaron are half-brothers?'

Ruth nodded and gave a great sigh, breathing out for a long time. 'There. I've told you. They could be twins. Look at Ellis' photograph.'

'Whew! Ruth!' Susan was blushing.

'I know. But as I said it is ancient history now. Only an aberration of the moment. Rhys saw Ellis as his own. Then we had Peter ... Rhys was ... is the best of husbands, the best of fathers.'

'Will you tell him?'

Ruth's laugh pealed out. 'Don't be silly. I'd not make Rhys unhappy. Not for anything. But I know. And Rhys will be happy that I am happy, whatever the reason. Don't you see? Now I know that in Aaron, we have a closer connection with Ellis than Rhys would ever know. He will never know.' Her voice sharpened. 'You promised, Susan. Hand on heart.'

Susan shook her head. 'I wouldn't tell him. I wouldn't tell anyone. Nothing would be served by it.'

Aaron came back from his tour of the factory at ten o'clock. He sought Susan out in the kitchen where she was writing a letter to Keziah.

And by coincidence, there is a man here who ChiChu and I knew in Spain. He speaks fluent Spanish, even some Catalan, so he should be a help. Oh, by the way, I saw Mr Strophair in the hospital. He's sitting there like the cat that got the cream. Can't see that what he's done is wrong at all. And guess who else I also saw? Jane Ann Golon! She was polishing the main stairs. Quite a privilege really. She must be behaving herself. But somehow she seemed less content than before. Less funny. I felt sad, seeing her.

She stared at the letter and realized that she would not send it. She'd take Aaron up to the farm. She could check on Barty and the girls and they could all think of a way to sort out this problem.

Aaron came through the door and she pushed the letter into an envelope. She smiled faintly at him. 'So what does it feel like to be the prodigal nephew?'

'They are very welcoming,' he said carefully. 'I was never greeted with such a welcome. I like them. They are fine, good people. I thought he might be like my father. But they are different. Very different.'

'It is strange to see you looking so much like those boys, yet speaking so strangely.'

Irritation flashed across his face. 'To me the way you speak is strange. In this country you're all obsessed with the smallest differences,' he said shortly. 'It must be living on such a small island that does it.'

For a second his temper called up her own and she wanted to take him down a peg or two; to ask him if he realized that his own father had been in this home up to no good; that the handsome man on the photograph was not his cousin but his half-brother. But she just shrugged her shoulders and waited a second. Then she said, 'About ChiChu . . .'

'Yes.' He leaned forward. 'I'll be honest with you, Susan. That's why I came.'

She frowned. 'You know this happened? That she was in hospital?'

He shook his head. 'Theo said something, but I wasn't clear. I had some leave and I thought I would come and visit her . . . and you.' He paused. 'You have been on my mind. Those times in Spain. Like a film over and over.'

She suddenly knew quite well that it was ChiChu, not herself, that was on his mind. 'What happened to the arm?' she said directly.

He shrugged. 'I had a close call in France recently . . .'

'Close call? What does that mean?'

'Well, there were shots. I was not the one killed.'

'So it's right what Theo says. You are a spy?'

He looked at her blandly. 'I had the close call in a certain place which is crawling with Germans. But I didn't know that makes me a spy,' he repeated. 'A colleague, Frenchman, was killed. Somehow that made me think what a waste of time it was to prevaricate in these days.

That was when I wished to see you and ChiChu. Somehow you were in my mind.'

'Well, you'll have your work cut out to see ChiChu.' She told him of the events of the last days. 'I need you to come there with me and talk to her; talk to Dr Tordoff. Make him let us bring her back. He will resist. She's been kind of signed over. It's hard to disentangle, once it is done.

He looked at her seriously for a moment, then smiled and it seemed to her for a second that she could trust him. Even with ChiChu. 'However we do it, it needs to be done soon,' she said. 'But first we need to go up to the farm and check on my son and the girls who are watching him and the farm. They are very good but there is so much to do. So much.'

'Not to the hospital?'

'Not just yet. I need to think how I can get her out. They're keeping her asleep. No point in going to see her till we work out a way of getting her out.' Her voice lightened. 'I think now we can do it between us. We have to.'

Chapter Twenty-Six

Wounded Soldier

Aaron's immaculate riding boots were splashed irretrievably by the time he had ploughed his way up to Goshawk Shield from the road. Judith laughed when Susan introduced him. She was struck by the incongruity of the immaculate uniform and the muddy boots.

She nodded at the injured arm. 'Wounded soldier, are we?'

Susan hurried upstairs to see Barty.

'Well,' Aaron kicked his knapsack into the corner and it settled like a khaki dog going to sleep, 'I've got convalescent leave for this. Don't mock.' He lifted the arm that was in the sling and winced. 'I've really come to see Miss Sabater and see if I can help. Susan says we have to check on things here first.'

'Here!' said Judith. 'Look at these hands.' She waved her hands before his face. 'Have you seen hands in such a state? We are really stretched out round here.'

He glanced round. 'Perhaps I could give a hand? One hand, that is.'

She laughed. 'As for round here, Keziah and I are perfectly capable of doing what should be done.'

He shrugged. 'It's just that I heard about Miss Sabater. I thought I could help. It seems in this family I'm always having to prove myself.'

Later that night Keziah and Judith were standing side by side at the sink washing the last of the dishes. 'Bowled over by the blond captain?' said Keziah. 'Eyes out like headlights there.'

There was no doubt that Judith had taken an instant shine to the captain who'd arrived like a wounded angel in their midst. She glowed in his presence and was sinfully extravagant with her Pond's Cold Cream, slathering it on her hands and face to compensate for the chapping qualities of the easterly winds which raged down the fell.

Aaron smiled at her efforts. Judith was pretty and she was uncomplicated. He'd met many like her in his travels. Even in her corduroys and thick jersey she had a trim figure, and her blonde hair, let down from its plaits, crackled in the light of the paraffin lamp. It was soothing to be asked innocuous questions about South Africa, to describe its long landscapes, its blood-stirring heat, its exquisite flowers. No awkward questions about an errant father. No suspicious looks in response to every statement.

She chattered away and Aaron found himself agreeing to go to a dance on Saturday night with her and Keziah. 'I'm on the injured list,' he warned. 'I won't be able to dance.'

'No matter.' She tossed her head and her blonde hair crackled into the air then settled again. 'We can tap our feet together. The band is a lot of old codgers but they make wonderful music. Believe me! You wouldn't imagine it in a small-town band.'

'I've things to do this week,' he said. 'Susan and I going to Priorton after ChiChu. I may not—'

She shook her head again. 'No matter. Saturday night, that's the thing. Four days away.'

Later, in their shared bedroom, Keziah said, 'That was a bit much, Judith. Talk about throwing yourself at somebody. You should be ashamed of yourself.'

Judith lay down on the bed and pulled the blankets up to her cheeks. 'Isn't he the most delicious, the dreamiest thing you ever laid your eyes on for months? There's more than a shortage of bacon and cheese these days. Have to make the most of what you can get your hands on. Haven't you heard there's a war on, you silly goose?'

Early the next morning Aaron found Susan in the dusty barn, milking the cow. 'You look pretty good at that,' he commended, nodding at her busy fingers.

'Should be,' she said, her voice muffled by the cow's warm flank. 'Been doing it since I was six, mebbe seven. Rose Clare, that'd be your grandma, wouldn't it? Rose Clare showed me how. And when I got older we shared this job, like we shared everything.'

'What was she like, Rose Clare?'

'She was the world to me. Brought me up, showed me how to go on. She was funny and kind. Irish. Did you know that? That she was Irish?'

He shook his head. 'I thought she was Welsh, like my father.'

'Always wore red petticoats.' Susan wriggled her shoulders but still kept up her rhythmic squeezing of the teats. 'Theo and her, they had their problems, like.'

'Problems?'

'Well, seems like Rose Clare was a better mother to me than she was to her. Learned by her mistakes, seems like. There, that's it.' She sat back on her heels then stood up.

She patted the cow on her neck and tipped a few more cakes in her trough. 'Was there something?' she said. 'Or did you just want a lesson in milking?'

'I want you to take me to the hospital today, to see Miss Sabater.' He lifted up the steaming pail and they set off towards the farmhouse.

'Well, I don't want to go until I can think of a copper-bottomed way of getting her out of there.'

He lifted the bucket on to the table by the sink. 'I suppose it is an impossible request,' he said. 'I don't suppose there's such a thing as a typewriter anywhere round here?'

She took the milk from him. 'You don't suppose wrong. There is an old one of Theo's in one of the top cupboards. I saw it when I was sorting out sheets when we first came here. In a box with all its fiddly bits. Theo must have tucked it away when she first went to London. She's got one of those modern Remingtons now.'

'Will you get it down for me?'

'Just give me a chance to stow this milk in the pantry,' she said. She returned and washed her hands at the sink. 'So, what is it you're up to?'

He winked at her. 'What I'm doing is working on the side of right, just as I always do.'

As she stomped upstairs in search of the typewriter Susan thought it was the wink that did it. A slight thing, a fluttering of a single eyelid; but suddenly she trusted him. He was all right. He really was all right, this grandson of Rose Clare. Theo might not be sure of him, but she was wrong.

She brought the box to his bedroom door and knocked. He took it from her and shut the door behind him. For the rest of the morning she could hear him tapping away, shuffling round. At noon he came down to the kitchen for his dinner, buttons shining, leather gleaming, ready for their journey.

Keziah kicked Judith under the table and rolled her eyes. Judith went red and continued to eat her soup.

'We'll stay overnight again in Priorton at Uncle Rhys and Ruth's,' Susan said. 'Try to get this thing sorted. Maybe Aaron can turn the screw on old Tordoff. You never know.'

'Don't worry about Barty,' said Keziah. 'We'll watch him like he was Princess Elizabeth. Give our love to ChiChu and tell her to get herself home, double quick. We've nearly finished the beet, but there's the barns to whitewash.'

Chapter Twenty-Seven

Operations

Dr Tordoff's secretary popped her head round the door. 'There's a Captain Maichin here to see you, Captain.'

Tordoff sat up straight in his chair. What a good thing he'd incorporated his military rank into his hospital life. In insisting on being addressed by his military title he was reminding those in his little universe that, through him, they were making their contribution to the war effort. He'd let it be known, during one of the regular staff whist parties, that the Government had wished to second him directly into the military but he had resisted this. He knew, he said, that his duty was on the Home Front, in his own community.

He stood up to greet the soldier as he came through the door and acquitted himself with a very sharp salute. He surveyed the tall, blond figure before him. 'Sit down, Captain Maichin, sit down, won't you!' he said briskly.

Aaron sat down, his glance flickering round the busy office. 'Thank you, Dr Tordoff,' he smiled slightly. 'But did I hear your secretary call you Captain?'

Tordoff coughed. 'Overenthusiasm, Captain. The staff see me as their surrogate in this action. I'm fortunate enough to be very active on the Home Front.'

'Vital work, so I'm told,' said Aaron.

'And you, Captain? Where might your theatre of operations be?'

Aaron shrugged. 'Well, unfortunately, just at the moment I'm driving a desk in London.'

'Have you seen action?'

'I was at Dunkirk, like a hundred thousand others.'

'I see you have a more recent injury.' Tordoff nodded at the sling. 'Did you get that at your desk?'

'Well, this came about on a bit of a bust-up. But generally I drive a desk.'

Tordoff nodded. He knew when to keep silent. The space between them throbbed with his discretion. 'I see. Well, then, Captain Maichin? What brings you to our neck of the woods? I thought it might be Home Defence business when I saw you, but—'

Aaron shook his head. 'No. I can see things are running here smooth as silk. Obviously in good hands.' He hesitated. 'It's another matter on which I need your help. It is official business in its own way.'

Tordoff leaned back and threw out his arms expansively. 'Anything, Captain. Anything in my power.'

Aaron looked him in the eye. 'You have a patient here. Maria Josep Sabater. Dark girl. Dark eyes.'

Tordoff frowned. 'The Spanish girl. Yes. She's been here a week. A bit of a handful, I'm afraid.'

'Well, Captain Tordoff, I can't say much but . . . it's essential I see her.'

Tordoff shook his head. 'It would be very hard. She's a very troubled young woman, Captain. Aggression. Manic behaviour. I can't think what you'd want with her.'

Aaron took out some papers from his small leather

satchel. He placed them on the desk. 'What I am going to show you, Captain Tordoff, is utterly, utterly confidential.' He spread out the sheets of official paper, letters and ChiChu's battered passport. Tordoff put on his glasses and peered at them. They were in French and Spanish and, using his Latin to decode, looked like instructions to an agent, a certain Miss M. J. Sabater. The picture was certainly the dark girl in the wide ward. 'What does this mean?'

'I am not absolutely sure why they want to recall her. She was my opposite number on an operation in the Pyrenees before the war. She had to rest up here in England, so I sent her to my relatives up here. Now the men upstairs need her back, something about further debriefings.'

'But she is in no fit state—' said Tordoff.

'Aftereffects of the action, I'd think,' said Aaron. 'You would know how well documented it is now, the aftereffects of war experience. Shell shock and all that.'

'Mmm. Mmm.' Tordoff peered at the papers again, trying to make sense of them, to look authoritative. 'So what, exactly, do you want me to do? She's under sedation.' He hesitated. 'Out cold, in fact.'

'I want you to hand her over into my custody. I have forms here, which we can sign . . .' he rummaged in his case again. 'Special release forms. It says the Ministry will take responsibility for her and you are in no way responsible for her after she leaves your care.'

Tordoff frowned. 'It is very irregular.'

'These are irregular times, Captain Tordoff. You especially should know that.'

Tordoff put his hand towards the telephone. Aaron leaned across and put a hand on his. 'At the outset,

Captain, I indicated that this was a matter of utmost confidentiality. You would not like it said that you had here, under sedation, a person who had information crucial to the war effort?'

'Well . . .' Tordoff sat back in his chair. 'The war . . .'

'Splendid,' said Aaron, standing up. 'Now I must emphasise that you say nothing to anyone. Not your colleagues. Not even my cousin, Miss Cornford. She knows nothing of this confidential matter. She merely wishes to care for Miss Sabater, who is her friend. Miss Cornford is a trained nurse, so you should trust her. As a fellow officer, you should trust me.'

Dr Tordoff stood up and proffered his hand. 'I had not realized who she was, that—'

Aaron nodded wisely. 'Deep cover, Dr Tordoff. Deep cover.'

Aaron hid his shock when he saw the shrunken figure on the bed, the gleam of eyeball showing through the half-open eye. He turned to Tordoff. 'Would it be entirely impossible to have an ambulance, Captain Tordoff? I came here by taxi, but looking at Miss Sabater . . .' It would do no good to tell the good doctor that he had come on the Favourite Service bus. 'I have to get her right up into Weardale for her convalescence. And her debriefing, of course. Miss Cornford is waiting downstairs.'

'Weardale!' Tordoff thought of the hospital allocation of petrol. 'The petrol—'

'I'll do my very best via the Ministry to get you some compensation for that.'

'Well . . . well . . . I'll order the ambulance for you.' Suddenly Dr Tordoff was weary of all of them: the dashing captain, the pusillanimous Nurse Cornford, the raving Spanish woman. He wanted his hospital back in its blessed routine. It was his business to deal with the insane, not with the flotsam and jetsam thrown up by war. Anyway, he had an important session with his troop to think about tonight. They were doing the identification of enemy planes, followed by drill, of course.

He couldn't understand why he had been taken with this fellow. Flashy uniform. But that accent! One of our Commonwealth brothers, no doubt. Still, one must tolerate them. We were at war, after all.

'How did you do that?' Susan held on to ChiChu's hand as the ambulance trundled round another bend.

Aaron smiled slightly. 'Subterfuge. Risking my career. If this got out, I'd be shot.'

'Shot? Well, Aaron—'

'Perhaps not shot. Booted out of my particular branch of the service, perhaps.'

'So why did you . . . ? Why did you do it?'

'I suppose . . . for you. For the family. For my Aunt Theo who still doesn't trust me. Kind of showing off, I suppose. Discovering I have a family.' He paused. 'But when I really think about it – and I would only tell you this, Susan – when I really think about it, I did it for Miss Sabater. From the day we met in Barcelona she has had such a look in her eye for me. Such contempt. I think I want to convince her that we're on the same side. That those foul things that happened to her family and friends in Spain can't be put at the door of soldiers who were there trying to help.'

Susan persuaded the ambulance driver to stop at Priorton so they could pick up their things. Ruth and Rhys were sad that they had to turn round and go straight back after a single night. Ruth came out to the ambulance to take a look at ChiChu, who was muttering and twitching now on her stretcher in the ambulance.

She turned to Aaron. 'I'm pleased to see this young woman because she brought you to see us, brought you home,' she said. Then she took both Aaron's hands and held them close. 'You know where we live,' she said. 'Now you know you will always have a home here. There's the factory. All for you, if you want it. There is a large space in our house and our hearts are here for you. Always.'

He found himself pulling her to him, embracing her. 'Well, Aunt Ruth, that is the nicest thing anyone has ever said to me. I can't deserve it.'

Then they were on their long, bumpy way up the dale. The ambulance driver shook his head at the impossibility of getting the ambulance up the farm track. Aaron cursed his injured arm, which made it impossible to carry ChiChu the last six hundred yards. 'Wait here,' said Susan.

She appeared ten minutes later on a tractor, dragging a wheeled sledge on which sat Judith and Keziah. Between them, they lifted ChiChu and the baggage on to the sledge. Aaron gave the ambulance driver a ten-shilling note and the man smiled for the first time on the long journey. They waved goodbye to him and set off together up the last bumpy stretch of the journey.

Aaron trudged through the mud beside Judith. 'So here you are,' she said, flashing him a wide smile. 'A knight in shining armour, rescuing the sleeping beauty?'

The smells are different, Avia. It's colder, colder. Not that sticky, sweet smell of the death place. There are voices. I hear Judith. You know, the one who the farmer hurt? And Keziah, the one who was in the mad hospital with Susan. And Susan, there she is murmuring, murmuring. Speak

*louder, Susan. Louder so I can hear. And Barty. I can
hear Barty. There is another voice. A man's. A man's. I
know that voice. I heard it in Spain. I know that voice.*

'What's she talking about?' said Keziah. 'What is she
muttering on about?'

Susan looked down at the slender figure tucked in now
in her own bed at Goshawk Shield. 'When I first heard it
I thought she was praying but she told me after that she
was talking to her grandmother.'

'But her grandmother is dead.'

'Yes. I know. She knows. I'm just happy to hear her
talking at all. Who knows what harm they've done to her
in that place?'

Chapter Twenty-Eight

No Flamenco

During ChiChu's first three days home Aaron stationed himself by her bed in the room she shared with Susan and Barty. He stoked the fire and swished the curtains. He marched about the room and talked to her about Catalonia. About Aragon where she fought for Spain. About Barcelona: the streets of the old city and some of the fine brave people he'd met there. About the press of people on the Ramblas and the excitement of people at the barricades talking, arguing, persuading people to their point of view. He talked of the early days of the revolution and the exultancy when the republican government was voted in. How the only thing to be then was a worker, and even the bourgeois merchants and capitalists pretended to be workers.

Each time she woke or half woke from this twilight sleep ChiChu could hear that crisp persistent voice speaking in her own language. She tried to answer but her lips and tongue were made of putty and would not respond.

Early on the Saturday morning of that week Susan was disturbed by routine sounds in their bedroom. She sat up.

'What is it?' she mumbled. 'What is it?'

'I hear cockerel,' came ChiChu's voice. 'Time I feed hens. Clear them out.' She was standing at the end of her bed, holding the iron rail tight.

Susan leaped out of bed and opened the curtains wide to let the light in. 'ChiChu. You're up! Let me see you.' She hugged ChiChu to her.

The girl pulled away. 'Ooh. Ooh, Susan. You hurt.'

Susan laughed. 'I'm sorry. I forgot about your ribs. But you're better! Better! Here! Sit down on your bed before you fall down.'

ChiChu sat down hard on her bed. She wrinkled her nose. 'I smell,' she said. 'I smell.' She put her hand to her shorn head and put her fingers just under her nose.

'Can you remember?' said Susan. 'Do you remember?'

ChiChu wrinkled her nose again. 'Toro's blood.'

Susan nodded. 'Yes. Poor old bull. But after that? Do you remember after that?'

ChiChu shook her head. 'I dreaming. Bad things. Nasty people.' She put her hands to her hair again. 'I bite nasty people. Then all is grey. Grey. Me, I feel sticky, like bread dough. Cannot move. Then a voice. A man's voice. Talking about home. Always talking.'

Susan nodded, smiling. She told ChiChu the story of the past week. 'And Aaron Maichin has been talking solid to you for three days.'

'I was in the mad hospital?'

Susan nodded.

'Where you worked? The mad hospital where you worked?'

'Mmm. The same man was in charge.'

A shadow crossed ChiChu's face. 'Like prison,' she

364

said. 'Small room with walls of dirty cloth.'

Susan nodded. 'But you were rescued.'

'You save me?'

Susan shook her head. 'Aaron saved you. He got you out. Captain Maichin.'

ChiChu touched her hair again. 'Captain Maichin?'

'Like I say, he's been sitting by you for two solid days, ChiChu. Like you say, talking, talking.'

'The man's voice?'

'The man's voice.'

Barty woke up then and beamed at ChiChu. He put up his arms. ChiChu pulled him on to her lap and tickled him under the chin. She looked up at Susan. 'A bath, I must have a bath.' She wrinkled her nose. 'I not smell this way since I was at the emplacement with Esteban.'

Susan went downstairs to announce to the others that ChiChu was in the bath playing with Barty. 'With a bit of luck she'll be down herself in half an hour.'

Judith looked quickly at Aaron and noted the smile of satisfaction on his face. 'Well,' she said brightly, 'if we rush to get the first round of chores done we can be back in time to see ChiChu make her grand entrance.' She looked at Aaron. 'Would it be too much to ask the help of your one good hand in feeding the hens?'

He jumped to his feet and grinned. 'At your service, *mademoiselle*.'

Keziah and Susan watched them make their way across the farmyard. 'I think our Judith has her eye on the captain,' said Keziah.

'Well, that's unfortunate for her,' said Susan. 'I'm not sure, but I think our captain has his eye on ChiChu.'

Keziah groaned. 'Oh-oh. Trouble.'

'Don't you worry about that, Keziah. You just worry

about those two cows who're so loaded up with milk, they're fit to burst.'

Susan went upstairs to rescue Barty from ChiChu's attentions and told her not to be too long, or the water would be cold. Later, in the bedroom, she rebound ChiChu's ribs. 'By, you're skinnier than ever,' she said.

ChiChu smiled at her. 'Now, Susan, I will eat and eat. Go, give Barty food. Stop noise.'

When Susan had gone ChiChu sat on the bed and pulled on her long socks. Now at last she was clean. She felt as clean as a new baby. Her hair, cut short like the pelt of a puppy, felt silky soft. She felt light and soft, like a shelled egg. The scalding water of the bath and the lump of yellow soap had taken a whole scale off her, outside and inside at the same time had been washed off. It had washed off the last of poor Toro's blood. It had scoured the blood of her father and grandfather, of Esteban and her *Avia* from her skin. The hot water had finally melted the cold feeling that had lodged itself inside her since that last time with Esteban on the escarpment. She felt new as a peeled walnut: all cracks and crevices but clean and clear.

She surveyed herself in the mirror. She had to find a safety pin to fasten up her skirt which was now too big. Her hands and arms were a little lost in her cardigan. She smiled. 'Now, *Avia*, to start again. It is all made good.'

She had to cling on to the banister and the walls to get all the way downstairs to the kitchen. They were all in there: Keziah at the stove, waiting for the kettle to boil; Judith, leaning back on the dresser, was showing off her trim little figure; Susan by the fire played pat-a-cake with Barty who was standing between her knees. At the table sat Captain Maichin.

They all turned and smiled at her. 'Your arm hurting,' she said to Aaron. 'A wound?'

Aaron lifted his arm slightly. 'Nearly mended,' he said. 'Just like you.' He stood up, took her arm and guided her back into the chair he had just vacated. 'Welcome back,' he said in Catalan.

'In English,' she said, her chin lifting up. 'Now I speak only in English. I not return to Catalonia with the man Franco there. So I not speak that language. Only English.'

During the next few days the house purred with the feeling of celebration. The war was only noted in the respectful silence with which they received the news at nine o'clock. They might have been an island in an ocean. They all pitched in with the farm chores so the work was completed early in the day. They all pitched in with the cooking so every meal was a miniature feast.

ChiChu took the hens back into her care and Aaron helped to feed and clean them out. Keziah laughed at the two of them making their way across the yard, saying how the halt was helping the lame. Judith looked on politely and said nothing.

While she went around her tasks ChiChu demanded the words for everything, and repeated it after whoever was willing to supply it. She listened carefully to their phrases and repeated them. She told them to tell her when she said things wrongly. On this she was determined. That now, for ever, she would speak only English.

'For ever?' said Susan.

ChiChu shook her head. 'Perhaps, when I go back to my own country, when those Fascists are swept away, I speak my own language. Until then, only English.'

After two days, ChiChu lifted the latch for the first time on the old dairy and entered the dimly lit space where Toro had spent his days. She hitched herself up on to the high stone stall. His rotting meal was still in his manger. The smell of him was in the air. 'Toro,' she whispered.

Aaron finished his particular task, the chopping of sticks for the fire with his good hand, and walked through the house and the yard. He pushed open the dairy door and peered round. 'Are you all right, ChiChu? Isn't it a bit dark to be sitting here?'

'Toro was here,' she said. 'Now he's gone.' Large tears were flowing unchecked down her cheeks. 'I remember.'

He stood very still. He'd seen her angry and wild, resentful, under pressure. But he had never seen her in tears.

He took a step towards her. 'ChiChu, I . . .'

Behind him the door was pushed open. 'Where are you, ChiChu? Susan's howling because the dinner—' Judith stopped and looked from one to the other. 'What is it?' she said sharply. 'Is there something wrong?'

ChiChu wiped her eyes on the sleeve of her cardigan and sniffed. 'Is nothing,' she said. 'Is Toro's place. Makes me cry like a girl. No *miliciana*.'

Judith smiled then and went and sat beside ChiChu on the high stall. She put an arm round her. 'Poor ChiChu,' she said. She looked up at Aaron, her eyes bright, inviting. 'That man was a beast of the first order. ChiChu here saved me once, right here, from his voracious advances. ChiChu went for him with a pitchfork. Saved me from a fate worse than death.' She looked at him, knowing the picture she was painting. 'You were a soldier then, ChiChu.'

ChiChu frowned. 'Vo-ra-cious. What this?'

Aaron laughed and held up his arms so that she could

jump down from the high stone stall. 'She means he was very, very hungry. As we are. Come on, let's see whether Susan has done some of her excellent potato hash or beef stew without beef.'

Judith held out her arms to be lifted down too. When she was safely on the ground she clung briefly to him, then linked his arm. 'Now, Aaron, shall we get this child in for her dinner? I think I'm pretty voracious myself.'

They had just finished the meal when Judith clapped a hand on her forehead. 'It's Friday!'

Keziah was stretching her legs before the fire. 'By gum, so it is! It's Friday! Go to the top of the class and give the pens out. What's so amazing about that?'

'The dance. It's Saturday tomorrow. We're taking the lovely captain to the dance!'

He looked up sharply. 'I don't know . . .'

ChiChu was sitting on the fireside chair washing Barty's sticky hands and face with a flannel. She looked up. 'I go,' she said. 'I go to dance.'

Susan protested. 'ChiChu,' she said, 'you're hardly off your back.'

ChiChu said, 'I am very, very strong.'

'Perhaps it is a bit soon,' said Judith hurriedly. 'It would be too much for you.'

ChiChu looked at her. 'I just sleep a long time. A good rest. Now I wake. My body aches still. But I am good. Good and strong.'

'Well,' said Aaron cheerfully, 'if we all go we can make sure that ChiChu is all right, can't we? She can show you how to dance the flamenco.'

'I don't know . . .' said Susan.

'We'll all take care of her,' said Aaron firmly. 'We'll have a jolly time. Judith and Keziah have had a hard week so they deserve a break. And ChiChu is beginning to wake up from her big sleep.'

'Why, man,' said Keziah. 'Yeh just mek her sound like Sleeping Beauty.'

Judith looked at her darkly. 'Don't be stupid, Keziah.'

'What have I said?' said Keziah. 'What have I said?'

ChiChu stood up and handed Barty over to Susan. 'What Sleeping Beauty?' she said.

'An English fairy story,' said Susan. 'Don't worry, just a bit of Keziah's nonsense. So. You are going to the dance?'

'Yes. But no flamenco. Only the gypsy ladies, the café women, do the flamenco. Not me.'

Chapter Twenty-Nine

The Red Citroën

The next morning a young, fair woman in smart country tweeds turned up at the kitchen door of Goshawk Shield. Judith greeted her enthusiastically and introduced her as her cousin Norma.

Norma handed her a small suitcase. 'Brought you the stuff you asked for, Jude.' She peered down at the clods of mud on her hand-made shoes. 'I left your car on the road. Your dad filled it with petrol and there's a spare can in the back. You didn't tell me the walk up from the road was so long.'

Judith looked at the others. 'Norma kindly brought my car over for me. And a few of my things. I dropped her a line. Lucky that she turned up today, don't you think?'

Norma accepted a cup of Camp Coffee but insisted on going straight off, as she had to get the train back to Newcastle at four o'clock.

'I'll take you back to the station,' said Judith. 'It'll be a change to be behind the wheel again instead of on shanks's pony.'

The two girls went off arm in arm down to the road to where Judith's low-slung Citroën was sitting on its haunches, a bright spot of pillar-box red in the greens and greys of field and fell.

Susan turned to Keziah. 'Now what's she up to?'

'Can't you guess? That Aaron. Making an impression. Decided to stop playing humble farm girl, at a guess. Can't blame her. I'd fancy him myself if I was taller.'

Susan smiled. 'Keziah, don't be so suspicious.'

Later that evening Judith presented herself for their outing to the dance. The case which Norma had brought proved to be a magical box of tricks: some kind of hair stuff so she could sweep up her hair high at the side; hot tongs to curl the back hair so it fell in a torrent of curls; cream and powder to pale her tanned skin and clear red lipstick for her full lips. She stood at the bottom of the stairs wearing a new dark green wool dress with semi-military epaulettes and twinkling brass buttons.

She smiled at their keen interest. 'I asked Norma to bring a few things,' she said. 'You get really sick of wearing the same old things, don't you?'

Keziah looked down at her own handkerchief-blouse made from curtain lining, then at ChiChu's hand-me-down and pinned-in outfit. 'Blimey!' she said. Then she made a mock bow to Judith. 'You shall go to the ball, Cinderella!'

Judith looked under her lashes towards Aaron, immaculate in his officer uniform, his arm finally out of its sling. 'And my glass coach awaits. Perhaps you could drive, Aaron?' She threw him a single key which he caught neatly. 'Shall we go?'

She took his arm and steered him through the door. They made a fine couple, walking down the yard.

ChiChu was scowling her dark scowl. 'I not going,' she said. 'I not going to dance.'

Keziah took her arm. 'Oh, you're coming, lady. You're bloody coming. If you think I'm gunna play gooseberry to them two you have another think coming.'

'Tilley lamps! Take lamps!' said Susan. 'How else will you find your way back up the fell at midnight?'

Susan watched them from the farm gate. Judith got into the front passenger seat. She leaned forward to remove an invisible speck from the immaculate walnut fascia. The other two tumbled into the back. Susan wondered briefly where the petrol had come from. Most cars these days were up on bricks, mothballed for the day when everyone could drive their cars again. Then she remembered something about Judith's father being in munitions on Tyneside. He'd have access to coupons, all right.

She cleared the kitchen, got Barty to sleep, then took a cup of tea up to her own little sitting room. She'd load the fire with the scrap wood so thoughtfully raked together by Aaron and get her feet up.

Before she put on the light and closed the curtains she leaned across the sill and looked through the narrow window. The wings of dark were settling on the fell, hiding the cottages and the vertical scratch of trees from view. The road that had recently led her friends away from the farm had sunk into blackness. The sky above was brighter, more luminous than the dense blackness of the land. The stars gathered in fierce bright groups in revolt at the blackout vacuum below. A twinkling light on the fell opposite caught her eye. Someone had left a light on, hadn't obeyed the blackout code. No. The light was moving. Someone was moving across the fell; probably finding their way home with their own Tilley lamps.

Susan closed the curtains and settled down beside the

fire to write a letter to Theo. She told her about ChiChu's rescue and that, after due consideration, Aaron Maichin passed muster. In his sturdy kindnesses he reminded her of Rose Clare. And hadn't he had a mother after all, to give him good qualities to compensate for his father's dark consequence? And now, after he had worked his magic for ChiChu, she felt they should put the past to rest and take him for himself. *No need to let the shadow of Edward hang over you both after all these years.* Rhys and Ruth had taken him to their hearts and had been particularly struck by his close resemblance to Ellis, their eldest. *Do you remember, Theo? Poor Ellis was in the Fleet Air Arm and was killed? Well, Aaron is the pot model of him. No denying it. Ruth in particular was very moved. I have some things to talk to you about this.*

Susan sealed the envelope, then set about writing two letters to Jake Stanton. She wrote the letters in twos in case just one of them got through to him in his far prison camp. Jake, whom she had met only a couple of times in the flesh was, in his absence, becoming a person in her life. She smiled at the thought.

Chapter Thirty

In the Mood

The arrival of the new band at the dance hall was an occasion in the town. The queue outside the dance hall snaked past the butcher's and ended right by the Methodist hall. The people stood on the wet pavement and stamped their feet. As they talked their breaths joined in the air.

The red Citroën was treated to a few whistles as it purred past the crowd of people and there was a ripple of pleasure as it came to a stop. People craned their necks to see what sort of exotic creatures would emerge from such a rare vehicle. There was a sigh of satisfaction when the immaculate blond captain handed out the elegant blonde woman in a tightly belted coat. They were certainly a fair match for the car. Then there was a mutter of greater curiosity as this same fair hero handed out a sturdy figure in a Burberry mackintosh, and a slender dark girl in a coat which was too big for her and bare brown legs. They were an odd quartet.

The double doors opened and the arrivals were forgotten in the rush to get into the heat of the hall out of the chilly night. The quartet from Goshawk Shield waited until the very end of the queue. They paid their money demurely and entered the brightly lit hall. The band was tuning up and by the time the girls had disposed of their coats to a tall woman in a wraparound pinny, the band was in full swing. Most of the men and a few of the women were in army uniform. Here and there were sailors enjoying a longed-for leave; an RAF type was telling stories of the air battle over London that stopped Hitler in his tracks.

The local women were in their Saturday best, meeting the challenge of wartime improvisation with resourceful but varying effect. Some of them were in military uniform. One girl was in land girl's kit. Keziah peered at her but didn't recognize her so she left her in peace.

The band had a big brass line-up so the music was loud and swinging. It swept to the walls of the hall in a wave and reverberated its length. The shining honey-coloured floor was webbed with couples dancing conventional quicksteps, interlaced by bolder couples dancing a kind of bebop which the soldiers had imported from other more cosmopolitan dance halls.

Judith, looking tall and elegant in her dark green, tapped her high-heeled shoe to the beat. Finally she could stand it no longer. 'Come on, Aaron. Shake a leg,' she said. 'Can you resist it?'

He laughed and shook his head. 'I've told you already,' he said. 'I cannot dance. Never had the time to learn.'

'I'll dance with you,' offered Keziah.

Judith threw her a chill smile. 'I don't think so,' she said.

Keziah laughed. 'Oh. Excuse *me*!'

Judith sat back and cast a casual eye around the hall at the tense, expectant clusters of soldiers near the door. It only took a single minute for a tall, dark sergeant in Canadian uniform to come across and ask her. She smiled meltingly at him and accepted his offer of a dance.

They swung away. Soon the Canadian was twirling her round and round. They made an elegant couple.

'I'll say one thing for our Judith,' said Keziah. 'She scrubs up very well and she can certainly dance.'

Young Constable Meadows, almost unrecognizable in civvies, with his hair nicely Brylcreemed, turned up and asked if he could have the pleasure. Keziah mimicked Judith's melting smile and was, in her turn, swung into the centre of the floor.

Aaron moved his chair slightly so he and ChiChu were face to face. 'And what about you, ChiChu?' he said. 'Can you dance?'

ChiChu shrugged. 'Judith teaches me. So I am beginner. The music is good.'

'Well, you can show me. Show me how to dance. Two beginners together.'

She frowned at him. 'You say no to Judith.'

He laughed. 'Judith frightens me. Come on, ChiChu. Look! There's a little corner there,' he said. 'You show me. No one will notice us.'

He took her hand and led her across to the corner, and she tried to show him how to do it, pushing him this way and that. In the end she clapped her hand on her forehead and said, 'I forget everything Judith tells me. I cannot do it.'

He looked at his shining shoes, now scuffed with ChiChu's footmarks. 'I don't suppose you can,' he grinned. 'As a dancer you are a very good soldier.'

She spluttered, then laughed, and by the time Keziah

and Judith came back to their seats, the two of them were giggling uncontrollably.

Judith frowned. 'What is it? Is there a joke?' she said.

'I teach . . .' ChiChu spluttered. 'I teach Aaron to dance. But I forget what you say. How to dance.'

'As a dance teacher,' repeated Aaron, 'she is a very good soldier.' He smiled across at ChiChu.

The music was starting up again. 'Well,' said Judith, picking up his hand and pulling him to his feet, 'If you want to learn to dance, you should come to the engine driver, not the oil rag.'

He allowed himself to be pulled to the floor. She placed his hand on her waist, whispered instructions in his ear and they began.

'What is oil rag?' said ChiChu.

'It's just Judith acting like a spoiled baby,' said Keziah rather shortly. 'Here, ChiChu, get up and I'll show you how to dance this one. It's a waltz. Can you remember?' She waved away the hovering Constable Meadows and concentrated on her role of teacher.

With Keziah ChiChu found it easier to remember all she'd been taught and they had fun practising, swinging past Judith and Aaron. 'Hey you two! How's this?' said Keziah. 'Ginger Rogers!'

Aaron begged off the next dance and the Canadian came and swept Judith away again. This time Constable Meadows was allowed to dance with Keziah.

'Do you want to practise?' Aaron shouted above a particularly loud blast of music. 'Would you like another go? You were dancing well there with Keziah.'

ChiChu shook her head. Then she put her hands on her ears. 'Too much noise,' she said. 'I cannot think.'

He took her hand and pulled her to her feet. 'We'll go

somewhere else,' he shouted. 'Somewhere where it's more quiet. Then we can talk.'

'Talk?' she yelled.

'We've never really talked, you and I. Not since Barcelona.'

She scowled. 'In Barcelona is not talk. You asked me questions. I not answer,' she shouted. 'That was not talk.'

He took her arm and guided her through the crowd.

Judith watched them depart over the shoulder of her Canadian. 'That's it then,' she said. 'That's it.'

'What was that, honey?' he said, steering her to a very nice back-dip.

She beamed up at him. 'Oh, nothing, Roy. I was just wondering. How long was this leave you said you had?'

Chapter Thirty-One

Hostage

Susan sat up with a start. Her pencil had fallen from her hand and the fire was down to a cool glow. She leaned over and put another chock of wood on it. She watched it carefully until she could smell it smouldering, then relaxed. A second later she heard it again. It was inside the house: not quite a noise but the sense that someone else was there, breathing the air of the house, disturbing the space.

She picked up the poker and made for the door. It creaked as she opened it. The corridor outside was pitch-black. 'ChiChu? Keziah?' she called. 'Are you back?' She was answered by a stillness: not a natural stillness but the stillness of someone holding their breath.

Further along the landing, below the door of the bedroom which she shared with ChiChu and Barty, was a pencil of light. She had left young Barty in there, in darkness, at seven o'clock. She felt her way along the wall. She put her ear to the door. She could hear Barty muttering and chuckling. She could hear the lower rumble of a man's voice.

She lifted the latch very carefully then smashed the

door open, brandishing the poker as she did so. 'What do you think—' She broke off.

Before her, grinning in the half-light of a Tilley lantern, was Barry Strophair. He was quite smart. His jacket was clean and the scarf tied round his neck was new, as was the cap, jammed slightly sideways on his head. By his side stood Barty, muttering rather sleepily but looking fairly content.

She forced a smile to her lips. 'Mr Strophair! This is a surprise.'

He looked at her. His face had an awful wildness. 'Ah have a message down here an' Ah thowt Ah'd come and see the bairn. Ah was showin' him his reflection in your mirror and we were decidin' who he teks after. We thowt we couldn't see a crack of likeness to the Gomersals. Not a crack. Yon feller your mother went with musta been quite different, like. That's allus considerin' she actually saw him. It can get quite dark in them shearin' sheds. They said it was a shearer. But then Ah looks at this bairn an' Ah say to meself, "Barry, yeh're off yer head." I'd forgotten the Eyetie, see? It was an Eyetie, wasn't it?'

She looked at the hand which was holding Barty tight. His fingernails were black and split at the ends. The house below was silent. There was no one to help her.

'The message, Mr Strophair!' she said. 'You said you were on a message.'

'Aye. Well, Ah gets meself out of the hospital, fine and dandy. But this nurse tells me the Spanish lass's gone already. Why, she's not fit to be out, her. They should keep her locked up. Ah went looking for her, see? Ah was just gunna tell her that Ah was sorry Ah'd missed her and she was to watch out for me next time. I was sorry I'd missed her. Ah'd 'a reminded her that she took me livelihood away, doing that. Messin' around with the bull. Makin' him move so I hit him.'

Susan swallowed the protest rising in her. 'Well, she's not here. You can see that, Mr Strophair.'

Barty was starting to whimper.

'Pity, that. But Ah have this other message too.'

'Give me the bairn,' she put out her arms. 'Give him to me.'

He pulled Barty to him and moved towards the window. 'Oh no, this whelp here, he's me hostage.'

'Hostage?'

'Ah telt yer Ah had another message.'

She let her arms fall to her sides. 'What message was this, Mr Strophair?'

'Well, Ah come here to get me money. Me sheep money that you and the Spanish lass and those other women stole from me.'

'We didn't steal—'

'Well, Ah don't have it. And you give me fake money for it, didn't you? That shows you stole it.'

'Listen. We did that, made the fake money, because we didn't have it. Just to keep you happy for that minute.'

'Well, missis, you can keep me happy too, and this bairn. You can find the money where you put it. And give it to me.' He lifted Barty up to show the child his face in the mirror. Barty started to chuckle. 'There. The bairn's all right. Yeh gan and get that package and Ah can be on my way.'

She smiled uncertainly at Barty. 'Don't worry, Barty. Be a good boy for Mr Strophair,' she said grimly. 'And I'll find your wretched money.'

The Citroën creaked on its brakes as the engine cut out

and the car settled on its springs. The narrow pins of permitted headlight illuminated the black stretch of water and then flickered out and they were sitting in the dark.

ChiChu laughed. 'I think we splash through the water,' she said. 'We go further, we go splash.'

Aaron wound the window down and peered out into the black night. 'Crikey! We nearly did splash through the water. Road leads down to here and sets off again opposite. It must be a ford.'

'Ford?' ChiChu's voice came to him in the darkness.

'Very low water which you can drive through, walk through.'

'Oh.' She wound down her own window and peered out. 'The car gets very wet. Judith will be very mad.'

He leaned back in his seat, patted his pocket and drew out his cigarettes. He offered her one. She shook her head. 'No. No cigarettes.'

He laughed. 'Too young. I forget.' His match flared in the darkness and died, leaving the glowing tip of his cigarette.

'Not too young,' she growled. 'I smoke cigarettes since age twelve. But I stop in the war. I stop because Esteban, he is so mad for cigarettes. I give him mine.'

'Esteban?'

'He is dead, Esteban.'

'Yes. But who was he?'

'Is like Barcelona. You ask questions. Questions. Questions.'

He drew on his cigarette and put his hand out of the window to flick off the fragment of ash. 'I ask about Esteban because I want to know about you. I want to know all about you.'

'Why?'

He was silent for a while. He sighed. 'I thought you'd trust me now. I ask you for myself. For no one else. I thought we could be friends when I got you out of that hospital.'

'Esteban.' She hesitated. 'He was my comrade. I loved him.'

'Like a comrade?'

The chill wind was cutting into the car. She shivered. He reached an arm behind her to wind up her window. When the window was up he left the arm where it was, behind her shoulders. She leaned her head back against the warmth of his arm and his hand came down and pulled her round to him. 'So who is this Esteban?'

'He was my sweetheart, my lover. He died in my arms. His hands were bloody stumps.'

'I am sorry.'

She stiffened, pulled away from him. 'Is all right if he suffer like that, if the Fascists did it. But is not all right, the way it happened.'

'Why not?' he said.

'Because he was killed by a bad guns left by a man who called him a Trotskyist traitor. One of Stalin's lackeys. Dogs.' She leaned forward and wrote ESTEBAN in the mist which was beginning to cloud the windows. 'Perhaps one of your friends. He left the guns. When Esteban shoot our enemy, his gun blows his hands off.'

'And was Esteban a traitor?'

She reached back and wrenched his arm away from her. 'Patriot! He was patriot!' She spat the words out. 'He was no traitor.'

He caught her hand and held it, still, on his chest. 'Don't be angry, ChiChu. I am jealous, that's all.'

'Jealous? What is jealous?'

He paused, glad that the darkness masked his uncharacteristic blush. 'It is me wishing that I were Esteban. That you loved me.' He dropped his half-smoked cigarette out of the window. Then, with her hand on his chest, he leaned and kissed her on the lips.

ChiChu fingered her lips. 'Esteban was my sweetheart,' she said. 'But there was not time. There was never time.'

He cleared his throat. 'And there's no time now, ChiChu. My arm is healed. I have to go tomorrow, back to the Army. Back to London.'

She put a hand on his. 'Will you shoot them, those Germans, Aaron? Like Esteban? Do you have a machine gun?'

She could feel him shake his head in the darkness. 'I do different things. Not exactly machine guns.'

She removed her hand from his. 'You are spy, like Susan says.'

He shook his head again. 'It's not like that. Whatever I do, I do my bit against Hitler. Like I would always. Like I did always, against Franco in Spain.'

'Does that mean killing your friends, your comrades?'

'War is complicated, ChiChu.'

'No. Is simple. You do what is right. Is not right to kill your comrades. Is right to kill the enemies of the people.'

He heaved a sigh that came from his polished boots. 'This is not the time nor the place, ChiChu.'

'Place?' she said, fearing and relishing the uncertainty in his voice. 'Why not the place?'

He took a deep breath and said very rapidly, 'ChiChu. I have been travelling and fighting one way or another since I was nineteen. In your country and here in Europe. In all that time I have never bothered with . . . women, not before. There were other things to do. Your face, that time in

Barcelona, I will never forget it. A fighter with shorn locks. A little Samson. And I've been seeing that little face ever since. Now they have shorn your locks again.'

'Aaron, Aaron,' she put her finger on his lips. 'Too fast, too fast. In Catalan, please, in my own tongue. My head whirls.'

When he tried to make the avowal in her own language, he was stopped by her lips and the feeling of the tips of her fingers through his hair. The sense of urgency and years wasted charged through them, welding them for a time into a single being born of war.

Strophair was holding on to Barty, following Susan from room to room as she looked under chairs and behind cupboards for the package. She grew impatient with the time it was all taking and started to throw cushions around and throw things off shelves at speed. 'Where did you put the dratted thing, Mr Strophair? Where?'

'Ah didn't put it nowhere, missis. You and them women put it somewhere. You stole it. Ah telt yeh.'

'We didn't!' she said. 'We didn't. Look, Mr Strophair, why don't you help me to look? Then we'll find it quicker. Put Barty down and help me look. Help me!'

He squeezed harder on Barty, who yelped. 'Not likely, missis. Like Ah say, this bairn is my hostage. Here, son, see yerself in the mirror.' He held Barty up to the mirror. 'Our Jack, he liked the mirrors. Would laugh himself daft, would our Jack.'

'You brought Jack up yourself, Mr Strophair?'

'Aye. No picnic after his ma died, bringing a bairn up.'

'I imagine.' She thought of the two of them, the man and the boy, with Goshawk Shield falling into darkness around them. 'It must have been hard.' As she talked she was pulling brushes and brooms out of the understairs cupboard, tipping up buckets, poking behind bars. 'It must have been a hard job, bringing up a lad on your own.'

'Yeh'd think he'd be grateful, wouldn't yeh? Not go off and get himself snaffled by the Germans. Leaving his dad on his own!' His tone was thin and bleak.

'Yes, you would, wouldn't you?' Susan opened the door to the bottle pantry with its rows of dusty jars and bottles, which in Rose Clare's time had been full of glowing jam and fruit. The bottles hadn't been disturbed in years. On the back of the door, equally dusty, hung Rose Clare's ancient crossover apron. Susan ran her hand down it, thinking of the childhood years when she'd stood on a stool beside Rose Clare, helping to stir the bramble jelly, the blackberry jam. Her hand encountered something in the pocket of this same apron. She drew out a package wrapped in oilcloth.

'Thank you, Rose Clare,' she breathed.

She put it behind her back. 'I've got it here, Mr Strophair. I've found your money.'

He stood before her, a dark shadow in the kitchen passage. 'Gi's it then.'

'No. Go into the kitchen. Take Barty into the kitchen,' she said. 'Go on!'

'Gi's it here.' He moved towards her.

'No,' she said firmly. 'Go back into the kitchen and I'll give it to you.'

He backed into the kitchen, not taking his eyes off her. Barty at last caught on to the atmosphere and started to whimper. Strophair backed into the brighter light of the kitchen. Susan caught her breath to see Barty's wide, dark eyes fill with tears.

'Now,' she said coldly. 'You put Barty over there behind the settle. On the floor. Right behind.'

'Now, missis,' said Strophair. 'Ah'm not—'

'On the floor.' She grabbed the fire tongs and jammed the package into their jaws. Then she held the package over the flickering fire. 'Or this lot burns.'

'It's me own money,' he said. 'Me own. From lambs Ah bred and reared meself. Gi's it 'ere.'

'That's my own son, Mr Strophair. I bred and reared him myself.' She thrust the tongs into the heart of the fire.

'Stop! Stop!' He lifted Barty high over the back of the settee and dropped him on to the floor. The child did not cry. He hauled himself to his feet, to peer with shining black eyes through the gap in the back of the settee.

Susan went to the door and opened it. She pointed the smouldering package at Strophair. 'Now, out! Out of my house!'

He moved slowly towards her. 'I only want what's mine.'

She pulled her arm back and threw the coal tongs, together with the smouldering money roll into the darkness outside. Strophair chased after it and Susan shut and bolted the heavy door behind him. She battered the door with the flat of her hand and pushed the heavy table behind the door. 'And good riddance to bad rubbish!' she shouted. 'Good riddance.' She could hear him stumbling around in the yard, cursing the dark.

She lifted Barty over the settle and set him on her knee. She scrubbed his damp cheeks with the corner of her nightie. 'There, love. The bad man's gone now. And there's nothing more to worry about. Not a thing. Didn't Rose Clare help us out of our mess?'

She was still on the settle two hours later when the others came back from the dance. This time they didn't leave the Citroën down on the road, but brought it bumping up the muddy track. When Judith, sulking in the back, protested, Aaron said easily, 'These Citroëns are like tanks, Judith. Four-wheel drive. I've driven them over much worse terrain in France many times.'

Despite compensating herself with the handsome Canadian, Judith was furious with Aaron for sticking to ChiChu, even more furious that he had taken ChiChu for a moonlight canoodle in her car. Her dignity prevented her from protesting out loud at this poaching. But who was poaching whom, she was not quite clear. Sometimes it was not only words that she found hard to read. Although she did not protest, she found it hard to join in the banal post-dance chatter, which was mostly Keziah wondering whether she should go to the pictures on Wednesday with PC Meadows.

In the front of the car ChiChu's mind was racing with words, into one language, into another. As the dark bulk of the dry-stone walls flashed past them she thought of that time with Esteban under a stone overhang in the sierra. They knew each other all right, as comrades, as friends and very briefly as lovers. That experience had been the crackle of childish fireworks, the rolling around in the dust of playful puppies. The time tonight with Aaron in the dark by the ford had been more like the collision of planets, a fusing of stars. She wondered why Keziah and Judith could not see this change in her.

Keziah had laughed out loud when Aaron explained that they'd had a ride down to the ford to see the river. 'Oh yes!' she said. 'Oh yes! I see!' Judith had scowled and talked a lot about the Canadian. But they had not seemed to notice this glow between herself and Aaron, as though tongues of lightning were still connecting them even when they were separate from each other.

Aaron handed ChiChu out of the car and held on to her hand as they went to the kitchen door. Unusually, it was bolted. They knocked on the door. Keziah forced her way from the back and banged hard on the door. 'Susan? What is it? Where are you?'

They heard the clatter of noise and the grinding of bolts coming out of their sleeves; the door opened, exhaling a gasp of hot air into the night. 'Come in, come in,' said Susan.

They crowded into the kitchen. Barty was fast asleep on the settle with a blanket over him. Beside him on the settle were the two long pokers.

'What is it?' said Keziah. 'That door is never locked. What's been happening here?'

ChiChu sat beside Barty and picked up a poker. 'The bad man,' she said. 'It was the bad man.'

'Strophair?' said Judith. 'He was here?'

'Strophair!' said Keziah.

'He came threatening Barty till I found his money. I found it and threw him out.'

'Where was it?' said Keziah. 'The money.'

'In the pocket of an old apron of Rose Clare's. In one of the pantries. He must have hidden it there one night when he was drunk.'

'You fended him off?' said Aaron, pulling the table back to the centre of the room.

'Barty is all right?' said ChiChu. 'Not hurt?'

'He giggled his way through most of it,' said Susan. 'But Strophair was threatening him. No doubt about it.'

'We should tell the police. Pronto,' said Aaron. 'The

man wants to be behind bars.'

Susan shook her head. 'He's more mad than bad. Just think – his son in a camp; his farm taken off him. He needs taking care of, not putting behind bars.'

'Perhaps I should go and see my friend Dr – sorry – Captain Tordoff,' said Aaron.

Susan shook her head. 'Leave it alone,' she said.

'Well, that settles it,' said Keziah. 'I'll go to the pictures with that PC Meadows, an' I'll keep going out with him so long as he keeps Strophair away from us. Out of our hair.'

Susan's glance dropped to Aaron and ChiChu's hands, which were still entwined. 'So what's this then? What have you two been up to?'

ChiChu unclasped her hand from Aaron's. 'Is all right, Susan,' she said. 'Leave it.'

They bolted all the doors and stoked up the fire with logs before they went to bed. Judith, in bed first, was grilled by Keziah, who was still brushing her hair. 'So he is very keen, this Canadian?'

'Keen as mustard,' said Judith. She turned over and pulled the blankets under her chin. 'They always are.'

Keziah forbore to mention Judith setting her cap at Aaron Maichin or Aaron's obvious pash on ChiChu. 'And will you see him again?' she said.

'He has one week's leave left. Wants to see me all the time.'

'Plenty of work here at Goshawk, mind. Remember there's a war on. You can't scarper off.'

'We don't work twenty-four hours a day, do we? And I have one more can of petrol for the car before I run out. Then we'll have to put it in the barn for the duration I suppose.'

'Mmm,' said Keziah, falling into the bed. 'Well, you'll have to give me a lift tomorrow night if I've got to grease around this policeman to keep Strophair off our backs. Judith? Judith?'

But Judith was snoring gently, dreaming of someone wearing a wide hat, riding a magnificent stallion across a wide prairie.

Susan and ChiChu were wide awake in their bedroom. Barty was fast asleep on the bed he shared with Susan. ChiChu had had a bath. She looked fresh and young in an old, much-washed nightdress of Theodora's. She had brushed her short hair till it crackled.

'Is all right with you, Susan?' said ChiChu, sitting on her bed. 'Does he frighten you? The bad man?'

Susan had plaited her hair and was tying it with black tape. 'I'm fine, ChiChu. How many times should I say? Strophair's a silly man and I got rid of him. Barty doesn't know that anything has happened. So he's fine. So it's all fine. Now get into bed and get some sleep.'

ChiChu didn't move.

Susan turned the lamp right down.

'Susan?'

'What?'

'Aaron is not spy.'

'I've worked that out.'

'Is not bad man.'

'I had worked that one out too. I just have our Theo to convince of that. I think she will never forgive him for having Edward for a father.' She wondered briefly what Theo would think of Edward having fathered Rhys's elder son, Ellis. Perhaps she knew already.

'Susan?'

'What?'

'I love him. I love him very much.'

Susan put a hand on ChiChu's where it was lying on the quilt. 'I know. I saw this when you came in tonight, despite the dramas.'

'He loves me.'

'So it seems.'

'I go to lie with him.'

Susan's hand clasped tighter on ChiChu's hand. 'No, ChiChu. I can't let you . . .'

ChiChu left her hand where it was but did not return the grasp. 'I go to lie with him. Now.'

'No!'

'I already lie with him by the river,' said ChiChu calmly.

Susan's grasp loosened.

'In Spain,' went on ChiChu, 'I lie with Esteban on the sierra. We play like children, but I lie with him.'

In the many months in England, it seemed to Susan, ChiChu had become younger and younger. Being a foreigner in a foreign land had made her an infant: one to be guided. She'd thought that it would be nice in the near future for ChiChu to have the childhood and young adulthood she'd missed in the revolutionary tumult of Spain. But here was ChiChu leapfrogging over all those preconceptions and growing up in the blink of an eye. She'd gone down to the dance a child and had come back a woman.

'ChiChu, I don't know what to say,' said Susan.

It was ChiChu's turn to grasp Susan's hand tightly. 'I am not child, Susan. I am *miliciana*. I fight for my country,' she paused, 'I choose you for my friend and I choose the person to lie with. I love the person.'

Susan sat up straight and hugged ChiChu. 'Of course, dear girl, what am I thinking? How could I stop you?'

'Aaron goes back tomorrow,' said ChiChu, standing up. 'Perhaps die next week.'

Susan nodded. 'Yes, ChiChu. You go. Go to him.'

Chapter Thirty-Two

I am *Miliciana*

They had made Aaron a shakedown bed in the empty bedroom over the porch. There were no curtains at the window and, faithful to the blackout regulations, Susan had informed him that he was not to use a lamp. He must go to bed in the dark. He didn't mind this too much. He'd slept in many more uncomfortable places.

The bare window framed the night sky. He watched the moon move from one frame to the other. On the darkest nights here as he watched he'd seen the lowering clouds split and clear suddenly so the moon and stars lit up the wide reaches of the night sky. He knew pilots who had cursed this feature of the English weather. These bright nights. The moon was their enemy.

He was sitting up smoking a last cigarette, contemplating the stars when the sneck rattled and the door squeaked open. His muscles tensed as thoughts of Strophair leaped to his mind. Then ChiChu slipped in, closed the door and stood with her back to it.

'You look like a moth,' he whispered. He leaped to his feet and took her into his arms. 'A fluttering moth.'

'A moth? What is this?' She smiled up at him.

He picked up the sides of her nightdress and fluttered it like wings in the air. 'It is white. It has wings.'

She still looked puzzled.

He dropped her nightdress and flapped his arms in the air, making buzzing noises with his mouth. Then he measured with his fingers the size of a moth.

She laughed. 'Ah, *papallona*!'

'I should know that,' he said. He looked towards the doors. 'Susan? What will she—'

'I say to Susan, I choose who I lie with. I am *miliciana*, daughter of freedom. I belong to myself.'

He laughed and put an arm round her shoulders. 'Come and see this wonderful sky.' They peered up into the blackness. 'This sky covers England and France where I will be soon. It covers South Africa, where I was born. And Catalonia, where you were born.'

'Mmm,' she breathed.

'I say to you, Maria Josep Sabater, that every night wherever I am, I will look at the sky and think of you.'

'I too, Aaron. I think of you.'

'And I say to you that when this show is over and we've trounced Hitler, you and I'll be married, tied together for ever.'

'No church,' said ChiChu, thinking of her father. 'No church.'

'No church,' he said. Then, from his little finger, he took a signet ring and slipped it on her forefinger. 'And I'll love you for all time. After time. I promise.'

She kissed the ring and kissed his cheek. 'All time,' she said. 'I love you all time.' She took his hand and led him to the shakedown bed. 'Now,' she said. 'I choose to lie with you.'

Later, lying in the darkness, listening to his breathing,

she closed her eyes. In her nostrils were the scents her grandmother carried round with her. 'Ah, *Avia*,' she whispered. 'My grandfather? Was he like this at the beginning?'

Epilogue

Dorey

A Sunday in October 1999

I am back in the small hotel by the whitewashed church, now restored to simple faith after its role as dressing station two generations ago. My rucksack is loaded with bits and pieces from the mountains and my shoulders ache.

The dark face of Jordi behind his battered desk in the hotel almost breaks into a smile. 'No train back to Barcelona,' he says. 'Is too late.' He will not speak to me in Spanish although I booked in last night in my best Castilian Spanish.

'I have to tell them,' I say. 'I have to tell my family in Barcelona that I will not be back tonight.'

I'm nervous as I hear the purring of the line at the other end. But they are not there, at the Hotel Lloret. 'They have gone out,' says young Francisco behind his desk. 'The old ones have gone to watch the dancing in the Plaça St Jaume. I will tell them you will not return tonight.'

In my small room I arrange the bits of stone and the bullet casing in a line on the bathroom shelf. I peer at their twin images through the mirror, hoping that might make them seem more significant. Perhaps I am fanciful. Perhaps that was not at all ChiChu's hillside, where she fought as a very young woman with Esteban and the other comrades. But she did pore over maps with me before we came away. She drew a circle round the very place then looked at me over her gold-rimmed glasses. 'We did use maps in those days, pet,' she said. 'Don't think maps were only invented with the Beatles.'

I know for certain that the little church next door to this hotel was the dressing station where Grandma Susan was a nurse. I checked that out back in England. The name of the church was in her letters to Aunt Theodora; the one I'm named after. Those were the letters which started this goose chase of mine. I still don't know whether it was a wild one.

The letters were in a big box of papers in Susan's room at Goshawk Shield where she lived most of her life. There was another box with Theodora's papers and journals. A note in Susan's neat handwriting said it was for me. *For Dorey, afterwards.*

There were letters in the box to and fro between Theodora and Susan from Spain and from Goshawk Shield; between Susan and Aunt Keziah, the one who married the policeman; between Keziah and Uncle Roy in Canada who wrote on Auntie Judith's instructions; between Susan and Grandpa Jake when he was in the prison camp, and afterwards; between Susan and Barty in Italy where he went to work; between Susan and my mother, Rosita, just before she and my father, Barty, were married.

My parents came from Italy for Susan's funeral. My father cried for his mother. My mother cried in the arms of her own mother, ChiChu. ChiChu endured it all with a stony face. My father walked with me through the rooms of Goshawk Shield and told tales of life when Jake and Susan were still alive; he told me how the life on the farm choked him and how pleased he was he went to university to study Italian, which after all was the language of his father.

Susan had not said much to me about those years. She and Grandpa Jake were busy farming at Goshawk, getting on with things. She carried on single-handed after he died. 'What you had to do,' she said, 'was do the next thing. Look forward. Always look forward.'

Old Jordi at the hotel here is the same. I was asking him about the little church in those days, and the fighting out in Aragon. 'All in the past,' he says, shaking his head. 'We look forward now.'

Two years of an aborted Spanish degree helped me to work my way through the papers and the public texts that hold some explanation, although much of that was contradictory. Some of the tale I chiselled out, bit by bit, from a reluctant ChiChu. She, too, would say, 'All in the past; you are obsessed with the past, Dorey,' shaking her head with its piled dark hair.

ChiChu and Susan! Could a girl have grandmothers so different? Susan up on her farm with her heavy aprons and her shining bottles of fruit; ChiChu down in her big house, wife of the leading manufacturer in Priorton. Different they were, but the greatest of friends, always. Even when they were quite old Susan used to watch over ChiChu like an affectionate mother pigeon. For as long as I can remember ChiChu's elegant mantelpiece has been ruled by a ghastly cat ornament. Pasted carefully on the underside is a card which says, *To my dark-eyed girl on her marriage, December 1945. Love Susan.*

ChiChu has been detached about it all, no more than amused at my interest in Spain, but always pleased to talk about her much-mourned friend, Susan. Then the pressure of university finally spat me, half broken, out of its machine. When I survived the short, sharp cure at Park View Hospital, ChiChu nursed me through the blank final stages of depression and became more tolerant of my curiosity. And now she has even allowed me to chivvy her to come here with me to be my guide in these last stages of the story. I think she might even be enjoying herself. Last Sunday she showed us how to dance the sardana in the church square, her elegant feet tapping in the circle alongside my dumpy Doc Martens.

On Monday we walked through the City Museum, moving from room to room, reading documents about the occupation of her city by Franco's Fascists. We watched flickering archive footage of the parade through Barcelona, led by prancing horses ridden by hawk-faced figures in swirling white robes. We studied the quiet face of a bespectacled general. A flickering film caught the sun glinting off Italian helmets as the soldiers marched down the broad avenue of the Ramblas: the trams halted and the people looked on.

In a darkened room we saw expressed in careful graphics the grotesque flush of executions which were the conqueror's *coda*. We saw the anxious faces of refugees hauling their families and baggage into the short-lived safety of pre-war France. I mention to ChiChu how much it reminds me of scenes on the television now from Kosovo and Chechnya. She shakes her head, her eyes dark with sorrow and I wish I hadn't said that.

We saw records: the careful documentation from the

prisons. On one of them, a dark-haired girl with a keen young Catalan face, reminded me so much of ChiChu that I wept. On the paper, this girl was described as a 'rebel'. There were no tears in ChiChu's eyes.

Finally, we saw the 'installation'. This was a room-size space ankle-deep in grey dust and burned books, symbolizing the thirty-six years of the dictatorship before this new democratic Spain was born. Presiding over it all was a portrait of Franco behind bulletproof glass.

Of course, I cried at all of this, but ChiChu just held my hand very tightly. We went to the Plaça Reial to recover. We sat under the colonnade for an hour drinking coffee (her) and gin (me). In front of us the trickling water of the fountain caught the sunlight and we laughed at a man playing football with his young son who was dressed in the strip of Barcelona Football Club. A man in plastic trainers and a battered coat made his way along the cafés under the colonnade and tried to sell cigarettes from a holdall.

I've been awake all night in the hotel by the little church, scribbling and thinking and smoking cheap Spanish cigarettes. Now I think I might have put it all together. There is so much I do know now; what I didn't know before seems so much clearer.

I return the motorbike to the garage and catch the first train. But the train stops at a small station outside Barcelona and we are all swept off the train by the officious guard and herded on to the station. Something strange happens. The good working knowledge I have of Spanish deserts me and all I hear around me is an impenetrable babble. I have no idea why we have been thrown off the train and no notion of when or whether we will get another. I wander around amongst the crowd, a greater and greater sense of panic bubbling up inside me. I go into the little bar and buy strong, cheap coffee in a glass and sit at the high stool, ignoring what now appear to be the malevolent glances of some workmen around a table and a woman with shopping bags by the door. I think of ChiChu defending Mr Walstein against those men in the café in North London. Then I drain my glass and grimace at the bitterness of the dark coffee. How terrible for ChiChu when she finally got to England, shut out by a wall of words.

I put my notebook on the stained counter and start to scribble, creating my own wall against these people. When the train arrives forty minutes later, the woman with the bags who has been watching me with interest nudges my arm to tell me it is here.

ChiChu sees me arrive. She's been watching from her little balcony high on the Hotel Lloret. She raises her silver-topped cane. Her voice floats down to me. 'Dorey! You're back!'

I ride up in the clanking pre-war lift and make my way to her narrow room. She merely tolerates my kiss, but I can sense her relief. 'For a minute,' she says, 'we thought we had lost you on the High Sierra.'

'No. No.' I shake my head. 'You don't get rid of me that easily.'

She leads me back on to the balcony and we are squashed there side by side. Below us whirl the noise and the perpetual movement of the Ramblas. A living statute of a Roman centurion draws a crowd. Someone puts a peseta in his bowl and the crowd starts back as the statue makes a sudden mechanical movement. Opposite him is a small stall with banners, giving out political leaflets. There is a poster of Che Guevara. One of the banners is red with a gold hammer and sickle. I remember those tales of barricades in this very space and the flags and banners with their revolutionary message draped from this very balcony.

'I looked for the place, ChiChu,' I say. 'I found it, the very place where you were. I found the gun emplacement, the piles of stones.'

'How would you know?' she mocks. 'It is not possible. There were many of those places.'

'I do know. I could hear it, feel it,' I say, looking into those deep eyes, still dark and very fine. 'I think I do know.'

She stares at me, then nods. 'There's some lemonade in the room,' she says. 'You must be very tired, child.' ChiChu has never spoken Catalan or Spanish in my hearing, even in these recent days in. Barcelona. My half-good Spanish has had to serve when we go out.

I bring out two glasses. 'How was your afternoon?' I say.

She nods. 'Very fine. Very fine. I've been sitting here watching the whole city parade before me. The women trotting along, the men walking on their heels like sailors. I looked hard at many faces and thought I knew them.'

'Did you go into the Old Quarter? Go where you used to live?'

She shakes her head. 'How many times do I tell you? It is there no longer. It was blown up. They all died. My grandmother's teeth were found in a tree many yards away.'

I lean over and kiss her cheek. 'Dear *Avia*,' I say.

She is about to say something when there is a disturbance in the room behind us. It's my grandfather laden down with supermarket carriers, bringing the bustle of the street with him. His face lights up when he sees me. 'Dorey! Back in one piece I see.' He's shrunk a little now, from his great height, but his bearing is still erect, military, and he still has a head full of silvery hair. He pulls out the bounty from one of his carriers: a bottle of fino sherry and three blue-rimmed glasses. He stands beside us inside the French window. 'So how are you, ChiChu? Ready for a small glass of the best sherry in the world?' It is still there, that last trace of his South African accent. ChiChu herself has no accent, unless you count that distinctive soft lift that says she comes from the North of England.

Grandpa draws a chair up behind us and hands out the sherry. He looks at me under his straggly silver eyebrows. 'What a good thing, Dorey, that you inveigled your grandmother to come home like this. I've been trying to get her here since 1975 when the old devil popped his clogs, but I could never, never do it. We should stay longer, ChiChu . . .'

ChiChu stared into her glass, flushing the shining liquid to and fro. 'No, no. You're wrong, Aaron. I've not come home. Tomorrow we all go home on the two o'clock flight. We need to get Dorey back to Goshawk Shield so she can write her story at last. Don't we?'

Grandpa laughs, pats my arm, then he kisses the top of her head. 'So we do. Although whether it'll quite make a story I'm not sure. We're just ordinary people. It was the times that were extraordinary. Don't you think?'